M.G. Webb

the
chickens
are out

cover photo: iStock.com/NikonShutterman

Printed in the United States of America
Published by Braughler Books LLC., Springboro, Ohio

First printing, 2019

ISBN: 978-1-970063-32-5

Library of Congress Control Number: 2019915840

Ordering information: Special discounts are available on quantity purchases by bookstores, corporations, associations, and others. For details, contact the publisher at:

sales@braughlerbooks.com
or at 937-58-BOOKS

For questions or comments about this book, please write to:
info@braughlerbooks.com

Braughler™
Books
braughlerbooks.com

To my wife Kathy

prologue

I'll never forget the day I met Kathy.

It was early in March, 2006, and it was a Monday. Back then my company, Stone Flooring Sales and Installation LLC, still had a storefront and warehouse in West Chester. We were slammed at that time. This was, of course, before the Great Recession.

Anyway, on that particular Monday, we were installing six jobs—two in Butler County, two in Hamilton County, and two in Warren County. On Mondays, I would close the store at noon, and then I would drive around all afternoon dropping by on jobs and doing measures. I liked to drop by every job as it was being installed. But this wasn't always possible—especially when we're installing six jobs at once and they're all over the map.

One of the jobs being installed that day was the dining area of a cafeteria at Miami University in Oxford. We were installing two thousand square feet of vinyl tile. It was a full days work for a flooring crew, but not a huge job.

The subcontractor I had on that job was a guy by the name of Ray Taylor. I've known Ray for about fifteen years. He always one of the first guys I call when I need a job done—whether its ceramic tile, carpet, VCT or wood. Because I never have a problem with his work. He takes pride in his work, and not everybody does these days.

It would make sense not to drop by Ray's job, because I didn't have anything to worry about on that one. So I didn't put it on my schedule.

I kept thinking about Ray, though. I had heard that he and his wife were getting a divorce, and the divorce was an ugly one—ugly enough to land Ray in jail a couple times. Ray's my friend. I wanted to see how he was doing, and show my support.

So Miami University was my second stop.

I arrived at the University at about 1:00 PM. I pulled into the drive for Lincoln Hall, and parked my van around back, which is where the cafeteria was.

I entered the building and walked down the hallway to the cafeteria. The archway leading into the dining area was blocked with a big X of two inch yellow tape. I had to smile. Most installers, including myself, would not have bothered to do that.

Ray and two of his guys were laying the field tile. I watched, standing where I could be seen, but I didn't say anything.

After a couple minutes, Ray saw me and waved. " Hey Mark. Be right there."

"No hurry," I said.

Ray was laying his tile toward another archway where, once he was close enough, he could step out of the cafeteria without stepping in glue.

I heard the outside door open and looked down the hall. A woman entered the building and was walking towards me. As she got closer, I noticed that she was pretty. She had short auburn hair. She was wearing tan pants and a black western style shirt. The shirt had a large horse's head printed on the front. I noticed her footwear too. She was wearing women's work boots, which I thought was unusual, but quite charming.

She walked up and stood next to me and started watching the guys lay tile.

"The cafeteria is closed today, ma'am," I said.

"Yes it is," she said.

She turned around and walked away. I looked over at Ray. He had just one more row of tile to lay before he could step out of the dining area.

I heard a clunk from the pop machine and I turned and looked. The woman pulled a Diet Coke out of the pop machine, opened it, and set the can on top of an empty newspaper rack, which was next to the pop machine. Then she took a granola bar out of the green canvas purse that she was carrying and began unwrapping it.

"Would you like to sit down, ma'am?"

She looked around. "On the floor?"

Ray and his guys had the chairs stacked in the hallway. I lifted one of the chairs off the top of the nearest stack and set it next to the newspaper rack.

She smiled. "Is that for me?"

"Yes."

She sat down in the chair, and said, "Thank you." Then she finished unwrapping her granola bar. "I only have twenty minutes between classes," she said. She took a bite of her granola bar, chewed, and then she took a sip of her Diet Coke.

"Do you teach here?" I asked.

She seemed puzzled. "Why did you ask me that question? Do you think I'm too old to be a student here?"

"No. No, of course you're not," I said. Then I added: "You just look so intelligent, that I thought you must be a teacher." That was true. She did look like an intelligent person.

A smile slowly came to her face. "Do you think teachers are intelligent? Not everybody thinks that."

"Well, some of them are and some of them aren't," I said. "I use to be a teacher."

"Oh really? What did you teach?"

"High School English."

"But you didn't like teaching, huh?"

"No, well, actually, I enjoyed teaching very much."

"Then why'd you quit?"

"Um." I was wishing I hadn't brought up this subject. "I had a disagreement with the principal. He suspended one of my students, and I felt the suspension was unwarranted."

"You quit over a disagreement?. I have disagreements with the head of the Biology Department all the time."

"Well this disagreement got physical."

She looked at me very seriously. "Physical, huh."

"He was in my face, wagging his finger. I don't even remember what he was saying. But that finger kept tapping my chest, and after five or six taps I pushed him away."

"Did you tell him you were sorry after you did that?"

"No. He pushed me back."

"Oh."

"And then I punched him." I showed her with a very gentle hook. "Boom."

"That's not good."

"No," I said. "It wasn't good at all. I knocked him down. When he sat up, his mouth was pretty bloody, and he was holding his jaw. I just said, 'I quit' and walked out."

"Hey Mark."

I turned around. Ray was walking up to me. He had a school boy grin on his face and an unlit cigarette hanging from his mouth. "Hey Ray," I said. "You guys are making good time on this one."

"You seem to be making good time yourself," he said, still grinning.

That comment embarrassed me. I looked at the woman. She smiled and chuckled softly.

"Ray, how's your schedule for next week?" I asked quickly.

"Ah, let me think." He pulled the unlit cigarette out of his mouth, thought for a minute, then said: "Wednesday and Thursday I have open, I think."

"Well I need you for a ceramic job. Could you put me down for Wednesday and Thursday?"

"Yeah, yeah. Will do, Mark." He began nodding his head. "Yep."

"So," I said. "How are you doing, Ray?"

"You probably heard about me and Deb."

"I heard you were getting divorced, yeah."

Ray began nodding his head again, and then he exploded: "That fuckin' bitch! She's fuckin' a guy half her age. In my house! In my fucking house! I'm not allowed to go within a hundred yards of that house, but the judge says I've got to pay the mortgage. Isn't that some shit!"

"Yeah, it is," I agreed.

Ray put the unlit cigarette in his mouth then pulled it right back out. "The guy Deb's fuckin' is a real piece of shit. Doesn't work. Drinkin' and fuckin' is all he can do." He held the cigarette up like a teacher holds a pencil up when making a point. "I've got a sixteen year old daughter in that house. And I still got my Glock. I told the judge that I couldn't find it. But I got it. And if that piece of shit ever touches my daughter, there will be hell to pay—if you know what I mean."

"Yeah, Ray, I know what you mean."

The woman had stopped chewing. She held her granola bar in one hand, her Diet Coke in the other, and stared at Ray. She looked frightened.

"For both him and Deb," Ray added.

"I get the picture, Ray."

Ray glanced at the woman. "Well I better go smoke my cigarette," he said. Then he walked down the hall and left the building.

"I apologize for my friend," I told the woman.

"Your friend, or your employee?" She took a bite of her granola bar.

"Whatever he is. I apologize for him. He's usually not like that."

"I should report him to the police." She took another bite from her granola bar.

"Why would you do that?"

"He's got a gun. He's not suppose to have a gun."

"I know. He shouldn't have the gun. That's wrong. But he's just talking crazy. He's really a very gentle guy."

"Yeah. Well some killers are also very gentle guys." She put the last piece of granola bar in her mouth, walked over to a trash can, and threw away her granola wrapper and her Diet Coke can. She covered her mouth with her hand, because she was chewing, and looked at me.

I noticed her eyes for the first time. Her face was nice to look at, but her eyes were stunning. They were gray around the outer edge of the iris, and light brown around the pupil. In between the colors merged, and her eyes sparkled.

"Um, I have to go," she said, still covering her mouth.

"I'll walk out with you," I said.

"Okay. I'd like that."

I began walking alongside her. "My name's Mark, by the way."

"My name's Kathy," she said. "I'm pleased to meet you, Mark."

"You know," I said, trying to think of a way to excuse Ray's behavior. "Divorce is rough on a person emotionally."

Kathy began walking slower. She turned to me. "I know that," she said. "My divorce became final two weeks ago."

"Oh. I'm sorry I brought that up. I'm divorced too. But I've been divorced for ten years."

"You don't have to be sorry."

"Oh, sorry about that," I said, and grinned.

We came to the door and I opened it for her. We walked outside. I saw Ray standing by the dumpster, smoking. I waved. He smiled and nodded.

"Are you still single?" Kathy asked.

"Um, well I never remarried, if that's what you mean."

"No, that's not what I mean," she said.

We came to the wide main sidewalk and turned right.

"Oh, you mean 'single' as the word is defined in Twenty-first Century American English," I said.

"Yes." She laughed. "Do you speak Twenty-first Century American English?"

"I'm learning it."

"I'm fluent in it," she said.

"Then. In that sense, yes, I am still single."

We came to the sidewalk which leads to the next building and Kathy stopped walking. "I get off here," she said.

She was looking at me. "Kathy, I've enjoyed talking to you."

"Me too," she said.

"Maybe we could meet up and talk again sometime?"

"I'd like that," she said.

"Um. How about Friday evening? Maybe we could meet at an Applebee's?"

"I like Applebee's, and Friday evening works for me." She fished around inside her purse for a minute and then took out a pen and a card. She wrote on the card. "I have to run. Here's my number." She handed me the card. "Call me."

"I'll call you tonight."

"Okay."

I watched Kathy until she entered the building.

I glanced at the card. It said "Kathy", spelled with a K, and her phone number was in the 937 area code. I put the card in my shirt pocket, and then I walked over to the dumpster and talked to Ray.

chapter 1

"Mark, I haven't seen Kathy in over a year. But there is a drastic difference. Maybe you don't notice because you see her everyday."

"No, Mom, I notice. Her intellect is deteriorating. That's why she's not working."

"Mark, Kathy is out of it. When we were all at the Mayberry Diner, she couldn't figure out what anybody was talking about. I watched her. She was confused."

"I know that, Mom. I'm very concerned."

"Don't just be concerned, Mark, take her to a doctor."

"Mom, I've discussed it with her. She doesn't want to go to a doctor."

"Don't discuss it with her, Mark. Just get her to a doctor!"

"Mom, to be honest, I don't think taking her to a doctor's going to do much good."

"Oh, Mark! In this day and age they have medication to treat almost everything, including—and I hate to use the word—but dementia.

"Alright, Mom. I've been wanting Kathy to see a doctor. I'll make sure she sees one."

"Make sure she sees one soon, Mark."

"I will, Mom."

"Okay. Well I'll let you go now, Mark."

"I'll talk to you later, Mom. I love you. Bye."

"I love you too, Mark. Bye."

I put my cellphone in my shirt pocket, grabbed my coffee, and went out to our back deck. It was Saturday morning, and it looked like it was going to be a nice day. The sky was clear and the air was warm. Our chickens were happily running around in what we called our "chicken yard"—which was a fenced in meadow at the back of our property.

Kathy was outside attending to the bird feeders. I watched her walk from bird feeder to bird feeder, pouring in seed from a plastic pitcher. She was wearing gloves and her suede winter coat with the hood pulled up over her head.

After she emptied the pitcher into the last bird feeder, which was the one that was farthest away, she started walking back to the house.

As she climbed up the steps to our deck, she said, "The chickens are all out."

"I see that."

Kathy went into the house, and then I went in.

"Kathy, do you think it's cold outside?" She was taking off her coat.

"Cold outside?" She looked at me with a confused expression on her face.

"Are you cold?"

"No."

"Kathy, you don't need a coat when it's this warm outside."

"I need my coat."

"Why?"

"Rosacea," she said, and she hung her coat on the back of a kitchen chair.

Kathy had told me that before, and she might have had rosacea at some time in her life. Although, since I've known her, her complexion has always been clear.

"Okay," I said. "Then why don't you see a doctor about it?"

"What?"

"You should make an appointment to see a doctor."

"What's appointment?"

"Kathy, you should see a doctor."

"We don't have insurance."

"That's okay. We have the money to pay a doctor."

"Can I play the music?"

"Yeah, Kathy," I said. "Listen to your music."

Kathy went into the living room and turned on her boombox. She played a CD from the band The Gall Stones, which was already in the boombox.

I went into the computer room and got on my computer. I googled health clinics near Spring Valley, Ohio. I scrolled through the search results until I found one that had Saturday hours. It was called Xenia Health Center. I got up and went into the living room.

The music was very loud:

Dog eat dog, day and night
Black is white and wrong is right
Dog eat dog, it's all good
All in the name of brotherhood

"Kathy!" I spoke very loud so she could hear me over the music.

She turned down the boombox. "What?"

"Where's your cellphone, Kathy?"

She thought for a moment. "Where's my cellphone?" She went into the kitchen, reached into her coat pocket, and pulled out her cellphone. She looked at the cellphone, then at me. "What to do?"

"Let's go into the computer room." She followed me into the computer room. She sat in front of her computer; I sat in front of my computer, which was still on.

"Kathy, I want you to go to a doctor for a check-up."

She looked at me. "Kay," she said.

I jiggled the mouse and the page that I had been looking at re-appeared on the computer screen. "I've found a doctor—or, actually it's a clinic, and I'd like you to call and make an appointment."

"Make an apartment?"

"No, not make an apartment. I want you to call the clinic and set up a time when you will go in for a check-up."

She looked at her phone, and then at me.

I looked at the computer screen. "Dial this number—" I began reading the number: "Nine."

"Nine." She opened her phone and pushed the nine button.

"Three."

"Three." She pushed the three button.

"Seven."

And so on.

After she finished putting the number in, she held the phone up to her ear. "Ringing," she said.

"Hello," Kathy said into the phone.

There was a pause.

"See doctor."

Another pause.

"Kathleen Stone."

"Yeah." Kathy looked at me. "Which doctor?"

"Any doctor," I said.

"Any doctor," Kathy said into the phone.

Kathy listened to her phone. Her eyes began darting about. She handed me the phone.

I held the phone up to my ear. "Ma'am, I can schedule you to see Dr. Doolittle on Thursday at eleven or at one," the woman said.

"Eleven would be fine," I said.

"Who is this?"

"This is Mark Stone. I'm Kathy's husband."

"Okay, Mr. Stone. I'll put Kathleen down to see Dr. Doolittle on Thursday, April 18, at eleven o'clock."

"Alright."

"Who is Kathleen's insurance provider?"

"We don't have insurance. We'll pay cash."

"The appointment will cost one hundred and sixty dollars. And that doesn't include blood tests, should Dr. Doolittle decide they're needed."

"Do you accept credit cards?"

"Yes, we do."

"We'll probably put it on a VISA."

"That would be fine."

"Great. We'll see you Thursday, then," I said.

I closed Kathy's phone and handed it to her. She set the phone on her desk. "The chickens need water," she said.

"You gave them water this morning," I said. "Do you think they need more water already?"

"Yeah," she said, and then she got up and went into the kitchen.

I followed her.

Kathy picked up the green gallon jug off the kitchen floor, took off the cap, and then put the jug in the sink and began filling it with water. While the jug was being filled, she took the lid off a plastic container that was on the counter. She measured out one level tea-spoon of powder from the container. I don't know what the powder was, but Kathy once told me that it's used to harden the shells on the hen's eggs. When the jug was full enough, she turned off the faucet, and poured the powder into the jug. Then she put the cap on the jug and shook it.

Kathy put the jug on the kitchen table and reached for her coat.

"You don't need your coat, Kathy. It's warm outside."

"I need my coat." Without looking at me, she put on her coat, grabbed the jug, and headed out the back door.

I went back into the computer room. I had a carpet job sched-uled for Thursday and Friday, and now, because of Kathy's doctor's appointment on Thursday, I needed to reschedule the carpet job for Friday and Saturday. I sat down at my computer table and pulled my cellphone out of my pocket. I went to my contacts, brought up Jim Conroy's phone number, and called him.

"Hello Mark."

"Hi Jim. Hey, I hate to bother you, but I've got a little bit of a problem."

"What kind of a problem, Mark? Doesn't sound like good news."

"Well, it's a scheduling problem, Jim. I don't think I'm going to be able to get to your job on Thursday. I think we're going to have to do it Friday and Saturday."

"Mark, I've got some bad news too. Saturday's not even possible. Sue and I are flying down to Atlanta on Saturday. I'm afraid it's going to have to be Thursday and Friday."

"Well you don't have to be there."

"No, Mark, I do have to be there."

"Um, let's see…I could move some things around and we could

do your job Tuesday and Wednesday."

"That won't work. The painters are going to be in there Tuesday and Wednesday."

"Alright, Jim. You know, I really wanted to get the job done next week, but—"

"You've got to do the job next week! We're moving in on the twenty-second."

"Well, okay then—"

"And Mark, you told me that you personally were going to install my carpet."

"I did say that."

"That's why I bought carpet from you. It did cost me a little bit more. But that's okay."

"Alright."

"See you on Thursday, Mark."

"Okay. I'll be there.."

"Have a nice weekend."

"You too, Jim."

I sat at my computer table thinking. I'd like to go with Kathy to her doctor's appointment, but she's capable of getting there by herself. The only problem is that she's never been to the Xenia Health Center, and she doesn't know where it is.

I jiggled the computer mouse to wake up my computer. The page reappeared on the screen, and I pulled up a map of the health center's location. It turns out, the health center is right across the street from the recycling center which she goes to about once a week.

I heard Kathy come in the back door. I turned off my computer and went out to the kitchen. Kathy set the green jug on the floor.

"Kathy, we're leaving," I said.

Her face lit up. "Are we going to the grocery?"

"No, not right now. We can go to the grocery tomorrow. Right now I wanted us to drive up to the clinic where you have an appointment next Thursday. So that you know where it is."

"Kay," she said, sounding disappointed. Then she looked at her purse, which was on the kitchen table. She thought for a moment before picking it up.

We went out to the deck, and I locked the back door. "Let's take the Honda," I said.

"We're taking Honda?"

"Yes."

She got the Honda keys out of her purse and gave them to me.

I started the Honda. "Now Kathy, I want you to remember this, because this is how you're going to get to your doctor's appointment next Thursday."

"I should write this." She took a note pad and a pen out of her purse. She flipped the note pad to a blank page.

I pulled out of our driveway, turning right to head toward Xenia. "Okay, we're going into Xenia," I said.

"You turn right?" she asked.

"Yes," I said.

"From house, turn right," she said, as she wrote on her notepad.

We drove into Xenia. "Turn left here, just like you're going to Kmart." I turned left. "Then you'll drive past the UDF and the Speedway, just like you're going to Kmart."

"Turn left. Go past UDF and Speedway," she said and wrote on her notepad.

"Okay, we're going through this light, but at the next light we're turning left, just like you would if you were going to recycling," I said as we drove through the light on Main Street.

"Turn left second light," she said and wrote.

"Just like you're going to recycling." I turned left at Dayton Avenue. "Turn left here."

"Turn left." She looked at me after she wrote this down, holding the pen ready to take her next note.

"Kathy, we're going to keep going straight at this light," I said, as I brought the Honda to a stop at Allison Avenue. "Then there will be two stop signs. Go straight at the first stop sign. Turn left at the second stop sign."

"Straight at light. Turn left second stop sign," she said and wrote.

The light turned green. I accelerated and kept straight. I stopped, then kept straight at the first stop sign, and then turned left at Progress Drive.

"You see," I said. "This is just like going to recycling." I turned right on the road where the recycling center was located. "There's your recycling, Kathy. But we're going over here." I pulled into the Xenia Health Center's parking lot, and then I pulled into a parking spot. I put the car in park. "Now you drive," I said.

"Me drive?"

"Yes, you drive."

We got out of the car and changed places.

She put the car in drive, pulled out to the road, and took us back on the same roads that I had driven to get us there.

There was one difference: When we got to Church Street, instead of turning right, she went straight, which took us into the Kmart parking lot.

"What are you doing? We're not going to Kmart."

She laughed. Then she drove between two parked cars.

"Kathy! What the hell are you doing?"

She made a u-turn and pulled back up to the light at Church Street. She laughed again. I think she was aware that I was looking at her like she was crazy. "This is how I go home," she said.

We did arrive home safely.

· · · · ·

I opened my eyes Thursday morning and glanced at the alarm clock on the dresser. It was 5:25 AM. I heard a noise in the kitchen. Kathy was up making coffee. I closed my eyes and drifted back into sleep. The bed moved as Kathy got back into bed. I opened my eyes. It was 5:36 AM. I smelled coffee. I heard the coffee maker rumble as it turned the last of its water into steam. I kept my eyes closed.

Kathy lay beside me, looking over my shoulder at the alarm clock. Very softly, she whispered, "Five fifty-five. Five fifty-five. Five fifty-five. Five fifty-five…" And then. "Five fifty-six. Five fifty-six. Five fifty-six. Five fifty-six. Five fifty-six…" And then, "Five fifty-seven. Five fifty-seven…"

Kathy would always tell me when it was five fifty-nine, because the alarm clock was set for six.

"I'm awake, Kathy," I said at five fifty-eight. I got out of bed and shut off the alarm.

I went out to the kitchen, and poured myself a cup of coffee.

Kathy came into the kitchen. She was still in her flannel pajamas, and she had a pair of my old tennis shoes on her feet. I had bought her a pair of slippers, but she seemed to prefer the old tennis shoes.

"Kathy, you have a doctor's appointment this morning at eleven o'clock," I said.

"I know."

"Okay, well, I don't want you to forget."

"I wrote it," she said. She showed me a note:

5:30   make coffee
5:59   wake up Mark
7:00   do recycling
8:00   feed chickens
8:01   open chicken door
9:00   feed wild birds
10:00 leave for doctor in X

"Kathy, I have one question," I said. "Why would you go to recycling, come back home, and then a couple hours later go back to the same area? Why not just do recycling a little bit later?"

She looked at me like I was crazy. "That won't work," she said.

"Alright, do it however you want. Just don't forget your doctor's appointment."

"I won't."

I shaved, took a shower, and got dressed for work. I filled up my coffee mug and kissed Kathy before going out the back door.

"Don't forget your doctor's appointment," I said one last time.

"I won't."

When I was about ten miles down the road, I realized that I had forgotten something. I had forgotten to check her cellphone to make sure the ringer was turned on.

I called four or five times that morning. She didn't answer. So the ringer was probably not turned on.

Although it didn't matter.

When I got home, the first thing I said to Kathy was: "How'd you doctor's appointment go?"

"I got three things."

"Three things"

"Yeah." She handed me a bag from the Kmart Pharmacy.

"What are these for?"

"Rosacea," she said.

I looked in the bag. She had a cream, which was for rosacea. She also had two other medications: Namenda and donepezil. These medications are used to treat Alzheimer's disease.

Kathy handed me a card. It was for her next appointment, which was in three weeks. "Doctor said you should come too," she said.

I nodded. I was definitely going to go with her on her next appointment.

chapter 2

May 8, 2013

We walked up to the reception window.

"Kathleen Stone is here to see Dr. Doolittle," I said.

"Dr. Doolittle isn't here today," the nurse said. "Dr. Raji will see her."

"Okay."

Kathy's appointment was at one. We were about fifteen minutes early. "Come on, Kathy, let's sit down."

We sat down in a large waiting area. Across the room, there was a young mother holding a baby. Another child—probably three or four years old—sat beside her. They were the only other people in the waiting area.

"Oh look," Kathy said, looking across the room. "She has the babies. Isn't that nice?"

"Yeah, Kathy, that's nice. Let's just wait for the doctor, okay?"

Kathy kept looking up at young mother with her two children.

"Kathy, the doctor's going to call us pretty soon. So let's just wait. Okay?"

Kathy stood up. She was staring at the young mother and her children.

"Kathy, sit down," I said.

She walked over to the three. "I listen to The Gall Stones," she said. "Do you like rock?"

The young woman reached for the hand of the child who was sitting beside her. "Yes," she said.

I had followed Kathy and was standing behind her.

Kathy continued, "They have a song, *Dog eat dog, day and night.* Isn't that funny? Dogs eating dogs."

The young woman smiled nervously and nodded.

"Kathy, let's sit down," I said. I put my hand on her shoulder.

Kathy glanced at me, and then at the young woman. "I'm from Ohio. I never heard of dogs eating dogs. But they're from California. I guess they have that problem in California. Their dogs eat dogs."

"Come on, Kathy," I said, and I steered her back to where we were sitting.

A few minutes later a door on our side of the room opened. A nurse stood in the doorway, looking down at a clipboard. "Kathleen Stone," she said.

"Come on, Kathy," I said. "That's us."

We followed the nurse down the hall to an examination room. There were two chairs against the wall. We sat down.

The nurse took Kathy's pulse. She listened to Kathy's heart. Then she picked up a blood pressure meter. She opened the cuff and looked at Kathy. "Kathleen, you're going to have to take off your coat," she said.

Kathy grabbed the front of her coat with both hands. "I need my coat."

"Kathy, let me hold your coat," I said. She let me take her hands off the front of her coat. "Stand up, please."

Kathy looked at me and then at the nurse.

"Nothing's going to happen to your coat, Kathy."

She stood up. I took her purse and helped her get her coat off.

"Kathleen, sit down for me, please," the nurse said.

Kathy sat down. I sat next to her, holding the coat and the purse. The nurse pushed up her shirt sleeve, took her blood pressure, and then left the room.

I looked at my cell phone. It was ten minutes after one. We waited. I looked at my cell phone again. It was twenty minutes after one.

At 1:32, the door opened. A dark skinned man wearing a lab coat walked in. He picked up the clipboard that was on the cart and looked at Kathy. "So, why are you here today, Kathleen?" His accent sounded Indian or Pakistani.

"Where's the doctor?" Kathy asked.

"I'm the doctor. I'm Dr. Raji," he said. He looked down at the clipboard, and then put it back on the cart.

Kathy eyed him suspiciously.

Dr. Raji stared at Kathy for a minute. Finally he asked, "Do you know where you are, Kathleen?"

Kathy seemed offended by the question, and she didn't answer.

"What county are you in?"

She didn't answer.

"Kathleen, what county are you in?"

She still didn't answer.

"Who is the president of the United States, Kathleen?" Dr. Raji put his left arm across his chest, held his chin with his right hand, and waited for an answer.

Kathy was getting angry. I believe she thought that Dr. Raji was trying to make her look bad. And, of course, she was right about that.

"What year is it? Can you tell me that, Kathleen?"

"Thirteen," Kathy blurted.

"What thirteen, Kathleen? A number comes before the thirteen."

"Um." Kathy was thinking.

"What number comes before thirteen?"

"Um...Nineteen-thirteen?"

"No!" Dr. Raji said quickly. "It's Twenty-thirteen."

He picked up the clipboard and looked at it. "Have you been taking your medications?" he asked, looking up.

"Yes," Kathy said.

Dr. Raji looked at me. "Has she?"

"Yes," I said.

"One is wrong," Kathy said.

"One of your medications is wrong?" Dr. Raji asked.

"Yeah."

"Which one is wrong?"

"For rosacea," she said.

He looked down at the clipboard. "Dr. Doolittle prescribed metronidazole for the rosacea."

"That's wrong," Kathy said.

At that moment I remembered something. So I told the doctor: "When we were first married, she was taking a pill for rosacea. But I never thought she had rosacea."

"Doxycycline?" the doctor suggested.

"Yeah. I think that's the one."

"That's the one," Kathy said.

Dr. Raji stared at Kathy for a minute. "Where's the rash?"

"The rash?"

"Yes, the rash!" Dr. Raji said. "I don't see a rash. Where's the rash?"

Kathy turned to me. "What's rash?" she asked.

I put my hand on my cheek. "It's a red, bumpy area on your skin," I said.

"You wife has Alzheimer's," Dr. Raji said to me. "Make sure she takes her medications."

"She takes her medications. She takes them on her own," I told him. "But are you sure she has Alzheimer's?"

"That's Dr. Doolittle's diagnosis, but I agree."

"So, you don't do any tests? Or anything?"

"There are no blood tests for Alzheimer's disease. We can only guess." He began writing on the clipboard. Without looking up, he said, "I'd like to see Kathleen again in a month or so. You can make an appointment at the front desk on your way out." He walked out of the room, still writing on the clipboard.

I stood up and looked at Kathy.

"Are we done," she asked.

"Yeah, we can go."

Kathy got up and I helped her put her coat on. I gave her her purse.

We walked down the hall toward the door which opens up to the waiting room. There was a window right before the door. I stopped and looked in. No one was sitting at the desk under that window.

Kathy opened the door and went out into the waiting room.

"Kathy, wait! Don't go," I said, catching up to her.

Kathy stopped walking. "You said we were done?"

"We need to pay them," I said.

"Kay."

We walked up to the window in the waiting room. I reached for my wallet, but Kathy also pulled her credit card out of her purse.

She looked at me. "Me pay?" she asked.

"Sure. Go ahead." I put my wallet back in my back pocket.

Kathy handed the nurse her credit card.

The nurse swiped the credit card and handed it back. "I'll have your receipt in a minute, Mrs. Stone. It has to print."

"Also," I said, "Dr. Raji wants to see Kathy again in about a month."

"I have two openings on the third of June."

"Do you have something a couple weeks later than that?"

"Let's see. I have a ten o'clock on the nineteenth of June."

"We'll take that one," I said.

The nurse wrote the appointment on a card and handed it to me.

Kathy started walking toward the door.

"Mrs. Stone," the nurse called out, "you're receipt is printing now."

"We don't need it," I said, and I followed Kathy out the door.

chapter 3

Kathy's next doctor's appointment—her June 19 appointment—fell on a week when my company, Stone Flooring Sales and Installation LLC, was doing a big job in Louisville, Kentucky. The job consisted of carpeting a lobby, and fourteen floors of hallways in a high rise apartment building called Jefferson Place.

This wasn't a job that I was eager to do, because I thought it was too far away. But the manager of the high rise, Jack Kline, talked me into going down there and giving him a price. So I drove to Louisville—it took me two and a half hours to get there. I looked the job over, and I bid very high.

That was on Wednesday, June 10. The next day Jack Kline called me. He wanted Stone Flooring to do the job. So I told him we'd start on Monday, June 17.

I didn't plan to spend much time on the job.

I subbed all the work out to three crews. I met them on the job Monday morning to get them started, and then I came back home. I was only there for about an hour.

On Tuesday I didn't go down there at all; and I didn't plan to go down there Wednesday either, because Kathy had a doctor's appointment on that day.

Then, at about 5:30 Tuesday evening, my cell phone rang. I looked at the number. It was a 502 area code. That's the area code for Louisville.

"Hello, this is Mark Stone."

"Mark, this is Jack Kline."

"Hi, Jack. What can I do for you?"

"We got a problem, Mark. A big problem."

"Alright, Jack," I said. "What's the problem?"

"Mark, your installers left the biggest damn mess I've ever seen. I mean, Jesus Christ! There's dirt everywhere! Pad pieces everywhere! Those boards with nails—they're everywhere. And people can step on them. The residents are bitching like hell."

"What floor are we talking about, Jack?" I asked, although I probably could have guessed.

"The forth floor," he said.

That would have been my guess. That was Bob Jones's floor. "You say they're not there anymore?"

"No," Jack said. "They left around two."

"Okay, Jack. I don't know what the hell's going on. But—"

"It's in the contract, Mark! You have to clean up at the end of every day! This has to be cleaned up today!"

"I know what's in the contract, Jack. And I'm sorry that the forth floor's a mess. Okay. But you know where I live. I can't do anything about it right now. I can promise you that, if that crew doesn't come back, someone will clean up that mess first thing in the morning."

"Mark, if someone steps on one of those nail boards, we could get sued. And if we get sued, you'll get sued—I promise you that! So you need to get down here and take care of this."

"I'll be down there tomorrow, Jack. It might be in the afternoon."

"In the afternoon! You're suppose to be overseeing this job!"

"I'll do what I can do, Jack."

"I'd better see you on the job tomorrow—in the morning."

I didn't like the tone of his voice, but, very calmly, I said: "Jack, I will take care of the problem. I promise."

"Tomorrow morning?"

"Tomorrow morning," I said.

"Okay, Mark, I'll see you tomorrow morning."

"I'll see ya, Jack."

I tried to call Bob Jones all evening. He wasn't answering his phone. The calls were going to voicemail, and his voicemail box was full.

· · · · ·

"It's five fifty-nine." I opened my eyes. Kathy was standing in the doorway.

"What?"

"It's five fifty-nine."

"Okay." I got up and shut off the alarm. "I'm up."

I went into the kitchen. The coffee maker was still filling the coffee pot. I waited for it to finish, and then poured myself a cup of coffee.

"Do you want a cup?" I asked.

"Yeah." Kathy took a box of Cocoa Puffs out of the cupboard. "Can I have supper?"

"Yes," I said.

Kathy poured the Cocoa Puffs in a bowl. She got a glass of milk out of the refrigerator, and added milk from the glass to the bowl.

I set her coffee down on the table by her bowl.

Usually, on mornings when I had to work, I would sit down at the table for a few minutes and drink coffee with Kathy. I didn't do that on this particular morning, because I wanted to get out of the house as quickly as possible.

So I carried my coffee with me to the laundry room. I got a pair of jeans out of the dryer, and then I went into the bedroom. I set my coffee on the dresser and got dressed. Then I went into the bathroom, setting my coffee on the counter near the sink. I brushed my teeth. I finished my coffee as I walked back to the kitchen.

I dropped my empty coffee cup into the kitchen sink, and unplugged my cellphone from its charger. I looked at the screen. It was 6: 13 AM. "Kathy, I've got to get going," I said.

"Kay." She put her spoon in the bowl and got up.

I filled my Speedway mug up with the rest of the coffee. I turned off the coffee maker. "Kathy, where's your cellphone?" I asked.

She bend down and reached into the pocket of her coat, which was hung on the back of her chair. She pulled out her cellphone and handed it to me. I checked the ring tone. It was set all the way up. "Okay," I said, handing the phone back to her. "Don't forget: You have a doctor's appointment at ten."

"I know."

I looked at Kathy. I didn't like sending her to the doctor alone, but I didn't know what else to do. "The president of the United States is Obama," I said.

"Wait." She got a note pad and a pen from her purse.

"President is—" She was writing.

"Obama," I said. "O-B-A-M-A

"We're in Greene County."

"Green?" She seemed confused.

"Yes. It's the name of a color also. But we live in Greene County."

"County. Greene," she said and wrote.

"It's Twenty-thirteen," I said.

She followed me to the back door. I gave her a kiss. "It's Twenty-thirteen," I said again.

"It's Twenty-thirteen," Kathy said.

I gave her another kiss and went out the back door.

· · · · ·

I pulled around back to the loading dock Of the Jefferson Place Apartments. It was 8:32 AM. I had made pretty good time getting down there.

I called Kathy. No answer. She might be feeding the chickens or something, I thought.

I went into the building and took the service elevator up to the forth floor. As soon as I stepped off the elevator, there was a pile of pad pieces. And there were a few pieces of the old tack strip. I stepped out from the alcove and looked up and down the hall. It was filthy all right. Jack was not exaggerating. It looked like they had scrapped up the old pad which was glued around the walls and they just let the pieces lie where they fell. They had knocked most of the old tack strip loose too.

I called Kathy.

"Hello."

"Kathy, what are you doing?"

"Doing? Feeding chickens."

"Okay. You have a doctor's appointment today at ten."

"Kay."

"Well, I'll be home about five, or maybe before that. I don't know."

"Kay."

"I'll see ya, Kathy. I love you."

"Kay."

"Bye Kathy."

"Bye."

Next I called Bob Jones to find out what time he was getting down there. He didn't answer his phone.

I put my phone in my pocket and headed down to my van. When I was coming down the steps from the loading dock, Ray Taylor pulled in. He parked his van next to mine.

I walked up to Ray's van. He rolled his window down. "What's up, Mark?"

"You got both your helpers with you today?"

"Yeah," Ray said. "Jamal's back there."

"Can I get you to loan me Jamal for a couple hours this morning?"

"Sure, Mark. What do you need help with?"

"Cleaning up Jones's mess."

"Yeah," Ray said. "We saw that."

"Ray, next time you see a problem like that, I'd appreciate it if you'd call me and give me a heads up. Jack Kline called me last night and he was raising all kinds of hell."

"You know, I thought about doing that. Sorry. I didn't."

"That's okay."

"Where is Jones anyway? He's usually already here by the time we get here."

"God only knows where he is. I been trying to get ahold of him since last night."

"Maybe he's in jail."

"That's crossed my mind," I said, laughing.

Ray turned his head to the back of the van. "Jamal, you want to work with Mark this morning?"

"It'll be a treat," Jamal said.

Jamal and I went over to the side of my van. I opened the side door and went in. "Let's see. We're going to need this." I handed Jamal a plastic trash can. I also handed him a broom, a roll of contractor bags, a shovel, two hammers, two pry bars, two scrapers, two pairs of knee pads, and two pairs of gloves. Jamal put everything except the broom and the shovel in the trash can.

We walked in with Ray, and his helper Steve. They both carried tool boxes. Jamal carried the trash can. I carried the broom and the shovel. We all took the service elevator together. Jamal and I got off at the forth floor. Ray and Steve went up to the sixth floor.

"Okay, Jamal, we're going to clean this mess up," I said.

Jamal chuckled. "I can't believe those dudes left it like this."

"Yeah, well, I'm not real happy about it."

I took the stuff out of the trash can and put it on a bench that was in the alcove. Then I put a contractor bag in the trash can. "What I want you to do is to pick up the big pieces of pad, and the big pieces of tack strip, and throw 'em in the can. Here's some gloves." I held out a pair of gloves to him.

"I don't need 'em," Jamal said.

"Alright." I dropped the gloves back on the bench.

Jamal got busy picking up the trash. I put on a pair of knee pads, and got down on the floor with a hammer and pry bar and began taking up the tack strip that was still nailed to the floor.

"What do you want me to do now?"

I looked up. The trash can was full already. "Do you know where the dumpster is?"

"Sure do. You want me to take the bag down there?"

"Yeah."

"Okay if I smoke a cigarette when I'm down there?"

"Go ahead."

Jamal pulled the bag out of the can, tied it up, and carried it over to the service elevator. He pushed the button to go down.

I got up and lined the trash can with another contractor bag. The elevator doors opened. Jamal got into the elevator with his full bag.

I called Bob Jones again. He didn't answer his phone again.

When Jamal came back, he resumed picking up the floor.

"Jamal, I'm going to go up to talk to Ray for a minute."

Jamal looked at me and shrugged. "Okay."

I chuckled. "Well I'm glad you don't care."

I took off my knee pads and pushed the button for the main elevator. Since I didn't have tools, or trash, or anything else with me, I was allowed to take it. If I were carrying a hammer, I would have had to take the service elevator.

The elevator doors opened, I got in and went up to the sixth floor.

Ray and Steve had all the old carpet up. It was rolled up in short rolls and stacked in the alcove by the service elevator. They were in the process of taking up the old pad. Ray was slicing; Steve was rolling. They were trying to minimize their mess, which I appreciated.

"You guys are moving right along," I said.

"We like to get done early," Ray said. He got off the floor. "Did you ever get ahold of Jones?"

"No," I said. "And that's a big problem, because I don't know who I'm going to get to replace him."

"I know of somebody," Ray said.

"Who?"

"Phillip and Zac."

"Your girl friend's sons?" I had some doubts about that.

"Yeah." Ray sounded confident in what he saying. "Phillip is a good installer, and Zac is a helluva helper. They've helped me plenty."

"How much experience does he have?"

"Mark," Ray said. "This isn't a hard job."

"No, it's not," I said. "Once you're got it laid out, then you've just got the one pattern match seam."

"I'd help him lay it out, and I could help him with the seam."

"Okay," I said. "Could you call him for me? See if he's available Thursday, Friday and Saturday."

Ray got out his cellphone. He tapped the screen a few times and held it to his ear. "Phillip, do you and Zac want to work Thursday, Friday and Saturday?"

Ray gave me a thumbs up.

"Keep him on the line," I said.

I called Bob Jones one last time. He didn't answer his phone, but his voice mail box was accepting messages. So I left one: "Bob, I don't know what happened to you. You left early yesterday. You left your floor a mess. I'd been trying to get ahold of you since last night. It's ten o'clock now. You're still not here. So I got somebody else."

I looked at Ray. "It' a go."

"Phillip, figure on working Thursday, Friday and Saturday," Ray said into his cellphone.

"Let me have the phone," I said.

Ray handed me his phone.

"Phillip, This is Mark Stone."

"How ya doin' Mark."

"I'm doing okay," I said. "Now, you and your brother can work Thursday, Friday and Saturday, right?"

"Yeah."

"This jobs in Louisville, Kentucky."

"I know that already."

"You'll need to be down here by about eight-thirty or nine at the latest."

"I know how to get up in the morning, Mark," Phillip said. "I've done that my whole life."

"Okay. I'm going to start you out on the forth floor. It'll be ready for carpet. If I'm not here by the time you get here, Ray will help you get started."

"Okay," Phillip said.

"I'll see you tomorrow, then."

"See ya."

I handed Ray back his cellphone. "Thanks."

"Your welcome," he said.

"Is Terry here yet?" I asked.

Ray pointed to the ceiling "Can't you hear 'em?"

"Yeah. I guess I can," I said. "I'm going to go up there."

It was only one floor up, so I took the west stairs. There were stairs at both ends of each hallway.

When I got up to the seventh floor, Terry, and his helper, Rob, didn't notice me. They weren't very far along on the take up, and they were cussing like sailors.

"Terry, they asked us to leave because you fuckin' dumped a beer on a girl's back," Rob said.

"You're full of shit!" Terry said loudly. "There's no God damned way I'd do something like that!"

"Dude," Rob said, "I fuckin' watched you do it. You were leaning up against a pole, and it looked like you fell asleep standing up."

"You guys need to watch your language," I said.

"Mark," Rob said, laughing. "I didn't see you there."

"Oh," Terry said. "Sorry." Terry realized that he had slipped. Jobs like these hallways look like no one is around. But there are two dozen doors on each hallway, and behind many of them people are listening. It's easy to slip up on jobs like that—especially when you're half drunk like Terry and Rob were.

"There are people behind those doors that can hear you guys," I said to Rob. "They don't need to hear that kind of language."

"Okay," Rob said, nodding. "You're right."

I looked at Terry "About what time are you guys going to finish tonight?"

"Probably seven. Maybe a little later. Eight at the latest."

"Well, work till your finished," I said. "Pick up all your scraps. Vacuum. And after six, remember: no hammering."

"Mark, why would we be hammering after six?"

"I don't know, Terry. I'm just saying. That's one of the rules. No hammering after six."

"They sure have a lot of rules on this job," Terry said.

"Yes they do."

"Did Jones ever show up?"

"No," I said. "I've got a new crew coming in tomorrow."

"Bob Jones is a fuckin' idiot," Rob said, with some anger in his voice.

"Watch your language," I said.

"Bob Jones is an idiot. Can I say it like that?"

"That's fine."

Terry laughed. "Rob worked one day for Bob Jones."

"Yeah. That day was a...frickin' disaster."

"Real good." I laughed. "Well, I'm going to go back down to the forth floor and finish cleaning up Jones's mess."

I took the elevator down to the forth floor.

When I got down there, I was surprised to see that Jamal was almost done with the cleanup. There was about sixty feet of the old tack strip left to take up; and then we'd be ready to sweep up and patch the floor.

"Jamal, you're making quick work of this," I said.

"I don't like to do it," he said. He taped his pry bar with his hammer and popped up a piece of tack strip. "So I do it fast."

"That makes sense," I said. I dragged the trash can behind him and picked up the tack strip he was popping up. We finished the whole wall in about five minutes.

"Alright," I said. "Jamal, start down there, at that end of hallway." I pointed to the east end of the hallway. "Sweep everything that way." I pointed to the west end of the hallway. "And sweep it clean. That's important."

"I know," Jamal said.

"I'm going to go get some patch, and we'll fill in these holes and cracks."

Jamal grabbed the broom and walked down to the east end of the hallway.

I took the service elevator down to the loading dock and went out to my van.

When I was in my van, I opened up a five gallon bucket of Dependable crack filler and looked inside. It was about half full of the white powder. I figured that would be enough. So I grabbed the bucket of Dependable, an empty bucket—for mixing—two trowels and a putty knife, and then I headed back up to the forth floor.

Jamal and I worked well together. When he was done sweeping, he mixed and poured the crack filler. I spread it on the floor with a trowel. In a little over an hour we were done.

Jamal helped me get my stuff back down to my van. He carried the garbage can full of tools. I carried the last trash bag, which had a few pieces of tack strip in it and some dirt. I threw the trash bag in the dumpster.

When we got to the van, I opened the side door, and Jamal loaded the trash can full of tools.

"Thanks a lot for you help, Jamal. I really appreciate it." I reached for my wallet.

"Glad to help," Jamal said.

I opened my wallet, pulled out a fifty dollar bill, and handed it to him. "Is that enough?"

Jamal smiled and nodded. "Yeah."

I looked into my open wallet. I wasn't going to pay Bob Jones anything for the work that he had done on the forth floor, so I could afford to be generous. "No it isn't," I said. I pulled out another fifty dollar bill and handed it to him.

"Wow! Thanks a lot, Mark. I'll work with you anytime."

"Well, okay. Tell Ray I said thanks."

"I will."

Jamal pulled a cigarette out of his pocket. He put it in his mouth and walked away. I got into my van.

As I was about to pull out of the parking lot, I saw Bob Jones's van coming down the road. He pulled into the parking lot. I rolled my window down. Bob stopped his van and rolled his window down.

"You're fired," I said.

"What!" He seemed very surprised.

"Check your voicemail," I said.

I rolled up my window and drove away.

It was about noon when I got on I-71 in Louisville to head back home.

Five miles down the road, my cell phone rang.

"Hello."

"This is Drake Memorial Hospital, I'm looking for Mark Stone," a woman's voice said.

"This is Mark Stone."

"Are you married to Kathleen Stone?"

"Yes. What happened?"

"We have your wife here in the emergency room at Drake."

"Is she alright? Was she in an accident?"

"No. She wasn't in an accident, and she's not injured. But she's here, and she needs someone to pick her up and take her home."

"Is there something wrong with her car?"

"So far as I know, there is nothing wrong with her car."

"Well, why can't she drive home?"

"Mr. Stone! Your wife is not allowed to drive!" The woman made that point emphatically. "Someone has to pick her up."

"Well, I'm driving now, but it's going to be at least two hours before I can get up there."

"Can you get here any sooner than that?"

"No."

"Okay," the woman said. "I'll have my supervisor call you. Good bye."

"Good bye."

Ten minutes later, my cellphone rang again.

"Hello."

"Hello. This is Sheila Henry at Drake Memorial Hospital. Am I speaking to Mark Stone?"

"Yes, you are," I said.

"Mr. Stone, how soon can you get here to pick up Kathleen?"

"Listen, like I told the other person who called: It's going to be a couple hours. I'm heading up there now. But I'm not in the area. I'm on I-71." I glanced at a sign at the side of the expressway. "I'm passing through La Grange, Kentucky.

"Where's that?" she asked.

"Kentucky? It's on the south side of the Ohio River."

"Is there anyone else you can send—a family member, a friend perhaps?"

"No. There's no one else."

"Well, your wife keeps trying to walk out of the hospital," she said. "We don't want to detain her."

"What the hell are you talking about! You won't let her drive her car. It sounds to me like you *are* detaining her!"

That sounded angry. I didn't expect that, and I'm sure Ms. Henry didn't either.

After a short pause, I asked, "How'd she get there, anyway?"

"The Xenia police pulled her over for driving erratically. She appeared to be confused, so the officer called an ambulance. And she was brought here to be checked out."

"Really." That surprised me. Kathy's always been a good driver.

"And now she's ready to go home."

"Well why don't you call her a cab? She's got a credit card. She can pay for it."

"No. She can't be home alone. That would be dangerous."

"She's home alone all the time. She'll be fine," I said.

"What if she wanders off?"

"She won't. She sticks to her routine when she's at home. She feeds her chickens. She feeds the wild birds. She doesn't wander off.."

"Just get here as soon as you can."

I looked at the speedometer. I was going 75mph. "I'm going eighty right now," I said. "It's still going to take me a couple hours to get there."

"That's all you can do, I guess," she said.

"Right," I said.

About ten minutes later, my cellphone rang again.

"Hello."

"Mr. Stone, this is Sheila Henry at Drake Memorial Hospital."

"Yes," I said.

"We sent your wife home in a cab," she said.

"Thank you." I breathed a sigh of relief.

"When you said that your wife has a routine when she's at home, that got me thinking. She was asking us about 'the chickens' a lot. So we got her a cab, and told her to go home and take care of her chickens."

"I really appreciate that," I said. "And that's what she will do when she gets home."

"I believe she will," Sheila said.

I slowed the van down to sixty mile an hour, which is a more comfortable driving speed for me. I only made one stop on the way home. I got off the expressway in Independence, Kentucky, went into a Speedway, bought a twelve pack of Budweiser, and then I got right back on the expressway.

It was a few minutes after three when I got home. I parked my van behind the house, finished my third beer, and put the empty cans back in the box with the full ones.

Kathy came out of the house. When I got out of the van, she was walking up to me. "A funny thing happened today," she said.

"Where's the Honda?" I asked.

"Kmart. They wouldn't let me have my car." She looked at me, waiting for some sort of reaction.

"Okay," I said. "Did you go see Dr. Raji?"

"I went. He wasn't there."

"He wasn't there?" That seemed odd to me.

"They said doctor's not here. But wait. I waited and left."

"You went to Kmart."

"Yes."

"Okay," I said, still puzzled.

"Are you hungry?"

"Can we have supper?"

"Yes," I said.

We went into the house. I threw my empty beer cans in the trash, and put the full ones in the refrigerator.

I warmed up some chili in the microwave and we ate supper.

chapter 4

June 20, 2013

    I slept in until 7:00 AM. I hadn't set the alarm on the night before because I didn't plan to go to Louisville or anywhere else in the morning. I had problems to deal with at home—especially the problem of Kathy's car being absent from our driveway.

    I made the coffee because Kathy was still in bed.

    When the coffee was ready, I poured myself a cup and went into the computer room.

    I called Ray first.

    "Yeah, Mark. What's up?"

    "Ray, it doesn't look like I'm going to make it down there today."

    "Okay."

    "I've got too much shit to take care of here."

    "Well you're the boss, Mark. You don't have to tell me about it."

    "No. I guess I don't," I said. "I never did get Phillip's phone number from you. I wanted to talk to him this morning."

    "It's on my cellphone. But hold on, I'll get it for you." Ray said something to Steve. "Mark, I got it. It's on Steve's cellphone too. Are you ready?"

    "Yeah."

    He read me the number and I wrote it down.

    "Thanks Ray. Hey, where are you guys anyway?"

    "We are three miles from Napoleon."

    "Okay."

    "Don't worry about Phillip," Ray said. "He won't fuck up. I'll make sure of that."

    "Thanks Ray. I'll probably be down there tomorrow."

"Okay. Have a nice day, Mark."

"You too, Ray."

I tapped Phillip's phone number into my cellphone, and then I tapped the green icon at the bottom of the screen.

"Yo."

"Is this Phillip?"

"Yessir."

"Where are you right now?"

"We're on I-71. It just split off from I-75."

"Okay. Ray will be down there when you get there. He'll show you where the carpet and the glue are in the garage."

"Right."

"We're doing all the floors exactly the same."

"Right."

"You're doing the forth floor. But take a look at the first or the second floor to see—"

"Right."

"Are you listening to me Phillip?"

"Right," he said, and then he laughed.

"Okay. It's a simple job. The Brown plush goes in the middle of the hallway. That's the elevator area."

"Okay."

"Okay. Now the sixty foot piece you'll need to split right down the middle."

"Okay."

"Cut it carefully because you only have a couple inches to spare."

"I'll make sure I do that."

"After you've made that cut, one piece will have a red diamond five inches from the cut edge."

"Uh huh."

"When you lay it out, put the cut edge of that piece on the front side of the hallway. Put the cut edge of the other piece on the back side of the other end of the hallway."

"So we're turning the carpet?"

"No."

"You're confusing me."

"I know I am." I chuckled. "We're not turning the carpet. But we're trying to get the tip a red diamond to touch the back baseboard along the entire length of the hallway?"

"Oh."

"I'm not going to be there today. But I'm going to try to get down there tomorrow."

"I'll probably get Ray to help me lay it out," Phillip said.

"That's a good idea," I said.

After talking to Phillip, I got up and went to the kitchen to refill my coffee cup.

While I was pouring coffee into my cup, Kathy came out to the kitchen. Rupert (our Jack Russel Terrier) was following her, wiggling and wagging his tail. His nails were clicking noisily on the laminate floor.

"Can I have supper?" she asked.

"Put Rupert out," I said.

"Put Rupert out?" she asked.

"Yes."

She got a Beggin' Strip out of the bag that we kept on top of the refrigerator. Then she went to the front door, opened it, and threw the Beggin' Strip out to the front yard. Rupert dashed out after it.

Kathy came back into the kitchen. "Can I have supper?"

"Yes," I said.

Kathy got the box of Cocoa Puffs out of the cupboard, and poured some in a bowl. I got the milk out of the refrigerator and poured some on top of the cereal.

"Do you want coffee?" I asked.

"Yeah."

I poured another cup of coffee and set it in front of her. Then I sat down at the table with my coffee.

Kathy took a sip of coffee and looked at me. "Do you have work today?"

"No."

She took a few bites of cereal, and then she asked: "Are the chickens out?"

"No. I haven't been out there. There still in."

"Kay."

After Kathy finished her cereal, she put her bowl in the sink. Then she prepared the chickens' water and put her coat on to go outside.

"I'll go out with you," I said. I grabbed the egg basket.

We went into the garage, and then into the chicken house, which is attached to the garage.

The chickens were all on the floor. It was a sunny day, and they wanted out. I stepped carefully around them to get to the back of the chicken house. Then I lifted open their little two foot by two foot door. They all rushed for the opening, clucking and bumping into each other.

Kathy picked up their water bowl. The bowl had some straw, and some feces in it. "This is messy."

"I'll rinse it," I said.

I took the bowl outside to our spigot and rinsed it. I brought it back in and gave it to Kathy.

Kathy filled the chicken's water bowl, and then she filled their food bowl.

I looked for eggs. I found two brown ones, two green ones and a white one in one corner; and another brown one in another corner.

"There's only one white egg," I said.

We have two leghorn hens. They're the ones who lay the white eggs, and they almost never take a day off.

Kathy pointed to beside a bale of straw. "They got that spot," she said.

Sure enough, there was a white egg and a brown egg in the spot that I was not aware of. I picked them up and put them in the basket with the others.

Kathy and I went back to the house. She filled the plastic pitcher with bird seed, and went out to feed the wild birds. I put the eggs on the counter and went into the computer room. It was three minutes after nine, which meant the Xenia Health Center was open.

I tapped the number into my cellphone and then tapped the green icon.

A woman answered the phone: "Xenia Health Center."

"Hello. This is Mark Stone. My wife, Kathleen, had an appointment yesterday at ten o'clock with Dr. Raji."

"I remember her," the woman said.

"Good," I said. "Do you remember if Dr. Raji was at that appointment yesterday?"

"Dr. Raji was not in yesterday."

"Okay then, why didn't you call Kathy and tell her that Dr. Raji wouldn't be there?"

"Mr. Stone, we tried to call your wife several times. She never answered her phone."

"Okay," I said, thinking that was probably true.

"One of our other doctors, Dr. Kennedy, looked at your wife briefly since she was already here, and your wife asked Dr. Kennedy for more metronidazole."

"You say she asked for more metro…metro…that cream?

"Yes."

"I think you misunderstood her. She doesn't even use that stuff."

"Mr. Stone, I don't think Dr. Kennedy misunderstood her. She asked for more metronidazole, and Dr. Kennedy asked me to call in another prescription for her at the Kmart Pharmacy."

"Alright," I said. I knew she was wrong about that, but I didn't want to argue with her.

"Dr. Kennedy also asked me to call Choice Care, which is a nursing service in Beavercreek, and see if they could send someone over to evaluate your wife."

"Evaluate her? I don't understand. Why would you bring in somebody from a nursing service to evaluate her?"

"Mr. Stone, your wife has dementia."

"I know that."

"Well we didn't think she should be driving."

"She drives fine."

"Mr. Stone, your wife is not lucid enough to drive a car."

"She might not be 'lucid', in your opinion, but she has a perfect driving record."

"Mr. Stone! I'm not going to argue with you."

"I'm not trying to argue with you," I said. "I'm just trying to find out what happened yesterday." Then I asked, "So what did this person from the nursing service say about my wife?"

"Mr. Stone, we asked Kathleen to wait fifteen minutes. And she sat down. But when the RN from Choice Care got here, she was gone."

"Okay. Thank you for the information," I said.

"You're welcome," she said.

I used to be a smoker. I quit about twenty years ago, and, usually, I don't think about smoking anymore. But, sometimes, I have a strong urge to light up a cigarette. This was one of those times.

I walked out to the deck and watched the chickens run around their yard.

Kathy emptied the plastic pitcher into the last bird feeder, and then she started walking back to the house. She stopped at the edge of the driveway and stared at the spot where the Honda was usually parked. Then she looked up at me. "I need my car," she said.

"I'm working on it," I told her.

I went back into the computer room and called the Xenia Police Department.

"Xenia Police. May I help you?" a woman said.

"Yes. My name is Mark Stone. And yesterday, my wife, Kathleen Stone, was pulled over by the Xenia Police. I just wanted to find out what exactly happened."

"Okay. I'm looking at the log. Did she get a ticket, do you know?"

"No. I don't believe she did."

"Oh, I found her name. She wasn't pulled over. But we received a call from the Kmart parking lot at 11:23 AM. Kathleen Stone was involved in that incident."

"Okay, so what happened?"

"That's not clear. Officer Price was the officer who responded to the call. Shall I have him call you?"

"Please do."

"Okay. Officer Price will call you as soon as he can."

"Thank you."

Kathy came into the computer room. She looked at me. I looked at her, waiting for her to say something.

Finally, I said, "Yes?"

"Can we go get the Honda?"

"We're going to do that, Kathy. But not now."

"I need my car."

"I know."

My cellphone rang a few minutes later.

"Hello."

"Is this Mark Stone?"

"Yes. I'm Mark Stone?"

"Mr. Stone, this is Tom Price with the Xenia Police."

"Thanks for calling. Are you the officer that pulled Kathy Stone over yesterday?"

"I didn't pull her over, Mr. Stone."

"You didn't? I was told that she was pulled over for erratic driving."

"Who told you that?"

"Someone from Drake Memorial Hospital—a nurse, I guess. She called me and told me that the Xenia Police had pulled over my wife for 'erratic driving'."

"No. That's not what happened, Mr. Stone," Officer Price said. "I responded to a call to go to the Kmart parking lot to see a Ms. Tami Anderson. Ms. Anderson is a nurse—an agency nurse of some sort, I believe. She is the one who reported your wife's erratic driving."

"Really?"

"Yes, really, Mr. Stone. Ms. Anderson said she followed your wife from the Xenia Health Center, and she almost caused four accidents on Main Street."

"Where did these 'almost accidents' occur?"

"On Main Street."

"I know 'on Main Street'. But where on Main Street? At the intersection of Progress; at the intersection of Allison? And what was she doing? Was she running red lights? Was she swerving out of her lane?"

"Mr. Stone, I don't know. I didn't observe your wife's driving. You'll have to ask Ms. Anderson those questions."

"And I intend to do that. But you just took Ms. Anderson's word for it and sent my wife off to the hospital."

"No, Mr. Stone, that's not what happened. When I got to Kmart, your wife was in the store. I took a statement from Ms. Anderson, and we waited for your wife to come out. She was in the store quite awhile. All she bought was some doggy treats."

"She enjoys walking around Kmart."

"And she's allowed to do that. But when she came out of the store, I talked to her. She seemed confused. So I thought it best to have her checked out."

"I see," I said. "Is her car still at Kmart?"

"We haven't done anything with it."

"Well, thank you for that."

"You're welcome."

I turned around in my chair. Kathy was standing in the doorway. "Can we go get the Honda?" she asked.

"I have one more phone call," I said.

Kathy left the room, and I looked up the number for Choice Care on my computer. I called them.

"Choice Care of Beavercreek, how may I direct your call?" a woman said.

"I'd like to talk to Tami Anderson."

"Just a minute," she said.

A radio station that plays 70's music started playing on my phone. I was listening to Boz Scaggs' *Lido Shuffle*. Then the music stopped.

"Tami is not available right now. May I ask who's calling."

"This is Mark Stone. Just have her call me. Tell her its important."

"Can she reach you at the number you're calling from now?"

"Yes."

"I'll tell her, Mr. Stone."

"Thank you."

I waited twenty minutes and then I called back.

"Hi. This is Mark Stone again. Is Tami Anderson there?"

"Tami will be in the field all day. I gave her your message."

"Could you give me her cellphone number. It's very important that I reach her."

"We've not suppose to do that, Mr. Stone."

"This is very important. Otherwise, I wouldn't ask."

"Well, I guess it'd be okay," she said, and then she gave me Tami Anderson's cellphone number.

I wrote the number down, said, "Thank you," and ended that call.

Then I tapped Tami Anderson's number into my cellphone and tapped the green icon. Her phone rang a few times, and then it went to voicemail. I called again a few minutes later, and again the call went to voicemail. This time I left a message:

"Tami, this is Mark Stone. Yesterday, you witnessed some errors in my wife's driving on Main Street, in Xenia. Please call me. I want to know exactly what you saw."

I immediately regretted leaving that message after I ended the call. Now that I'd spilled the beans, if Tami Anderson didn't want discuss the incident with me, she wouldn't call.

And I really wanted to know what happened, because Kathy wouldn't normally take Main Street from that area in Xenia to go to Kmart. Normally she would take Dayton Xenia Road.

Of course, it was possible that Kathy mistakenly turned right instead of left on Progress Drive. And then, thinking she was somewhere else, she turned left on Main Street. And then, feeling lost and confused, she created one dangerous situation after the other all the way down Main Street. And all this time, Tami Anderson was one car behind her, observing her driving.

But she did end up at Kmart. How did that happen?

It seemed much more likely that when Kathy left the Xenia Health Center, she turned left at Progress Drive and took Dayton Xenia Road to Kmart. And Tami Anderson, having been told by the people at the Xenia Health Center that Kathy was probably going to Kmart, turned right at Progress Drive and took Main Street to Kmart. Horns might have been honking in the traffic in front of her—or they might not have been. But when she arrived at Kmart, she saw Kathy getting out of her car—or Kathy was already in the store. Either way, she concluded that Kathy must have driven erratically. So she call the police and lied about what she had witnessed.

I had the feeling that Tami Anderson didn't want to talk to me.

Kathy came into the computer room. "Can we go get the Honda?"

"Kathy, did anything unusual happen when you were driving yesterday?"

"They wouldn't let me have my car."

"Yeah. I guess that's unusual. But I mean: When you were actually driving, did you almost hit someone, or did someone almost hit you? Did anything like that happen?"

"It did not."

"It did not?" I asked.

"It did not," she said again.

"Okay. Let's go get the Honda."

I drove us up to Xenia in the van. When I pulled in the Kmart parking lot, I saw the Honda. It was parked by itself. I pulled up next to it.

"Okay, Kathy," I said. "I want you to follow me home."

"Kay."

"Alright then," I said.

"Alright then," she said, and she got out of the van.

I waited until she got the Honda started, and then I made a U-turn. I pulled up to the light at Church Street, and put my left turn signal on. I glanced in my rear view mirror. Kathy pulled up behind me. She put her left turn signal on.

On the drive home, I kept a close eye on the rear view mirror to assess Kathy's driving. She was using her turn signal properly, and she kept the Honda in the center of the lane. Nothing erratic about that.

When we were on Route 42 coming out of Xenia, we started out in the left lane. Without signaling, I hopped over to the right lane. I looked in my rear view mirror. Kathy's right turn signal started blinking. Then she slowly merged into the right lane behind me. About a mile from our house, I hopped back into the left lane. I watched in the rear view mirror as Kathy's left turn signal came on and she slowly merged into the left lane. When her left turn signal stopped blinking, I put my left turn signal on. I kept glancing up at the rear view mirror. She was dead center in the lane behind me, with no turn signal blinking. One hundred yards from our house, Kathy's left turn signal started blinking.

I turned left into our driveway and parked the van. Kathy came in behind me and parked the Honda.

I walked over to the Honda as Kathy was opening the car door.

"Open the trunk, please?" I asked.

"Open the trunk?"

"Yes."

She opened the trunk of the Honda, and we went into the house.

I picked up a laundry basket full of cardboard and opened the back door.

"What are we doing?" Kathy asked.

"Recycling," I said.

"Kay," she said, and then she picked up the laundry basket that was full of plastic bottles.

We carried the baskets out to the Honda and loaded them into the trunk. We went back into the house. I picked up the laundry basket with the papers. She picked up the laundry basket with the glass. As I was loading my basket into the Honda, I noticed a red folder which was labeled *Drake Memorial Hospital*.

Curious, I opened the folder and looked at the papers inside. These were Kathy's discharge papers from yesterday. There were eight pages. On the last page, in a section titled *Doctor's Recommendations*, the doctor wrote, "No driving alone!"

I wasn't really surprised by the statement. The exclamation point offended me, a little bit.

Kathy loaded the glass into the Honda. I closed the trunk lid and went back up on the deck to lock the back door.

When I turned around, Kathy was opening the passenger door of the Honda. "You're going to drive," I said.

She waited until I came down the steps. "Me drive?" she asked.

"Yes. You're going to drive."

She walked around the back of the car and got in on the driver's side. I got in on the passenger side.

She got out her key and started the Honda.

"Do you know where the recycling station is in Xenia?"

She looked at me. "Yes."

"Okay, that's where we're going."

She put the Honda in reverse and backed out of her parking spot, turning the steering wheel to align the car with the driveway. Then she pulled up to the road. She looked both ways. It was clear.

So she pulled out of the driveway, turning right, and we were headed to Xenia.

She had control of the vehicle. So I sat back and kept an eye on the speedometer.

She slowed to about forty-five for the flashing yellow light at Paintersville Road. After that, Route 42 becomes a four lane divided highway. She increased her speed. Fifty, fifty-five, sixty, and her speed was still increasing.

"Slow down!" I said. "The speed limit is fifty-five."

"I'm going the speed of traffic."

"Well. Yeah, I guess you were. But don't go over sixty, please."

"Kay."

We were coming up to the Route 35 Bypass, which is on the south edge of Xenia, when Kathy turned on her left turn signal. She got into the left lane. She slowed down and turned left. Now we were on the on-ramp to the Route 35 Bypass.

"What are you doing?"

Kathy laughed. "Going to recycling," she said.

"Oh."

She stayed in the right lane on the westbound Route 35 Bypass. I glanced at the speedometer.

"Going sixty," she said.

"Okay."

She got off the Route 35 Bypass at the Main Street exit, headed east a short distance, and turned left at Progress Drive. She turned left at Green Way Boulevard, and we arrived at the recycling station.

"I guess that way is faster," I said.

Kathy laughed.

Kathy popped the trunk lid open, and we began emptying our laundry baskets into their assigned dumpsters. I walked the last basket, the cardboard, over to the cardboard dumpster. When I got back, Kathy was already in the car, in the driver's seat. I closed the trunk lid, and took the passenger seat.

"Let's go to Kmart," I said.

"Go to Kmart," she said.

"Yes. Kmart."

Kathy pulled out of the recycling station onto Green Way Boulevard. She put on her left turn signal, stopped at the stop sign at Progress Drive, and then she turned left onto Progress Drive. She put on her right turn signal, stopped at the four way stop sign at Dayton Xenia Road, and then she turned right on Dayton Xenia Road.

"Okay," I said to myself.

"What?"

"Nothing," I said.

Kathy drove us to Kmart going the back way—which is the way I thought she would go. Kathy's never been a fan of driving on Main Street.

We went inside Kmart, bought a case of Budweiser and a bag of Meow Mix, and then Kathy drove us back home.

Kathy shut the car off and took the keys out of the ignition. She turned and looked at me. "What now?" she asked.

I thought for a minute. "Case dismissed," I said.

chapter 5

Late Summer, 2013

Kathy continued to take the Namenda and the donepezil which Dr. Doolittle prescribed back in April. Those two medications cost us over $400 a month. But the cost, by itself, didn't bother me too much. What bothered me was that Kathy was taking a medication to treat a disease—Alzheimer's disease—which I didn't think she had.

Kathy definitely had dementia. But, in my opinion, Kathy had Frontal Temporal Dementia, which is much different than Alzheimer's disease.

It also bothered me that those expensive drugs—Namenda and donepezil—seemed to have no effect on Kathy.

So I did some internet research, and here's what I found out: Studies show that some patients with moderate Alzheimer's Disease show some improvement in memory when taking memantine (Nemenda) and donepezil. Studies also show that patients with Frontal Temporal Dementia did not benefit from taking memantine or donepezil. Some of those studies suggested that, while the FTD patients did not benefit from taking the drugs, the drugs didn't harm them; other studies suggested that the Alzheimer's drugs caused the FTD patients to become more confused.

I couldn't think of a good reason for Kathy to be taking the Alzheimer's drugs, but discontinuing her medications was a medical decision. I didn't want to make that decision myself. I needed to talk to a doctor about it. So I googled "doctors near Spring Valley, Ohio". The doctor on the list who was closest to us was Dr. John Brenneman. He was located in Bellbrook.

I called his office.

A woman answered the phone: "Dr. Brenneman's office."

"Hi. I was wondering: Is Dr. Brenneman accepting new patients?"

"Yes he is."

"Great," I said. "I'm calling for my wife Kathleen. She has dementia."

"Would you like to make an appointment for your wife?"

"Yes."

"Does you wife have any other medical problems besides the dementia?"

"No. Dementia is the problem."

"The earliest appointment I have is on Friday, August 30 at 2:30 PM."

"That would be fine," I said, although I would have preferred an earlier time.

"What is your wife's name?"

"Kathleen Stone."

"And who is Kathleen's insurance provider?"

"We don't have insurance."

She didn't say anything for a minute, so I asked: "Is the deal off, or what?"

"No, Mr. Stone, Dr. Brenneman will see Kathleen," she said. "But you will need to bring in one hundred and eighty dollars cash. We also take all major credit cards. We do not accept checks."

"That's fine. We're not going to cheat you."

"Okay, Mr. Stone. We will see Kathleen, and you, on Friday, August 30, at 2:30 PM. Please come in fifteen or twenty minutes early to complete the new patient paperwork."

"Alright. We'll be there."

· · · · ·

Dr. Brenneman's office was in a modern, ranch style, brick office building on the West side of Bellbrook. The sign in the front said that Dr. Brenneman was in Suite D. I drove around the building. Suite D was in the back. I parked the PT Cruiser.

"Let's go in, Kathy."

Kathy looked at me. "Is this for you, or me?" she asked.

I thought about her question. "For both of us," I said.

"Kay," she said.

I opened the glass door and followed Kathy into Dr. Brenneman's waiting area, which, I thought, had a very interesting set-up. The chairs were set up in rows. They all pointed in one direction—toward a wall with a large screen TV. CNN happened to be on when we walked in. There were eight rows, and each row had eight chairs. So the room could seat sixty-four people. But there was no one there except us.

I tapped lightly on the frosted glass window. A nurse opened it. "Oh, I'm sorry," she said. "Are you Mr. Stone?"

"Yes," I said.

"I have some forms for you to fill out." She handed me a clipboard with a stack of papers clipped to it.

Kathy and I sat down in the third row. I began filling out forms.

"I have to use the bathroom," Kathy said.

"Okay." I said. I looked around. I didn't see any restrooms. So I got up and went to the frosted window, which was still open. "Excuse me," I said to the nurse. "My wife has to use the restroom."

"Of course," the nurse said. She got up from her desk and came around and opened the hallway door. She stood holding the door open. "Ma'am. Ma'am, the restroom's in here."

Kathy looked at her.

"Kathy," I said. "You said you have to use the bathroom." I pointed to the hallway. "The bathroom's right in there."

Kathy got up. She walked toward the hallway.

"I'll hold your coat," I said.

"I need my coat!"

"Kathy, you don't need to take your coat into the bathroom."

She thought about it, and then she took her coat off and handed it to me.

"The restroom's right there, ma'am," the nurse said, pointing to a door.

Kathy walked down the hallway, opened the door, and went into the bathroom. She didn't shut the door.

"I'll send her back out when she's done," the nurse said.

"She didn't shut the bathroom door," I said.

"I see that," the nurse said, and then she closed the hallway door.

I went back to my seat and put Kathy's coat on my lap. I picked up the clipboard and pen. I had two more forms to fill out.

I finished the forms and turned the clipboard in to the nurse at the window. While I was standing there, the bathroom door opened, and Kathy came out to the hallway.

I didn't hear the toilet flush. "Um," I began.

"Yes," the nurse said. "You were about to say something?"

"No. Well, yes. Uh, when will the doctor see us?"

An older woman passed Kathy in the hallway and came out into the waiting area.

"He can see you now. But I need payment of one hundred and eighty dollars," she said.

"I have the cash," I said. I pulled a one hundred dollar bill and four twenties out of my wallet. I gave it to her.

"Follow me," the nurse said.

We followed her down the hall to a room, and we went in and sat down.

"I need my coat" Kathy said, after a couple minutes.

"Not right now," I said.

"We should leave," she said, a couple minutes later.

"Let's wait a little while longer," I said.

The door opened. A gray haired man in a white lab coat came into the room. A stethoscope hung from his neck. "I'm Dr. Brenneman," he said. "How are you folks today?"

"Fine," I said.

The doctor put the stethoscope in his ears. "We're going to have a look at Kathleen today," he said.

As the doctor listened to her heart, Kathy gave me a dirty look, and I felt a little bit guilty for misleading her about the purpose of this doctor's appointment.

Dr. Brenneman checked her blood pressure. "One twenty-five over eighty-five. That's pretty good," he said.

He picked up her wrist and counted her heartbeats. "One hundred and five," he said. "That's slightly high."

He held the stethoscope in various places on her back and asked her to breathe. Kathy didn't follow his directions very well, but he still said: "Sounds good."

Dr. Brenneman took the stethoscope out of his ears. "Is she taking any medications?" he asked me.

"She's taking Namenda and donepezil."

"Uh huh."

"Her doctors in Xenia think she has Alzheimer's. But I don't think that's what she has."

Dr. Brenneman looked Kathy in the eye. "Kathleen, what is today's date? Do you know?"

"No, Dr. Brenneman, she doesn't know that. And why should she? She's not working. She doesn't watch the news. Today's date is just not information that's important to her. Why don't you ask her about something that she should know?"

"Does she still drive?"

"Yes."

"Does she have her own car?"

"Yes."

Again, the doctor looked Kathy in the eye. "Kathleen, what color is your car?"

"Color?" Kathy turned to me. "What's 'color'?"

"She does forget things like that," I said. "Sometimes she'll call cows 'chickens'. She's not very good at calling things by their right name."

"Did her doctors in Xenia order a CAT scan for her?"

"No. They did not. They said there's no tests for Alzheimer's."

Dr. Brenneman shook his head. "No," he said. "You can't diagnose Alzheimer's with a CAT scan alone. But you can rule things out. She might have had a stroke."

"I don't know about that," I said. "But I don't think the medication that she's taking is helping her."

"We can discuss her medications some time in the future," he said. "Right now, she needs a CAT scan. That's the next step. So let's get that done."

"Okay," I said.

"Talk to Debbie at the front desk before you leave."

After he left the room, I gave Kathy her coat. She put the coat on, and we walked out of the room. I stopped at the window in front of the front desk.

"I'll wait in the PT Cruiser," Kathy said.

I looked at Debbie. "I'll be right back," I said.

I followed Kathy out the door. I aimed the remote at the PT Cruiser and unlocked it. Kathy got in on the passenger side and sat down.

I came back in and walked back up to the window.

"Will she be all right out there by herself?" Debbie asked.

"She'll be fine."

"Dr. Brenneman referred Kathleen to Clear Creek Medical Imaging for the CAT scan," she explained. "They will call you, probably on Monday or Tuesday, to set up an appointment for the scan. After she gets the CAT scan done, call us and make another appointment to see Dr. Brenneman."

"Alright," I said. "I'll see you some time in the future."

"Have a nice rest of your day," she said.

· · · · ·

The call came Monday morning.

"Hello."

"Hello. This is John with Clear Creek Medical Imaging. I'm calling to speak to Mark Stone."

"Hi, John. This is Mark Stone."

"Dr. Brenneman's office said that you were the contact person for Kathleen Stone. Is Kathleen your mother?"

"Kathleen's my wife. But I am the contact person."

"Kathleen has been referred to us for a CT scan."

"Yes. I know. I was told you'd be calling to set up an appointment. Uh, the only day I have open this week is Friday. Do you have times available on Friday?"

"We're not open on Fridays."

"Oh. Okay. Well, next week we can't do it. But any day the following week—"

"We have appointments available on the eighteenth," he said.

"That would work."

"Do you prefer mornings or afternoons?"

"Mornings," I said. "As early as possible."

"We have a nine o'clock?"

"That would be perfect."

"Okay, I'll put Kathleen down for nine o'clock, on Wednesday, September 18."

"We'll be there."

"One more thing, Mr. Stone. Dr. Brenneman's office informed us that you would be self-pay."

"Yeah. So."

"So we will need you to bring in a certified check in the amount of twenty-four hundred dollars at the time of the appointment."

"What! Did you say twenty-four hundred dollars?"

"That's the price of the procedure, Mr. Stone."

"Wow," I said. "I did not expect the price to be that high. I was expecting four, maybe five hundred dollars—something like that."

"The price of the procedure is twenty-four hundred dollars, Mr. Stone."

"Yeah. I know that. Does that include tax and everything?"

"That includes tax and everything."

"Okay. Let's see…Do you accept credit cards?"

"We do accept MasterCard and Visa. But there is a five percent convenience charge added to credit card payments."

"Well of course there's a convenience charge! So that would be—"

"An additional one hundred and twenty dollars if you put it on a credit card, Mr. Stone."

"Yeah. Listen, uh, John, I'm going to have to think about this. I'll call ya back on that appointment."

"Do you want me to scratch out you wife's name?"

"Well, uh, yeah. Scratch her name. I'll get back with ya."

"Okay."

I didn't need to think about it very long. We had been getting mail about the grand opening of the Health Insurance Marketplace for the ACA, or Obamacare, for the last three months. Open enrollment was going to begin on October 1, and that was less than a month away. I was already planning to buy us insurance. And now, faced with a very costly medical procedure that Dr. Brenneman ordered for Kathy, the best course of action, it seemed to me, would be to delay the CT scan until we had a health insurance policy. Once we had insurance, we could go ahead and get the CT scan done and we wouldn't have to worry about the cost. Because, well, we'd have insurance.

chapter 6

Early in October, 2013, I purchased an Obamacare policy for Kathy and me. Our health insurance coverage was set to begin on January 1, 2014.

The insurance company, Buckeye Blue Shield, sent us a booklet explaining their rules for using the insurance. They also sent us a thick directory of all the health care providers in their network in the state of Ohio.

Now I already knew that Kathy needed to have a CT scan done on her brain. The booklet explained to me how to get this procedure covered by our insurance. First, I would have to take Kathy to a primary care physician. The primary care physician would have to refer her to a specialist—in this case a neurologist. Then, if the neurologist ordered the CT scan, it would be covered.

I looked in the directory for Dr. Brenneman's name. Unfortunately, his name was not on their list of primary care physicians. So I circled another name: Dr. Carla Smith. Her office was in Waynesville, which was also close to us.

On the second of January, at nine o'clock, I called Dr. Smith's office.

"Dr. Smith's office," a woman said. "May I help you?"

"Hi. My name's Mark Stone. I'd like to make an appointment for my wife, Kathleen Stone."

"Is Kathleen a patient here?"

"No. We have Buckeye Blue Shield insurance, and Dr. Smith's name is in their preferred provider directory. It also said that you're accepting new patients."

"That's correct," she said. "We accept Buckeye Blue Shield insurance, and we are currently accepting new patients."

"Okay, then. As soon as Dr. Smith can see Kathleen—"

"Is Kathleen sick right now?"

"No. She's not exactly healthy either. Kathleen has dementia. This has been going on for a couple years."

"I see," she said. "Would January fifteenth be convenient for you and Kathleen? That's on a Wednesday."

"That would be fine."

"Is ten o'clock too early for you?"

"No. The earlier, the better," I said.

"Okay, Mr. Stone," she said. "We look forward to seeing you and Kathleen on Wednesday, the fifteenth, at ten o'clock."

"And we look forward to seeing you," I said.

. . . . . .

Kathy and I sat in the PT Cruiser. "Okay, Kathy, let's go in."

"You go in," she said.

"Kathy, the doctor's going to take a look at you. That's all. It won't take long."

"I don't want that."

"I know you don't, Kathy. But you have to go in."

"I have to go in?"

"Yes. We're going to go in. And we're going to come right back out. And then we can go get the chickens their food, okay."

"I have to go in, huh?"

"Yeah."

Kathy, very reluctantly, got out of the car. We walked into the office building. A sign said that Dr. Smith's office was in suite B. I opened the door with the "B" on it, and we went into Dr. Smith's office.

"I'm Mark Stone. This is my wife Kathleen," I told the nurse at the front desk.

"Good morning Mr. and Mrs. Stone," she said. "I have some paperwork for you to fill out." She handed me a clipboard. "And I need to see Kathleen's insurance card."

I handed the nurse Kathy's insurance card, and then I turned to

Kathy and said, "Okay, Kathy, let's sit down."

Kathy looked around the room. It was a small waiting room. There were about ten chairs, all of them empty. "Where to sit?" she asked.

"I don't know. Sit anywhere." I sat down. I tapped the chair next to me. "Sit right here."

Kathy sat down next to me.

I finished the paperwork and took the clipboard back up to the front desk. "All finished," I said to the nurse.

"Thank you. And here's your wife's insurance card." She handed me Kathy's insurance card.

When I turned around, Kathy was standing. "Are we done?" she asked.

"No, Kathy. We haven't seen the doctor yet." I went back to my chair and sat down.

Kathy remained standing.

"Kathy, please sit down."

She sat down.

After about a minute, she said, "I don't think doctor's going to see us."

"The doctor will see us," I said. "Let's just wait."

"Kay," she said. "Let's just wait."

She sat quietly for a couple minutes, and then she said, "I think we should just leave."

The nurse came into the waiting room. "You can bring her on back," she said. "Dr. Smith is ready to see her."

"Okay, Kathy. Let's go see the doctor."

We followed the nurse down the hall. She opened the door to a small examination room. We went in and sat down.

"Dr. Smith will see Kathleen shortly." The nurse left, leaving the door open.

"Kathy, will you take your coat off?" I asked.

She clutched at the front of her coat. "I need my coat. It's cold out."

"It's cold outside. It's not cold in here," I said.

Dr. Smith came in. She stood in front of Kathy and looked at her.

She smiled and said,"Hi, you must be Kathleen."

Kathy stared at her.

"Does she prefer to be called Kathleen or Kathy?"

"Either one," I said.

"Kathleen, I'm Dr. Smith."

"Kay," Kathy said, still clutching the front of her coat.

"Will you take your coat off for me, Kathleen?" Dr. Smith asked with a smile.

"No," Kathy said.

Dr. Smith chuckled. "She wants to be difficult." She put the stethoscope in her ears. "Kathleen, I'm going to listen to your heart."

Dr. Smith looked at me. "You're going to have to help me. Could you open her coat."

"Sure," I said. I got up and turned to face Kathy. "Kathy, I'm going to open your coat." I grabbed ahold of each of her hands, and I gently pushed them to her sides. Kathy looked me in the eye the whole time, and she put up no resistance. Her own hands opened the coat.

I stepped aside, and Dr. Smith slipped the chest-piece of the stethoscope under the coat. She listened to Kathy's heart, and then to both of her lungs.

Dr. Smith took the stethoscope out of her ears. "This is going to be challenging," she said, looking at Kathy. "Now I have to take her blood pressure."

"Is she going to have to take her coat off?" I asked.

"Maybe not." The doctor looked over Kathy's coat. "She has a lot of room in those sleeves." She picked up Kathy's left arm. "I think we can bunch the sleeve up to her shoulder. I can take her blood pressure over her shirt. That's thin material." She started pushing the coat sleeve up Kathy's arm.

"Could you hold this?"

"Sure," I said. I held the wadded up sleeve on Kathy's shoulder.

Dr. Smith wrapped the cuff of the blood pressure meter around Kathy's arm muscle. "This isn't ideal, but it will work," she said. She put the stethoscope in her ears and pumped up the cuff. She looked at the dial, and said, "Okay. Real good."

She let the air out of the cuff and took it off Kathy's arm.

I helped Kathy get her coat sleeve straightened out.

"Now I need to get her weight," Dr. Smith said. "The scale's out in the hall."

"Kathy, you need to get up," I said.

Kathy stood up. "Are we done?"

"Almost," Dr. Smith said.

We followed Dr. Smith down the hall to the scale.

"Kathleen, could you step up on the scale for me?" Dr. Smith asked.

I took ahold of Kathy's hand and arm and nudged her. "Come on, Kathy."

Kathy looked down at the bottom of the scale, and she wouldn't budge.

"Come on, Kathy," I said again.

"I think she's afraid to get up on the scale," Dr. Smith said.

"I don't understand why," I said. "It's a four inch step up. She climbs up and down our deck steps all day long."

"That's different," Dr. Smith said. "How much does she weigh?"

"Probably between one hundred and thirty and one hundred and thirty-five."

"Give me a number."

"One hundred and thirty two," I said. "That's on her driver's license."

She wrote that number down as she was walking away from the scale. "Follow me, please," she said. She walked into a small office and sat down at a desk. Then she looked up at me. "You can sit down."

I sat down on one of the chairs beside the desk. "Kathy, sit down please," I said.

"She can stand if she'd like," Dr. Smith said. Then she looked directly at me. "When did you begin to notice her dementia?"

"Probably about four years ago."

"In 2010?"

"Around then," I said. "But I didn't automatically think 'Oh, this is dementia'. I thought, at first, that it might be schizophrenia. I'd read, years ago, about a form of schizophrenia where the person speaks in 'word salads'. She did that sometimes. But, then again, she didn't seem to be insane. So I thought that it couldn't be schizophrenia."

"She hasn't seen a neurologist yet, I take it."

"No. That's the main reason we're here."

"I'm going to refer her to a neurologist. Do you know a neurologist that you'd like me to refer her to?"

"No. I don't know any neurologists."

"Unfortunately, I don't know a good neurologist either," Dr. Smith said.

"Well, it's got to be somebody on Buckeye Blue Shield's preferred provider list."

"Of course."

"Then, I guess, we'd prefer the closest one to Spring Valley. That's where we live."

"We can do that," she said. "I'll have Gina send over a referral to a neurologist near you, and you should get a call from them in the next few days. If you don't hear from them in about a week, let us know."

"Okay."

"I'd also like to get some blood work done on Kathleen." She handed me a form. "Fill this out, and take it to wherever she gets the blood work done. On the back, there's a list of labs where you can go to have it done. I recommend that you do this at least three or four days before she sees the neurologist."

I turned the paper over. "Alright. We'll probably get it done at Drake Memorial Hospital."

"You can go to any of those labs on the list. And you don't need an appointment."

Dr. Smith stood up and turned to Kathy. "We're done, Kathleen." She smiled and took Kathy's hand. "Now that wasn't so bad, was it?"

Kathy smiled back and chuckled.

• • • • •

I drove into Drake Memorial Hospital's parking lot and parked the PT Cruiser as close as I could to the Main Entrance. Drake has four different entrances. But since I didn't know where in the hospital they do the blood tests, going in the main entrance seemed the most reasonable choice.

I turned off the car and took the keys out of the ignition. I turned to Kathy. "Let's go in."

"Kay," she said.

We went into the main entrance and walked up to the information desk.

"My wife's here for blood tests," I told the guy behind the counter. "Where do they do that?"

"They do that in the emergency department. Do you know where that is?"

"I think so."

He stood up and pointed. "Take that hall all the way to the end. That's the ER. The lab is right behind their double doors, on the right. Ask somebody at the desk there. They'll show you where it is."

"Okay. Thank you."

Kathy and I walked down the hallway to the ER. We went up to a desk where a woman was sitting. "My wife needs to have some blood tests done," I told her. "Do you know where they do the blood tests.?"

The woman looked at Kathy. "You look awful familiar," she said.

"Do you know where they do the blood tests?" I asked again.

"Yeah." She got up and pushed a button to open the double doors. "That hallway right there." She pointed. "Go down there. It's the first door on the right."

"Thanks," I said.

Kathy and I went down the hallway to the first door on the right. I opened the door and we went in.

A young woman stood behind a counter. "Are you here for blood work?"

"My wife is."

"I'll take that," she said.

I handed her the form that Dr. Smith had given me.

She looked at the form for a few seconds and then put it down. "Kathleen," she said. "I'm going to take you to a room back here, and then I'll get your blood. Follow me please."

We followed her to a small room. She turned the light on and then went over to a cabinet and began putting medical instruments on a tray. With her back still to us, she said, "You're going to have to take your coat off for this, Kathleen."

To my astonishment, Kathy took her coat off and handed it to me.

The young woman put the tray on top of a small cart. "Sit down, Kathleen. Make yourself comfortable."

Kathy sat in the chair next to the cart, which was the only chair in the room.

The young woman began rolling up Kathy's shirt sleeve. "You're going to feel this, but it won't hurt." She bent over and wrapped a tourniquet around Kathy's arm muscle. She tapped Kathy's vein with her finger. Then, looking at Kathy's arm, she said, "I remember this vein."

She straightened up and looked at Kathy's face. "I've drawn your blood before," she said, and then she started laughing. "Look at you. Sitting there all calm and peaceful."

She turned to me. "The last time I drew her blood, she put up a fight. It took three of us just to get a blood sample."

I wasn't in the mood to joke around about the day that Kathy was detained at Drake Memorial Hospital, so I might have sounded angry when I said: "Yeah, well if I were in the situation that she was in that day, it would have taken six of ya! And you wouldn't be laughing about it now!"

"Forget I mentioned it," the young woman said.

"Sorry. I didn't mean to go off on you like that."

"I probably touched on a sore subject."

"You did."

She drew Kathy's blood, took the tourniquet off, and put a band-aid on her arm. "That's it, Kathleen. You can go home to your chickens now."

Kathy chuckled.

I helped her put her coat on, and we walked out of the hospital through the emergency room. It was about the same distance to the PT Cruiser as the main entrance.

After we got into the car, Kathy asked me: "Did I do good?"

"Yes," I said.

"Good," she said.

"I'm going to go to Rural King for the chicken food, okay," I said, and then I started the PT Cruiser.

"We need a back up for the wild bird seed," she said.

I pulled the car out of the parking lot. "We have an unopened bag of wild bird seed at home," I said.

"We need a back up."

"Alright, I guess we can get another one."

I drove the back way to Rural King, avoiding Main Street. I parked the car, and we went in the store.

I picked up a flat cart at the front of the store, and started pushing it down the front main aisle. Kathy walked beside me.

When we were next to the gun and hunting department, Kathy said, "We need wild bird seed."

"Yeah, I know." I pulled the cart down the narrow aisle up to the forty pound bags of wild bird seed. I picked up a bag off the top of the stack and put it on the cart.

"Can we get two?" Kathy asked.

"I guess," I said. "It's cheaper here than anywhere else." I loaded another bag

I pushed the cart back to the animal food section of the store. I found the chicken feed aisle, and pulled the cart up to the pallet of layer crumbles. I loaded four fifty pound bags on the cart, and then pulled the cart back out to the main aisle.

"Rupert needs some Little Bites," Kathy said.

"I just opened a bag of Little Bites yesterday," I said.

"We need a back up."

"Okay, the dog food's down here." I pushed the cart and she walked beside me.

A man with a boy, who was probably eight or nine, were walking toward us.

As they were passing us, Kathy looked down at the little boy, and asked, "Do you like chickens?"

The boy looked up at her. "I don't know any chicken's," the boy said.

"We have chickens and they like to run around. But the chickens don't like snow. They don't like snow because they don't have shoes."

"That's funny," the boy said.

They started walking away. "Dad, did you know that chickens didn't have shoes?" I heard the boy say. "No, I didn't," the dad said, laughing.

I loaded a bag of Little Bites on the cart.

"We need a back up for the cats," Kathy said.

I pushed the cart up to a pallet of Ally Cat. I picked up a bag.

"That won't work," she said.

"Kathy, I don't think they have Meow Mix."

An employee of the store was walking by and must have overheard me. "We have Meow Mix," he said. "It's not with the other cat food. I'll take you to it."

We followed him to the pallet of Meow Mix.

"How many bags do you want?"

"One," I said.

"Two," Kathy said.

"Two it is," he said, and he loaded two bags of Meow Mix on the cart.

"Well, I think we have enough stuff," I said, pushing the cart to the front of the store.

"Do they have Hershey?" Kathy asked.

"They probably do," I said.

When we were passing the candy aisle, I stopped the cart. "I'm going to get you some Hershey." Kathy waited by the cart while I went down the aisle and picked up a package of six Hershey chocolate bars.

"Can I have a Hershey?" Kathy asked when she saw the package in my hand.

"Wait till we pay for them," I said.

I pushed the cart up to the check out counter. I handed the girl the package of Hershey bars first. She rang them up and put them in a yellow plastic bag. Then she came out from behind the counter to ring up the bags of feed.

Kathy grabbed the yellow bag, opened the package of Hershey bars, unwrapped one and took a big bite.

"She must be hungry," the girl said, and then she looked for the bar code on the Meow Mix.

After we paid for everything, she asked, "Do you need help loading?"

"Yes. That would be nice."

"Ron, could you help him load?" she said to someone behind us.

"Glad to," Ron said. He was the guy who helped us with the Meow Mix.

Ron followed us out to the PT Cruiser. Kathy got in and finished eating her candy bar. I opened the Hatch of the PT Cruiser, and Ron and I took turns loading bags into the back of the car. After Ron loaded the last bag, I shut the hatch.

"Thanks a lot," I said.

"No problem," Ron said, wheeling away the cart.

I got in the car and drove us home.

chapter 7

The next day I had to do a small carpet job.

Or, to be more precise, I had to do a small piece of a big carpet job—a very big carpet job. My company, Stone Flooring, was under contract to do all the carpet and all the vinyl in a new seventy-two unit apartment complex in Mason. I had Terry doing all of the vinyl. Ray, Phillip, and I were doing the carpet.

On Thursday, January 16, we had two units in one building scheduled for carpet; and also, the steps and landings of another building was scheduled for carpet. I gave Ray and Phillip each a unit to do. I did the steps and landings because it was smaller yardage-wise—forty-four compared to ninety. But also, because no one else wanted to do the steps and landings.

I left my house at seven and drove to Middletown to pick up my helper Chuck. Chuck had been working for me for the last couple months. He had no driver's license because he owed so much in child support. So, most of the time, I had to pick him up, which I was getting tired of doing.

I parked my van in front of Chuck's dad's trailer. Usually Chuck sees me from a window and comes right out. He didn't do that this morning, so I honked my horn. I waited a couple minutes, and then I went up to the porch and knocked on the door.

Chuck's dad opened the door. "Yeah. What do you want?"

"Sorry to wake you up. I'm here for Chuck." I said.

"He's not here."

"Do you know where he is?"

"He didn't come home last night."

"He was suppose to work with me today."

"Yeah, and he said he'd come home last night, too. But he didn't."

I shook my head and said, "Okay."

"Do you want me to try to call him?" his dad offered.

"Don't bother. He's out of minutes."

It didn't bother me that I wouldn't have help that day. The job was small, and Chuck couldn't do much anyway. He could vacuum and pick up scrapes, and that's it. So I didn't really need him. But I didn't appreciate having to drive all the way to Middletown to find out that he wasn't going to show up for work.

When I drove into the apartment complex, I noticed Phillip's van and Ray's van both parked in Building D's parking lot. I didn't stop to talk to them. I parked my van in front of Building C, carried my tool box in, and got to work.

It was a few minutes after nine o'clock. I was drilling a hole in a piece of tack stripe on the basement floor when I thought I heard something. I took my finger off the trigger switch and pulled my hammer drill out of the hole. My phone was ringing.

"Hello."

"Hello. This is Lisa with Sugar Valley Diagnostics. May I speak with Mark Stone?"

"This is Mark Stone. Who did you say you were with?"

"Sugar Valley Diagnostics. We're a clinic that specializes in neurological disorders."

"Oh, yeah. I didn't expect you to call so soon."

"You're wife's doctor, Dr. Smith, referred her to us for a consultation."

"Right. My wife needs to see a neurologist."

"I have an appointment available on Monday, February 3, with Dr. Vanderberg."

"February 3?" I was scheduled to start a big carpet job on February 3. "Do you have any other days available?"

"Dr. Vanderberg has an opening on Tuesday, February 4, at 9:20 AM."

"That will work," I said.

After I got off the phone with Lisa, I walked over to the D building.

Phillip was doing Apartment 1; Ray was doing Apartment 2. Both were basement apartments, and I was hearing the high-pitch grinding of hammer drills coming from both sides of the hallway.

I walked into Apartment 1. Zac was drilling holes in the tack strip with a hammer drill and Phillip was coming behind him pounding in masonry nails. "Wow. You guys are noisy," I said.

Zac stopped drilling.

Phillip got up from the floor. "What's up?"

"How's your schedule looking for February?" I asked him.

"We don't have anything scheduled for February yet. Except, we'll probably do a couple of these units for you," he said. "Why?"

"I've got a big job coming up the first week of February and I'm going to need help."

"How big?"

"Six hundred and fifty yards. It's a whole house in Lebanon. We're just doing the carpet."

"Don't you have Chuck?" he asked.

I shook my head. "I don't think Chuck's going to work out," I said.

"I noticed that he doesn't like to work too much," Phillip said, chuckling.

"No, he doesn't. I think the idea of work makes him nervous. When he sees that there's a little something for him to do, he has to go out to the truck and smoke."

Phillip started laughing. "I'm sorry. It's not funny, but it is funny."

"Yeah. And that's not even the worst of it. Originally, he told me that his girl friend would take him to the job site every day. Well that lasted two whole days. So I got stuck with driving all the way to Middletown to pick him up for work. Well this morning, I drove to Middletown to pick him up, and guess what! He wasn't there."

Phillip nodded. "That's not good," he said.

"No," I said. "I need to work with someone who's dependable, has their own transportation, and knows what they're doing."

"You want both me and Zac, right?"

"Yeah, I want both of you guys," I said. "My situation now, with my wife having neurological problems—"

"Ray told me about your wife," Phillip said. "I'm sorry to hear about that."

"Yeah. Well, it is what it is. But, anyway, there are going to be times when I can't be on the job. For instance: this big job in Lebanon. The job starts on the first Monday in February. Well, I already know, Tuesday morning, I won't be there. I have to take my wife to see a neurologist. But I'll want you and Zac to be on the job."

"So how will we work that out with the pay?" Phillip asked.

"I haven't figured that out yet," I said. "It would depend. Obviously, the less I'm on the job, the higher your percentage of the installation goes."

Phillip nodded. "You been fair with me so far. I guess I can trust ya until I can't."

"Thanks, Phillip. I appreciate that."

I went back to the C building and got down on the floor. I picked up my hammer and a masonry nail, and pounded the nail into the hole I had drilled in the tack strip.

· · · · ·

Sugar Valley Diagnostics was in a large rectangular brown brick building. The parking lot was also large, and it was full of cars. I drove the PT Cruiser up and down the rows before finally settling on an outside spot on a middle row.

I parked the car, picked up the forms that Dr. Vanderberg's office had sent me to fill out, and looked at Kathy. "Let's go in."

"Kay," she said.

Kathy and I entered the building. In the lobby, on a wall facing us, there was a large black sign which listed every business and medical practice in the building. We walked up to the sign and I looked for Sugar Valley Diagnostics. It was on the forth floor, Suite E. This just confirmed information that I already had.

We took the elevator up to the forth floor. As soon as we stepped off the elevator, there was another black sign listing medical practices on that floor. This one had arrows. It pointed us in the direction of Sugar Valley Diagnostics.

I opened the door to Suite E and followed Kathy into a small waiting room. We walked up to the reception window.

"Kathleen Stone is here," I said to the nurse. "Do you want these?" I handed her the forms in my hand.

"Yes, I'll take those, Mr. Stone," she said. "Dr. Vanderberg will see Kathleen in a few minutes.

We sat down in the waiting room.

After a few minutes, the door on the side of the waiting room opened, and the nurse called out, "Kathleen Stone."

"That's you, Kathy," I said.

We followed the nurse down the hall to an examination room. We went in and sat down.

Kathy was being unusually patient today. I looked at her. She was blinking slowly. After about five minutes, her eyes closed and her head bend forward slightly. She had fallen asleep. I considered waking her up, but decided, if she's that tired, I'd just let her sleep. Because there was no telling when the doctor would come in and look at her.

I looked around the examination room. It was pretty typical. It had a small desk, two chairs next to the desk, which was where we were sitting, a supply cabinet across the room, and an examination table in the middle of the room.

Kathy was still asleep twenty minutes later when Dr. Vanderberg opened the door.

"Hello! You must be Kathleen," he said to Kathy.

Kathy opened her eyes and looked at him.

"Do you know who I am?" the doctor asked.

"No," Kathy said in a flat tone of voice.

"Do you know what I do?" he asked.

Kathy didn't answer that question. She just looked at him.

"What does a person that looks like me do?" he asked her.

I looked him over. A stethoscope hung from his neck, and he was lifting the chest piece to call attention to it. But other than that: He wasn't wearing a lab coat. He was wearing a red and black plaid shirt, and tan khaki pants. He looked like a farmer with a stethoscope. Or maybe a veterinarian—but that was a stretch.

"I'm a brain doctor," he said, as he sat down at the small desk.

"I never would have guessed that," I said.

"What's that?"

"Nothing," I said.

Dr. Vanderberg turned to Kathy. "What floor are we on, Kathleen?"

"Floor?" She seemed confused.

"The floors on this building are numbered," I said. "One, two , three, four. What number did I push when we got on the elevator?"

"Five," she guessed.

"No, Kathleen, we're on the forth floor." He looked at me. "You're not suppose to help her."

"Sorry."

"What county are we in?"

She didn't answer.

"To be fair, Dr. Vanderberg," I said, "we are very close to the county line."

"Yes, we are." He looked at Kathy. "What state are we in, Kathleen?"

"Ohio," she said proudly.

"What month is it?"

She didn't answer.

"Do you know what day it is today?"

Kathy looked confused, and his question didn't seem clear to me either, so I asked: "Do you want her to give you the date, or the name of a day of a week, such as Saturday, Sunday, Monday, et cetera?"

"Either one," he said.

"Saturday," she guessed.

"No."

"Can you tell me what year it is?"

"Twenty-thirteen," she said.

"No."

"Kathleen, I want you to spell the word 'world' backwards," he said. "The word is spelled W-O-R-L-D. Now spell it backwards."

"Backwards?" she asked.

"Yes, spell it backwards."

Kathy looked confused.

"Doctor Vanderberg, she doesn't understand what you want her to do," I said.

The doctor folded his arms on his chest and leaned back in his chair. "Kathleen, you haven't been yourself lately." He bent forward, rested an elbow on the desk, and looked at Kathy. "Are you having problems with your memory?"

"People lose memory when they get fifty," she said.

Dr. Vanderberg shook his head. "Not like this," he said. "No, not like this." He looked over at me. "Is she still working?" he asked.

"No. She hasn't worked for a couple years."

"What did she do?"

"She was a Biology professor," I told him.

"Biology professor!" He looked at Kathy. "That's a lot to forget."

Then he looked at me. "Is she still driving?"

"Yes."

He shook his head. "That's dangerous. She should not be driving a car."

"People with dementia drive all the time," I said.

"And people use bad judgment all the time," he said, irritably.

"That's true," I said.

Dr. Vanderberg looked down at his desk and began writing something. "I'm going to order some tests," he said, without looking up. "She should have a CT scan and an EEG, and then I'd like to see her again."

"Okay."

He got up from the desk. "We do the EEG's here. Make an appointment with the nurse before you leave."

"Will do."

In the ten seconds or so that it took Kathy and I to get out of the examination room, Dr. Vanderberg was no where to be seen in the hallway. He must be busy, I thought, and he's hurrying from one examination room to another.

Kathy and I walked out into the waiting room and went up to the reception window.

"Dr. Vanderberg wants Kathleen to get a CT scan and an EEG," I said.

"We don't do CT scans here," the nurse said, "But we do the EEG. Would you like to schedule that now?"

"Sure," I said. "We're here right now, we might as well get it over with."

"I'm sorry, you misunderstood me," she said. "Our technician is not here right now. She could probably fit you in this afternoon."

"That's alright," I said. "Let's just do it another day—as early in the morning as possible."

"She only works in the afternoon."

"Then let's do it as late in the afternoon as possible."

"We can schedule her for tomorrow at three o'clock."

"That will work," I said.

She filled out a white appointment card. "So that's Wednesday, February 5, at 3:00 PM—which is tomorrow," she said and she handed me the card. "Now this is a list of places where she can get the CT scan done." She handed me a sheet of paper.

I looked at the list. "Does she need an appointment for that?" I asked.

"Yes, but any of those places should be able to schedule her in a day or two," she said. "Would you like to schedule her follow up appointment now?"

"Might as well."

"Would you prefer a morning or an afternoon appointment?"

"Morning, as early as possible," I said.

"Okay, I'll schedule her for Wednesday, February 26, at 9:20 AM."

"That's fine," I said.

She gave me another appointment card.

Kathy and I went out to the car, and I drove us home.

As soon as we got in the house, Kathy asked, "Can I play the music?"

"Yes," I said.

I changed my shirt, and then I went out to the living room.

"Kathy," I said. Then, a little louder: "Kathy!"

She turned off her boom box. "What?"

"I have to leave for a few hours. I should be back by six."

"Do you have work?"

"Yes."

"Kay."

She walked to the back door with me. I gave her a kiss, and went out the back door. I walked to my van, got in, started it, and then I looked back at the house. Kathy was still looking at me through the window in the back door. I waved at her. She didn't wave back. I'm not sure that she understood the gesture.

I arrived at my carpet job in Lebanon less than a half hour later. My van was loaded with all the carpet, so I backed up the driveway to the garage door.

I carried my tool box into the house and set it in the kitchen.

The first floor and the upstairs looked like they were already stripped and padded. So I went downstairs to the basement.

"You guys are moving right along," I said.

"We're good," Phillip said as he kicked a roll of pad across the floor.

"No doubt about that," I said. "I'm going to need some help unloading the carpet."

"Zac!" Phillip said.

Zac came out of the exercise room. "What do you need?"

"I need your help carrying carpet. Come on."

I followed Phillip and Zac up the stairs and out to the garage. We found the button that opens the garage door. Then they began unloading the carpet. I got my seaming iron, my weights, my crab jack, and a roll of seaming tape out of the van and set them in the kitchen.

"Put the piece marked 'hall and steps' in the great room," I told Phillip.

"Whatever you say, boss," he said.

I seamed the upper hall together in the great room, and then took it upstairs and installed it. It was a few minutes before five o'clock when I finished.

I went back down to the basement. Phillip and Zac had finished padding and were picking up the scrapes.

"Gentlemen, why don't we call it a day," I said.

"It's a day," Zac said, and laughed.

"Suits me," Phillip said.

"Why don't you guys try to get here at about nine tomorrow," I said to Phillip.

He nodded. "Okay. We can do that."

"Well, I'll see you tomorrow, then," I said.

"See ya tomorrow," Phillip said.

"See ya later alligator," Zac said.

We packed up our tools and left.

I got home before 5:30. Kathy was on the computer, playing Solitaire, when I came in the house—which was good. I had been trying to come home at least half an hour before the time that I told her I would. Otherwise, when I parked the van, she would be either looking out the window of the back door—on cold days like this one—or standing near the driveway, waiting for me.

I was on the job at 8:00 AM the next morning, and I got right to work. Before Phillip and Zac got there, I had all five of the upstairs bedrooms rolled out and seamed to the hallway. I was seaming the side piece on to the master bedroom carpet when Phillip walked into the room.

"Damn! You started early," he said.

I moved the seaming iron. Then I looked up. "Yeah. I did," I said. "I wanted to get a jump on things because I have to leave in the early afternoon."

"Your wife again?"

I moved the seaming iron again, and then I pulled the weight ahead on the seam. "Yeah. I'm taking her to get an EEG."

"What's that?"

"That's that test where they attach wires all over your head."

"Oh, okay. What do you want us to do?"

"Just a minute. I'll show you." I moved the seaming iron. "You're going to install the bedrooms up here. You're going to need your kicker, your wall cutter—"

"Yeah, yeah. I know what tools I need to install carpet."

I moved the seaming iron and pulled the weight ahead. "Also, bring up my crab jack, and my cordless drill. Those are in my van."

"And a crab jack is—?"

"I used it in the hall yesterday" I moved the seaming iron.

"It's also called a mini-stretcher."

Phillip walked out of the room.

"And bring up the can of dry wall screws!" I yelled after him. "It's in my van!"

I finished the seam and unplugged the seaming iron. Then I picked up my knee kicker and started out the door. Phillip was coming up the stairs with Zac behind him. Both of them were carrying tools.

"Let's start at the room at the end of the hall," I said.

I went into the bedroom at the other end of the hall. Phillip and Zac came in behind me with tools in their hands.

"Your first stretch is going to be right there," I said, and I pointed across the room from the doorway.

"I've kicked in a room or two," Phillip said.

"Well we're not going to be kicking in these rooms." I got down on the floor and folded a corner of the carpet back. "Zac, I'm going to need the drill and the dry wall screws."

"Okie-dokie." He put the crab jack on the floor, and then handed me the cordless drill and the can of dry wall screws.

"Phillip, your first stretch is right across from the doorway."

"Right, Mark," Phillip said. "This is the second time you told me what I already know."

"Okay," I said. "So here's something you don't know: I'm going to reinforce a ten inch section of tack strip." I put three dry wall screws in the tack strip.

Phillip nodded. "That's what you did alright."

"Looks more like about a foot to me," Zac said.

"Okay." I picked up the crab jack. "The width of the blade of the crab jack is ten inches. That's why I reinforced the strip. Now watch."

I hooked the blade of the crab jack behind the tack strip and cranked the handle, stretching the carpet.

"That'll get it tight," Phillip said. He seemed impressed.

"It'll get it a lot tighter than you can get it with a knee kicker."

"I can see that," he said.

I kicked the carpet onto the tack strip with my knee kicker from the corner of the room up to the crab jack.

"I think I'm going to like that tool," Phillip said. "How much do those cost?"

"About three hundred dollars or so, last time I checked," I said. "But anyway, every three feet you'll get a stretch with the crab jack, and then you'll kick up to it with your kicker."

"Right," he said.

"So you'll have three stretches on the front wall, and three more stretches on this wall."

"I think I can handle that."

"Okay. We'll be stretching in all these bedrooms with the crab jack. And the den. And the exercise room. The only rooms we'll use the pole stretcher in are the great room, and the main area in the basement."

"Sounds like a plan," Phillip said.

"I'm going to go downstairs and seam up the great room," I said.

"Just remember the yellow square goes next to the red square."

"Don't forget the green line in the middle," Zac said.

"He loves that kind of work," Phillip said to Zac.

"Oh, I do," I said. "I just love pattern match seams."

I went back into the master bedroom to get my seaming iron and my weight, and then I carried my tools down to the great room.

While I worked on the seams in the great room, I kept checking the time on my cell phone. I finished the first thirty foot seam at 11:30. The second one I finished at 12:40.

I wanted to work until one o'clock. So I cut the carpet for the steps. They were going to go on in three runs. I cut the runs, rolled them up, and set them at the floor near the bottom step.

I went upstairs to check on the progress Phillip and Zac were making. Phillip was in his third room. Zac was vacuuming another room.

"Well, I'm going to have to get out of here," I said to Phillip.

"Good luck with your wife's EEG," he said.

"Yeah. I cut your steps for you. If you don't get to them, that's fine. We're in good shape time wise on this job."

"I'll get to 'em."

"Okay. Whatever. I'll see ya tomorrow."

"See ya."

. . . . .

I checked my cellphone when Kathy and I entered Dr. Vanderberg's waiting room. We were four minutes early. I told the nurse at the reception window that Kathleen was here for her three o'clock appointment, and we sat down.

At one minute after three o'clock a woman in a long white lab coat came out into the waiting room. She looked at me. "I'm ready for Kathleen," she said.

I stood up and then Kathy stood up.

"Oh, not you sir," she said. "I only need Kathleen."

"I know but—"

"Sir, you are not allowed to come back with her. Only she can go."

I shook my head slowly. "Alright then."

"Kathleen," she said. "Come with me."

Kathy looked at me.

"Go with her, Kathy," I said. "I'll be right here. I'll wait for ya."

Kathy reluctantly followed the EEG technician out of the waiting room. I sat down, picked up a *National Geographic,* and looked at pictures.

Ten minutes later, the EEG technician brought Kathy back. "I can't do the test," she said. "She won't let me put the electrodes on her. She keeps pulling them off."

I put the magazine down and stood up. "Well what did you expect?"

I was going to suggest that I go in and help, but she suddenly turned around and left the room.

I walked over to the reception window. "My wife did not get the EEG done," I said to the nurse. "So we won't be charged anything for this. Right?"

"Did you wife cancel the appointment?"

"No, she did not. Your technician canceled the appointment."

"In cases like that, typically, there is no charge."

"Okay," I said, and we went home.

chapter 8

The next day I called Drake Memorial Hospital to make an appointment for Kathy to get a CT scan done. I made the appointment for Wednesday, February 19, at 10:00 AM. I could have chosen an earlier date. But I picked the nineteenth because I didn't have any work scheduled on that date, and the nineteenth was still a full week before her follow up appointment with Dr. Vanderberg, which was scheduled on February 26.

. . . . . .

On February 17, two days before the appointment for the CT scan, I got home from work about six o'clock. It was cold and raining and already almost dark.

When I pulled in the driveway I noticed that the Honda was not home. That was unusual.

I remembered that, when I left that morning, Kathy mentioned that she was going to go to Kmart and then to recycling. But she always did those things in the morning, and she was always home by the time I got home.

I went into the house. "Kathy! Kathy!" I called. She wasn't home. Where could she be?

I didn't know what to do. I called her cellphone, hoping she had the ringer turned on, and hoping she would answer. She didn't. I called again. No answer. Then again. No answer, but that time I left a message on her voice mail.

I was beginning to wonder whether I should call the police, or maybe the hospital. But once I thought about it, it seemed to me that if she were in an accident—or something else happened—someone would have notified me.

I called her again. No answer. Then I called again.

"Hello," Kathy said.

"Kathy, where are you?"

"Don't know."

"Are you driving?"

"No."

"Are you in your car?"

"Yeah."

"Are you parked somewhere?"

"Yeah."

"Okay. Do you see any street signs?"

"No."

"Kathy, are you parked on the street?"

"No."

"Are you at a gas station?"

"No."

"Kathy, I want you to get out of your car and see if you can find a street sign."

I heard the car door close, and I said: "Kathy."

"What?"

"Did you find a street sign?"

"No."

"Okay, Kathy. What's around you? What do you see?"

"A store, I think."

"Okay," I said. "I want you to go into the store."

She didn't say anything, so I said: "Kathy. Kathy." I heard a bell. "Kathy."

"What?"

"Are you in the store?"

"Yeah."

"Is there anyone else in the store?"

"One."

"Okay, give that person your phone please."

I heard some conversation, but I couldn't make out what was being said. Then a man's voice came on the phone: "Hello."

"Hello. Um, I wonder if you can help me. My wife has dementia. You probably noticed that."

"Yeah," he said.

"Could you tell me where she is?"

"This is Higgins Auto Parts."

"Higgins Auto Parts. Where is that?"

"We're in Ottawa, Ohio."

"Ottawa, Ohio? Where is that?"

"It's in Northwest Ohio."

"Northwest Ohio. Wow," I said. "Okay, I'm going to pick her up. Do you mind if she waits there?"

"We're about to close."

"I'll get there as soon as I can. Do you mind if she waits in her car?"

"I guess she can," he said. "She's been parked out back for a couple hours now anyway."

I asked him for the address. He told me what it was and I wrote it down. Then I asked him to give the phone back to Kathy.

"Kathy," I said.

"What?"

"I want you to go back to the Honda and wait for me. I'm coming up there to pick you up."

"Kay," she said, and then she hung up.

I went out to my van and put the address in my GPS. According to the GPS, it was a one hour and fifty minute drive. I was determined to beat that time.

On the way up to Ottawa, I called Kathy several times. She never answered her phone. So I didn't know what to think. Had she been robbed? Was her cell phone and her purse now in the possession of a gang of juvenile delinquents? Having never been to Ottawa, I had no idea what kind of neighborhood she was in.

All I knew for sure was that it was cold; it was raining; and I was in a hurry.

I got to Higgins Auto Parts in one hour and forty minutes.

I drove around back. The lights on the van shined on the back of the Honda. Kathy was sitting in the driver's seat. The hood of her coat covered the back of her head.

I parked the van next to the Honda and got out. I opened the driver's door on the Honda.

"Are you all right?"

"Yeah." she said.

"Okay. Well, get in the van. It's warm," I said.

She got in the van, and I got back in the van. Then I called AAA. We had an AAA Plus membership, which meant we could get a tow of up to 100 miles for free.

The lady from AAA told me that the tow truck would be there in twenty minutes.

So we waited.

A six pack of beer sat on the floor next to the driver's seat of the van. Two bottles were empty; four were full. Kathy eventually noticed the beer. She pulled one of the full bottles out of the six pack.

"Kathy, I know you're thirsty, but don't drink that," I said. I gently took the beer out of her hand. "We'll go to McDonald's, okay."

When the tow truck arrived I got out of the van.

The driver rolled his window down. "What's wrong with it?"

"It won't start," I lied.

"Does it turn over?"

"No."

"Is the battery dead?"

"It's not the battery," I said.

"Okay. Where's it going?"

I gave him our address in Spring Valley and he put it in his GPS. Then he looked at his GPS screen. "That's over a hundred miles," he said.

"I know."

"I'm gonna have to charge ya for the extra miles."

"I know that too."

"Yer part of it's a hundred and thirty dollars."

"Okay." I looked in my wallet. I had nothing but twenties. So I gave him seven twenties.

"I don't have change right now," he said.

"That's okay."

He backed his truck up to the back of the Honda, and tilted the bed.

Then he got out of his truck, and he got down on the ground. He hooked two chains to the Honda's chassis.

"Put it in neutral," he said.

I put the Honda in neutral.

He climbed back into his truck, and he slowly pulled the Honda onto the truck's bed, and then he lowered the bed into a horizontal position. Then he opened his door, got out of the cab of the truck, and got up on the truck's bed. He opened the driver's door on the Honda, put the car in park, and took the keys out of the ignition.

"Here ya go," he said, as he tossed me the keys.

I caught Kathy's car keys, and I put them in my pocket.

The driver jumped down from the truck's bed, tied all four of the Honda's wheels down, and then he got back into his truck and drove away.

I drove to a McDonald's on the outskirts of Ottawa, which I had noticed on the drive up. I pulled into the drive-thru lane.

Kathy got out of the van. "We should go in," she said.

"Kathy, we're in the drive-thru lane," I said. There was already a car behind us.

"I think we should go in."

I put the van in park and walked around to her side of the van. "No. We're going through the drive-thru," I said. "Please get in." I helped her get back in the van.

I pulled up to the menu board.

"May I take your order?"

"Yeah. I'll take two double cheeseburgers, two medium cokes, and two value fries."

"That will be $5.58 at the first window."

Before we got to the first window, Kathy got out of the van again. "I think we should go in," she said.

"Kathy, we can't," I said. "We're in line to get our food. Please get back in the van."

She looked at the line of cars ahead of us and then at the line of cars behind us, and she got back in the van.

We picked up our food and drinks. I gave her a double cheese-burger out of the bag. She wasted no time with it. Her double cheeseburger was almost gone before we were even back on the road.

We were about fifty mile from our house when my cellphone rang.

"Hello," I said

"I just dropped your car off," the tow truck driver said. "Sorry about your driveway."

"What about the driveway?"

"I rutted it up pretty bad."

"That's okay," I said. "Hey, how'd you get down there so quick?"

"Seventy-five or eighty the whole way."

"Wow."

"Time is money in this business."

"In every business," I said.

"Well, you have a nice night."

"You too," I said.

Kathy and I got home an hour later.

As soon as we got in the house, Kathy took off her coat, and asked, "Can I use the bathroom."

"Yes," I said.

She went into the bathroom and peed for a very long time. It dawned on me that she probably hadn't used the toilet all day.

After she came out of the bathroom. Kathy went straight to bed.

I took a beer into the computer room and turned on the TV. The keys to the Honda were still in my pocket. As I watched the news and drank beer, I considered what I was going to do with the keys. Putting them back in Kathy's purse was the most obvious option. But I didn't feel comfortable doing that. So I put them in a bottom drawer in my desk, underneath a pile of papers.

· · · · ·

Kathy didn't mention her car keys until Wednesday morning—that was the nineteenth, the day her CT scan was scheduled.

She was standing in the kitchen, fumbling around inside of her purse. "Can't find keys to the Honda," she said. Then she looked at me.

"You don't need them," I said. "I'll drive us there in the PT Cruiser."

"I need my keys," she said.

I refilled my coffee cup. "They're not in your purse, huh?"

"You had them."

"Oh, that's right. I did have them." I took a sip of coffee. "They were in my pocket. I forgot to take them out."

"Are they in your pocket?" she asked.

"No. Not now," I said. "They were in my pocket yesterday, when I was working. Then Dr. Vanderberg showed up on the job, and he asked to see the keys to the Honda. I remembered that they were in my pocket. So I pulled them out of my pocket. Then he grabbed them."

"Doctor grabbed the keys to the Honda?"

"Yes. I told him to give them back to me. But he wouldn't. He said, 'No', and then he left."

"Doctor wouldn't give them back?"

"No." I said. I looked at the clock on the stove. It was nine fifteen. "Kathy, we'd better get going." The appointment was for ten, but I didn't know where the Radiology Department was located in Drake Memorial Hospital. So I wanted to allow us plenty of time.

We went out the back door. I locked up the house. Then we got into the PT Cruiser and drove to the hospital. I parked the PT Cruiser as near as I could to the Main Entrance.

We entered the hospital and walked up to the information desk.

"We're looking for the Radiology Department," I said to the guy at the desk.

He stood up. "Sure," he said. "You go this way." He pointed. "Right past the gift shop, there's a hallway. Turn right. You'll take that hallway past the elevators to another hallway. Turn left. Take that hallway till it dead ends. Turn left again. You'll pass carpeted hallways on your left. Go down the second carpeted hallway you come to. Down, almost to the end of that hallway, on the right, is Radiology."

"Um, okay," I said.

"You'll see signs with arrows along the way," he said.

"Good."

We followed the arrows on the wall around to the other side of the hospital. We came to a set of double doors. A sign above the doors said RADIOLOGY in large black letters.

We went in and walked down a hallway. Hospital rooms with their doors open were on both sides of us. We walked up to a nurses station. Two nurses were sitting behind the counter.

"My wife's here for a CT scan," I said.

"What's her name?" one of the nurses asked.

"Kathleen Stone."

"Okay. I have her here somewhere." She searched the counter top in the nurses station. "Here it is." She handed me a clipboard. "I need someone to sign."

I picked up the pen and looked at paper on the clipboard. It was a legal form guaranteeing the hospital that they would get paid. I printed Kathy's name and filled in the date. Then I put an x on the line for the patient's signature. "Kathy, you need to sign this," I said. I handed her the clipboard and the pen.

"Where to sign?"

"Sign next to the x." I pointed to the x I made.

Kathy signed her name next to the x. I took the clipboard from her and gave it to the nurse.

"Kelly. Could you take them outside for a CT Scan."

"Outside?" I asked.

"We're remodeling," she said. "It's temporary."

Kelly took us out of Radiology the same way we had come in. Then we went down the main hall to an outside exit. She opened the door. Kathy and I stepped out of the building. The air wasn't cold because we were now on a sidewalk enclosed by a long, clear plastic tent. We followed Kelly down the side walk and then up a couple steps into a trailer.

The trailer was about the size of a typical construction trailer. It had two rooms, not counting the bathroom, which was off to one side. A technician sat at a small desk in front of a computer.

"Who do we have here?" she asked.

"Kathleen Stone," Kelly said.

"I'll be with her in a minute," she said, as she looked at her computer screen.

I looked through a window of the door going into the other room. In the middle of the room, there was a white tubular machine. It was bigger than a refrigerator. The front of the machine looked like a giant donut. A gurney stuck out of the front of the machine like a huge tongue.

"So that's the cat scan machine," I said.

"That's it," the technician said.

She finished whatever she was doing on the computer and got up. She looked at Kathy. "Does she have any metal on her clothing—other than the coat?"

"No," I said. I looked at Kathy. "Kathy, let me have your coat."

She grabbed the front of her coat with both hands. "I need my coat."

"Kathy, let me hold it for you. Just for a minute."

She, very reluctantly, let me take her coat off her.

The technician picked up a small plastic basket off a table next to the door. "Put your purse in the basket, Ma'am."

"No," Kathy said.

"Ma'am, you can't take your purse in there. Please put your purse in the basket."

"No. I keep my purse." She clutched her purse tightly.

The technician turned to me. "She can't take her purse in there, it has metal on it."

"Kathy, put your purse in the basket," I said.

"I keep my purse," she said.

The technician reached for the purse.

"I keep my purse," Kathy said, pulling the purse away from the technician.

The technician sighed and shook her head.

"Kathy, let her have your purse," I said.

"I'll give it right back," she said.

"No. I keep my purse."

The technician was thoughtful for a moment, and then she asked Kathy: "Will you let your husband hold your purse?"

Kathy looked at me. I could tell that she was thinking about it.

"Kathy, let me hold the purse," I said. "I promise: I won't let anyone else touch it. If someone wants to touch it. I'll tell them 'No'. No one is allowed to touch it."

She looked at the technician. "He holds it?"

"He holds it," she said.

Kathy handed me the purse.

The technician took Kathy into the other room.

I sat down in a chair, holding Kathy's coat and purse. I waited.

The technician came out of the room. She stood in front of the door and looked through the window for a little while. Then she went back in.

A little while later, she opened the door for Kathy. Kathy came out of the room.

I helped Kathy put her coat back on, and then I gave her her purse. "No one messed with your purse," I told her.

chapter 9

On Saturday morning, February 22, I was sitting in the computer room, drinking coffee. Kathy appeared in the doorway. She was wearing her coat because she had just finished feeding the chickens.

I looked at her. Finally, I said, "Yes?"

"Can we get the Honda going?" she asked.

"I'll take a look at it," I said. "I'll fix it if I can."

I already knew that I could fix the car.

I had given her back the keys after I had come home from work on Thursday evening. I told her that I had gone to Dr. Vanderberg's office and demanded that he give me the keys, and he did. I don't know if she believed my story, but Kathy was happy to get the keys to her Honda back. But on Friday, when she tried to start the Honda, it wouldn't start. When I came home Friday evening, she told me: "The Honda won't go." I promised her that I'd look at it in the morning.

"I need my car."

"I know you do, Kathy," I said. "And I'm going to take a look at it."

She filled her plastic pitcher with bird seed, and went out to feed the wild birds.

I went out to the kitchen, opened a drawer, and got a 10mm open end wrench. Then I put my coat on and went outside. I opened the hood of the Honda and put the support rod in place. Then I leaned over and reached behind the battery. I felt around until I got my fingers on the red battery cable. I pulled the cable up, wiggled it onto the positive terminal of the battery, and tightened it down with the wrench.

I shut the hood, and then I got into the driver's seat. The keys were already in the ignition, so I started it. I revved the engine a couple of times, and then I shut it off, putting the keys in my pocket.

I went over to my van, and I picked up my old GPS off the console. I had just bought a new GPS, and I wanted Kathy to have my old one. I put the old GPS in the glove box of the Honda, and then I went back into the house.

I sat down at the kitchen table, and when Kathy came back into the house, I said: "I fixed the Honda."

"You fixed the Honda?"

"Yes. I fixed the Honda."

"You fixed the Honda."

"Yes."

"Kay," she said, and she started to take her coat off.

"Kathy, let's go for a drive," I said.

"Are we going to the grocery?" she asked.

"Sure. We could do that."

We went outside. "Let's take the Honda," I said.

"Me drive?"

"No. I'll drive since I know where we're going."

We got into the Honda, and I drove to the UDF at Church and Second Street in Xenia. We went in and picked up a case of Budweiser and a Hershey chocolate bar.

When we left the UDF, I turned right on Second Street, and then left of Bellbrook Avenue.

"Are we going home," Kathy asked.

"Yes," I said.

I drove down Lower Bellbrook Road until I was outside the Xenia city limit. Then I pulled into a church parking lot. It was empty except for a couple cars close to the church.

I stopped the car, and opened the glove box. I took out the GPS.

"Kathy, do you know what this is?" I asked, holding the GPS in front of her.

She looked at the object uneasily.

"I don't expect you to know what this is. You've probably never seen one before. I'm just going to show you what it does. Okay." I picked up the charger on the end of the power cord. "See this thing here. Now watch." I plugged the charger into the 12 volt outlet on the dash. The screen on the GPS lit up. "Did you see that. I plugged it in here." I pointed to the outlet. "And that turned it on."

Kathy looked out the window.

"Kathy, please pay attention," I said. "Now look."

She looked at the screen of the GPS.

"This says 'Where To?' I'm going to push the button." The next screen came up. "Okay. Now here are my choices. This middle one says 'Go Home'. That's what we want to do." I tapped the house icon. A map with a green "Go!" button came on the screen. "Do you see that, Kathy?" I put the GPS down. "Now let's switch places. I want you to drive us home."

I opened my car door, got out, walked around the back of the car, and opened Kathy's door. "You drive," I said.

"I think you can drive," she said.

"Kathy, I want you to drive. I want you to use the GPS to get us home."

"I think you can get us home."

"I'm not going to," I said. "You're going to drive us home."

"I think you can drive us home," she said.

"No. I'm not going to."

Kathy closed her car door. I stood outside the car looking at her. She looked back at me.

After two or three minutes, I walked around to the driver's side of the car and got in. "Okay, Kathy. Now watch." I pressed the green "Go!" on the GPS.

"Proceed to the highlighted route," the GPS said.

I pulled out of the church parking lot and continued south on Lower Bellbrook.

"In five hundred feet, turn left," the GPS said.

"Did you hear that Kathy? It's telling me where to turn to get home," I said.

"Look! They have the chickens," she said, as she noticed about a dozen black cows in a pasture.

"Those are cows, Kathy," I said.

I turned the GPS off. I didn't need it. I knew where I was.

When we got home, I put the GPS back in the Honda's glove box.

I wanted to believe that there was some chance that Kathy would use the GPS if she ever got lost again. But deep down I knew, even with coaching by me or someone else, there was no way that she would be able use the GPS to get herself home.

· · · · ·

On Monday morning, February 24, my cellphone started ringing. I got up off the floor, walked outside, and answered it.

"Hello."

"Hello. This is Lisa at Sugar Valley Diagnostics. Am I speaking to Mark Stone?"

"Yes, I'm Mark Stone."

"Dr. Vanderberg would like your wife, Kathleen, to get an MRI before her next appointment," Lisa said.

"Well the appointment's in two days," I said. "And I'm at work right now. I doubt whether we can get that done before the twenty-sixth."

"Would you like to reschedule Kathleen's appointment for a later date?"

"Yes. Let's do that," I said.

"The next available appointment he has is on Friday, March 21 at 11:00 AM," Lisa said.

"That would be fine," I said. I opened the door of my van and picked up a note pad and a pen. "Okay. What was that again."

"Friday, March 21 at 11:00 AM."

I wrote the date and time on the note pad. "Thanks. I got it," I said.

Later on that day, I went back out to my van and called the Radiology Department at Drake Memorial Hospital. I made an appointment for Kathy to get an MRI on March 6 at 1:00 PM.

· · · · ·

March 6 was a sunny day. The snow had nearly melted, and the chickens were running around in their yard.

We left the house, in the PT Cruiser, at about 12:15 PM. I drove us to Drake Memorial Hospital, and I parked in a side parking lot because it was closer to Radiology than the main parking lot.

Kathy and I entered the hospital through a side door. Then we went through the double doors into Radiology.

"Kathleen Stone is here," I told the nurse at the nurses station.

"She's early," the nurse said.

"I know."

"That's okay," she said. "Just follow me."

We followed her into one of the rooms off the hallway in front of the nurses station. The room was a fully equipped hospital room. It had a bed, a television, a couple chairs. There was even a bathroom.

"Do you want to watch television?" the nurse asked.

"Sure," I said.

She picked up a remote and turned it on. "Here. Turn to whatever you want." She handed me the remote. "Kelly will be in in a few minutes to help Kathleen get into a hospital gown."

"A hospital gown?"

"Yes. She has to wear a hospital gown."

"She didn't have to wear a hospital gown for her CT scan."

"Well she has to wear one for her MRI. Is that a problem?"

"Um. It might be," I said.

After the nurse left, I set the remote on the dresser, and walked over to Kathy. "Kathy," I said. "Let me take your coat."

"Take my coat?"

"Yes. Please. Let me take your coat."

"Kay."

She let me help her take her coat off. "I'll hold it for you," I said.

"Kay."

"Let's sit down," I said.

"Sit down?"

"Yeah."

"Kay."

We sat down in the chairs.

Kelly came in a few minutes later. "Well hi! Kathleen," she said, smiling. "It's nice to see you again."

Kathy looked up at Kelly. Her eyes followed Kelly as Kelly walked to the closet. She took a hospital gown out of the closet. She held it up. "Kathleen, I'm going to need you to put this on," she said. "Can you do that for me?"

Kathy clutched her purse.

Kelly took the hospital gown off the hanger and laid it on the bed. "I may need your help with this," she said to me.

"Alright."

Kelly walked over to Kathy and stood in front of her. "Kathleen, I need you to stand up for me."

She looked at me. "Could you take her purse?"

"I'll try," I said.

I got in front of Kathy and put my hands on her purse. "Kathy, let me have the purse."

"No!" she said, firmly.

"Come on, Kathy" I said. I wiggled the purse, and then, as gently as I could, I pulled it out of her hands.

Kathy got up. "I want that!" she said.

I backed up to the window, holding the purse. Kathy was coming at me, reaching for the purse.

Kelly was now behind Kathy. She quickly pulled Kathy's shirt up over her head and off her body.

Kathy turned toward Kelly. "Give me it!"

Kelly bunched the shirt up into a ball and tossed it to me over Kathy's head. I caught it.

Kathy turned toward me. "Give me it!"

"Um," I said.

Kelly quickly pulled the gown over Kathy's head.

"I don't like that!" Kathy said, gabbing the material of the gown with her hands.

Kelly got in front of Kathy and held her wrists.

"I don't like that!" Kathy said.

Kelly released Kathy's wrists and turned to me, shaking her head. "This isn't going to work," she said.

Kelly helped Kathy take the hospital gown off. "Give her back her shirt," she told me.

I gave Kathy her shirt. She put it on. Then I handed her her purse.

"Her doctor's just going to have to give her something to calm her down," she said. "We can't even get a hospital gown on her. She's never going to lay still for forty-five minutes to get an MRI."

"The MRI takes forty-five minutes?"

"Yes. And she has to lay still all that time."

"Oh. I didn't know that."

"Well her doctor did."

"So, we're not going to do the MRI today?"

"No," Kelly said. "Sorry. But we can't do it today. Her doctor's going to have to give her something that just about knocks her out."

"Okay then," I said. "Kathy do you want your coat." I helped her get her coat on.

"Call her doctor," Kelly said. "Tell him that we can't do this unless he gives her a powerful sedative. And figure on being here most of the day. We're not going to let her leave until the sedative has worn off."

"Why? She won't be driving."

"That doesn't matter. We still want her to be able to walk on her own before she leaves the hospital."

"Alright," I said. "I guess we'll see ya next time."

"Yeah. And hopefully we'll get this done." She looked at Kathy. "Kathleen, you want to get your MRI over with, don't you?"

Kathy just stared at her.

Kelly laughed. "I think that means 'No'."

We left the hospital and walked out to the PT Cruiser. We got into the car. I put the keys in the ignition, and then I turned to Kathy. "Kathy, I'm sorry," I said.

"Can we go to the grocery?" she asked.

"Sure. Let's go to Walmart." I started the car. "We need to get the Hershey."

chapter 10

The next day I was doing the steps and landings of Building E in Mason Manor. That was the seventy-two unit apartment complex we were doing. This was a nice job to do on a day when I needed to make phone calls.

At nine o'clock I was nailing tack strip onto the back of the steps. I put down my hammer and took my cellphone out of my pocket. Then I sat on a step and called Dr. Vanderberg's office.

"Sugar Valley Diagnostics. May I help you?"

"I hope so," I said. "I'm Mark Stone. My wife, Kathleen, is a patient of Dr. Vanderberg's."

"I know who you are."

"Is this Lisa?"

"Yes."

"Okay, Lisa, here's what happened: Yesterday I took my wife to Drake to get an MRI. They couldn't do it. She was not cooperative *at all*. The nurse—at Drake—said that the only way they're going to be able to do the MRI is if she's given a powerful sedative."

"Can you hold for a minute? I'll ask Dr. Vanderberg what we should do."

"Yes," I said.

While I waited, I held the phone to my ear with one hand, and with the other, I lined up and nailed the tack strip on the next four steps leading up to the next landing. I sat down on the landing.

"Hello. Are you still there?"

"I'm here," I said.

"I talked to Dr. Vanderberg, and he prescribed a sedative for her. Which pharmacy do you use?"

"We'll use the Walmart Pharmacy, in Xenia," I said.

"Okay, Mr. Stone, as soon as I get off the phone with you, I'll call it in. You'll be able to pick it up this afternoon."

"Alright."

"Now, you're going to give her the medication before you take her for the MRI the next time," Lisa said. "And Dr. Vanderberg wanted me to tell you that when she's on this medication, you must watch her carefully. The medication might make her very sleepy, and we don't want her falling down and injuring herself."

"Right. Thanks," I said.

"You're welcome."

I finished the tack strip, and then I padded the four landings, and all twenty-four steps before eleven o'clock. Then I went out to my van to take a break.

I sat in the van and stated eating my roast beef, ham and Swiss cheese sandwich. I ate about half, set the sandwich on the console, and pulled my cellphone out of my pocket. I called Radiology at Drake Memorial Hospital.

"Radiology. How may I help you?" a woman asked.

"Hi. This is Mark Stone. Yesterday, my wife, Kathleen, was there for an MRI. But she wouldn't cooperate, so it wasn't done."

"I remember that."

"Well, I've got some medication lined up for her. So, we're ready to try again."

"Okay, Mr. Stone. What day would you like to reschedule the MRI for?"

"Next Wednesday, in the morning, if that's possible."

"I have a ten o'clock on Wednesday, March 12."

"That will work," I said.

"I'll put her down."

"Thanks."

After I finished my sandwich, I went back into the building and opened the door to a lower unit. Then I came back outside, and I used a rock to prop the outside door open.

I pulled the twelve foot long roll of carpet out of the van and got my right shoulder under the middle of it. I lifted the front end of the roll so that the weight of the carpet roll balanced on my right shoulder. Then I carried the carpet into the building, down to the lower unit, and I dropped it on the floor.

I rolled the carpet out and turned it upside down.

I went back out to my van. I got my straight edge and closed the back doors of the van.

Coming back into the building, I moved the rock so that the front door would close. I went back into the lower unit. I changed the blade on my knife, and I got on the floor and started cutting carpet.

I cut the four landings first. I rolled them up, one at a time. I carried them to where they were going to be installed, and rolled them out.

Then I cut the carpet for the six standard steps and put that in place.

I cut eighteen thirty-six inch by twenty-seven inch pieces for the suspended steps.

I got the step ladder from the kitchen in the unit where I cut the carpet, set it up on entryway, and began stapling the thirty-six by twenty-seven inch pieces of carpet to the backside of the suspended steps with my tack gun. I stapled a piece of carpet to the backside of the last suspended step at one o'clock.

I was making good time. I wanted to be done by four, and it looked like I was going to make it.

I installed the basement landing first, and then I kicked on the six standard steps. Next I kicked on the six suspended steps going up to the second floor landing and finished up the back of them with my tack gun. I installed the second floor landing, and kicked on a suspended step going up to the mid-floor landing.

Phillip and Zac came into the building. I looked at my cellphone. It was two-forty.

"Are you guys done already?" I asked. They had done a unit in Building F.

"Yep," Phillip said. "Just came over to see how you're doing."

"Are you checking my work?"

He walked around, looking over the carpet that I had installed, and nodded. "Looks good," he said.

"Thanks," I said.

"You use the crab jack on these little landings?" he asked, pointing to the crab jack on the second floor landing.

"I use the crab jack for everything," I said.

"I gotta get one of those," he said.

"That's what I keep telling you." I got my knee kicker in position to kick on the next suspended step.

"I'll kick on the steps for ya," Phillip said.

"You don't have to do that," I said.

"I know I don't," he said. "But I help out my buddies. You just do the two landings."

"Okay." I got my crab jack and my wall cutter and I went up to the mid-floor landing.

"Zac, get me my kicker," Phillip said to Zac.

I finished the landings. Phillip kicked on the last eleven suspended steps. Zac finished the back of the last twelve suspended steps with my tack gun. And we were all done at three-thirty.

"I appreciate your help," I said. "What do I owe ya." I pulled out my wallet.

"Nothing," Phillip said. "I was just helping you out."

"I insist."

"I won't take anything," he said.

I pulled a fifty dollar bill out of my wallet and handed it to him. "Put that towards getting yourself a crab jack," I said.

"Since you put it that way," he said. He folded the bill and put it in his pocket. "Zac, pick up these scrapes for Mark."

"Yes sir," Zac said. He picked up the scrapes and put them in the black contractor bag.

"I don't have the address to Monday's job," Phillip said.

"I don't have it on me. I'll have to text it to you," I said. "But I'm going to need you to stop at Southland Monday morning and pick up eight rolls of half inch eight pound pad."

"I can do that. You say the jobs in Centerville?"

"Yeah. South Centerville. It's off of 741."

"Okay."

"I'm going to stop at Pro Source in the morning to get the carpet."

"Is it just one roll."

"Yeah. It's one two hundred yard roll of carpet."

"So it's one big roll."

"Yeah."

"What time do you want to start?" he asked.

"Try to get there between nine and ten," I said. "I'm going to try to be there at nine."

"Okay. See ya Monday," he said.

"See ya," I said.

Phillip and Zac left the building, and I packed up my tools.

I got in my van to drive home at three-forty. I had told Kathy that I'd be home at five. Now I thought that I might get home before four.

I pulled in my driveway at exactly four o'clock.

The Honda wasn't in the driveway.

I shut the van off and finished the beer I was drinking. I had a bad feeling in the pit of my stomach.

I pulled my cellphone out of my pocket and called Kathy. I didn't expect her to answer on the first attempt.

"Hello," someone said. It was a man's voice.

"Hello," I said. "Who is this?"

"This is Deputy Collins with the Greene County Sheriff's Department."

"Is Kathy all right? Was she in an accident?"

"No. She wasn't in an accident. I have Kathleen Stone right here. Who is this?"

"This is Mark Stone. I'm her husband."

"What's wrong with her?" he asked.

"She has dementia."

"Oh, okay. I knew something was wrong with her as soon as she got out of the car—once we finally got her pulled over. I thought she was going to walk into traffic."

"What did she do?"

"She was speeding."

"How fast was she going?"

"She was going forty-five in a school zone on Dayton Xenia Road."

"Oh," I said. "She probably didn't notice she was in a school zone."

"Probably not," he said. "I'm not going to let her drive, you know."

"Can I pick her up?" I asked.

"Where are you?"

"I'm in Spring Valley. Where is she?"

"We've got her at the intersection of Route 35 and Orchard Lane."

"I know where that is. I'll be there in ten minutes."

"Okay. We'll be right here waiting."

I was good to know that Kathy was safe—in some trouble, maybe, but safe.

I took my twelve pack of Budweiser—minus two—into the house and put it in the refrigerator. Then I came back outside, got into the PT cruiser, and headed up there.

I was going west on Route 35, coming up on Orchard Lane, when I saw two black Greene County Sheriff's cruisers pulled over on the right side of the highway with their red and blue lights flashing. As I got closer, I could see the Honda sitting in front of them. I pulled the PT Cruiser in behind the second one.

Two sheriff's deputies, one male and the other female, were standing in front of the Honda, chatting. I got out of the PT Cruiser and went over to the edge of the road. I saw Kathy as I was walking up to the deputies. She was sitting in the back of the first cruiser.

"I'm Mark Stone. I'm Kathy's husband," I said.

Deputy Collins, the guy I spoke to on the phone, handed me two tickets. He was a big guy, probably about six foot three. "You might want these," he said.

"Not really," I said, as I took the tickets.

I looked at them. One was for speeding—going 45mph in a school zone. The other one was for reckless operation. "What's with the reckless operation ticket? Was her driving erratic?"

"No, nothing like that," he said. "In Ohio, an officer can issue a citation for reckless operation with any speeding violation that exceeds the speed limit by 25mph or more. So 45mph in a school zone is also reckless operation."

"Oh. I didn't know that," I said.

"How are you planning to get her car home?"

"Um, I guess I'll come back to get it in a cab."

"Okay, but we can't leave it here." He pointed to the gas station on the corner. "Why don't you drive her car over to Certified and then walk back over."

"Alright."

I got into the Honda. The key was still in the ignition. I started it, drove it around the corner and across the street to the Certified gas station, and parked it. Then I walked back over to where the deputies were.

"Okay. So I can take her now?" I asked Deputy Collins.

"I'm not going to let her out of the car here," he said. "Why don't you drive you car over to Certified and I'll follow you over there."

"Alright."

I got into the PT Cruiser and drove that over to Certified. I parked it next to the Honda.

I got out of the car and looked over at the deputies. They chatted for a couple more minutes, and then she got in her car and drove off. Deputy Collins got in his car, drove over to where I was, and parked on the other side of the Honda.

I walked over to the deputy's car. He rolled down the window. "Park her car somewhere where she can't see it," he said.

"Alright."

I got into the Honda, started it up, and drove around to the back of the building. I parked, and put the keys in my pocket. Her purse was on the passenger seat. So I picked it up.

When I came back around to the front of the building, I went in and told the cashier what was going on. I told him that I'd pick the Honda up in an hour or so. He was fine with that.

I put Kathy's purse in the PT Cruiser and walked back up to deputy's car. "Can I have her now?"

"She's all yours." Deputy Collin's got out and opened the rear door of his cruiser. "Ma'am," he said. "You can go home with your husband."

Kathy got out of the deputy's car, and I opened the passenger door on the PT Cruiser.

"Kathy, get in," I said, putting a hand on her back.

"No. I need my car," she said.

I nudged her. "Come on, Kathy. Get in the car."

She grabbed the edge of the car door and wouldn't budge. "No. I need my car."

"Kathy, you have to get in," I said, putting a little more pressure on her back.

"No. I need my car."

"I was afraid this would happen," Deputy Collins said. "I'll take her home."

He opened the rear door of his cruiser. Then he grabbed Kathy by the elbows, holding them behind her back. He backed her up, sat her in the back of his cruiser, and closed the door.

"I'll follow you," he said.

"Okay."

I got into the Pt Cruiser and started it up. I pulled out to Orchard Lane, and turned left at Route 35. With Officer Collins behind me, I was very careful to keep my speed at exactly the speed limit.

I pulled into my driveway, parked the PT Cruiser, and got out of the car.

Deputy Collins was a couple seconds behind me. He pulled in and stopped behind the PT Cruiser. He got out of his car and opened the rear door. "You're free, ma'am."

Kathy got out of the deputy's car and walked up to me.

I reached in the window of the PT Cruiser and grabbed her purse. "Here's your purse, Kathy," I said, handing her the purse.

"Kay," she said. She put the strap of the purse on her shoulder and walked toward the house.

Deputy Collins was watching her. "Does she have a house key?" he asked.

"Yeah," I said. I watched Kathy on the deck as she fumbled around inside her purse. She finally found her house key, opened the door, and went in.

"I'm going to hold on to her driver's license," Deputy Collins said. "So she's not allowed to drive."

"That's fine with me," I said.

"Under certain circumstances, Ohio law allows me to confiscate someone's driver's license. It's called a security suspension," he explained. "Your wife will get a letter from the BMV in a few days telling her what she needs to do to get her license back."

"She probably never get her license back," I said.

"No," he agreed.

After Deputy Collins left, I went into the house. Kathy was filling her plastic pitcher with bird seed.

"I'm going to feed the wild birds," she said.

"Alright," I said. Then I went into the computer room and opened a phone book. I needed the number of a taxis. I called Purple Cab of Xenia.

"Purple Cab."

"I need a cab in Spring Valley."

"Where in Spring Valley?"

I gave him our address.

"Where ya going?

"Orchard Lane and Route 35."

"I'll send somebody to get ya. It'll be about twenty minutes."

I went outside to wait for the cab. Ten minutes later, an old green Buick pulled in the driveway.

The young woman who was driving rolled down her window. "Did you call a cab?"

"Yeah," I said, and I got into the back seat of the car.

"Where you going?" she asked.

"Orchard Lane and Route 35."

She pulled out of my driveway and headed up Route 42.

"Are you going to Enterprise?"

"No. I'm going to that gas station—Certified."

"Oh."

"I'm picking up a car," I said after a couple minutes of silence.

"Did you buy a car?"

"No."

She pulled in to the gas station.

"Go around back," I said.

She drove around to the back of the building.

"That Honda right there is what I'm picking up."

She stopped behind the Honda. "The fare comes to twenty-four dollars," she said.

I gave her a twenty and a ten.

"Thanks," she said.

I got out of the car.

"Do you want me to wait to see if it starts?" she asked.

"It will start," I said.

She drove off, and I started the Honda and drove home.

I went into the house. Kathy was listening to her boom box. When she saw me, she turned the music down. "What?" she asked.

"Nothing," I said.

She turned the music back up.

I got the 10mm open end wrench out of the drawer in the kitchen and went outside. I opened the hood of the Honda and put the support rod in place. Then I loosened the bolt on the positive terminal of the battery and pulled the battery cable off. I pushed the cable way down in back of the battery so that it couldn't be seen.

chapter 11

On Sunday, while Kathy and I were grocery shopping, we picked up Kathy's prescription from the pharmacy at Walmart. The drug that Dr. Vanderberg prescribed was named Ativan, 1 mg. There were only three pills in the bottle. The instructions said to take one or two pills an hour before the MRI.

When we got home, I put the bottle of pills on the top shelf of an upper kitchen cabinet.

I didn't get the bottle of pills down from the shelf until nine o'clock, Wednesday morning. Her appointment for the MRI was at ten, and we were ready to go.

I poured a glass of milk and took a pill out of the bottle. They were small.

"Here, Kathy. Take this." I held out my hand holding the small pill.

"Take this?"

"Yes."

She put the pill in her mouth.

"Here's some milk." I handed her the glass of milk.

She drank about half a glass of milk, and then set the glass on the counter.

"Are you done?" I asked.

She looked at the glass of milk. "No," she said. Then she drank the rest of the milk, and she put the empty glass in the refrigerator.

I took the empty glass out of the refrigerator and put it in the sink with the dirty dishes.

"We need to get going," I said.

"Are we going to the grocery?"

I thought about it. "We can, I guess. We have something else to do first"

"Kay."

We got into the PT Cruiser and I drove us to Drake Memorial Hospital.

The pill that I gave her didn't seem to have any effect on her. So, when we were inside the hospital, I stopped at a drinking fountain. "Kathy, stop," I said.

"What?"

I took the pill bottle out of my pocket and opened it. "I want you to take another one of these." I gave her a pill.

She put it in her mouth and swallowed it.

"Do you want a drink of water?"

She looked at the drinking fountain.

"Get a drink of water," I said.

She got a drink of water from the drinking fountain, and we went back to Radiology.

We checked in at the nurses station, and a nurse led us to a hospital room. It was not the same room we were in before, but one exactly like it.

"Kelly will be in to help you in a few minutes. Just make yourselves at home."

I sat down. A remote for a television was on the table next to me. I picked it up and aimed it at the television screen on the wall and pushed the power button. The blue light came on, and then the picture appeared. I surfed the channels until I found CNN.

"Kathy, why don't you take your coat off?'

She was standing under the television, holding the front of her coat closed with her left hand and holding her purse like a football with her right. "No," she said.

"Would you sit down, please?"

"Kay."

She sat down in the chair next to me and glanced up at the television from time to time.

Kelly came in. "How are you folks today?"

"Good," I said.

She stood in front of Kathy and smiled. "And how are you today, Kathy?"

Kathy eyed her suspiciously.

Kelly turned to me. "Did you give her her medication yet?"

"Yes," I said. I took the pill bottle out of my pocket and showed it to her. "I'm suppose to give her one or two of these. I gave her one before we left, and another one about twenty minutes ago. So she's already had two."

"Let me see that?"

I gave her the pill bottle and she looked it over. "Ativan!" she said, laughing. "This is what her doctor gave her? Ativan!"

"Yeah," I said.

"You've got to be kidding me."

"Are those not strong enough?"

She chuckled. "No." she said. She handed me back the pill bottle.

I looked at the bottle. "There's one left. Should we give her that one too?"

"Listen," Kelly said. "You could give her Ativan till the cows come home and it's not going to help. It's like giving her aspirin."

I looked at the pill bottle. "Her doctor seemed to think that these would just about put Kathy to sleep."

"Then he's not very smart," Kelly said.

"He seems to have a thriving business," I said.

"He has a thriving business because he's a neurologist, not because he's smart."

I shook my head. "So this was just a waste of time?"

"Well," Kelly said, calming down some. "We're here. I suppose we might as well try." She looked at Kathy. "Kathy, will you take your coat off for your old friend Kelly?"

"No," Kathy said.

"Kathy," I said, "please take your coat off. I'll hold it for you. Nothing will happen to it."

"No," Kathy said again.

"Now we're wasting more time," Kelly said.

"Yeah."

"Her doctor is suppose to be the smart one here, and he's the one who wants her to get an MRI," she said. "So he needs to come up with a plan. Something that will work. Not Ativan. That's just stupid."

"I'll talk to him," I said. "I don't think he has a very good grasp of the situation."

"Well tell him," Kelly said. "He knows that your wife has to be co-operative. She has to lay in that MRI machine for forty-five minutes."

"You mentioned that," I said.

"Hopefully he'll have another idea," she said.

"Yeah. Something that will actually work," I said.

"Right," she said.

"Are we done?" Kathy asked.

"Yes, we're done," Kelly said. Then she looked at me. "Enjoy your day, Mr. and Mrs. Stone."

"You too," I said.

Kathy and I walked out to the PT Cruiser. We got in and I started the car.

"Can we go to the grocery?" Kathy asked.

"Sure," I said. I thought about it for a minute and said: "Let's go to Kmart." We didn't really need anything. But Kmart was going to close at the end of April. So I thought they'd probably have some good deals.

We pulled into the Kmart parking lot. A huge yellow banner hung over the big letters of the store's name. It said "STORE CLOS-ING SALE".

I parked the car, and we went in.

Inside the store there were other big yellow signs. One said "EVERYTHING MUST GO". Another said "50% to 90% OFF EVERYTHING". I picked up a shopping cart.

"Can I have the Hershey?" Kathy asked.

"If they have it," I said. I looked around. There were no bags of pet food or salt in the front of the store. Most of the shelves were empty or nearly empty. "Let's go back to the shoe department," I said. "I need another pair of tennis shoes."

We went back to Footwear. Only a few pairs of men's shoes were left on the shelves. Most were size twelve. I wear a size nine.

There were also quite a few pairs of shoes lying on the floor. They looked either very big, or very small. I wasn't going to get down on the floor and look for a size nine.

"Can I have the Hershey?"

"Let's go look at the toys first," I said. I pushed the cart back to the toy department.

Kathy took off down an aisle. "Is Hershey down here?"

I left the cart and followed her down the aisle. "No, Kathy. Hershey's not down here."

A young couple with two small children were at the back of the aisle. Kathy walked up to them, stopped, and looked down at the two children. "Oh look! Isn't that nice? You have two." She looked up at the man. "I have two."

The man looked at her. "What?"

"The one, Andrew, when he came out his face was messy," Kathy said. "There happened to be a doctor right there and he said I pushed too hard. Isn't that funny? I pushed too hard."

"Okay," the man said, nodding.

"I'm sorry," I said. "My wife has dementia."

"She's no problem," the man said.

"My grandma's like that," the woman next to him said.

I noticed a set of plastic golf clubs for toddlers on the shelf. It was 60% off. "Are you going to buy that?" I asked the man.

"No." he said.

I took it off the shelf. "I'm going to get that for my grandson," I said.

"Go for it," the man said.

"Come on, Kathy. Let's go find the Hershey," I said, and I carried the toy golf clubs to our cart.

I pushed the cart along the back main aisle of the store, looking for something interesting to buy. I stopped when I noticed the Craft Beer Making Kit. It was only 50% off, but I thought I might have fun with it some day. So I put it in the cart.

Kathy broke loose and took off down an aisle in Electronics. I followed her. She picked up a CD from a table. "Is this the Hershey?" she asked.

"No, Kathy, that's not Hershey." I took the CD out of her hand and put it back. "Now let's go find the Hershey."

I pushed the cart to the aisle that used to be the food, candy and beverage aisle. There was almost nothing left. "Kathy, they don't have the Hershey," I said. I noticed a box of fruit and nut bars on the shelf. I picked them up. "This is the best we can do," I said, and then I dropped the box in the cart.

She took the box out of the cart. So I opened the box and gave her one of the fruit and nut bars.

I was pushing the cart towards the cash registers when a 95% off sticker caught my eye. It was for one of those two gallon cans of popcorn. I don't usually buy those, and I didn't want the popcorn. But at that price, I could feed the popcorn to the birds and then I'd have a nice can. I put the can in the cart.

We got in line at the cash register. When we were next, and I was putting our items on the conveyor belt, the cashier looked at Kathy and said: "Well, hi Kathy. I see you brought your husband with you this time."

Kathy chuckled.

As the cashier was ringing up our items, she asked me: "Did she ever find the Kmart in Beavercreek?"

"I didn't know she was looking for it," I said.

"Yeah," she said. "We drew her a map." She rang up the last item. "That comes to forty-seven, thirty."

I reached for my wallet.

"I pay," Kathy said. She opened her wallet and got out her Kmart rewards card and her credit card. She swiped them both.

"You have two hundred reward points," the cashier said.

I loaded our items back into the cart. "Was that last Friday that you drew her a map to the other Kmart?"

"Well I didn't. Our manager drew her the map. But yeah, I think it was last Friday. She wanted Meow Mix, and we didn't have any."

"You don't have much of anything," I said.

"No, we don't, not anymore," she said. "She was looking for it though. She was walking all over the store: 'Is the Meow Mix over here? Is the Meow Mix over here?' She was so funny." She stopped talking and looked at me. "I don't mean that in a bad way," she said.

"I understand," I said.

"So our manager called Beavercreek to find out if they had Meow Mix. And yes they did. Cuz they're not closing. Not yet anyway. And then he drew her a map to show her how to get there."

"Well she never found it. But we bought a bag of Meow Mix a couple days ago at Walmart," I said.

"I'm glad you got your Meow Mix, Kathy," she said, as we were leaving.

Kathy smiled.

When we got home, Kathy turned on her boom box and listened to music. I peaked into her purse, which she had put on the kitchen table. I was looking for the map. It wasn't in her purse.

I went out to the Honda. On the floor, in front of the passenger seat, there was a piece of paper. I picked it up and turned it over. It was the map

The way the manager had shown Kathy how to get to the Beavercreek Kmart was: Go west on Dayton Xenia Road, turn left at Trebein Roar, turn right at Route 35, turn left on Factory Road, turn right on Indian Ripple Road and that takes you to the Beavercreek Kmart. He drew the roads at the top of the page, and marked the Kmart with a big X. Below that he wrote the directions down, step by step.

So Kathy wasn't lost the other day when she got the tickets. She was still on the map. Following the manager's directions, she would have taken Dayton Xenia Road. She did. She was suppose to turn left at Trebein Road and right on Route 35. She must have done that to get to the intersection of Orchard Lane and Route 35, where the deputies had her pulled over. And the next intersection was Factory Road.

Kathy was on her way to the Beavercreek Kmart. The speed limit on Dayton Xenia Road was 45 mph. She just didn't notice when she drove into a school zone, and so she didn't slow down.

Anybody could make that kind of mistake.

chapter 12

March 21, 2014

Kathy and I entered Dr. Vanderberg's waiting room. It was five minutes before eleven o'clock. Her appointment was for eleven. I walked up to the reception window. "Kathleen Stone is here for her appointment," I told the nurse at the desk.

"Have a seat please," she said.

Kathy and I sat down.

An older couple were also in the waiting room. His hands were shaking badly. I think he had Parkinson's Disease.

The woman kept looking over at Kathy and me. She might have been wondering what was wrong with Kathy. Or maybe she was wondering what was wrong with me—I don't know.

The door on the side of the waiting room opened. The nurse stood in the doorway and smiled. "John," she said, very sweetly, "we're ready for you to come back."

The older couple got up. He shuffled slowly toward the door. She held his arm and walked beside him.

A few minutes later the door opened again. "Kathleen Stone," the nurse said.

"Come on, Kathy, that's you," I said. We got up.

"Follow me, please," she said.

We followed her to the same examination room we were in before.

"Sit down, Kathy," I said, as soon as we entered the room.

I remained standing. I didn't feel like sitting at that moment. "Kathy, are you going to sit down?"

"Are you going to sit down?" Kathy asked me.

"Okay, I'll sit." I sat down and Kathy sat down next to me.

The nurse was still in the room. "Has she been taking her medication?" she asked.

"Yes," I said.

"Any changes in mood, or behavior, or anything else?"

"Well, uh, yeah. I guess," I said. "She's not driving anymore because she got a ticket."

"She got a ticket?" the nurse asked, and I saw a flicker of anger in her eyes.

"Yeah," I said.

"So she was driving?"

"Well, yeah. That's how you usually get tickets. Isn't it?"

"Dr. Vanderberg is not going to be happy to hear that," she said.

"Oh well," I said.

The nurse left, and we waited.

After about twenty minutes, Kathy said, "I have to use the bathroom."

"Okay," I said. "I'll try to find it for you. Stay here." I got up and went to the door. "Stay in the room." I opened the door and looked out. I could see many doors. All of them were closed, and none of them had any markings identifying them as bathrooms.

I stepped out into the hallway. I walked down to where it dead ends into another hallway. I heard a noise and turned around. My wife was right behind me. "Kathy—"

"I have to use the bathroom."

"Okay." I looked both ways, up and down the hallway we abutted. There were more doors. All of them were closed. And none of them had any markings except for numbers.

The nurse came out of one of the rooms and saw us. "What are you doing out in the hall?" she asked.

"She has to use the bathroom," I said.

"Oh," she said. She walked over and opened a door that was across the hall from us. "There's the bathroom."

"Oh, door number five," I said. "I should have known."

"Can I use the bathroom?" Kathy asked.

"It's right there," I said.

Kathy went into the bathroom and I closed the door behind her.

The nurse stood there looking at me.

"I'm going to wait for her," I said.

"I guess that'd be okay," she said, and then she walked away.

I waited by the door while Kathy used the bathroom. After a couple minutes, the door opened.

"Wash your hands, Kathy," I said.

"Kay." She turned the water on and held her hands under the stream. Then she turned the water off. I handed her a couple paper towels and she dried her hands.

I looked in the toilet. She didn't flush. Usually, I would flush the toilet for her. That's what I do at home. But I didn't feel like flushing the toilet, for whatever reason. So I didn't.

We went back to the room and sat down.

A few minutes later the nurse came by. "I'm going to close this door," she said.

"Are we making too much noise?" I asked.

A few minutes later Dr. Vanderberg entered the room. "How are you folks doing today?" he asked in a not so friendly tone.

I didn't bother answering.

The doctor sat at his desk. He began looking through papers, writing notes on some of them. "So she's been driving?"

"Yeah. But she got a ticket and the officer took her driver's license," I said.

"That burned me up when she told me that," he said.

"What do you think you know about her driving, doctor?" I asked.

He looked up from his papers. "I think she has a significant cognitive impairment, and you can't see it!"

"How do you know what I see!" I said. "Have you seen an MRI or an EEG on me. Because I don't remember having that done!"

"I think a two ton vehicle in you wife's hands is dangerous," he said. "She shouldn't be driving."

"Well how many tickets have you had, doctor? How many accidents? She's had two tickets in her life. And zero accidents. So maybe you shouldn't be driving."

He looked back down at the papers on his desk. "So she's not driving now?"

"No," I said.

The doctor was looking at papers, writing notes, looking at papers, writing notes.

"What are you gonna do, doctor, pronounce a diagnosis?" I asked.

He turned to face me. "Yes," he said.

"Based on what?" I asked. "You didn't get an EEG. You didn't get an MRI. Are you basing you diagnosis on five minutes of stupid questions? Really?"

Dr. Vanderberg threw his pen on the desk. "Now you don't like my assessment," he said. He looked straight ahead for a few seconds. Then he turned to me. "Your wife has Alzheimer's Disease." He said this viciously: "Very advanced Alzheimer's Disease."

I shook my head. "I disagree. I think she has Pick's Disease."

Dr. Vanderberg leaded back in his chair and rubbed his forehead. "So you think this is FTD?"

"Yes, I do," I said. "I've been reading about the different types of dementia, and I think her symptoms fit Pick's Disease much better than they do Alzheimer's Disease."

"Does she repeat what you say?"

"Yes. She repeats what you say. She's obsessed with counting things— particularly her chickens. Her first noticeable symptom was trouble naming things. And she seems to remember things—except, not words."

"Hmm. You might be on to something," he said.

"Well, does the cat scan show you anything? She's did have that done."

He shook his head. "No. Cat scans aren't clear enough to tell us if this is FTD. But, there is another test that would. It's called a PET scan."

"Pets?" Kathy said. "We have a dog, two cats, and a bunch of chickens."

Dr. Vanderberg smiled and patted her hand. Then he looked at me. "So what do you want to do? Do you want to find out?"

"Yes I want to find out," I said. "If she doesn't have Alzheimer's, then the medication she's taking is probably not right for her."

"Right. It's probably not."

He turned to his desk and started writing something. "I'm going to put in a request for a PET Scan to her insurance company. Now I'm not sure what they're gonna want to do. If they approve the scan, then someone will be calling you to schedule it."

"Okay," I said.

" I want to see Kathleen again in a month or so," he said. "Make an appointment with the nurse before you leave."

"Alright." I got up. "Come on Kathy, we're done."

Kathy and I walked out to the waiting room and up to the reception window.

"Dr. Vanderberg wants to see Kathy again in a month or so." I told the nurse at the desk.

She looked at the appointment calender that was sitting in front of her. "Does Wednesday, April 23 work for you?"

"No. Let's make it on a Friday. I prefer Friday appointments."

"How about April 25. That's on a Friday."

"No. Could we make it later than that? Maybe early May?"

"Dr. Vanderberg will be on vacation the first Friday in May, but he has a one o'clock appointment available on May 9."

"I'd prefer a morning appointment, if that's possible."

"How about Friday, May 16 at nine o'clock?"

"That will work," I said.

The nurse filled out an appointment card and gave it to me. I put the card in my pocket. Kathy and I went out to the PT Cruiser, and we drove home.

When we got in the house, Kathy went to the living room and turned on her boom box.

It was only noon, and there was nothing I had to do. I opened the refrigerator and got a 25 oz. can of Foster's Lager. I opened the can and took a sip.

I walked into the living room with the beer. Kathy didn't even notice me. She was standing in front of the boom box listening to The Gall Stones.

I put my beer down on a table and got behind Kathy. I turned her around and kissed her. Then I kissed her again.

Kathy chuckled. "Are we going to do it?"

"Yes," I said.

"Kay," she said. She turned off the boom box and went to the bedroom.

I picked my beer up off the table and took it to the refrigerator. Then I went to the bedroom.

Kathy's shirt and bra were already off when I walked in the room. She giggled and unbuckled her pants. She pulled off her pants and panties and slipped into bed.

I chuckled a little bit as I began unbuttoning my shirt.

chapter 13

Kathy was scheduled to appear in court for her speeding and reckless operation tickets on Tuesday, April 1 at 9:00 am. She had to appear at Fairborn Municipal Court.

Fairborn is about twenty miles from where we live, so, on the morning of her court appearance, we left the house at about eight.

At eight-thirty, we were in the parking lot of the Fairborn Municipal Court building. I had never been to this courthouse before. The building, it seemed to me, was remarkably unimpressive. It was a plain, one story brick building, in a mostly abandoned shopping center.

I pulled the PT Cruiser into a parking space and turned it off. I turned to Kathy. "Kathy, leave your purse in the car," I said.

"Why?" she asked.

"We're going into that building," I said. "You won't need your purse. It will be safe out here. We're going to lock the car. You can even hide it under the seat if you want. But leave the purse in the car."

"Leave the purse," she said.

"Yes. Leave the purse."

"Kay," she said, and she put her purse on the floor.

We entered the building and got in line to go through the metal detector. Kathy wanted to walk around the metal detector. I held on to the sleeve of her coat. "Kathy, stay with me," I said.

There were three people ahead of us in the metal detector line. After they had gone through, and it was our turn, I wanted Kathy to go through first.

"Does she need to take off her coat," I asked the police officer who was watching the line.

"No," he said.

"Kathy, walk through that thing like those other people did," I said.

"Kay."

Kathy walked through the metal detector. She set off the alarm.

"Hold it right there, ma'am!" another police officer said.

Kathy raised her hands like she was under arrest. The officer was approaching her with a handheld metal detector. She probably thought it was a gun.

The officer waved the device up and down her body. It beeped around the front of her coat. "It's just the zipper," he said. "She's fine."

I put my wallet, my keys, my change, and my cell phone in the basket on the conveyor belt.

"You're going to have to take off your belt," the officer said. "That's a metal buckle."

"Okay." I took off my belt and put it in the basket.

I walked through the metal detector without setting off the alarm. Then I waited for the basket. It passed through the x-ray box and arrived at the other end of the conveyor. I put my belt back on and put my items back in my pockets.

I took Kathy's tickets out of my pocket and we walked over to the information desk. An older man was sitting behind the desk.

"I'm not sure where we're suppose to go," I said.

"Let me see those," he said.

I handed him the tickets.

He looked at them. Then he pointed down the hall. "Go to the first window—that's Window A. She'll tell you what to do." He gave me back the tickets.

"Thanks," I said.

Kathy and I got in line at Window A. There were only two people in front of us, and they were together. It was a mother and her teenage son.

"Do they have my driver's license?" Kathy asked.

"You'll have to talk to the judge about that," I said.

We stepped up to the window. I handed the woman the tickets. "My wife's suppose to be in court at nine," I said.

She looked at the tickets. "Could you wait a minute?" she asked.
"Okay," I said.

She walked away from the counter.

"Do they have my driver's license?" Kathy asked.

"No, Kathy, she doesn't have your driver's license," I said. "That's something you'll have to ask the judge about."

"Kay," she said.

The woman came back to the counter. "They want you to sit and wait outside Courtroom B." She leaned over the counter and pointed across the hall. "Do you see that wooden bench over there."

I turned and looked. "Yes."

"You can sit anywhere along that wall."

"Okay," I said.

"Is my driver's license back there?" Kathy asked.

"No, honey," the woman said. "Your driver's license is not back here."

We went over to the wooden bench across from Courtroom B and sat down. Courtroom B's doors were both opened.

I watched as other people entered the building. After going through the metal detector, everyone went up to a window. Most then went into Courtroom B. But a few people came over and sat on a wooden bench. There was plenty of room. The hallway was wide, and there were benches on both sides. So no one had to sit near anyone else.

I couldn't see what was going on in the courtroom so I watched the people on the benches. Many of them had lawyers. Those were the guys—mostly guys, anyway—wearing suits and carrying briefcases. There were also a group of the same kind of suit wearing people going in and out of an office near where Kathy and I were sitting. Those people didn't carry briefcases.

The suit wearing people—who I guess were the prosecutors—talked to the briefcase carrying people; and the briefcase carrying people talked to the suit wearing people and to the people sitting on the benches—who, I guess were defendants, their families and witnesses.

A police officer came out of the courtroom and told a woman, who was wearing a suit: "Court is about to begin."

The woman walked around the hall talking briefly with briefcase carrying people. I guess she was spreading the word.

The briefcase carrying people, and most of the people sitting on the benches, started filing into the courtroom.

The police officer closed the door and stood outside the courtroom.

The hallway was nearly empty. There was a young couple. She was holding a baby. Across from them there was a young woman taking to a man with a briefcase. And there was Kathy and me.

I got up. "Come on, Kathy," I said.

Kathy got up. "Are we done?"

"Um, let's go find out," I said. We walked over to Window A.

"Were we suppose to go in the courtroom?" I asked the woman behind the counter.

"They know you're there," she said. "They'll be with you in a minute."

"Okay," I said.

Kathy looked at me. "So what to do?"

"Let's go sit down," I said. "Come on." We went back over to the bench and sat down.

"Do they have my driver's license?" she asked.

"You'll have to ask the judge," I said.

A young woman wearing a suit walked over to us. "The judge will see you now," she said.

"Okay," I said. I got up, and then Kathy got up.

We followed the woman to the courtroom doors. The police officer opened one of the doors and we went in. He closed the door behind us.

"Wait right here," the woman whispered to me.

"Okay," I whispered. I took ahold of Kathy's hand and held it tightly so she wouldn't go anywhere.

The judge was hearing a case. The defendant was speaking:

"Your Honor, I don't drive. Not since my license was suspended, anyway. I quit. Cold turkey. I don't need the trouble. But my girlfriend had a headache. She needed some Tylenol. Her head hurt so bad that she couldn't drive. Now I'm the type of person who doesn't like to see suffering. I don't like to see human beings suffer. I don't like to see animals suffer. Or even a dog—I don't like to see a dog suffer."

"Mr. O'Keefe," the judge said. "I've heard enough."

"I apologize, Your Honor," the defendant said.

"I find you guilty, Mr. O'Keefe. And I hope you do quit driving, because I'm going to extend your driver's license suspension for one additional year. So you won't have a driver's license for sixteen months from now—at the earliest."

The defendant hung his head. "Yes, Your Honor."

"And I'm going to fine you one thousand dollars plus court costs."

"Your Honor, I don't have that kind of money." You could hear the anguish in his voice. "Oh my God!"

"And," the judge continued, "I'm going to sentence you to the county jail for a period of six months."

"Six months!" The defendant began to cry. "I'll lose everything. Everything."

"Mr. O'Keefe. Mr. O'Keefe!" he said again to get the defendant's attention.

"Yes, Your Honor."

"Mr. O'Keefe, I will suspend your jail sentence, and all but one hundred dollars of your fine."

"Thank you, Your Honor."

The judge smiled. "I just wanted to see you suffer, Mr. O'Keefe."

The bailiff and the court reporter chuckled. I looked around at the other people in the courtroom. No one else seemed to be amused by his remark. I wasn't either.

The defendant left through a side door, and then the bailiff stood in front of the judge's bench. He spoke in a loud, formal voice:

"Now hearing case number C-11292014, The State of Ohio versus Kathleen Stone."

"That's us," the woman said. "Let's go."

We followed her up the aisle into the well lit area in front of the judge. "You two stand over there," she said.

Kathy and I got behind the defendants podium. She sat down at a table.

The judge looked at her. "Are you representing the state in this matter, Ms. Harris?"

"Yes, Your Honor."

"So what happened?" the judge asked.

"The defendant, Kathleen Stone, was clocked at going 45mph in a school zone during restricted hours. Sargent Collins, the Sheriff's deputy who clocked her, followed her with his lights flashing for three miles from Dayton Xenia Road where the offense occurred to the intersection of Route 35 and Orchard Lane in Beavercreek."

"Was she charged with fleeing?" the judge asked, looking down at his docket. "I don't have that here."

"No, Your Honor, she was not charged with fleeing," Ms. Harris said. "She was cited for speeding, and for reckless operation because her speed was so excessive in a school zone."

"I see," the judge said, and then he turned and looked at Kathy. "And what do you have to say, Ms. Stone. Did this happen?"

"I need my license," Kathy said. She stepped out from behind the defendant's podium and took a couple steps toward the judge's bench.

"Ma'am!" the bailiff shouted. "You're not allowed to approach the bench."

"Kathy, come back," I said.

Another police officer—a big guy—stepped between her and the judge. His hand was on his gun.

Kathy looked at him and then joined me behind the defendant's podium.

"Ms. Stone, you've been cited for speeding and for reckless operation of a motor vehicle. How do you plead?"

"Do you have my driver's license?" Kathy asked the judge.

"How do you plead, Ms. Stone?" the judge demanded. "Guilty, or no contest?"

Kathy remained silent.

"Guilty or no contest, Ms. Stone?"

Again, Kathy choose to exercise her right to remain silent.

"Guilty or no contest, Ms. Stone, which is it?"

"Your Honor," I said. "I know I can't represent my wife. But I will tell you this: she doesn't think she's done anything wrong."

"Okay," the judge said. He began nodding his head angrily. "Okay," he repeated. He continued to nod his head. "It's not guilty, then." He banged his gavel.

The big police officer came over to me. "Step this way, sir," he said. He was ushering us out the door.

"Mr. Stone," Ms. Harris said. "Wait outside. Don't leave yet."

"Okay," I said.

The big police officer opened the side door

Kathy and I left the courtroom and entered a narrow hallway. I walked along slowly toward the main hallway. Kathy walked beside me.

"Are we done?" Kathy asked.

"Almost," I said.

I heard the door open and close behind me. Then I heard footsteps.

"Mr. Stone," Ms. Harris said. She had caught up with us and was walking beside Kathy. "Just have a seat where you were. I'll get you a date for her pretrial."

"Okay."

Ms. Harris went on ahead. Kathy and I walked out to the main hallway. We walked over to where we were sitting. "Let's sit down," I said.

"Sit down?"

"Yes." I sat down, and then she sat down.

Ms. Harris brought some papers out to me about five minutes later.

"This is what happened today." She handed me a paper with the Fairborn Municipal Court letterhead. "And this one is for her pretrial. You'll also get one in the mail." She handed me another paper with the court's letterhead. "Her pretrial is scheduled for April 16 at eleven o'clock. That's on a Wednesday. It's going to be held in Courtroom C. Do you know where that is?"

"It's right around the corner, isn't it?"

"Right. Just turn where the hallway turns and there it is."

"I think we can find it," I said.

"I'm sure you can," she said. "We'd like you to come in about a half hour early. And when you come in, you can just have a seat—where you're sitting now would be fine. And someone—probably me—will talk to you."

"Okay," I said.

"You know," she said. "It would have worked out fine if she had pleaded guilty or no contest. I was there to request leniency for her."

"Really," I said. "Well, thanks for telling me."

She laughed, and said, "You're welcome."

. . . . .

On April 16, we arrived at the courthouse at twenty minutes after ten o'clock.

I asked Kathy to leave her purse in the car. She put the purse under the seat, and we went into the building.

We went through the metal detector, then walked along the main hallway. I looked over at Window A. There was no one behind the counter—which was fine, because we didn't need to go to Window A today.

There were people running back and forth across the hallway, going into rooms or down narrow hallways, but I didn't see anyone sitting on the benches. We passed the spot where we were sitting on the day of her first court appearance. I wanted to sit farther down the hall, where we could see the doors of Courtroom C. So we walked a little further, and then we sat down.

There was one other guy, and his lawyer, sitting on a bench. They were sitting very close to the doors of Courtroom C. He was wearing an orange jumpsuit. Two deputies were standing near the guy and his lawyer.

Ms. Harris walked up to us. "Good morning, Mr. and Mrs. Stone."

"Good morning," I said.

She stood in front of Kathy. "Kathleen, I have a deal that I'd like to offer you. Would you come with me to my office, please?"

Kathy looked at me.

"Yes, she will." I stood up. "Come on, Kathy."

"Mr. Stone, you can go with her. But you're not allowed to help her make the decision. Do you understand? You're not allowed to help her in any way."

"I understand," I said.

We followed her back to her desk in the DA's office. She stood behind her desk; we stood in front of her desk.

"Kathleen, you've been cited for reckless operation, and for speeding," she said. She put her hands on top of her desk, where there was a copy of each citation.

I looked down at the citations. I don't think Kathy noticed them.

"If you plead guilty to speeding," Ms. Harris continued, "then I will drop the reckless operation." She pulled the reckless operation citation off her desk.

Kathy looked at me.

Then Ms. Harris looked at me. "Now don't you say anything."

I folded my arms, and looked straight ahead, at the wall. I kept my face expressionless.

A young man in a white shirt and a tie looked up from his desk. He seemed interested in the negotiation.

"Kathleen, look at me. Don't look at your husband," Ms. Harris said. "Now what do you want to do? Will you plead guilty to speeding if I drop the reckless operation?"

Kathy looked at Ms. Harris, and then she looked at me.

"Kathleen, don't look at your husband. Look at me."

Kathy looked at her and asked: "Do you have my driver's license?"

The young man chuckled quietly.

"No, I don't. But we're not talking about your driver's license right now," Ms. Harris said. "I'll tell you what: I'll drop the speeding if you plead guilty to the reckless operation." She put the reckless operation ticket back on the desk and pulled off the speeding ticket.

Kathy looked down at the reckless operation ticket.

"Now don't you say anything," Ms. Harris warned me.

My arms remained folded. My face remained expressionless. I did, in fact, have an opinion on which one of the deals was the better deal. But I kept my opinion to myself.

Kathy looked at me, and then she looked at Ms. Harris. "Do you have my driver's license?"

The young man burst out laughing. "I think they're going to have to drop this one," he said.

"She's not going to take a deal," Ms. Harris said. "You two can wait outside. I'll get you when it's time to see the judge."

"Okay," I said. "Come on, Kathy."

Kathy and I went back out to the bench and sat down.

Ms. Harris came out of her office and walked down the hall to Courtroom C. A police officer opened the door for her and she went into the courtroom.

She came out of the courtroom a couple minutes later. She walked up to us.

"The judge is ready to hear Kathleen's case," she said.

"Come on, Kathy," I said.

Kathy and I followed Ms. Harris down to Courtroom C's double doors. The police officer opened one of the doors, and we went into the courtroom.

"All rise," the bailiff said.

We were in the aisle, and we stopped walking. People on both sides of us began to stand.

"Hear ye! Hear ye! The State of Ohio, Court of Common Pleas, Sixth Circuit, is now in session. The Honorable Julie Radcliffe presiding," the bailiff announced.

The judge, who was already sitting at the bench, said, "You may be seated."

"It's show time," Ms. Harris said. We followed her up the aisle. She opened a gate, which we went through. Then she pointed to the defendants podium. Kathy and I stood behind the podium. She stood behind a table.

"Please raise your right hand," the bailiff said.

I raised my right hand. Ms. Harris raised her right hand. Kathy looked around. She appeared to be baffled.

"Do you swear to tell the truth, the whole truth, and nothing but the truth?" the bailiff asked.

"I do," I said.

"I do," Ms. Harris said.

"You may sit down," the judge said to Ms. Harris.

Ms. Harris sat down at the table.

"This is a pretrial hearing for case number C-11292014, The State of Ohio versus Kathleen Stone. The charges are speeding, 45mph in a school zone during restricted hours; and reckless operation of a motor vehicle. Do you understand these charges being brought against you, Ms. Stone?"

Kathy stared at the judge.

"I asked you a question, Ms. Stone. Do you understand the charges that have been brought against you?"

Kathy looked at me, and then back at the judge.

"I'm waiting for your answer, Ms. Stone. You do not have the option of not answering my question. You must answer. I could hold you for contempt of court. Do you understand that?"

"Your Honor," I said. "You should know that Kathy has dementia."

The judge looked at me. "And who are you?"

"I'm Mark Stone. I'm her husband."

"Mr. Stone, she is allowed to represent herself, but you are not allowed to represent her. That would be practicing law without a license."

"But what I'm saying is she can't represent herself," I said.

"Which is why you need to hire an attorney," the judge said. "You can represent your wife in most venues, Mr. Stone. But not here. This is a court of law. If you represent her here, you are committing a crime. Do you understand?"

"Yes, Your Honor."

"I'll give you two weeks to get an attorney," the judge said, and she banged her gavel.

I looked over at Ms. Harris.

"We'll send you a letter with your new court date," she said. "You can leave."

"See ya," I said.

"Bye," she said.

And then Kathy and I went home.

· · · · ·

The next day, I went into our computer room, took the current edition of the Dayton Area Yellow Pages down from the shelf and opened the book up to Attorneys. There were several pages of advertisements, and a huge number of names and telephone numbers listed. I started by reading the small ads with no pictures. The key words I was looking for were: DUI, Traffic Law or Misdemeanor.

I didn't think that Kathy's case was going to be very difficult for a lawyer to handle. She was clearly not competent to stand trial—that was the most important fact of her case. And the court didn't need to be convinced of it—they already knew it. It was just a matter of having a person with the right credentials saying it to them and putting it on the court's record. So my idea was to call around, get prices, and hire the cheapest lawyer I could find.

I made phone calls and explained the situation to several lawyers. I got four or five quotes between eight hundred and fourteen hundred dollars.

One lawyer rejected the whole idea of an "incompetency defense" in Kathy's case. "That's just not done in traffic cases," he said.

"Well, I'm sure it's unusual," I said. "But in this case, that's what has to be done."

"I don't think they'll go for it," he said.

"Thank you for your time," I said.

The last one I called was a lawyer by the name of Martin Wright. I explained the situation to him, and then he asked for the case number.

I looked at a letter from the court, which I had in front of me. "The case number is C-11292014," I said. "The prosecutor on the case is Ms. Harris."

"Debbie?" he asked.

"Yeah. I think that's her first name."

"I'll tell you what I'll do," he said. "I'm going to take a look at the case on the court's website, and I'll probably call Debbie. And then I'll get back to you, with a price, if I want to represent your wife. But I'll get back to you, one way or the other, in fifteen or twenty minutes."

"Okay. I look forward to hearing from you," I said.

After I got off the phone, I went to the refrigerator and got a Budweiser. I came back to the computer room, turned on the television, and watched an old episode of *The Rifleman* while I waited for Mr. Wright to call.

My cellphone rang a half hour later.

"Hello."

"Hello. Is this Mark."

"Yeah. This is Mark."

"Mark, this is Martin Wright. I'll represent Kathleen for five hundred dollars. How does that sound?"

"That sounds very reasonable. You've got the job. What time does your office close? Kathy and I can head up there this afternoon to get the money to you."

"You don't have to come to my office," he said. "Just send me a check in the mail. Put the case number on the memo line, and put a note in with it so my secretary knows what the check is for."

"I'll do that right away," I said.

"And one more thing, Mark," he said. "Kathleen probably won't have to make another court appearance. I'll call you if she needs to. But she probably won't."

"That would be fine," I said.

He chuckled. "I didn't think you'd mind that," he said. "Well, good luck to you, Mark."

"Thanks," I said. "And good luck to you."

I wrote the check, and a simple note, which said:

Dear Martin Wright,

Thanks again for taking Kathleen's case. Please keep me informed. Hopefully, everything will go smoothly.

Sincerely,
Mark Stone.

I wrote his office address on the front of an envelope. Then I folded the note around the check, put it in the envelope, and sealed the envelope. Later that day I put the envelope in a mailbox.

At least once a day, for the next week or so, I checked the court's website for new entries in Kathy's case. One evening, on April 22, I noticed a new entry. Martin Wright was now listed as defense counsel.

The entry was dated for that day.

I kept going back to the court's website, expecting to see that motions had been filed. Nothing seemed to be happening. So, on Friday, April 25, I called Martin Wright. He didn't answer his phone, so I left a message on his voice mail:

"Martin, this is Mark Stone. My wife's court date is coming up. It's on the thirtieth. And I was just wondering what was going on with her case. Please give me a call. Thank you."

Monday afternoon, on April 28, my cellphone rang.

"Hello."

"Hi, is this Mark?"

"Yeah."

"Mark, this is Martin Wright. I've got some good news. The court has dismissed your wife's case."

"That is good news," I said.

"Her case was dismissed 'without prejudice'. That means that they could bring the case back. They won't. But that's what that means."

"Right. I'm not going to worry about that," I said.

"No. That's nothing to worry about. It's over."

"Well, thanks again, Martin."

"Have a nice day, Mark."

"I'm doing just that," I said.

chapter 14

One of the things that Kathy did, as part of her daily routine, was to go to the mailbox at the side of the road and get the mail. In 2014, she no longer opened, or read, any of the mail. She would just get the mail out of the mailbox, bring it in the house, and put it on my desk. Sometimes, when there was no mail in our mailbox, Kathy would take the mail out of our neighbor's mailbox, and bring that in and put it on my deck. This happened frequently. But no one ever made it into a big deal. When I found our neighbor's mail on my desk, I would just take it back out to their mailbox and put it in. I never even brought the issue up with Kathy.

On Friday, May 2, among the letters that I found on my desk when I got home were two letters from the Ohio BMV. They were both addressed to Kathy.

I opened one of the letters from the BMV. This was the letter that Deputy Collins told me she would get as a result of him taking her driver's license. I was expecting that letter. I read it. It explained that a law enforcement officer, Deputy Collins—and the letter actually named him—had reason to believe that Kathy was suffering from "a disability or medical condition" which prevented her from "safely operating a motor vehicle". The letter went on to explain what she needed to do to get her driver's license back. First, she would have to send the BMV a letter from a doctor stating that she had no known disability or medical condition that would prevent her from safely operating a motor vehicle. Then she would be allowed to take the written test. And if she passed the written test, she would be allowed to take the road test. If she passed that test too, her driving privileges would be reinstated upon the payment of a $150.00 reinstatement fee.

The second letter was almost, word for word, identical to the first letter. It was different in two respects. One was that instead of a law enforcement officer, it was a "medical professional" who had reason to believe that she was suffering from a "disability or medical condition" which prevented her from "safely operating a motor vehicle". And the "medical professional" was not named. The other difference was that instead of a letter from a doctor, they were requiring a signed and notarized statement from an MD that he or she has examined her and she has no "physical or mental condition" which would prevent her from safely operating a motor vehicle.

I put both letters, along with a booklet of Arby's coupons, a letter from AARP, and a letter from a company selling replacement windows in our recycling bin.

. . . . .

The following Monday, I found another interesting letter on my deck when I got home. It was from our health insurance company, Buckeye Blue Shield. I opened the letter and read it.

I had been expecting this letter too. This was the letter where Buckeye Blue Shield explains why they refuse to pay for a PET scan for Kathy. In a nutshell, the letter said that Buckeye Blue Shield considers the PET scan an "experimental" procedure. And they would not approve it, because "clinical observation" could be used to achieve to same result.

I did not agree that the PET scan was an experimental procedure. It's pricey—it costs five thousand dollars or so. And it's new. But it's beyond the stage where the scientists and engineers who invented the PET scan haven't gotten all of the bugs worked out. It works.

I think by "experimental" Buckeye Blue Shield meant that it was too expensive. And I could accept that. Many things are too expensive: luxury cars, yachts—this list could go on and on. I've told others, and I've been told many times myself, "That's too expensive." So I can understand that.

And apparently, Buckeye Blue Shield felt that, to save money, good old fashion "clinical observation" should be used to diagnose a patient like Kathy. I guess I agreed with that too.

Now "clinical observation" would involve the doctor forming a trusting relationship with his patient. It would involve him showing her pictures of objects, and animals, trying to get a sense of the severity of her language deficit. It would involve questioning her, trying to get a sense of her reasoning deficit. It would involve talking to me, her husband. What skills did she once have that she no longer has? What strange habits has she acquired?

The problem for us was: Dr. Vanderberg didn't have time for "clinical observation". He was a busy man.

It was only four o'clock in the afternoon. So I picked up my cellphone and went to recent calls. I found the number to Dr. Vanderberg's office and tapped it.

"Sugar Valley Diagnostics."

"Hi. This is Mark Stone. My wife, Kathleen, has an appointment on the sixteenth."

"Yes, Mr. Stone," Lisa said.

"I'd like to cancel that appointment."

"Would you like to reschedule her appointment for another date?"

"No. I don't think so," I said. "You wouldn't happen to know of a good neurologist, would you?"

"What?"

"Nothing," I said.

"Is there a problem?"

"Of course there's 'a problem'," I said. "We wouldn't be going to see a neurologist if there weren't a 'problem'."

"I mean, do you have a problem with Dr. Vanderberg?"

"I just don't think that guy's going to work out for us."

"We're sorry if you're dissatisfied."

"It's okay. I just think we'd be better off going somewhere else."

"That's your choice, Mr. Stone."

"Yes it is."

"Well, I hope things work out for you and Kathleen," she said.

"Thanks," I said. ""Bye."

"Bye," she said.

Okay. So now what do I do? Kathy was still taking Namenda and donepezil, which, if she had Alzheimer's Disease, might have improved her cognition. But I never thought Kathy had Alzheimer's disease, and I still didn't. I was convinced that Kathy had FTD, and the drugs that she was taking might make her condition worse. Kathy had been taking the Alzheimer's medications for close to a year by then. And I had no way of knowing whether they doing nothing at all, or they were making her more confused.

Getting Kathy correctly diagnosed would have been nice, I thought.

The Buckeye Blue Shield Preferred Provided Directory was setting on the corner of my desk. I slid it in front of me and opened it to the Neurology pages. There was a long list of neurologists. I was sure that Dr. Smith would refer us to whichever one I wanted. But I didn't know anything about any of them, except for Dr. Vanderberg. There were three listings under *Neuropsychologist*. Would one of those be more helpful? Probably not. There was one listing under *Neuropsychiatrist*. Arnold Pick and Alois Alzheimer were neuropsychiatrists, and those guys had no problem doing "clinical observation". Would this one guy who's listed in the directory do "clinical observation"? My educated guess was: no. He'd probably be too busy to bother with that.

Okay. So what do I do now? I closed the directory, leaned back in my chair, and let my mind wander.

My thoughts drifted back to a Sunday morning in January, 2009. Kathy and I had been married for eleven months. We were still living in our house in Ross, but we had just bought a house in Spring Valley. So we were packing up some of our things, getting ready for our eventual move.

We were in the living room. She was taking pictures down from the walls, wrapping them in bubble wrap, and carefully fitting them into a cardboard box. I was taking books—mostly hers—off a bookcase and stacking them in a box. A piece of paper slid out of a biology textbook as I was taking it down from the shelf. I put the book in the box, and picked the paper up off the floor. It was Kathy's birth certificate.

"Should this be with the books?" I asked. "This is your birth certificate, Kathy."

"No," she said. She sat on the floor wrapping a framed finger painting that one of her children had done. "It belongs with my important papers. I used it as a bookmark one day."

"Oh," I said.

She laughed. I think I was giving her that look that I gave her when she did something that I would never do. "I'll get it in a minute. Let me finish this," she said. Then she started folding and taping the bubble wrap around the picture.

I looked at her birth certificate. I had seen the document before—when we went to the courthouse to get our marriage license, for instance. But I had never read it.

Her mother's maiden name was Tkach. "How do you pronounce your mother's maiden name?" I asked. "Is it ta-kotch?"

"No, it's Tkach." She spit the word out. All the sounds were there, and it was one syllable.

"Ta-kotch," I said.

"No, it's Tkach."

"Ta-kotch."

She laughed. "It's Tkach. It's a Ukrainian name," she said.

"Oh," I said. "Your father's last name: Petrenko. That's Ukrainian too, isn't it? And I can pronounce that one."

"Yes, his name is Ukrainian also. But the father listed on my birth certificate is not my biological father."

"Stanley is not your biological father?"

"No, he's not," she said, suddenly becoming very serious. "But he raised me as if I were his own, and for that I will be forever grateful to him."

"Uh-huh," I said. "But the mother listed on your birth certificate is your biological mother?"

"Yes. The mother on my birth certificate is my biological mother."

"Hmm."

"My biological father got my mother pregnant, and he wanted to marry her. So my mother asked her mother for permission. But her mother said: 'No. I will not give you permission to marry that man because he is a Shepard.' So my mother didn't marry him."

"He was a shepherd?"

"Yes. His name was Charles Shepard. He was a Shepard."

"So what was wrong with being a Shepard?"

"I don't know. I asked my mother, and she didn't know either. But her mother insisted that she not marry into the Shepard family. And she obeyed her mother."

"And she never knew why?"

"Apparently not."

"Have you ever met your biological father?" I asked.

"No," she said. "I wanted to meet him when I was in high school. But my mother told me that he had become a terrible alcoholic, and so that was bad idea. So I never did meet him."

"Uh huh," I said. I took a sip from my can of beer and I dropped the matter.

I always wondered what was wrong with the Shepard family. Kathy's story seemed so peculiar. I doubted that the Shepards were a family of "terrible alcoholics". There had to be more to it than that. This was a mystery. But back in 2009, it didn't seem like a mystery that needed to be solved. In 2014, however, with me convinced that Kathy had FTD—a disease that is often known to be hereditary; and, with her taking medications—based on what I believed was a misdiagnosis—which might be worsening her condition; things were different.

"Can we have supper?"

Kathy had come into the computer room and I hadn't noticed. "What?" I said.

Kathy laughed. I had been deep in thought, not asleep, but I think she thought that she had woken me up. "Can we have supper?" she asked again.

"Yes. Of course."

I got up and went to the refrigerator. I took out the big pot of chili that I had made over the weekend. It was a good batch of chili. In addition to the five pounds of ground beef, the onions, the different colored peppers, the tomatoes, and all the other ingredients that I always use, I put in sliced mushrooms and diced celery. I put the pot on the counter and scooped out enough to half fill a large glass bowl. I put a lid on the bowl, and put it in the microwave oven for five minutes.

Kathy sat at the table, drinking milk, while the chili was in the microwave.

When the microwave beeped, I opened it up, pulled out the glass bowl of chili and set it on the counter. Then I split the chili up into two regular sized bowls. I put one of the bowls in front of Kathy. She immediately started to scoop the chili into her mouth. I put the other bowl in front of the place where I sit at the table. I sat down.

I was on my forth or fifth bite of chili, and Kathy was half done with her bowl. Then she stopped eating and began staring at the remaining chili in her bowl.

"Aren't you going to eat the rest of it?" I asked.

"I think the chickens should eat it," she said.

"Don't you like it?"

"I think the chickens should eat it."

I got up, got the pot of chili out of the refrigerator, and put it on the counter. I got a dog bowl down from the cabinet and put a few scoops of chili in it. Then I put the dog bowl on the table. "This is for the chickens," I said.

Kathy chuckled. "Kay," she said. She had already started eating again.

I put the pot of chili back in the refrigerator, and then sat down to finish my chili.

Kathy finished her chili. "Can I have supper?" she asked.

I took a bite of chili. "Do you want more?"

"Yeah," she said.

I got the pot of chili out of the refrigerator again and filled her bowl. I put her bowl in the microwave, set the timer for two minutes, and returned the pot to the refrigerator.

When the microwave beeped, I took out Kathy's bowl and gave it to her. Then I sat down and ate my chili.

We finished eating at about the same time, and we put our bowls in the sink.

"Let's go feed the chickens," I said.

Kathy picked up a loaf of bread that was on the counter. "They like these things," she said.

"Okay, we can give them some bread," I said, I took four slices of fresh bread out of the plastic bread bag, and then tied the bag in a knot to reseal it.

We went out the back door. Kathy carried the dog bowl. I carried the bread. The chicken's saw us walking toward the chicken yard, with food, and they flocked around the gate.

I opened the gate and Kathy and I stepped into the chicken yard. I held the bread high, because some of the chickens were jumping up, trying to get it. Kathy was doing the same with the dog bowl. We walked about ten yards into the chicken yard and Kathy put down the dog bowl full of chili. The chickens surrounded the bowl, pecked at the chili and swallowed small bits. When one got ahold of something big, like a slice of mushroom or a hunk of pepper. She— and it was always a hen that got the big piece of food—would dash off, away from the group, and eat her catch in peace.

I was tearing the bread in long pieces and throwing them to the chickens. I was trying to get a piece of bread to our rooster. The Brown Leghorn rooster was the biggest, and, with silky reddish brown plumage on his breast and around his neck, and huge black tail feathers, the most elegant bird in the flock. He was also the slowest. Every time he managed to get a piece of bread in his beak, one of the hens would snatch it from him and dash off with it. He was too much of a gentleman to even get mad about it.

The bowl of chili was gone in a matter of seconds. I was still throwing strips of bread. At one point, all twelve hens had a pepper, or a mushroom, or a piece of bread in her beak, and I was able to get a piece of bread to the rooster. He dropped it on the ground and ate it without being disturbed.

Kathy picked up the dog bowl. "The chicken's are fun, huh?' she said.

"Yeah," I said. I looked around at our flock, still enjoying their snack. "I like our chickens," I said.

"I'm glad," she said.

Kathy and I went back into the house.

"Can I play the music?" Kathy asked.

"Yeah," I said, as I opened the refrigerator.

She went into the living room and turned on her boom box.

I got a beer from the refrigerator and went into the computer room. I opened the beer, turned on the television, and watched the news.

A half hour later, Kathy came into the computer room. "I'm going to lay down," she said.

"Okay," I said. "I'll be in after awhile. There's some business that I have to take care of."

"Kay," she said.

I got up to give her a goodnight kiss, but she turned around and left the room before I could get to her.

I took the *Greater Dayton White Pages* down from the shelf and set it on my desk. I opened the directory to the S section and found "Shepard". As it turns out, there are four different spellings of that name. There's "Shepard", "Sheperd", "Shephard" and "Shepherd". Between the four spellings, there were almost two hundred listings in that phone book.

But there was only one Charles Shepard, and that seemed like a logical place to begin my search. I waited until eight—because I didn't want to interrupt anybody's supper—and then I tapped the number into my cellphone and tapped call.

After a few rings, someone said, "Hello."

"Hello. I'm looking for a Charles Shepard."

"I'm Charles Shepard."

"The Charles Shepard I'm looking for is in his eighties, or maybe even his early nineties." (I was guessing that Kathy's biological father was born around 1930 because her mother was born in 1930.)

"Mister, I think you've got the wrong Charles Shepard. I was born in 1982."

"Okay, maybe I'm looking for your grandfather? Or a great uncle? Or someone else in the family?"

"No," he said, "not by that name. Grandpa Shepard's name was Bernie. And he had two brothers—John and Clyde. I've got an Uncle Red, and Uncle Billy. They're Shepards. But the only Charles Shepard I know of is me."

"Well, I appreciate your time. Sorry I bothered ya."

"That's okay, Mister. Wish I could've helped you more."

"Have a nice evening, Charles," I said.

"You too, Mister."

I picked up my pen and put a black dot next to the name Charles Shepard in the phone book. The black dot, I decided, would mean that I had spoken to a person at that number.

There were two C Shepards listed in the phone book. I called the first one. The phone rang three time, and then the call went to an automated voicemail system. I picked up a red pen and put a red dot next to that name. The red dot would mean that I had called that number but had not spoken to anyone.

I called the next C Shepard. The phone rang.

"Hello." It was a woman's voice.

"Hello. I'm looking for a Charles Shepard."

"You have the wrong number."

"Alright, but maybe you can help me. The—"

"Dude! You have the wrong number! Okay? You called the wrong person. My name is Charlene Shepard. Okay? Not Charles, Charlene. Okay?"

"Okay. Thank you," I said.

She hung up.

I made about a dozen more phone calls. None of them turned up any leads.

At nine o'clock, It seemed to me that it was getting too late to pester the Shepards. Besides, I was tired of making phone calls to people I didn't know. So I put a bookmark on the page I was using. I closed the phone book and put it back on the shelf.

I went out to the kitchen and got the pot of chili out of the refrigerator. I divided most of the chili up into four plastic food storage containers. I put the four containers in the freezer, and then I put the pot of chili, which still had a couple meals left, back in the refrigerator.

I went to the bedroom. Kathy was already asleep. I turned on the alarm on the alarm clock. Then I remembered something that I needed to do. I went back out to the kitchen and took the coffee filter, with the used coffee grounds, out of the coffee maker. I put in a fresh filter, and scooped in some fresh grounds. Kathy makes the coffee in the morning, but the last few days, she hasn't changed the coffee filter or put in fresh grounds. So this morning my coffee had the look and the taste of warm dirty water.

I went to bed, knowing that tomorrow morning my coffee would be better.

chapter 15

At eight o'clock, the next night, I got the phone book down from the shelf and set it on my desk. I opened it up to the bookmarked page, which was the page with the Shepards. There were fifteen ink dots—ten black ones, and five red ones. I called the next name on the list: Eric Shepard.

The phone began ringing.

"Hello."

"Hello. Am I speaking to Eric Shepard?"

"Yes, this is Eric."

"Eric, my name is Mark Stone, and I'm looking for an old man who might be a relative of yours. His name is Charles Shepard."

"Charles Shepard, you say?"

"Yes, Charles Shepard."

"I have a cousin by the name Charles Shepard," Eric said. "But he's not an old man."

"The Charles Shepard I'm looking for would be in his eighties or maybe even his early nineties. He might even be dead already."

"No, my cousin's not the Charles you're looking for. He's in his early thirties. What's this about, anyway?"

"This is regarding an inheritance. I can't be more specific unless I'm talking to Charles himself, or to one of his relatives."

"Oh. Okay, then."

"Can you think of a Charles Shepard in your family that has passed away in the last twenty years or so?"

"No, I can't. I wish I could."

"Okay. Thank you, Eric. I appreciate your time."

"No problem."

I made eighteen more phone calls. For the most part, the Shepards I talked to were friendly and cooperative, like Eric. Some were suspicious of me. One Shepard even told me to get a job.

At about ten minutes after nine o'clock, I made my twentieth call of the night. It was to Marvin Shepard.

"Hello," a young man, or boy, said.

"Hello," I said. "Am I speaking to Marvin Shepard?"

"Just a minute."

A few seconds later another voice came on the line: "Hello, this is Marvin. How can I help you?"

"Marvin, my name is Mark Stone. I'm looking for a man who might be a relative of yours. His name is Charles Shepard. He'd be in his eighties or early nineties by now. He might even be dead."

"What do you want him for?"

"It's a very important matter," I said. "It involves an inheritance."

"An inheritance, you say?"

"Yes, that's what I said. And, I can't be more specific about that unless I'm talking to an actual relative of Charles Shepard."

"Well, I had an uncle named Charles Shepard, but he's been dead for—" I heard him ask someone else in the room: "Mary, when did Uncle Charlie die?"

I heard her say: "Oh Lord, that was back in 1992."

"Mark," he said. "My Uncle Charles died in 1992."

"He might be the one that I'm interested in," I said.

I heard the woman in the room ask: "Who's that on the phone?"

"Some guy. I think he's got some money for Uncle Charlie," he told her.

"Give me that phone," she said to him.

"Hello," she said on the phone.

"Hi," I said. "My name's Mark Stone, and I'm trying to get some information about your late relative, Charles Shepard."

"Do you have some money for him?"

"No," I said. "I don't."

I heard her tell Marvin: "He says he doesn't have any money for your uncle."

"He said something about an inheritance," Marvin told her.

"So what's this about an inheritance?" she asked me.

"It's not money," I explained. "My wife may have inherited a medical condition from her biological father, whose name is Charles Shepard."

"Your wife's father's name is Charles Shepard, you say?"

"Yes."

"Then that must be a different Charles Shepard," she said. "Because Marvin's Uncle Charles didn't have any daughters."

Marvin must have been standing right beside her, because I could hear him plain as day. He said, "Wait a minute! He might be right."

"Right about what?" Mary asked him.

"Uncle Charlie might have had a daughter," he said. "I remember, one time—when I was a boy, I spent the weekend over at Uncle Charlie's and Aunt Ruth's house. And they had a fight over—what I thought I heard was—his daughter. So I asked my mom about it when I got home."

"And what did your mother tell you?" Mary asked him.

"She told me not to poke my nose into other peoples business," Marvin told her. "And it is true that when Uncle Charlie was older he had a medical condition."

"He went insane," Mary said.

This I heard very clearly because he raised his voice: "No, he did not go insane. He had a medical condition that runs in the Shepard family. Now give me that phone!"

"Hello, this is Marvin again," he said on the phone.

"Yeah, Marvin."

"Mark, this medical condition that your wife has, does it affect her mind?"

"Yes, it does," I said. "And if she has the same disease that her biological father had, it would help us a lot to know what the doctor's said about his disease."

"Yeah. I imagine it would help," he said. "But I'm not the best person to talk to about that, Mark. His wife—my Aunt Ruth—is still alive."

"Do you have her phone number?" I asked.

"Yes I do," he said. Then I heard him say: "Mary, would you go get the red address book for me?"

"Why do you need it?" Mary asked.

"He wants Aunt Ruth's phone number," Marvin said.

"You can't give him your Aunt Ruth's phone number," she said.

"Why not?"

"Because he's just some guy on the phone. We don't know him."

"Mary, he says he's married to Uncle Charlie's daughter. She would be my cousin. If she has the same disease that Uncle Charlie had, then I want to be helpful—if I can."

"Give me the phone," Mary said.

"Mister," she said on the phone.

"My name's Mark Stone. Please call Mark," I said quickly.

"Okay then, Mark, even if you are who you say you are, Ruth Shepard might not want to talk to you."

"I know that," I said. "And, of course, that would be her choice."

"Here's what I'll do, Mark," Mary said. "You give me your phone number, and any other information you want me to pass on, and I'll give it to Ruth Shepard. Then if she wants to talk to you, she can call you."

"That's fair enough," I said, and I gave her my phone number.

"Okay, What else do you want me to tell her?"

"Let's see," I said. "My wife's name is Kathleen. She was born in 1955. Her mother's first name was Helen. And the disease that she now has is a form of early onset dementia."

"Okay, I got it," she said. "I'll call Ruth tomorrow morning, and give her your information. Then if she wants to call you, she'll call you."

"Okay."

"Okay, then. Bye."

"Bye," I said.

· · · · ·

The next day, I was on a glue down carpet job with Phillip and Zac in Blue Ash. We were carpeting a new building that was going to be a dental clinic. The job was two hundred and ninety yards, so we planned to take two days.

At about eleven o'clock, when I was spreading glue, my cell phone rang. I got up off the floor and started walking toward the front door. I pulled my phone out of my top pocket. "Hello, I said.

"May I speak to Mark Stone?" a woman asked.

I could tell by her voice that she was elderly.

"This is Mark Stone," I said. I went out the front door, and started walking towards my van.

"My niece, Mary, called me and told me that you called her and had some questions about my late husband."

"Yes. I did call Mary, and I do have some questions about your late husband, Charles," I said. I opened the driver's door of my van and I climbed in and sat down. "I take it that you already know that your late husband had a child by another woman."

"Oh yes, I knew about Kathleen," she said. "Kathleen was a secret. But she was a secret that everybody knew about. I knew her mother when she was pregnant with Kathleen."

"Well, Mrs. Shepard—"

"You can call me Ruth."

"Okay, then, Ruth," I said. "I'm married to Kathleen."

"That's what Mary said."

"And these last few years, my wife's intellect has been deteriorating."

"Mary said that Kathleen had dementia. I was so sorry to hear that. Charles had dementia. It runs in the Shepard family."

"That's what I want to talk to you about," I said.

"So what do you want to know?" she asked.

"Well, Ruth, I have many questions. And I'm at work right now. I was wondering if I could meet you sometime. Maybe for lunch, at a Frisch's Big Boy or some place like that?"

"Why don't you just come to my house?"

"That would be even better," I said.

"I live in Columbus, you know."

"No, I didn't know that. But that's fine. May I come over tomorrow?"

"Anytime after eleven," she said.

"Okay, I'll be there tomorrow morning. Now what's your address?"

Ruth gave me her address, and I wrote it on a note pad. Then I
got off the phone. I left the note pad on the console of my van and
I went back into the building.

Phillip and Zac were spreading glue on the floor in the area where
I was spreading glue before I left the building. I waited for them to
finish, and then I helped them drop the carpet into the wet glue.

Zac grabbed the roller and began rolling out the bubbles in the
carpet.

Phillip looked at me. "What's wrong with you? You're not suppose to take a break when you're spreading glue."

"There's a right time to take a break, and a wrong time to take a
break," Zac said, as he moved the roller back and forth.

I laughed, and said. "Sorry."

"Just don't let it happen," Phillip said, and smiled.

"Okay," I said. "Um, Phillip, do you think you and Zac can finish
this job without me tomorrow?"

"Sure," Phillip said. "Do you have something else to do?"

"I am going to meet with the widow of Kathy's biological father."

"Is that who you were on the phone with?"

"Yeah."

"That should be interesting," he said.

"Yes it should," I said.

We got back to work, and at four o'clock we had the main area
and both hallways done.

"Let's call it a day," I said.

"It's a day," Zac said.

While Zac vacuumed, Phillip and I walked around and looked at
the rooms that were not yet done.

"So, tomorrow you'll have seven rooms to do," I said.

Phillip nodded. "Yep," he said. "That's the exact number I come
up with—seven."

"That's a lot of work, Phillip. Do you want me to call Chuck to
see if he's available?"

"Absolutely not," Phillip said. "If I'm in charge, I don't want
Chuck on the job. Zac and I got this."

"Alright," I said. "Don't worry about the cove base. We can do that Friday morning."

"No, Mark, we'll get the cove base up. We might as well finish the job."

"Well, if you get the cove base up that's great," I said. "But you don't have to worry about it."

"I'm not going to worry about the cove base, Mark."

"Good," I said. "I don't want you waking up in the middle of the night from a bad dream, screaming, 'Oh my God! We don't have time to put up the cove base! Oh no! The world's coming to an end!'."

Phillip laughed. "That won't happen."

"Well good," I said.

Phillip got a few tools, and a bottle of seam sealer, out of my van. Then he and Zac drove away in his van. I made sure the doors were locked, and then I left the job site.

chapter 16

May 8, 2014

I pulled my van out of our driveway at about twenty minutes after nine o'clock. I was driving the van to Columbus, rather than the PT Cruiser, because I told Kathy that I was going to a carpet job. The van backed up that story, whereas taking the PT Cruiser might raise further questions.

As soon as I was on the road, I plugged in my new GPS. Ruth Shepard's address was already in the GPS—I put it in there last night. So I tapped *Recently Found*. Then I tapped her address, and then I tapped *Go*.

For a few seconds, the GPS fell into its *Acquiring Satellites* mode. Then it said: "In one quarter mile, turn left." It drew me a map, and estimated my time of arrival at 10:45 AM.

I turned left.

There were a couple reasons why the 10:45 ETA wasn't going to happen. One was that my van was ten years old; it had a six cylinder engine with two hundred and fifty thousand mile on it; and I didn't drive it fast. The other was that I wasn't going to take the route the GPS had planned for me. I was coming up on SR 380, and the GPS was going to ask me to turn left and head toward Xenia. That section of SR 380 was boring—cornfields on both sides of the road. If I turned right on SR 380, on the other hand, and headed south, there were trees on both sides of the road. Then I could pick up I-71 on US 73 near Harveysburg. That's what I wanted to do.

When I got on I-71, from US 73, my GPS had already adjusted the ETA to 10:52 AM.

Traffic was light on northbound I-71. So it was a quiet, pleasant drive. Or, I should say, it was a quiet, pleasant drive until I got into

Columbus. Inside the I-270 circle, it was bumper to bumper, sixty mile an hour, watch out for orange cones driving. I kept two hands on the wheel, my eyes on the road, and I listened to my GPS. I breathed a sigh of relief when the GPS had me exit the interstate.

When I turned onto Ruth Shepard's street, my ETA, according to my GPS, was 11:09 AM.

I pulled into Ruth Shepard's driveway.

Ruth Shepard had a nice home. It was a two story, red brick, older home. It wasn't too big, and it wasn't too small. The bushes were perfectly manicured, and she had different colored flowers in a flower garden in front of the porch. What I found most impressive, though, were the blue wooden shutters. They weren't the vinyl or aluminum decorations that people attach at the side of their windows and call "shutters". These were real shutters. They hung on heavy iron hinges, and—if they still worked—you could shut these shutters over the windows if you wanted to.

I stopped the van next to the sidewalk that leads to the front porch. The blacktop driveway continued around to the back of the house where there was a two car garage. I didn't see any cars back there. So I decided to leave my van right there.

I got out of my van, walked up the sidewalk, climbed up the porch steps, and knocked on the door.

A small woman with long white hair opened the door. She smiled, and asked, "Are you Mark Stone?"

"Yes," I said.

"Please come in."

I stepped into the house, and she closed the front door. We stood in her foyer, for a moment, just looking at each other. To break the ice, I said, "I'm very glad that you agreed to talk to me."

"Well I'm glad you found me," she said. "I always wondered what became of Kathleen. I worried about her."

"Really," I said, puzzled.

"Let's talk in the kitchen," she suggested.

"Sure," I said, and I followed her down the hall to the kitchen.

"Please sit down," Ruth said.

I pulled a chair out and sat down at the kitchen table.

"Would you like some coffee?"

"Yes, I would. Thank you."

"How do you drink it?"

"Black."

She took two cups down from a cabinet and set them on the counter. She filled the cups from a warm pot of coffee which she had taken off the warmer of a very old, but clean, Mr. Coffee coffee maker. Then she carefully set the pot back on the warmer and brought the cups over to the table. She set one of the cups in front of me, and the other she set across from me, which is where she sat down.

I took a sip of coffee. "This coffee is very good," I said.

Ruth smiled. "So, Mark—may I call you Mark?"

"Please do," I said.

"So, Mark, what is it that you want to know?" She leaned forward, folded her arms on the table, and looked at me.

"Well," I said. "I guess I'm curious about a lot of things. Um. You just mentioned that you worried about Kathleen. Did you ever meet Kathleen?"

"No. I never met her. I only saw her one time. That was at her college graduation."

"You attended her college graduation ceremony?"

"Yes. Charles and I were in the audience. Kathleen didn't know we were there—not that she would have recognized us."

"Kathy said she never met her biological father."

"She didn't."

"So, why did you and Charles go to Kathleen's college graduation?—if you don't mind me asking."

"Charles paid for Kathleen's college education. Is that a good enough reason?"

"Yes," I said, nodding. "Yes it is." I took a sip of coffee, thinking that already this interview had taken an unexpected turn. I took me a moment to think of my next question: "Didn't it bother you that your husband was paying for Kathleen's education? I mean—she wasn't your child."

Ruth laughed. "Now isn't that a silly question," she said. "Of course it bothered me, Mark. And we use to have fights over it.

But I always understood why Charles wanted Kathleen to get a good education."

"And why was that?" I asked, and then I quickly added, "I'm sorry if it seems like I'm interrogating you."

"No, no, Mark, I understand. You want to know. And I'll tell you," she said. "Kathleen was Charles' daughter. He was responsibly for her existence, and—God bless him—he took that responsibility very seriously. She was a Shepard, just like he was a Shepard. And, of course, he didn't know, when he was young, that he was going to get Pick's Disease—"

"Is that what the doctors called his disease? Pick's Disease?"

"Well," she said, "our doctor called it Pick's Disease."

"I'm sorry," I said. "I interrupted you."

"Oh, you're fine, Mark," she said. "As I was saying: Charles didn't know that he was going to get that disease. But he knew that the disease ran in the family. And, I think, it was something that was always at the back of his mind. Charles use to say, 'I'm a Shepard, and my brain might have an expiration date stamped on it. So I've got to make the most of it.' He was a firm believe in education—for himself, and for his children. He was a lawyer, but even after he got his law degree, he went to night school and got a masters degree in Neuroscience."

"That sounds like Kathy," I said. "She has four college degrees, including a PhD in Zoology."

Ruth smiled. "Well good. I glad to hear that."

I took a sip of coffee. "Did it bother Stanley at all that Charles was paying for Kathy's college education?"

Ruth laughed. "Of course it bothered Stanley. Stanley was the father that Kathleen knew. He was the one that provided for her since she was born. And at first, he refused to accept Charles' money. He said that Kathleen could go to a state college, which is what he could afford. But that wasn't good enough for Helen. She wanted Kathleen to go to Ohio Dominican University, because Kathleen was exceptionally smart—and she didn't get that from Helen! I'll tell you that. But Ohio Dominican University is very expensive. It was more than Stanley and Helen could afford. So Helen came to Charles and asked for money. And Charles was more than happy to help out—because

Kathleen was a Shepard in blood. She was his biological daughter. But then, Stanley refused to accept the money—like it was dirty or something. Helen finally talked him into it. But he would accept the money under one condition: Charles had to agree *never* to have any contact with Kathleen. Because Stanley didn't want her to figure out where the money for her college came from. Charles wanted to help Kathleen, so he agreed to that."

Ruth lowered her head and began shaking it slowly. She clenched her hands into fists. Then she suddenly looked up at me. "Doesn't that take the cake!" she asked. "Charles put that girl through school. And he isn't allowed any sort of contact with her because that would injure Stanley's ego? We should have told Stanley to go to Hell! I'm still angry about that."

"Yes," I said. "That takes the cake." I took another sip of coffee. "Um, do you mind if I ask you a question?"

Ruth gave me a funny look. "Isn't that's what you've been doing, Mark. You're asking me questions. I'm answering them. So, yes, you may ask me a question."

"You might not like this question."

"If I don't want to answer the question, then I won't answer it," she said. "I promise."

"Okay," I said. "Here's the question: Was Charles an alcoholic?"

"What! No. Who told you that?"

"When Kathy was in high school, she wanted to meet her biological father. But her mother told her that Charles was a 'terrible alcoholic'. So meeting him was not a good idea."

"Helen told her that! That woman was the most spiteful, ungrateful witch I have ever known. They didn't do that child any favors by lying to her like that, you know."

"I agree."

"Is Helen still alive?"

"No."

"Well she lucked out there," Ruth said. "Because I would have hunted her down and kicked her ass!"

Ruth calmed down, and then asked me, "Would you like some more coffee?"

"Yes. Please." I finished the coffee in my cup.

Ruth got the coffee pot and refilled both of our cups.

"Are you hungry? Would you like a donut?"

"That sounds good." I said.

Ruth went back to the counter and got two small plates down from the cabinet. She opened a carton of Krispy Kreme Donuts. "I shouldn't eat these," she said, putting a glazed donut on each plate. She set the two plates on the table, and she put a napkin beside each plate. Then she sat down.

I took a bite of the donut. "Ruth," I said, "you mentioned Charles' 'children'. Did you and Charles have any children together?"

"We did," she said. "Thanks to me."

"Thanks to you?"

"That's right. It was thanks to me," she said. "Charles didn't want to get me pregnant. He said that because he might pass on 'defective genes' to a child, the responsible thing for us to do was to not have children. Kathleen was an accident. She was the result of a broken condom."

"So Charles didn't want to have children, but you did."

"No. That's not true. We both wanted children. But Charles wanted us to adopt them."

"And you wanted to roll the dice?"

"Um. I suppose you could put it that way," she said. "I was on Enovid."

"Enovid? What's that?"

"The pill."

"Oh, birth control pills."

"Right," she said. "So, as I was saying, I was on the pill. And we went to the adoption agency. And before we could even look at the babies, they wanted to visit our home. Then they wanted to look at our tax returns. Then they wanted us to take parenting classes. Oh my word! They made the process so complicated. And all I wanted was a baby."

I chuckled. "So you figured there was an easier way to go about it."

"Well," she said, "I don't know if it was easier, but it was certainly simpler. I quit taking the pill. I never told Charles. When I got pregnant with Frank, in 1961, I told Charles 'nothing is one hundred percent'. And then, when Peter came along in 1963, I said, 'maybe this Enovid is not as great as they say it is'."

"So you and Charles had two sons together?"

Ruth nodded. "Yes. Charles and I had two boys."

"Okay," I said. "You know I'm going to ask this question."

"How are they doing?" Ruth said.

"Yes. How are they doing?"

"Well. Peter was killed in a motorcycle accident in 1989."

"I'm sorry to hear that."

"Oh that all right, Mark. That was a long time ago."

"And how's Frank doing?" I asked.

"Frank? He seems to be to be doing okay. He's fifty-two now, and, since his fiftieth birthday, he gets an MRI done on his head every year. Nothing's shown up so far, knock on wood. But, you know, with Frank, I don't think he'll get Pick's Disease."

"Really. Why is that?"

"I don't know," she said. "I think, maybe, because Peter was so intellectual—just like his father."

"Kathy was very intellectual—once upon a time."

"Right. Kathy was probably like Peter. When Peter was killed, he was in the PHD program at Yale. He was almost finished."

"Oh really. What was his field of study?"

"Philosophy. Peter wanted to be a philosophy professor."

"That's interesting," I said.

"Of course, I'm not saying Frank's not smart," she said. "Frank is smart. He got good grades in school. And he went on to college He went to Ohio University. And he got a degree in accounting. Now he's an accountant—and a good one. But he was never the intellectual type—if you know what I mean."

"Yeah," I said. "I know what you mean. I think I'm that kind of guy, too. I'm smart—at least I think so. I'm fairly well educated—I have one college degree. But I never consider myself the smartest guy in the room."

"Right. That's how Frank is?"

"Um. You said that Frank is getting an MRI done on his brain every year—now that he's turned fifty. Do other Shepards do that too?"

"Well, Mark, that would depend on what kind of insurance they have, I suppose. But, yes, I've heard that some of them get tested," she said. "Of course, not all of the Shepards have to worry about Pick's Disease. Now Marvin Shepard—you've met Marvin, I believe."

"I've talked to him on the phone," I said. "I've never met him in person."

"Well, anyway, Marvin, I think, is fifty-five now. But his father, Clyde Shepard, whose seventy-nine or eighty now, never got the disease. So Marvin doesn't have to worry about it. He won't get the disease either."

"I see," I said.

"Now Ester—she's eighty or eighty-one now—she didn't get Pick's Disease. But Janet—that's Charles youngest sibling—she did. Janet died in 2005, and she had just the one daughter: Barb. Barb is about forty-five now, and I hope she starts getting tested when she turns fifty. But who knows? That poor baby has lived such a tough life."

"Uh-huh," I said.

"Not that the tests will make any difference. She'll either get the disease or she won't."

"That's true," I said.

Ruth nibbled on her donut, and I pushed the last quarter of my donut in my mouth. Then I wiped my fingers off with my napkin and took a sip of coffee.

"It seems I've been doing all the talking," Ruth said. "Tell me, Mark, how is Kathleen doing?"

"Well," I said. "She's got dementia. That much is obvious. And her doctors say that she has Alzheimer's Disease. I think they're wrong. I've always thought that what she has is FTD—which is the same disease that you're calling Pick's Disease."

"FTD—that's the term that Charles' neurologist used," Ruth said. Then she added, "Wait a minute. I believe there was a 'b' in front of those letters."

"Was it bvFTD?"

"I believe it was."

"That's behavior variant Frontal Temporal Dementia," I said.

"If I were a doctor, I think that would be my diagnosis of Kathy's condition. Either that, or PPA, which is Primary Progressive Aphasia. Or maybe even lvFTD, which is language variant Frontal Temporal Dementia. All of these diagnoses are subcategories of one syndrome, and that syndrome is called Frontal Temporal Lobar Degeneration—or FTLD. The diagnosis that a doctor decides upon, with FTD patients, depends on which symptoms are initially the biggest problem. For example, if the patient's language deficit is the biggest problem at first, they're diagnosed with lvFTD or PPA. If the patient's behavior is the biggest problem at first, they're diagnosed with bvFTD."

Ruth took a sip of coffee. "Mark, you just went intellectual on me," she said.

I laughed. "Yeah. I guess I did. Sorry, I've just been reading so much about FTD, and the brain, and all that."

"But it's all Pick's Disease, right?"

"Right."

"Okay. I know Kathleen has dementia," Ruth said. "But other than that, how is she doing?"

I thought about her question for a moment, and then I said, "Well, a couple months ago, she lost her driver's license."

"What was her crime?" Ruth asked.

"Speeding."

"Speeding? Why that's not too bad. Did she run from the police, or anything like that?"

"No," I said. "I think she ignored them for a little while, hoping they'd go away. But she pulled over."

"Charles hit a parked car, and then he ran from the police officer who saw it happen."

I nodded. "Okay. That's worse than what Kathy did."

"Charles was a lawyer, you know. And he was on his way to court, and he was running late. So he was probably speeding. Anyway, he made a turn and he crunched the side of a car. Not just a dent, mind you—he crunched up the whole side of that car, and he crunched up the whole side of his car to boot. A police officer was driving down that street, and he saw the whole thing happen. So he put on his siren. But Charles didn't stop. So the officer followed Charles two miles to the courthouse. Charles parked his car, and the officer pulled in behind him. Then Charles just grabbed his briefcase. He got out of the car, and he just started walking up the courthouse steps, like nothing had happened."

"Did he go to jail for that?"

"He did," she said. "But not for long. One of the partners in his law firm, Sam Whitaker, bailed him out and brought him home. Sam told me what happened. Sam and I sat at this table and talked for a long time. Sam told me how bad things were getting at the office, and how bad things were getting in the courtroom. Charles was messing up cases. He thought that it was time for Charles to retire."

"So then you knew."

"I had a feeling, before that, but yes. After that discussion with Sam, I couldn't deny it anymore. When Sam left, I went out to the living room. Charles was sitting in his chair. He had been sitting there the whole time. He knew we were talking about him, but he didn't care. I said, 'Charles, I'm going to take you to see the doctor.' He said, 'That would be an apropos ruler.'"

"He said that would be an apropos ruler?"

"Yes. He used to use the term 'appropriate measure' quite a bit. I think that's what he meant."

"Probably," I said. "So did he retire?"

"Not then. Charles had some say in the matter, you know. It was his law firm at first. It became Shepard and Whitaker when he had more business than one lawyer could handle. Then it became Shepard, Whitaker and Young when they had more business than two lawyers could handle. Now he did stop driving. He had to stop driving because his key to his car wouldn't work anymore. That was my doing. When they fixed his car, after the wreck, I had them change the ignition key. And I never gave him a copy of the new key. So when we got the car back, it just sat in the driveway. He tried to start it, but he couldn't start it with the key that he had, which was the old key."

"Did the court suspend his driver's license?"

"Yes, they did. But you can drive a car without a driver's license. You can't drive a car without a key."

"Some people can."

"That's true, Mark. I'm sure some of Charles' clients could have started the car for him. But he couldn't do it."

"So, I guess you had to drive him to work?"

"Yes, Mark, I drove him everywhere. I drove him to the office. I drove him to court. On his last case, I drove him to court every day, and I stayed with him. It was a very serious case. It was a murder case. The defendant, his client, was an obese black man. His gun had been missing for several years. But he never reported it. He always thought that he misplaced it. Then the gun turns up on a crime scene. It had been used to commit a murder."

"That's not good," I said.

"No," Ruth said. "It wasn't good. But that's all they had. There were no prints on the gun. There was no evidence that put Charles' client at the murder scene at any time. His client didn't even know the murder victim."

"So he was charged only because his gun was used to commit the murder?"

"Yeah. They had no idea who committed the murder. But his gun was used, and he was a black man with a criminal past, so…"

"So he was charged," I said.

"Yeah."

"Did Charles mess up that case?"

"Well, he didn't do his best work in the courtroom—I can tell you that. He wasn't too bad questioning the witnesses. And they were his own questions. But Sam Whitaker had looked them over and made corrections. Then Peggy typed up the corrected version of the questions. So, in court, all Charles had to do was read the corrected version of his questions off a page on his clipboard. And he did okay with that. But when he got up to give his closing argument, he didn't pick up his clipboard. And I was thinking, 'Oh no.' Because everything was written down for him. Then he started to walk back and forth in front of the jury, just babbling. He called the victim 'the dead thing' several times. And the gun he called a 'tube'. The jury looked very confused. I was too. At the end of his argument, he walked over to his client and put his hand on his shoulder.

Then he looked at the jury very seriously, and said, 'This one hasn't seen its tube in five years.' The jury broke out laughing. Why are you smiling, Mark?"

"I'm sorry," I said. "But it is kind of funny."

"Maybe you think so, Mark, but the judge didn't. The judge called Charles and the assistant prosecutor up to bench and the three of them had a long talk. When Charles turned around, I could see he was mad. Boy was he mad! Then the judge declared a mistrial."

"Ruth," I said, "I didn't mean that it was funny that Charles messed up his closing argument. I meant—"

"That's okay, Mark. I get it. What he said was kind of funny."

"So, did he retire after that?"

Ruth nodded. "He had to. The judge reported his conduct to the bar association, and they scheduled a hearing. But he had been diagnosed with Pick's Disease by that time. So, that's what we told 'em, and they agreed to drop the matter if he would retire. So he retired. Thank God."

"You know," I said. "I think Kathy had similar problems the last couple years she taught."

"Oh!" Ruth said. She seemed interested. "Was Kathy a teacher?"

"She was a college professor." I said.

"What did she teach?"

"Biology, mainly. But she also taught chemistry sometimes."

"Where did she teach?"

"All over," I said. "She was working as an adjunct professor when we got married. And so, she was always looking for new contracts. When we met, she was teaching at Miami University in Oxford. Then she taught at a technical school in Cincinnati—I can't remember the name of the place—for about a year. Sometimes she taught at more than one college in the same semester. In 2009—I think it was—she was teaching a class at Urbana University, and, as soon as that class was over, she had to run to her car and drive all the way to Edison State College to teach another class."

"Did she get to the point where she just couldn't do it?"

"Well," I said. "Like Charles, she got to the point where she wasn't allowed to do it."

"I see."

"She had taught for years, and had a bunch of material organized in power point presentations on flash drives. Towards the end, I think, she was just going to her classes and plugging in a flash drive and showing the students pictures with words. She might have read them the words."

"You know," Ruth said, "when Charles was reading his questions off a clip board in court, I had the feeling—and I'm sure the judge and the jury had the same feeling—that he didn't understand the questions he was asking."

"Right," I said. "I'm pretty sure Kathy was that way too. I never sat in on any of her classes. But, one time, I was standing behind her while she had a presentation that she was going to give up on her computer. The word 'pseudopod' was up on the screen. I couldn't remember what that was, so I asked her: 'What's a pseudopod?' She just said, 'Don't know'."

"She had forgotten?"

"Apparently she did. And, I didn't say anything to her. But I was thinking: 'Shouldn't you look it up?' But she didn't seem fazed by it. So…That was the last course she taught. And she didn't even finish that one. The head of the biology department relieved her of duty half way through and he finished teaching the class himself. That was in 2011. She never found work after that."

Ruth took a bite of her donut. "So, Mark," she said, while chewing. "You haven't told me how you're doing."

"How am I doing?"

"Yes, Mark, Kathleen's disease affects you too."

"Yeah, I guess it does," I said. "We can't do a lot of the things that we used to do. We used to go to concerts all the time. And in the summer, every weekend we'd go to a fair or a festival of some kind. Now I can't even take her to a restaurant. She's too restless. She just can't sit and wait for the meal to come to the table. About a month ago, I took her to Red Lobster. I wanted to have a nice dinner in a nice restaurant—just like we used to do all the time. So we ordered steak and lobster—or, I should say, I ordered it. I ordered two, actually—one for her and one for me. So, anyway, we ate our salads.

Then she was done. She wanted to leave. I tried to explain to her that the main courses were coming. But she either didn't understand, or she didn't care. She insisted that we leave. So, I had to turn the order into a to-go order. She waited in the car, while I waited for them to finish cooking, and then bag our steaks and lobsters."

"Charles was like that too," Ruth said. "He wouldn't even sit still for his own son's funeral."

"What did he do?" I asked. "You don't have to tell me if you don't want to."

"I'll tell you what happened, Mark," she said. "The priest was up in the pulpit delivering his sermon. Charles and I and Frank and his wife, Emma, were sitting in the front row, of course. So, while the priest was preaching, Charles gets up and walks up to the casket. He puts his hand on the casket, and he says, 'This one stopped.' Then he started laughing. I stayed in my seat. But I was saying, 'Sit down, Charles. Sit down.' He just stood there and, I swear, he was laughing at me. So finally, Sam Whitaker went up there. Sam patted Charles on the back and said, 'Charles, please sit down so the priest can talk.' Because the priest—he quit preaching during all this. Then Sam said, 'Come on now, Charles, let's sit down.' But Charles wouldn't budge. Then Charles said, in a very loud voice—and the whole room could hear: 'A priest, a rabbi, and a monkey went into a bar.' And he burst out laughing. So, Sam—I could see he didn't know what to do at that point. He looked at me and said, 'Let's take Charles outside.' So we took Charles outside. And we're standing there, on the steps of the church. And Charles says: 'Don't you get it? A priest, a rabbi, and a monkey went into a bar.' Sam said, 'I think I should take him home.' So I gave Sam our house key, and then I went back in and sat down. I was quite upset."

"Were you mad at *him*?"

"Yes I was, Mark," she said. "But I was mad at myself too. I shouldn't have brought him there in the first place."

"Maybe not," I said. "But I think anybody could understand why you would take him to his own son's funeral."

"Because I didn't want people to ask questions about him," she said. "And they didn't. After the priest finished his sermon, and everyone walked past the casket, I stood out in the hall. Everyone was coming up to me. They'd say, 'So sorry about Peter.' But they were thinking, 'Sorry your husband is demented!' I'm sure that's what they were thinking."

"Probably," I said.

"No I'm sure of it, Mark," she said. "Anyway, I was glad, as I was standing there getting hugged and kissed on the cheek, when the funeral director came up to me and reminded me that we had a problem. We were short a pall bearer. Someone had to replace Sam Whitaker because Sam was—well, he was at my house babysitting Charles. So I had to go look around for Frank. I asked Frank who could we get. He suggested his cousin Marvin. So that problem was solved. And then Jon Young asked me if I'd like to ride with him to the cemetery. I said no. I like Jon, but I wanted to be alone. So I drove myself to the cemetery. And I stood alone by the grave as the priest said a prayer and they lowered Peter into the ground."

Ruth looked at me. "That was in 1989," she said. "The day after the funeral, I started looking at nursing homes."

"So you put Charles in a nursing home?"

"Yes, Mark, I did. It wasn't just his behavior at Peter's funeral. It was a lot of things—a whole lot of things." Ruth became thoughtful for a moment, and then she continued: "He took up shoplifting—as a hobby. Does Kathleen do that? Does she steal things?"

"No, I don't believe she's ever stolen anything," I said. "Although it has crossed her mind. A couple weeks ago, we were buying some feed for our chickens, and they weren't sure if they had what we wanted. So we ended up going back to the loading dock, and loading four bags of the feed in our PT Cruiser before we paid for them. Once the bags were loaded, Kathy says, 'We should just leave.' I said, 'No, we have to pay for the Purina Layer Crumbles.' She said, 'You think we should pay, huh?' I said yes we should, and she said okay."

"She deferred to you, which is good," Ruth said. "But Charles wouldn't do that. He would just get stubborn and loud. We got thrown out of a Walgreen's one time because he shoved a bottle of sunscreen in his pocket and refused to put it back on the shelf where it belonged."

"That must have been embarrassing."

"It was."

"I hope I never have to put Kathy in a nursing home."

"Well, it's good that you can still hope that," Ruth said. "With me, I was on the verge of a nervous breakdown. I hated to do it, but I had to for the sake of my own sanity."

"Uh-huh," I said.

"Oh, the nursing home wasn't so bad, Mark," she said. "The worst part of it, I thought, was the loss of his freedom. They had to put him in the escape proof unit—or, what they called the dementia unit. Because they were worried about him escaping. So he couldn't wander around like he could here, and go out in the yard if he wanted to. But Charles didn't seem to mind. He made some friends."

"So, was the unit he was in like a jail?"

"No, Mark. It was nothing like a jail. It was just a section of the building—and a big section—that had alarms on the exit doors. So if you left, an alarm would sound."

"And then would a security guard grab you?" I was trying to picture the place.

"No, Mark. A nurse would grab you. Charles used to set off the alarm. They all did. There were about twenty of them. And yes, sometimes they tried to exit the unit. But mostly they stayed in their section of the building. They had a nice activity room. They could also go into each others' rooms and look through each others' things. The first year he was in there Charles would spend his days just walking around talking at people. No one could understand what he was saying. But he was always talking. Then he stopped talking. He didn't utter a single word for the rest of his life."

"Uh-huh," I said. "You say he died in 1992?"

"Yes. He died in March of 1992."

Ruth looked out the window. I looked too. A squirrel jumped from branch to branch on one of her trees. The squirrel disappeared from view, and she turned back to face me.

"It was early September, in 1991, when Charles quit walking. No one knew what was wrong. He just couldn't walk anymore. So we put him in a wheelchair. Then he got to the point where he couldn't sit up in his wheelchair. So I bought him a geri chair. He was having more and more trouble moving, and couldn't move the left side of his body at all. Then. On February 10, 1992, he died. They said he had sepsis. I have no idea how he even got that."

'That's ah—" I said.

"That's life, Mark," she said. "It ends. We all die." Then she looked out the window again.

"Ruth," I said, "I should be going. I really appreciate you taking the time to talk to me." I got up from the table.

"Oh, don't mention it. I've enjoyed our little chat." She got up from the table.

She walked me to the front door.

"Now don't be a stranger, Mark," she said. "Your welcome to come and visit me anytime."

"I'll try to do that," I said. "I've enjoyed our chat too."

chapter 17

Kathy got her first prescription for Namenda and donepezil back in April, 2013. That prescription was written by Dr. Doolittle, a doctor at the Xenia Health Center, on the first, and only, time that she saw him. Her prescription was renewed by another doctor—Dr. Brenneman—who she saw one time in late August, 2013.

In May, 2014, Kathy was still taking Namenda and donepezil every day. She had been taking those medications for over a year.

I never thought Kathy had Alzheimer's disease—which is what those medications are meant to treat; and I never thought that she benefited in any way from taking them. With that said, I was reluctant to discontinue Kathy's medications, because that's a medical decision, and I'm not a doctor.

But it was time for me to take action.

When I got home from Columbus, and went into the house, I heard The Gall Stones playing loudly in the living room. I opened the kitchen cabinet where Kathy kept her vitamins and her prescriptions. I grabbed the Namenda and the donepezil, and I took the two bottles of pills with me to the living room. Kathy was standing in front of her boombox. I walked up next to her.

"Kathy," I said.

She turned down the boombox. "Are you home?" she asked.

"Yes." I held up the pill bottles. "You don't have to take these anymore."

"Don't take these anymore," she said.

"No. Don't take these anymore."

"Don't take these anymore," she said again.

I shook my head. "No."

"Can I play the music?"

"Yes."

She turned up the boombox. I took the pill bottles to the computer room and put them in a desk drawer.

. . . . .

I kept a closer eye than usual on Kathy for the next few days, I watched her walk out to the garage, and I watched her walk around, filling the bird feeders with bird seed. Nothing changed with these activities. Whenever I saw her at the back door, counting the number of chickens that were out—which was several times a day—I'd stand behind her and I'd count them too. Sometimes she missed one or two, but usually she got them all. So nothing new there either.

At about ten o'clock on Sunday night, after she had been off the Alzheimer's medications for ten days, Kathy came into the computer room and asked me: "You work tomorrow?"

"Yes."

"What time?"

"I'm going to get up at six."

"I'm going to lay down," she said.

"Okay."

She left the room. I continues to sit, watch television, and drink beer.

About twenty minutes later, when I needed another beer, I got up and went to the kitchen. As I was tossing my empty beer can into the recycling bin, I noticed that the coffee pot was full of water, and it was setting next to the coffee maker. I walked over to the coffee maker. I pulled out the grounds compartment and looked inside. I saw a new filter and fresh—never used before—coffee grounds.

Kathy had not made coffee in the morning in months. But now, it appeared that that's what she was planning to do. And she was planning to use fresh coffee grounds.

I drank a couple more beers, and then I decided to go to bed.

When I went into the bedroom, I noticed that the red alarm dot on the alarm clock was already glowing. I checked the setting for the alarm. It was set for 6:00 AM. Kathy must have set the alarm.

. . . . .

I awoke the next morning to the smell of fresh coffee. Kathy was in bed, beside me, apparently looking at the alarm clock. "Five fifty-seven, five fifty-seven, five-fifty-seven, five fifty-seven, five fifty-seven," she whispered. "Five fifty-eight, five fifty-eight, five fifty-eight, five fifty-eight—"

I got out of bed and turned off the alarm.

I went out to the kitchen and got myself a cup of coffee. Then I shaved, showered, and got dressed.

When I was ready to leave, I filled my mug up with coffee.

"I'll be back at four," I said, thinking I didn't have much to do that day.

"Back at four," she said.

"Yes," I said. I gave her a kiss. Then I asked: "Why did you make coffee this morning? You haven't done that lately."

"Wanted to," she said.

"Well I'm glad of that," I said. I gave her another kiss and then I left.

As I was driving away from our house, I was thinking about that answer. I believe, in her own way, Kathy had just told me that she has more energy now that she was off the Alzheimer's meds.

chapter 18

Kathy and I went for over a year without going to see a doctor. Between March of 2014 and April of 2015, neither of us had any reason to go to a doctor. I was never sick during that time. Kathy, of course, still had Pick's Disease, which is incurable. And I was aware that doctors prescribe anti-anxiety medications and/or antidepressants to treat the symptoms of her disease. But Kathy wasn't depressed; and, when she was at home, she was never anxious. So why go to a doctor?

But all good things come to an end.

One morning, in late April, 2015, as I was leaving the house in the morning, Kathy pointed to her right foot and said, "That one's messy."

I looked down at her foot. The foot was in a work boot which appeared to be clean enough. "It looks fine to me," I said. I gave her a kiss, and I left for my job.

When I came home later that afternoon, Kathy was in the yard pouring bird seed in the bird feeders. I watched her walk from one bird feeder to another. She was walking with a slight limp. I also noticed that on her right foot she wasn't wearing a work boot. She was wearing one of my old tennis shoes on that foot.

I went in the house and got a beer out of the refrigerator. Then I went out to the deck.

Kathy finished feeding the wild birds and started walking towards the house. When she came up on the deck, I pointed to her right foot and asked: 'Why do you have that on your right foot?'

She pointed to the foot. "That one's messy," she said.

"Okay," I said. I thought that I'd better take a look at the foot so I followed her into the house. When we were in the kitchen, I said,

"Kathy, sit down."

"Sit down?"

"Yes," I said. "Sit down, please."

She pulled out a kitchen chair. "Here sit?"

"That would be fine," I said.

She sat down in the chair. I set my beer on the table and got down on the floor. I took off the old tennis shoe, which wasn't tied, and then I peeled off her sock.

Her big toe and the two toes next to it were red and swollen. Across that corner of her foot there was about a two inch crease. The crease had dashes of scab along it, like the skin had been broken. It looked like she had dropped something heavy on her foot.

I looked up at her. "Kathy, we should have a doctor take a look at this foot."

Kathy just looked at me.

"Also, you need to take a shower."

"I stink?"

"Well," I said. "You don't smell too bad now, but you're beginning to."

"Can I play the music?"

"Yes," I said.

Kathy went to the living room to stand in front of her boombox and listen to music. I went to the computer room to call Dr. Smith, her primary care physician. I took the first open appointment, which was 9:00 AM on Friday, May 1. That was three days away.

. . . . .

Thursday night—the night before Kathy's doctor's appointment—I set the alarm clock for seven-thirty. But I got up around seven Friday morning and shut the alarm off so that it wouldn't ring.

Kathy usually got up before I did, but not on this morning.

I started the coffee, and then I showered, shaved and brushed my teeth. Kathy was still in bed.

I sat at the kitchen table, drinking coffee, until eight. Then I walked over to the bedroom doorway. "Kathy," I said. "You need to get up."

She didn't say anything.

I walked over to her side of the bed. Her eyes were open and they came up to meet mine.

"Kathy."

"What?'

"You have to get up. You have a doctor's appointment."

"I don't think I do," she said.

I walked back out to kitchen. I took a sip of coffee and looked out the window on our back door. The sun was up and the sky was clear. The chickens would want out. So I went out to the chicken house to open their door.

When I came back in the house it was ten after eight. I went to the bedroom.

"The chickens are out," I said.

"Kay," Kathy said.

"You need to get up. We have to leave pretty soon."

She didn't say anything.

"Kathy, please get up. You have to go to the doctor."

"I don't think I can do that," she said.

I came back to the kitchen and sat down at the table.

Now I could understand why Kathy didn't want to go see a doctor. Going to doctors for her dementia had done us no good. But this was different. She had an injured foot. This was much simpler than a degenerative brain disease. This was something that could be seen with the naked eye. You could see the red and swollen toes. You could see the crease on that corner of her foot. You could see the scabbing. And there might be broken bones in there. She might need a splint. Or she might need a tetanus shot, or some antibiotics. With this "messy foot", a doctor might be helpful.

At eight-thirty I went back into the bedroom.

"Kathy, the doctor can help with your messy foot," I said. "Now please get up. Or we're going to be late."

"I don't think I can do that," she said.

I went to the computer room and I called Dr. Smith's office.

The phone rang twice, and then someone said: "Dr. Smith's office, may I help you?"

"This is Mark Stone. I'm Kathy Stone's husband."

"Yes Mr. Stone."

"I can't get Kathy out of bed," I said. "There's no way we can make the nine o'clock appointment."

"Would you like to cancel her appointment, Mr. Stone?"

"Is there any way Dr. Smith could see her this afternoon?"

"No, Mr. Stone. I'm sorry, Dr. Smith doesn't have any appointment available today. Would you like to reschedule Kathleen's appointment for another day?"

"Uh, yeah. I guess," I said.

"The earliest I have is on Wednesday, May 6."

"I guess I'll take it."

"I can do morning, or afternoon on Wednesday."

"Let's do afternoon," I said.

"I'll put Kathleen down for 1:00 PM, Wednesday, May 6."

"We'll see ya then," I said.

"Good bye, Mr. Stone."

I wrote "Smith 1 PM" on the May 6 square of my desk calender. But I wasn't going to tell Kathy about this appointment. I wasn't going to make that mistake again. It'd be easier to get her there, it seemed to me, if I just told her that we were going to the grocery store.

I went back into the bedroom. "Kathy, you can stay in bed. We're not going to the doctor, today," I said.

I went back out to the kitchen and sat at the table and drank coffee.

I heard Kathy making some noise in the bedroom. A few minutes later she came into the kitchen wearing a work boot on her left foot and my old tennis shoe on her right foot. She went up to the window in the back door and started counting: "One, two, three, four, five, six—"

"They're all out," I said.

She turned and looked at me. Then she turned back to the window. "One, two, three, four, five, six, seven, eight, nine." She turned and looked at me again. "Nine are out," she said.

"Okay," I said. "I didn't feed them and I didn't get the eggs. I just opened their door."

She picked up her green gallon jug and took it over to the sink and began filling it with water.

When she was ready to go out to the chicken house, I picked up the egg basket. "I'll get the eggs," I said.

She walked to the back door with a slight limp. She stopped, before opening the door, and pointed to her right foot. "That one's messy," she said.

"I know," I said, and then I followed her out to the chicken house.

· · · · ·

Tuesday night—the night before her afternoon doctor's appointment with Dr. Smith—Kathy was up later than usual. When I went to bed, at a few minutes after eleven o'clock, she was standing in front of her boombox, listening to The Gall Stones. I was tired, but I didn't fall asleep, because the bedroom door was open, and the music from the living room was fairly loud.

After a few minutes the music stopped.

I closed my eyes, expecting that Kathy would soon get into bed. When she didn't, I opened my eyes. Kathy was standing in the doorway, leaning against the door frame.

"Kathy, are you coming to bed?"

She didn't say anything.

"Kathy?"

"What?' she said.

"Are you coming to bed?"

She put both hands on the door frame and she sank to her knees. Then she crawled over to her side of the bed, but she didn't get into bed,

I got up and turned on the light, and then I went over to her. Her left shoulder and left arm and her head were on the bed. Her right hand and both knees were on the floor. "Kathy, what's wrong? Do you need help?"

She didn't answer.

On Kathy's side of the bed, there was a dresser, and next to that, a chest of drawers. The space between the furniture and the bed was about eighteen inches. That where Kathy was—in that narrow space.

I couldn't do much to help her. I squeezed in between her and the dresser. But I couldn't get on the floor to lift her. All I could do was get my left arm under her right shoulder, grab the bed post with my right hand, and lift. So that's what I did.

But that alone wasn't going to get her into bed. I needed her to help.

"Come on, Kathy. You have to help," I said.

She didn't help—for whatever reason. She was awake, but she was completely dead weight.

I went out to the kitchen and got a beer out of the refrigerator. I opened the beer and sat down at the table. I pondered the problem, hoping an idea would pop into my head. It didn't.

I finished the beer, and then I went back into the bedroom. Kathy was in the same position. But now she was asleep. I decided to turn the light off and lay down myself. Soon I was asleep.

The alarm wasn't set, but I woke up at six. I got out of bed and turned the lights on.

Kathy was still in the same position—her head and her left arm on the side of the bed, both knees and her right hand on the floor. And she was still sleeping.

"Kathy, wake up!" I said. "Wake up!"

"What?" she said, groggily, without even opening her eyes.

I squeezed in between her and the dresser. "Come on Kathy, let's get you into bed," I said. I got my left arm under her right shoulder, my right hand on the bedpost, and I tugged up—which is the only thing that I could think of to do.

Again, she didn't help, and I wasn't able to get her into bed.

I went out to the kitchen and made a pot of coffee. I poured a cup, and I sat down at the kitchen table. I drank coffee until seven, hoping that Kathy would come walking into the kitchen. That didn't happen.

At seven o'clock, I went back into the bedroom and tried again. Kathy seemed to be half awake, but I still couldn't get her into bed.

I came back out to the kitchen. I picked up my cellphone and sat down at the table. I unlocked the screen and just looked at the icons for awhile—until the screen darkened. Then I tapped the screen to light it back up. I tapped the phone icon. And I tapped in 9-1-1.

"9-1-1. What is your emergency?"

"Um, I'm not sure this is an emergency," I told the dispatcher. "The situation is this: My wife kind of collapsed in the doorway when she was going to bed last night. She crawled to the bed. But she never crawled into bed. She's got her head and an arm on the bed. But that's all. The rest of her is on the floor. And I can't lift her onto the bed. She's been in that same position for about eight hours now."

"What is your address?"

I gave her our address.

"And what is your name, sir?"

"Mark Stone."

"Okay, Mr. Stone, I'll send out the paramedics right now."

I got a Beggin' Strip from the bag on top of the refrigerator and went out to the living room. "Rupert," I said, holding up the Beggin' Strip.

Rupert stood up in his dog bed. He yawed and wagged his tail.

I opened the front door and threw out the Beggin' Strip. Rupert ran out after it, and I closed the front door.

Then I went out to the back deck and waited for the paramedics.

I heard a siren, and a couple minutes later, the paramedics pulled into our driveway in their shiny red EMS truck. The truck stopped, and the siren went silent.

I walked down to the truck as the paramedics were climbing out of their vehicle.

"Are you Mark Stone," the driver, who was an older, stocky man, asked me.

"I am," I said.

I explained the situation to the older paramedic as we walked toward the house. Two younger paramedics followed behind us.

We went into the house, and then into the bedroom.

"Do you see where she is? I couldn't get in position to lift her," I said.

"She is pinned in there pretty good," he said. He looked at the younger paramedics. "Chip, get back there and hold her head up. Billy, help me move this bed."

Chip climbed over Kathy and got into position where he could hold her head and left arm up. Billy, and the older paramedic, each grabbed a bed post on my side of the bed, and they pulled the bed away from Kathy while Chip held her up. They moved the bed a couple feet.

Chip gently laid Kathy's head and arm down on the floor.

"Billy, help Chip flip her over and put her up on the bed," the older paramedic said.

Chip and Billy rolled Kathy over on her back, and then they picked her up and laid her on the bed.

Kathy was awake. But she looked tired—too tired to comment on what was going on around her.

"Let's put this bed back," the older paramedic said.

The four of us each grabbed a bed post, and we wiggled the bed back over to the original dents that it had made in the carpet.

Kathy closed her eyes. She looked comfortable.

"We should probably take her to the hospital," Chip said.

"I agree," the older paramedic said. Then he looked at the younger two. "Well don't just stand there. Get the gurney."

The two younger men left the room.

They came back a couple minutes later, rolling a gurney. They squeezed the gurney in next to my side of the bed. Then they picked Kathy up and laid her on it.

Kathy seemed fully awake now. She pointed to her right foot. "That one's messy," she said.

The younger paramedics wheeled Kathy out the back door. They stopped on the deck.

"We're going to have to carry her down those steps," the older paramedic said.

The younger paramedics held on to the handles of the gurney while the older paramedic pulled a lever which drew up its wheels.

"Careful now," the older paramedic said, as the younger paramedics slowly descended the steps of our deck.

When they got down to the ground, the older paramedic pulled the lever in the other direction to bring the wheels of the gurney back down. They wheeled Kathy to their truck and loaded her in the back.

"Are you taking her to Drake?" I asked the older paramedic.

"Yeah," he said. "Unless you want us to take her somewhere else."

"No. Drake is fine," I said. "I'll follow you there."

"Okay," he said.

He got in his truck, turned it around, and pulled out of our driveway. He drove away without the siren.

· · · · ·

I noticed the paramedic's vehicle parked in front of the emergency room entrance when I pulled into the hospital parking lot. I found a parking spot close to the entrance. I parked the PT Cruiser and went into the ER.

I walked up to the front desk. "I'm here to see Kathleen Stone," I said. "I'm her husband."

"She just got here," the man at the desk said. "Just have a seat. I'll let you know when you can see her, Mr. Stone."

I sat down in the waiting area. I was the only one there.

A couple minutes later, the double doors opened and the paramedics pushed out the empty gurney. The older paramedic followed the younger two, who were rolling the gurney. He waved at me and said, "Good luck."

I waved back. "Thanks," I said.

A nurse come out. She talked to the man at the desk for a moment and then she came over to me. "You can see your wife now, Mr. Stone," she said. "Follow me, please."

"Okay," I said. I got up and followed her.

We went through the double doors, and then we turned right and went down a hallway. On the right side of the hallway there were several small rooms with glass doors. Some of them had curtains drawn across them. Kathy was in the forth small room. When we came in, she was leaning on the railing of a hospital bed. She had her weight on her left foot.

"She wouldn't stay on the bed," the aide who was in the room with Kathy said.

"Ma'am, you have to stay on the bed until the doctor sees you," the nurse said.

"Are the chickens out?" Kathy asked her.

"No ma'am. We don't have any chickens here," the nurse said. "Now get back on the bed."

The aide put her hand on Kathy's left wrist. Kathy tightened her grip on the railing. The aide looked at the nurse. "She's resisting," she said.

"Can't she sit in a chair until the doctor gets here?" I asked. I walked over to the other side of Kathy. I put my left hand on top of her right hand; and with my right hand, I tried to gently loosen her grip on the railing. "Come on, Kathy. Let's sit down," I said to her.

"I suppose she can sit in a chair—for now," the nurse said.

Kathy allowed me to loosen her grip on the railing, and I held her hand as she limped over to the chairs against the wall. She sat down, and I sat in the chair next to her.

"Stay in the room with her," the nurse told me before leaving.

The aide followed her out of the room and closed the sliding glass door.

Kathy looked at me. "I think we should go," she said.

"Kathy, we're here anyway. Let's let them take a look at your foot. Okay."

She thought about it, and then said, "Kay."

After a few minutes, Kathy said again, "I think we should go."

"We need to stay," I said.

"We need to go," she said.

Kathy got up and limped to the door. I followed her. When she put her hand on the door handle to open the door, I put my hand on the handle below hers, and I held the door shut.

"We need to go," she said.

"No, we need to stay."

A nurse—one I hadn't seen before—came up to the door. She was carrying an odd shaped plastic pan and a plastic bag with other things in it.

I removed my hand and let Kathy open the door.

"Does she have to use the bathroom?" the nurse asked.

"Probably," I said. Then I turned to Kathy. "Kathy, do you have to use the bathroom?"

"Yeah," she said.

"Come with me, ma'am. I'll show you where the bathroom is," the nurse said.

Kathy looked at me.

"I'll go with her," I said.

"Sure," the nurse said. "Right this way."

We followed the nurse down the hall. Kathy had no shoes and a sore foot, so we moved much slower than the nurse did.

The nurse stopped, and waited for us, outside of the bathroom.

"I'm going to go in with her," the nurse said. "Because I need to get a urine sample."

"Okay," I said.

The nurse opened the bathroom door and looked at Kathy. "Here it is, ma'am. Here's the bathroom."

"Do you have to use the bathroom?" I asked.

"Yeah."

"Well there it is. Go in and use it," I said.

Kathy went into the bathroom. The nurse followed her in and closed the door.

A couple minutes later, the nurse came out holding a plastic bottle with a yellow liquid in it. "I got a sample," she said. Then she added: "She'll be out in a minute. She finishing up."

Kathy came out of the bathroom.

"She doesn't flush the toilet," I said.

"Don't worry about it," she said. Then she looked at Kathy. "Come on, ma'am. Let's go back to your room."

The nurse lead us back to the room. We went in and sat down. The nurse closed the sliding glass door.

We waited, and after awhile, a young woman opened the door and rolled a small cart into the room. "Well how are you folks today?" she asked.

"Not so good," I said.

"Do you remember me?" she asked.

I looked at her. I didn't remember her at first, but then I did. "Oh yeah," I said. "You took a blood sample from Kathy a little over a year ago."

"Yup. And I'm here to get another one." She looked at Kathy.

"You remember me, don't you Kathleen?" She rolled up Kathy's shirt sleeve, and then she picked up a tourniquet from the top of her cart. "I know you remember this," she said.

Kathy chuckled.

The young woman wrapped the tourniquet around Kathy's upper arm. She tapped a vein with her finger, and then stuck a syringe in the vein and drew blood. She put the blood filled syringe back on the cart. Then she poked Kathy with another syringe and got a second sample of blood.

"There. That wasn't so bad, now was it?" she said.

Kathy chuckled again.

"You folks have a nice day," the young woman said.

"We'll try," I said.

She pushed the cart out of the room and closed the door.

Another nurse came in after we had been waiting for a very long time—it was close to noon. When she came in, she walked right up to Kathy and asked, "Ma'am, why are you out of the bed?"

Kathy didn't say anything.

"She felt move comfortable sitting over here," I said. "We've been waiting for over three hours to see a doctor."

"Well she's not the only patient we have today!" the nurse said.

"I would hope not," I said.

"Dr. Mason will see her in a few minutes," the nurse said. "Right now, she needs to get up on the bed so I can take her vitals!"

I stood up and turned toward Kathy. "Come on, Kathy," I said.

"Are we going?" she asked as she rose from her chair.

I took her by the hand and walked her over to the bed. "The doctor's going to look at your foot. And then we'll go. Just sit down on the bed please."

"Kay," she said. She sat down on the bed.

The nurse put the stethoscope on her ears and listened to Kathy's heart. Then she moved the chestpiece around to Kathy's back. "Take a deep breath," she said.

Kathy continued to breathe normally.

She picked up Kathy's hand and put an oximeter on her fingertip. She held Kathy's hand up by her wrist for a few seconds, and then she took the oximeter off her finger. She went over to a computer which was on a counter at the back of the room and typed something on the keyboard. Then she picked up a blood pressure meter, which was on the counter, and came back over to Kathy.

As she wrapped the cuff of the blood pressure meter around Kathy's arm, she asked, "Do you know where you are?"

Kathy didn't answer.

The nurse pumped up the cuff. "Can you tell me what year it is? Do you know?"

"She has dementia, okay? And she doesn't care what year it is, or who the president is, or what county we happen to be in. She doesn't worry about that stuff anymore," I said.

"They told me that she has dementia," the nurse said. "I'm just trying to get an idea of how severe it is."

She deflated the cuff, took it off Kathy's arm, and then put the blood pressure meter back on the counter. She typed something on the computer.

The nurse turned around and looked at Kathy. "Do you have any pets?" she asked.

"We have a dog, two cats and a bunch of chickens," Kathy said.

"What are their names?" the nurse asked.

Kathy appeared to be confused by the question.

"What's your dog's name?' the nurse asked.

"Rupert."

"What are the cats' names?"

Kathy looked at me.

"Can you remember?"

Kathy looked at the nurse, and then she looked back at me.

"Can you remember one of the cats' names?"

"She knows their names when she sees them," I said.

"And who might this young man be?" the nurse asked Kathy as she pointed at me.

"That's Mark," Kathy said, in sort of a snide tone of voice.

"And what is his relationship to you?"

"We're married," Kathy said in the same tone. "Isn't that nice?"

The nurse nodded her head slowly. She seemed surprised that

Kathy had all that knowledge. After a couple of minutes—when Kathy's remarks had sunk in—she said, "Yes, that is nice."

An unshaven man wearing light blue scrubs came into the room. A stethoscope hung from around his neck. "I'm Dr. Mason," he said.

"I'm Mark Stone," I said.

"Are you the husband?"

"Yeah."

Dr. Mason looked at Kathy. "You must be Kathleen," he said. "So, why did you come to see me, Kathleen?"

Kathy didn't answer.

"She has an injured foot," I said.

Dr. Mason looked at me. "I wasn't asking you," he said. Then he turned to Kathy. "Does your foot hurt?"

Kathy pointed to her right foot. "That one's messy," she said.

"Messy?" Dr. Mason asked. "How is it messy?"

"That one," Kathy said, still pointing to the foot.

Dr. Mason looked at the nurse. "What's wrong with her?"

"She has dementia," the nurse said.

"Dementia?" The doctor looked at Kathy. "She looks a little young for dementia." He looked at me. "Did all this begin with a blow to the head?"

"What!" I said.

The doctor looked at the nurse. "We'd better check this one out. She needs a CT scan on her head. Stat!"

"Ma'am, you have to lay down on the bed," the nurse said to Kathy. She pushed Kathy's shoulder down on the bed.

Then the doctor and the nurse began to roll the bed out of the room.

I followed them down the hall a short ways. "She's got a foot injury, not a head injury," I explained to the nurse. "Why in the hell would you do a head scan?"

"We have to check for internal bleeding," the nurse said. "That's the law."

"What!" I said again. I stopped walking. They pushed the bed around a corner and out of sight.

I went back to the room.

Twenty minutes later, two nurses rolled the bed, and Kathy, back into the room. Kathy looked scared.

Then Dr. Mason came into the room. He opened a drawer in the cabinet and got out a pair of scissors, and he began cutting the sock on Kathy's injured foot. When the sock was cut almost to the toe, he peeled it off her ankle and foot.

"You know, doctor," I said. "I know of a way to take a sock off without using scissors. I guess they don't teach you that in medical school, huh?"

Dr. Mason gave me a dirty look, and then he looked down at Kathy's injured foot. "What happened to her foot?" he asked me.

"Why don't you tell me, Sherlock? You're the detective."

Dr. Mason looked up at me. I saw a flash of anger in his eyes, but he didn't say anything.

He looked down at Kathy's foot. "Clean and dress the wound," he said without looking up. "And give her a point nine saline IV." Then he walked out of the room.

One of the nurses—the one who had quizzed Kathy—said to the other: "Maddie, wash her foot with the antibacterial soap. I'm going to go get the gauze and the saline solution."

She left the room. Maddie turned the water on at the sink. She put some water in a stainless steel pan, took a bottle of soap and a sponge out of the cabinet, and then she began washing Kathy's foot.

The other nurse came back in and put a roll of gauze on the counter. She rolled the IV pole next to bed, and hung the bag of saline solution on it. She poked the IV needle in Kathy's arm and taped it in place. Then she left the room.

Maddie finished washing Kathy's foot. She dried it with a towel, and she wrapped the wound with gauze. "That should be good for now," she said. Then she left the room.

I sat down in a chair and watched the fluid from the bag of saline drip into a tube which curled down to the needle in Kathy's arm.

The nurse came in with another bag of fluid. She hung it on the IV pole, and then she hooked it into the flow of the saline solution. "Your wife has an infection," she said. "We're giving her antibiotics, which, we think, should be given through the IV. So we're going to admit her."

"She's not going to like that," I said.

The nurse left for a moment and came back with a clipboard full of papers. "You need to sign these," she said.

I looked at the stack. There must have been thirty pages. "All of these?"

"Just sign where you see a red x, initial where you see a red dash."

"Fine," I said. I went through the papers signing on lines, and putting my initials in various spots. I didn't read anything.

Two male nurses came in and started to move the bed and the IV pole out of the room.

"Where are you taking her?" I asked.

"The fifth floor," one of them said. And they pushed Kathy out of the room.

I finished signing and initialing the papers and took the clipboard up to the nurses station. "My wife's up on the fifth floor," I said, as I handed the nurse the clipboard.

"She hasn't been assigned a room yet," the nurse said.

"But she is up on the fifth floor, right?"

"Yes, but you can't go up and see her—not until she's assigned a room. That might take an hour or two."

"Okay, then," I said.

It was three o'clock in the afternoon. I hadn't eaten all day. As I walked out of the hospital, I had a three way debate going on in my head. That debate was between Wendy's, McDonald's and Burger King.

chapter 19

After eating a Whooper and a medium fry at Burger King, I called Drake Memorial Hospital: "You have a new patient there named Kathleen Stone. Has she been assigned a room yet?"

"Kathleen Stone, let me see," the woman said. "Yes. Kathleen Stone is in room 504. Would you like me to put your call through to her room?"

"No," I said. "I'll just go up there."

I went back to the hospital, and I took the elevator up to the fifth floor. I located the room, without help, and went in.

Kathy was in bed, covered up with a sheet. She was wearing a hospital gown. The IV pole was next to her bed and an IV needle was still in her arm. She was sleeping peacefully.

I looked around her room. It was much nicer than I would expect in an older hospital like Drake Memorial. It had just one bed. But the room was big. The chest of drawers, and the dresser looked new. I looked in the bathroom. It was clean, and the fixtures looked fairly new. A flat screen TV was on the wall above the chest of drawers and opposite the bed. A night stand sat next to the bed, and a phone sat on top of the nightstand. Next to the night stand, there was an armchair, which also looked new.

"Kathy," I said, quietly. "Kathy."

She didn't respond. So I let her sleep.

I sat down in the armchair and looked out the window. The room had a nice view of the parking lot, and beyond that, some trees. I relaxed for a few minutes, and then I went back over to the bed.

"Kathy," I said. She was sleeping soundly.

I didn't want to bother her, so I went home.

. . . . .

The next day I did a carpet job in Middletown with Phillip and Zac. We finished the job—which was a ninety yard job with furniture and take-up—a few minutes after five o'clock. I drove to the hospital as soon as I left the job.

I got to the hospital around six and went straight up to the fifth floor. I walked into Kathy's room.

The back of Kathy's bed was raised and she was sitting in an upright position. She was staring down at a food tray which sat on an overbed table in front of her.

"Hi Kathy," I said.

She looked at me and pointed to her foot. "I need to get this thing going," she said.

"Yeah, you do," I said.

I looked at her tray of food. It had a fish sandwich and french fries on the main plate, a small bowl of coleslaw, strawberry shortcake on a smaller plate, and a glass of milk. She hadn't touched any of it except the milk.

"Aren't you going to eat?" I asked.

"No."

"Why not?" I picked up the fish sandwich. "This is fish, Kathy. You like fish. Why don't you taste it?"

She pointed to her foot again. "I need to get this thing going."

"Okay," I said, and put the sandwich back on the plate.

I walked over to the armchair and sat down. I looked out the window at the view. It had been a physically grueling day, and I was tired. I almost fell asleep.

Something started beeping, and I jumped out of the chair. I looked around the room. I didn't know where the beeping was coming from, at first, but soon discovered that it was coming from a metal box which was clamped to the IV pole.

A nurse came in with a bag of saline solution.

"Why is that beeping?" I asked. "Is something wrong?"

The nurse pushed a button and turned off the alarm. "It's nothing to worry about," she said. "The alarm just tells us that she needs another bag of saline."

She hooked up the full bag of saline solution, and then she looked at Kathy's food tray. "Ma'am, you have to eat," she said. "You're not going to get better if you don't eat."

"Did she eat lunch?" I asked.

The nurse shook her head. "She didn't eat lunch, and she didn't eat breakfast either."

"Okay," I said, thinking. "Um, is there a candy machine on this floor?"

"No. There are vending machines as you come into the main lob-by—"

"I know where they are down there," I said.

I waited until the nurse left, and then I asked, "Kathy, do you want the Hershey?"

"Do they have the Hershey?"

"Yeah," I said. "I'll go get some."

I took the elevator down to the first floor. Then I went through the main lobby to the vending machine area. I bought her two regular Hershey milk chocolate candy bars. I also bought a granola bar. Kathy liked those too.

When I got back to Kathy's room, I gave her a Hershey candy bar.

She chuckled. "Hershey," she said, looking at the candy bar and smiling. She unwrapped the candy bar and gobbled it down.

I gave her the granola bar next. She ate that almost as quickly.

So I held up the other Hersey bar. "Do you want to eat this now, or do you want to save it for later?" I asked.

Kathy grabbed the candy bar out of my hand. She unwrapped it and began eating it, but at a more normal pace.

"Now tomorrow, do you want me to bring you some chili when I come up here?" I asked. Because I knew she liked chili.

"Chili?" she asked.

"Supper," I said

"Supper?"

"Yeah, supper," I said. "When I come up tomorrow, I'll bring you some supper."

"Bring supper?"

"See you tomorrow, Kathy," I said, and I kissed her on the fore-head.

"See you tomorrow," she said.

• • • • •

For the next few days, I stopped at Wendy's on my way to the hospital and picked up a large chili for Kathy. She enjoyed eating the Wendy's chili. But over the weekend, she started to eat some of the hospital food as well.

On Monday afternoon I got to the hospital around four o'clock. Carrying the Wendy's bag, I went up to the fifth floor. I went to Kathy's room. A doctor and a male nurse were standing at the foot of Kathy's bed.

Kathy noticed when I entered the room, and she said to the doctor: "I think you all can leave so I can get going."

The male nurse looked at the doctor and laughed. "I think she's giving us the boot."

The doctor smiled at Kathy. "We'll leave now, Kathy. We won't bother you anymore, today."

When the doctor turned around, he noticed me. "Are you her husband?"

"Yes. Are you her doctor?"

"My name's Dr. Wilson. I'm her attending physician right now."

"I'm Mark Stone," I said, and I shook his hand.

"Could I speak to you in the hall for a minute, Mr. Stone?"

"Sure," I said. I set the Wendy's bag on the dresser and stepped out into the hall.

"Your wife's condition, as far as the infection goes, is improving," the doctor said. "But we're concerned that the infection has reached the bone."

"Oh," I said.

"A specialist is coming in tomorrow morning to do some tests, and when we get the results we'll know something."

"So, if the infection has reached the bone, what then?"

"Well, she might lose some toes."

"Uh-huh," I said, nodding slowly. "Would she still be able to walk?"

"She'd probably still be able to walk. But she might need a cane or a walker."

"Oh. Well we don't want that," I said.

"No we don't," the doctor said. "But let's not be pessimistic right now. Let's find out first."

"Okay," I said.

"How long has she had the dementia?" he asked, changing the subject.

"Four, maybe five years."

"What causes it? Do they know?" he asked.

"She has Pick's Disease," I said. "It runs in her family."

"I thought it was FTD," he said, folding his arms and nodding. "Well, Mr. Stone, it's been nice meeting you."

"Likewise, Dr. Wilson," I said.

He walked down the hall, and I went back into Kathy's room.

"Do you want supper?" I asked, picking up the Wendy's bag.

"Supper?"

"Yeah." I pushed the button to bring the back of the bed up, and then rolled the overbed table in front of her. "I brought you some chili." I took the top off the chili container and put the container on the table. Then I gave her the spoon.

Kathy ate about half the chili, and then she put the spoon down and looked at me.

"Don't you want anymore?" I asked.

"I think you can eat," she said.

I looked at the chili. I was hungry. "Okay," I said, and I finished the bowl.

Then I pushed the overbed table back against the wall and I lowered the back of the bed.

Kathy pointed to her foot. "I need to get this thing going," she said.

"You will," I said, hoping her infection hadn't reached her bone.

I sat on the side of the bed. After a few minutes, Kathy closed her eyes and went to sleep, and I went home.

．　．　．　．　．

On Wednesday morning, I got a call from the hospital with some good news: The tests on Kathy's foot came back negative, which meant her infection had not gotten into her bone.

When I went to the hospital later that afternoon, just as I was about to enter Kathy's room, someone behind me said, "Mr. Stone."

I turned around. "Yes," I said.

A small woman in a pants suit walked up to me. A large black tote bag with a shoulder strap hung to her side. The bag was full of papers.

"Are you Mark Stone?" she asked.

"I am," I said.

"Good. You're the one I'm looking for. I have something for you."

"Alright," I said, not sure that I wanted what she had to give me.

"I can give it to you in your wife's room."

"Um, okay."

I went into Kathy's room. The back of Kathy's bed was tilted up and the overbed table was in front of her. "Hi Kathy," I said.

Kathy just looked at me.

The woman sat the tote bag on the overbed table. She took a card out of a side pocket and handed it to me.

"I'm Sandy Hawkins," she said. "I'm the social worker here at the hospital."

I looked at the card and nodded.

She pulled a packet out of the tote bag and handed it to me. "This is a list of rehab facilities in the area."

"Rehab facilities?"

"Yes. Your wife is going to be discharged to a rehab facility."

"Really. I didn't know that."

"Oh, I'm sorry. I assumed they told you."

"No, they didn't," I said. "Do you know when she's going to be discharged?"

"Soon. Maybe tomorrow."

"That is soon."

"So, I need you to pick three rehab facilities, and number them one, two, three—first choice, second choice, third choice."

"Should I go out and look at the places?"

"If you have time."

"Well I won't. So I'll just do it now."

"That's fine. Just leave it at the nurses station. I'll pick it up later."

"Okay."

She looked at Kathy and smiled. "Her eyes are moving back and forth. She's probably wondering what's going on."

"She has a pretty good idea what's going on," I said.

"Do you think so?"

"Yes," I said. "I think there's more going on in her head than people give her credit for."

"Maybe so," the social worker said. "Well, I'll leave you two alone."

She left, and I sat down in the chair and looked over the list. It was a long list but I didn't have any trouble narrowing it down. Anything in Dayton was out of the question, because I don't like driving in Dayton. Anything north of Dayton or west of Dayton was out also; because those places were too far from our house, and I'd have to drive through Dayton to get to them. I ended up picking: Saint Leonard's Senior Living and Rehab, which is a few miles west of our house, for my first choice; Liberty Nursing Center, which, like Saint Leonard's, is in Centerville—only its a couple mile farther from our house—for my second choice; and Lebanon Health and Rehab, which is a few miles south of our house, as my third choice.

When I finished circling and numbering my choices, I took the list up to the nurses station and gave it to the nurse.

"Don't leave yet," the nurse said. "Dr. Wilson wants to see you."

"I wasn't going to," I said.

As I was going back into Kathy's room, I noticed a food cart coming down the hall. "Supper's coming," I told her.

She didn't say anything.

A couple minutes later, an aide carried in a tray of food. "Here ya go, Ms. Kathy," she said, setting the tray on the overbed table. "Doesn't that look good?"

After she left, I looked over the meal. It did look good. They served her meat loaf, mashed potatoes and green beans. The desert was cherry pie.

"I'll open this for you," I said. I opened the carton of milk and poured it in the plastic cup they provided.

Kathy began drinking the milk.

"Do you want ketchup on this?" I asked, pointing to the meatloaf. I opened a packet of ketchup with my teeth and squeezed it on the meat.

Kathy put her cup of milk down and looked at the food.

"Eat," I said.

"Eat," she repeated. She picked up her fork, stabbed a hunk of meatloaf, and put it in her mouth.

Dr. Wilson came into the room. "Mr. Stone," he said, and he gave me a nod. He looked at Kathy. "How are you today, Kathy?" He looked back at me. "She seems to be eating well."

"I think her appetite is back," I said.

"They told you the good news, I assume."

"You mean that her infection didn't go to her bone? Yeah, I was very relieved to hear that, believe me."

"I imagine you were," the doctor said.

"They also told me that she's going to be discharged to a rehab facility."

"Yeah. We've done all we can do. There's no reason for her to be here anymore. Now, she will be on the antibiotic drip for a few more days, but they can do that at the nursing home."

"Do you have any idea when she's going to the nursing home?"

"She'll be discharged as soon as they find a facility for her to go to. So, probably tomorrow—maybe tomorrow morning, maybe to-morrow afternoon."

"Okay."

Dr. Wilson extended his hand. "Mr. Stone." I shook hands with him. "Good luck," he said.

"Thanks," I said.

The doctor left. I sat down on the edge of Kathy's bed and watched her eat.

The social worker poked her head in the room. "Mr. Stone." She was holding up the list of rehab facilities that I had turned in at the nurses station. "Thank you."

"Oh, you're welcome," I said.

"I'll call you tomorrow morning when she's placed."

"I'd appreciate that," I said.

After Kathy finished eating, I pushed the overbed table against the wall. "I'm going to go home," I said. I kissed her on the forehead. "See you tomorrow," I said.

"See you tomorrow," she said.

chapter 20

When I got home, I called Phillip.

"Yeah Mark," Phillip said, answering his phone.

"Phillip," I said, "I don't think I'll be able to work tomorrow."

"Your wife again?"

"Yeah. They're going to transfer her to a rehab facility sometime tomorrow. But they can't give me a time when that's going to happen."

"Just sometime tomorrow?"

"Yeah. And I think I should be at the facility when she gets there. So, I don't want to be clear out in Okeana when I get the call."

"I understand, Mark," he said. "Do you want me and Zac to work?"

"Well, you can if you want."

"Zac wants all the work he can get," he said. "He's going up to Columbus this Sunday to see his girlfriend. So he needs money."

"Alright," I said. "You guys can strip and pad the job tomorrow if you want to."

"We want to," Phillip said.

"Okay, you're going to have to pick up six rolls of half inch eight pound pad at Southland."

"I can do that," he said.

"And you might as well pick up a box of wood strip."

"Right."

"Alright then," I said. "The key to the front door is under the mat. If Ronnie stops by—that's the owner of the house—tell him I'll be there on Friday. And if you have any questions, give me a call. I'm sure I'm not going to be busy."

"I think I can handle it, Mark."

"Then I'll see you on Friday," I said.

"See ya."

· · · · ·

The next morning, at nine o'clock, I called the number on the card that the social worker at the hospital had given me.

"This is Sandy," the social worker said, answering the phone.

"Sandy, this is Mark Stone."

"I was just about to call you, Mr. Stone," she said. "Saint Leonard's was full, but I did get Kathleen placed at Liberty. She going to be taken over there this morning."

"About what time? Do you know?"

"The transport service said they pick her up about ten. So...however long it takes them to drive there."

"So she should get there between ten-thirty and eleven," I said.

"That sounds about right," she said.

"I'm going to try to be at Liberty when she arrives."

"I think she'd like that, Mr. Stone," Sandy said.

· · · · ·

I put the address in my GPS, and the GPS led me to a sign next to a blacktop driveway which went through a wooded area. The sign said *Liberty Nursing Center* and there was a red arrow under the name pointing towards the woods.

I drove through the wooded area—which was probably about five hundred yards—and then I came to a clearing. I could now see the building housing Liberty Nursing Center. It was a sprawling, one story brick building with a hip roof.

On the street side of the building there was an entrance which identified itself as the *Jefferson Wing* entrance. I didn't know whether that was the main entrance, so I continued to drive around the building. On the side of the building there was an entrance which identified itself as the *Roosevelt Wing* entrance, and in the back there was the *Reagan Wing* entrance.

I drove back to the front of the building, parked the PT Cruiser near the Jefferson Wing entrance, and went into the building. I walked into a lobby and up to a frosted window which was slid open. There was woman sitting behind a desk near the window.

"Kathleen Stone is suppose to be coming here this morning. She should be here right about now," I said to the woman.

"Well I don't think she's here yet," she said. "But let me check." She looked at her computer screen and clicked the mouse a couple times. "She's been assigned to Reagan," she said. "That's in the back of the building—"

"I think I know where it is," I said. "Thanks."

I went outside and got back into the PT Cruiser, and then I drove around back. I parked near the Reagan Wing entrance and went into the building.

This part of the building looked completely different from the part I had just left. Instead of a small lobby, I walked into a large open area. There were two dining areas, each with ten to twelve table. The dining areas were carpeted with a green, red and yellow patterned carpet. The tablecloths on the tables alternated red and green. Chandeliers hung from the ceiling in the dining areas. There was also a nurses station not far from the entrance door.

I walked up to the nurses station. A nurse sat behind the counter. "May I help you," she said.

"Yes. Kathleen Stone is suppose to be coming here from Drake Memorial Hospital this morning," I said.

"We know," the nurse said. "She's been assigned to room 708. But she hasn't arrived yet. You can have a seat and wait if you like."

I sat down at a table with a green tablecloth, and waited.

The nursing home was perfectly silent at first. But after awhile, I heard a noise. Then the noise stopped. Then I heard it again. Then it stopped again. I heard it again, and then I saw a nurse pushing a large medication cart out of a hallway. She turned a corner at the nurses station and went down another hallway. The noise stopped, for a moment, and then started again.

A little while later, an old man in a walker went up to the nurses station. "Excuse me," he said.

"You're in room 631, Mr. Miller," the nurse said in a very loud voice.

"Excuse me?" the old man said.

"Didn't you hear me?" the nurse asked in an even louder voice. "I said you're in room 631."

"Where is room 631?" he asked.

She pointed down the hall. "Go straight down that hall and take your first right."

The old man moseyed down the hall. A few minutes later he came back. He went up to the nurses station. "Do I have a room here?" he asked the nurse.

"You're in room 631," she said in a loud voice.

At about noon, I heard a beeping noise coming from outside, and then I saw the red blinking lights cast upon the wall. I got up and looked out the front door. An ambulance was backing up to the building.

The ambulance stopped, and a man got out. He came around to the back of the ambulance and opened the back doors. I could see another man inside the ambulance unfastening a gurney. Once the gurney was unfastened, they slowly pulled it out of the ambulance and lowered the wheels.

They rolled the gurney inside the building.

Kathy lay flat on her back covered with a white blanket, and she was a strapped to the gurney with two straps. One strap was around her thighs, and another strap was around her shoulder and chest. Her eyes were open wide. She looked scared.

"She's going to room 708," the nurse told the men. "Follow me."

The men pushed the gurney down the hall, following the nurse. I followed the gurney.

The nurse went into room 708, and the men pushed the gurney into the room behind her. I went into the room too.

"Sir, could you please wait outside until were done in here?" the nurse said to me.

"Sorry," I said, and I stepped out of the room.

When the men pushed the gurney out of the room, I went back in. "Can I come in now?" I asked the nurse.

"I'm not done yet, but I guess," the nurse said grudgingly.

"Hi Kathy," I said.

Kathy was looking intently at the nurse, who had a needle in one hand and her arm in the other.

"Ma'am, relax you're arm and let me put this in," the nurse said. She held Kathy's arm and waited. "Relax your arm, ma'am."

Kathy and the nurse appeared to be in a stare-down. "If you relax your arm, this won't hurt. If you won't relax your arm, it will hurt. It's up to you ma'am."

Finally, the nurse put the needle in Kathy's arm. "There we go," she said. Then she hooked in the bag of IV fluid.

"How long is she going to be on the antibiotic drip?" I asked.

"Sunday is her last day on the antibiotics." The nurse put a piece of tape over where the IV needle went into Kathy's arm. "She's all yours," she said, and then she left the room.

I walked up to the side of the bed.

Kathy looked at me. "Are the chickens out?" she asked.

"Yes," I said. "I opened their door this morning, and they all went out. And I fed them and gave them fresh water."

"Kay," she said.

I could have also mentioned that I picked up eight eggs. But Kathy was never concerned about their egg production—that was more my thing.

I noticed that her right foot was no longer bandaged. It was in a hospital sock, like her left foot. "Does your foot still hurt?" I asked.

"Foot?" She seemed confused by the word.

I pointed to her right foot. "That thing," I said.

"I need to get that thing going," she said.

"You'll get it going," I said.

I sat in the chair next to the bed, found the remote (It was attached to a bed post.), and turned on the television. I watched CNN. Kathy didn't pay much attention to the television, but it didn't seem to bother her.

A few minutes later, they brought in Kathy's lunch tray. It was a light lunch—a ham and cheese sandwich, chips, apple sauce and milk. She ate all the food on the tray, and drank the milk, quickly.

I stood up. "Do you want me to get you another sandwich, Kathy. Are you still hungry?"

She closed her eyes and went to sleep. So I made my exit.

· · · · ·

I went to the nursing home to visit Kathy late the next day. Because we didn't finish our carpet job in Okeana until seven o'clock in the evening, and it took me almost an hour to drive to the nursing home from Okeana.

On Saturday, and again on Sunday, I didn't have to work. So I went to the nursing home in the morning.

On Sunday morning, at about eleven o'clock, I was sitting in the chair next to Kathy's bed, watching television, and Phillip called me.

"Yeah. Phillip. What's up?" I said into my cell phone.

"Are we going to need Zac tomorrow?"

"Um. Why, doesn't he want to work?" I asked.

"He wants to go to a concert with his girlfriend tonight. And if he does that, he won't make it back till tomorrow."

I thought about it. "That's fine," I said. "We can get by without him. We're just doing a kitchen and a hallway in laminate."

"I know," he said. "Should we start a little earlier, maybe?"

"No," I said. "I told the homeowner we'd be there at ten o'clock. Let's stick to that. The jobs not that big. We'll be done by five, six at the latest."

"Okay. I'll tell Zac that we don't need him."

"Tell him to have a good time at the concert," I said.

"Right. Well, you know, that's not really what he's after."

"I understand that," I said, chuckling. "I'll see you tomorrow at ten."

As soon as I got off the phone, Kathy said, "I have to use the bathroom."

"I'll get a nurse," I said.

I went out to the hall. I didn't see anyone, so I went up to the nurses station. "My wife has to use the bathroom," I told the nurse who was sitting behind the counter.

"I can help her," she said. She got up and came out of the nurses station. Then she started walking down the hall towards the room.

I followed her.

She entered the room, and then she opened the top dresser drawer and got something. "Come on, Ms. Kathy. Let's go to the bathroom."

"What's that?" I asked.

"What?"

"That," I said, pointing to the plastic undergarment.

"This." She held it up. "It's a diaper."

"Doesn't she have regular panties in her drawer?"

"Yes. But we'd rather have her use a diaper. Just to be safe," she said. Then she moved the IV pole to where Kathy could grab ahold of it. "Grab on to this, Ms. Kathy."

Kathy grabbed on to the IV pole and pulled herself out of bed. She started walking toward the bathroom, using the IV pole as sort of a rolling cane.

"Let go of the pole now, Ms. Kathy," the nurse said. "You can't take that in with you." The IV pole had an electronic box attached to it, and it was running out of cord.

Kathy let go of the pole and went into the bathroom. The nurse followed her in and closed the door—but not all the way, because Kathy was still hooked to an IV tube.

I waited.

The toilet flushed. A few moments later I heard the facet running. Then Kathy came out of the bathroom. She walked toward the bed, ignoring the IV pole.

The nurse quickly grabbed the IV pole and moved it closer to Kathy. "Be careful, Ms. Kathy, you'll pull out your IV."

Kathy sat down on the bed, and then she lay back and stretched out the arm that had the IV needle in it. She sighed.

"I'll bet she'll be glad when she's done with that IV," I said.

"Her and me both," the nurse said. "She's got one more bag after this one. Then she's done. She'll be done sometime this evening."

"You'll like that, won't you Kathy?" I asked.

"Like that," she said.

I hung around the nursing home for a couple more hours—until after Kathy's lunch—and then I left.

· · · · ·

On Monday morning, when I got to the customer's house—which was in Monroe—at ten minutes till ten o'clock, Phillip was already there. He was in the driveway, sitting in his van.

I parked my van behind his. We got out of our vans at the same time.

"You're raring to go this morning, aren't ya?" I said.

"I want to get this job done," Phillip said.

"I know you haven't done much laminate," I said. "But laminate is easy. And this is an easy laminate job. You just snap it together, and you cut a piece once in a while. So its snap, snap, snap, cut. Snap, snap, snap, cut."

"It's a snap, huh?"

"Yep," I said. "Let's go tell Mrs. Collins that we're here."

We went up to the front porch and rang the doorbell.

Mrs. Collins, who is an older woman, opened the door. "Good morning, gentlemen," she said. "I've swept and mopped the floor for you."

"Thank you," I said. I pointed to the front yard. "I just wanted to let you know that we're going to be setting up the saw in your front yard. That will keep the sawdust away from everything."

"That would be fine," she said. "Please come in." She held the door open for us.

Phillip and I went through the doorway and walked into the kitchen.

"Let's put this table in the family room," I said.

We pulled the four chairs out and carried the table into the family room. Then we carried the chairs into the family room.

"What about the refrigerator and stove?" Phillip asked.

"Leave 'em where they are," I said. "This isn't like carpet. We can move 'em when we get to 'em."

Phillip nodded. "I think I like installing laminate."

"Alright. Get the boxes of laminate and the rolls of underlayment out of the back of my truck. Stack about half of the material right here in the hall—make sure we can get through. The other half, stack on the porch. I'm going to get the tools out and set up the saws."

"I'm on it," Phillip said.

He unloaded the flooring, while I unpacked the tools, set up the saws, and rolled out a couple swipes of underlayment.

"That's the last box," Phillip said, stacking the box of laminate on top of the others in the hall.

"Bring that one in here," I said.

Phillip brought the box of laminate into the kitchen. He laid it on the floor and I unwrapped it.

"Okay, we're going to start on that wall," I said, pointing to the window wall.

"Why that wall?" Phillip asked.

"It's an outside wall. It's the longest wall. That's the easiest place to start."

Phillip nodded. "That makes sense."

I went over to the corner that I was going to start in and put my knee pads on. "Hand me a couple planks," I said to Phillip. He handed me two planks of laminate. I put one plank in the corner. "Now, I don't want this to be to tight against the wall," I said. "So I'll put in some spacers." I put in three spacers in various places between the plank and the wall. "I'm using the eight inch side of the spacer."

"Why don't you use the quarter inch side of the spacer?" Phillip asked.

"It's a small area," I said. "If we were doing a basement, or something like that, I'd probably use the quarter inch side."

"Makes sense," he said.

I showed him how to snap the planks together using a hammer and a tapping block. We came to the end of the first run of planks. I cut the last plank, and we used the cut off end to start the second run.

Then my phone rang.

I took my cellphone out of my pocket and held it to my ear. "Hello," I said.

"May I speak to Mark Stone, please?"

"This is Mark Stone."

"Mr. Stone, this is Lavern at Liberty Nursing Center. I wanted to assure you that everything is all right with your wife, but we moved her to a different room. Her new room number 421."

"Why did you move her to a different room?" I asked.

"This morning your wife became very active. She tried to leave the building several times. We wouldn't let her. Then she tried to climb out a window. So we thought it'd be best to put her in a more secure unit."

"A more secure unit?"

"Yes. She's on Kennedy Hall. That's our secure unit."

"Room 421, you say?"

"Yes. She's in room 421."

"Okay. Thanks for letting me know," I said.

"You're welcome, Mr. Stone."

When I got off the phone, Phillip asked: "Was that about your wife?"

"Yeah," I said. "She's not on the IV drip anymore—this is her first day off. And apparently she tried to escape the nursing home—several times. She even tried to climb out a window."

Phillip laughed. "I guess she got that foot goin', didn't she? Oh, I'm sorry. I shouldn't laugh."

"No, that's okay," I said. "It is kind of funny. She finally got her foot goin', and now she's in a 'more secure unit'—whatever that means."

"It means that she's locked up in a cell," Phillip said.

"You make it sound like she's in jail," I said.

"That's what it's like," he said. "My mom used to work at a nursing home, and she used to tell us about it. If a patient wouldn't cooperate, they were locked up in a cell. And if they didn't behave themselves in the cell, they were given a shot that knocked them out. They didn't put up with any bullshit."

"Are you sure she didn't work in a mental hospital?" I asked.

"No. It was a nursing home."

"Okay. Well, hand me a plank."

Phillip handed me a plank. I snapped it in, and then he handed me another plank. And then another—until we were at the end of the second run. I marked the last plank on the second run, and he took it outside and cut it. I snapped the last piece in, and then I started the third run with the cut off piece.

"Do you want to go check on your wife?" Phillip asked. "I think I have the hang of this."

"It's not rocket science, is it?"

"No, it's not," he said.

I thought about it, and then I said: "You know, the nursing

home's not far from here. Why don't we do two more runs. And then I'll help you move the stove over to that corner." I pointed to the corner.

"That works for me," Phillip said.

So we did two more runs with me, on the floor, snapping the planks together; and him handing me the planks, and cutting the planks that needed to be cut. Then we moved the stove onto the new laminate flooring in the corner.

"Okay," I said. "I'll probably be gone an hour—maybe a little bit longer. If you get all the way across the room—I don't think you will, but you might—don't move the refrigerator out. Wait for me to do that."

"I promise that I will not move that refrigerator by myself," he said.

"Okay, I'll see you in a little while," I said.

I went out to my van, got in, and drove up to Liberty Nursing Center. I parked near the Reagan Wing entrance and entered the building.

"My wife's been transferred to another room. She's in room 421 now. Do you know where that is?" I asked the nurse at the nurses station.

"Yes, I know where that is," the nurse said. "Your wife's been moved to Kennedy Hall." She pointed down the hall. "That's down this hallway all the way to the end. Turn left. Then go all the way down that hallway until you come to a set of double doors. That's Kennedy Hall. Ask a nurse to let you in."

"Thanks," I said, and I started walking down the long hallway. I turned left at the end of the hallway—which is the only way I could turn without exiting the building—and I started down the next hall. That hall wasn't as long. At the end of it there was a nurses station on my right, another hallway to my left, and a set of closed double doors straight ahead.

I pointed to the double doors. "Is that Kennedy Hall in there?" I asked the nurse at the nurses station.

"Yes it is," she said. "Do you want in there?"

"Yes, my wife's in there."

"Just press that big red button on the wall and go in. But go in quick—the alarm's only off for a few seconds."

"Okay." I pointed to a big red button on the wall which was about shoulder high. "This button?"

"That's the button," she said.

I pushed the button, opened the door, and quickly slipped into Kennedy Hall. I pulled the door closed behind me.

I looked at the room numbers. The first room on my right was 429. The first room on the left was room 428. As I walked down the hallway, the numbers descended. I came to room 421.

I looked in Kathy's new room. It wasn't as nice as her room in the Reagan wing. It was small. The furniture was pretty beat up, and there was no television.

And Kathy wasn't in the room.

I looked down to the far end of the hallway. I saw some people, so I started to walk down there.

A nurse's aide came out of one of the rooms. She looked at me quizzically. "May I help you?" she asked.

"I'm looking for Kathleen Stone. I'm her husband," I said.

"Oh, you must be Rupert," she said.

"No. My name's Mark," I said.

She looked confused. "Well, then, who's Rupert?"

"Rupert is our dog," I said.

"Oh, okay." She began laughing. "Rupert is her dog. And we thought that he was her husband. That's funny."

"Do you know where she is?" I asked.

She stopped laughing. "Yeah. I'll take you to her."

We walked down to the end of the hall and rounded the corner. The nurse's aide pointed. "There she is."

Kathy was sitting on the floor against the wall, holding her face in her hands. She was surrounded by three female patients. One was in a wheelchair; one had a walker; and the other was standing without assistance.

I walked up to Kathy and touched her shoulder. "Kathy," I said.

"Don't you touch her!" the old woman in the walker said, angrily.

"Doreen," the nurse's aide said, "that's her husband."

Doreen smiled at me. "Well hi there, Rupert," she said.

"Hi," I said.

I turned to Kathy and held out my hand. She took my hand and looked up at me. "She looks tired," I said to the aide.

"She wore herself out," the aide said. "Since she got here she's been running between this door—" She pointed to the double doors close to us. "—and the one you came in, trying to leave. These three have been following her around."

"Kathy, do you want to get up?" I helped her get to her feet by pulling her up with my hand.

"Are the chickens in?" Kathy asked me.

"Yes, the chickens are in," I said. "And they're up." (Of course, that wasn't true. In the morning before I left for my laminate job, I fed the chickens and opened their door.)

"I need to get going," Kathy said. She pulled free of my hand.

Then the nurse's aide got between Kathy and the double doors.

"The chickens," Kathy said.

"Don't worry about the chickens. I'll let them out," I said, wishing I had answered her question more honestly.

"It's time to go back to your room now, Kathleen," the nurse's aide said. She grabbed ahold of Kathy's arm.

"Come on, Kathy," I said. "Let's go to your room."

The nurse's aide held on to Kathy's arm as she steered Kathy around the corner and down the hall toward her room. I walked along on Kathy's other side.

"What do you mean that your chickens are 'up'?" the nurse's aide asked me.

"That means they're up on the ceiling joists," I said. "That's where they go to sleep at night."

"Are the chickens up?" Kathy asked.

"Probably not," I said. "But I'll go check on the chickens in a little while, okay Kathy? Is that okay?"

"I go," Kathy said.

"No, Kathleen," the nurse's aide said. "You have to go to your room, now." She steered Kathy into room 421.

I followed them into the room.

"Does she go by Kathleen or Kathy?" the nurse's aide asked me.

"Kathy," I said.

"Kathy," the nurse's aide said to Kathy. "I know you're tired. And that foot's still healing. So I want you to lay down and get some rest."

"Foot?" Kathy asked.

I pointed to her right foot. "That thing," I said.

She pointed to her right foot. "That thing?"

"Yeah, Kathy," I said. "Now just lay down, okay?"

"Kay," she said. She laid down on the bed, and the nurse's aide covered her with a blanket. Then the nurse's aide left the room.

I sat down in a chair close to the bed. I didn't talk. I just watched Kathy, hoping she would go to sleep so I could leave. But her eyes were open. She was watching me.

Kathy moved over to the edge of the bed. She patted the mattress beside her. "You lay down right here," she said.

"I have to go pretty soon," I said. "I have to finish a job."

I watched her, and she watched me. After awhile, Kathy began blinking slowly, and then she closed her eyes. I waited a couple minutes, and then I got up and left.

I was heading towards the double doors that I had come in through when someone behind me said, "Mr. Stone." I turned around and stopped. It was the nurse's aide.

"Mr. Stone, if you're leaving, someone has to let you out. Those doors have an alarm," she said as she walked up to me.

"Oh, sorry," I said. "I didn't think about that."

I walked up to the keypad with her. She began punching in numbers.

"The chickens," someone said.

I turned around, and there was Kathy.

"Kathy, you need to stay here," I said. "I'll be back in a couple of hours. Right now, I'm going to go feed the chickens."

"Let me worry about her," the nurse's aide said. "When that light turns green, you just go."

"Okay," I said.

"Okay. I'm going to enter the code again." She punched in the numbers on the key pad and the green light came on.

I quickly opened the door, slipped out, and pushed the door closed behind me.

· · · · ·

When I got back to the job, Phillip was installing the laminate in the hallway.

I walked into the kitchen. It was all done except for underneath the refrigerator. "Wow," I said. "You got a lot more done than I thought you would."

Phillip chuckled. "Once you got out of the way things went pretty quick," he said, as he got up. "I'm gonna hit a cigarette."

"Go for it," I said. "I'll take over."

Phillip went outside to smoke a cigarette, and I measured and cut four planks to finish up the hallway. When he came back in, I was just starting the foyer. We did that together, and then we moved the refrigerator out and did behind it.

"Alright," I said. "Get the quarter round out of my truck and put it on the porch. I'm going to get a couple measurements."

"I'm on it," he said.

I got my measurements and walked out to the saw. "Hand me two sticks of quarter round," I said to Phillip, who was on the porch near the pile of quarter round.

He handed me two sticks of quarter round. I cut one stick square, and the other one at a 45 degree angle. "Now, come here Phillip. I want to show you this."

Phillip approached, and, with a coping saw, I cut out the bare wood on the cut end of the piece of quarter round with the 45 degree angle cut.

"Why are you doing that?"

"You'll see," I said. "Let's go in the house."

We went into the kitchen, over to the corner where our pieces of quarter round were going. I held the square cut piece in place against one side of the corner. "Put a couple nails in that," I said.

He picked up the nail gun and shot two nails in the piece of molding.

I set the coped piece of molding against the other side of the corner, pushing the coped end tight against the square cut molding.

"Put a couple nails in this," I said.

Phillip picked up the nail gun and shot a couple nails in that piece of molding.

"What do you think of that corner?" I asked.

Phillip nodded. "I like it. It looks tight," he said.

"Right," I said. "You know, if you miter your inside corners, you might save a little bit of time. And most of your inside corners might come out looking pretty good. But there's always going to be that one corner that you're just not happy with. And, when you're driving away from the job, you're thinking about that one corner."

Phillip chuckled. "You might lose sleep over that corner."

"You might," I said. "Okay, I'll cut 'em, you nail 'em."

Phillip nailed the molding just as fast as I could measure and cut it. We were done with the quarter round in less than an hour. We moved the refrigerator and stove back in place. Then we moved the table and chairs back into the kitchen.

The job was finished.

"Are you going to go back up to the nursing home?" Phillip asked, as he loaded the trash can full of scrapes into my van.

"Yep," I said. I loaded the saw into the van. "I told Kathy That I'd be back. So…"

"I'll see you tomorrow, Mark," he said. He walked over to his van.

"Alrighty," I said. I got in my van, backed out of the driveway, and headed back up to Liberty Nursing Center.

chapter 21

On Monday, June 8—three weeks after Kathy had been moved to Kennedy Hall—I arrived at Liberty Nursing Center to visit her at about 8:00 PM. I parked my van, and entered the building through the Jefferson Wing entrance, because it was the closest entrance to Kennedy Hall.

I walked through the lobby—which was always deserted after business hours—and then I went down Jefferson Hall to the double doors. I pushed the red button, and quickly slipped into Kennedy Hall.

Amber—who is a day shift nurse—was behind the counter at the nurses station. She noticed me. "I have something for you," she said. Then she began looking around behind the counter.

"You're here awful late, aren't you?" I asked.

"Something came up and Peggy had to call off. So yeah. I'm still here. Unfortunately."

"Well, look at bright side, Amber. You'll get a bigger paycheck," I said.

She looked up and smiled. "Now you know my secret," she said. "That's the real reason I'm here: I need money."

"Don't we all," I said.

"Oh here it is," she said. She picked up a white envelope and handed it to me. "This is for you."

I looked at the envelope. Except for having my name on it, it was blank. "What is this?" I asked.

"It's a subpoena," she said, and then she smiled again.

Amber came out from behind the counter. "Kathy's in the activity room," she said. "She's been waiting for you."

I followed Amber into the activity room—which was directly across the hall from the nurses station.

Kathy was sitting at a table across from an old white haired woman. There were several other patients in the room. And the television was on, but no one seemed to be watching it. Everyone seemed to be in their own little world.

Amber walked up to Kathy. "Kathy, guess who's here?"

Kathy turned around. When she saw me, her face lit up. "Are we going?" she asked, getting up from her chair.

"No, we're—" I started to say. But Kathy walked right past me and left the activity room.

I followed her out, and then Amber came out of the activity room.

Kathy was standing next to the double doors.

"Now why are you standing over there?" Amber asked Kathy.

"The chickens," Kathy said.

"Mark can feed your chickens," Amber said, and then she looked at me. "Have you been feeding her chickens?"

"Every morning," I said.

"See, Kathy, you don't have to worry about your chickens." Amber took Kathy by the hand and led her away from the doors. "Your wife's getting pretty slick," she said. "She stands in the corner by the door, and when the door opens from the outside, she slips out—and she doesn't set the alarm off. She did that twice today."

"That's pretty clever," I said, laughing.

Amber let go of Kathy's hand, and opened the half door to go back into the nurses station. But she stopped, half way in, to watch Kathy.

Kathy was eying the medication cart which was parked in front of the nurses station. On top of the cart there were four or five one ounce plastic cups. Each cup had pills in it.

Kathy reached over and picked up one of the cups.

Amber grabbed Kathy's wrist. "Kathy, give me that," she said. "Those aren't for you." She took the cup out of Kathy's hand and put it back on the cart.

"Just curious," Kathy said.

"Do you want some hot chocolate?" Amber asked her.

Kathy didn't answer. But she seemed interested.

"You do want hot chocolate, don't you?" Amber looked at me. "Take her back into the activity room, please."

"Sure," I said. Kathy was already looking at me. So I walked into the activity room and she followed me.

I pulled out the chair that Kathy had been sitting in and Kathy sat down. I sat down in a chair next to her.

I opened up the envelope, took out the paper, and unfolded it. The letter was from Liberty Nursing Center. I scanned the page and didn't see the words "amount due" anywhere on it.

Amber brought in two cups of hot chocolate. She set one in front of Kathy, and the other one in front of the old woman sitting across from her.

I put the paper back in the envelope, unread.

"Do you want a cup of hot chocolate?" Amber asked me.

"Yes, thank you," I said.

Kathy reached across the table for the cup of hot chocolate setting in front of the old woman. I grabbed her wrist before she could get to it. "Kathy, that one's not yours. You drink yours."

"Kay," she said.

I let go of her wrist, and she took a sip out of her own cup.

Amber brought me a cup of hot chocolate. "Thanks," I said.

I relaxed and enjoyed my hot chocolate—for about a minute. Then Kathy got up from the table.

"Kathy, where are you going?"

Kathy walked out of the activity room.

A nurse's aide, Casey, had been standing in the corner watching the patients. "She'd better not be going into Anna's room," Casey said.

"Is she going in my room?" Anna got up from the table and grabbed her walker.

I hurried to get out of the activity room in front of Anna.

Now Kennedy Hall is an L-shaped hall. At the bottom side of the L, there are three separate spaces. At the corner of the L there is a large room. Next to that there is a lounge area. And the nurses station is next to the lounge area.

The large room was Anna's room. The door was closed, and Kathy was about to open it.

"Kathy, don't!" I shouted.

"What?" Kathy said, as she opened the door.

"That's my room!" Anna shouted.

I reached Kathy before she went in. "Kathy, you can't go in there," I said. I put my arm around her and steered her in the opposite direction.

"Just curious," Kathy said.

"Call the police!" Anna shouted.

"Anna, she didn't do anything," Casey said.

"She's a crook! And so is that crazy nut!" Anna pointed at me.

"Anna, that's her husband," Casey said.

"No he's not. He found her in the street, and he makes money off of her."

"Anna, that's not very nice," Casey said, laughing.

I started laughing too. "Come on, Kathy," I said. "Let's go to your room."

I took Kathy by the hand, and we walked down the hallway, toward her room.

"Here's your room, Kathy."

She pulled free of my hand and continued walking down the hall.

"Where are you going?"

I followed her down to the double doors that lead to outside of the unit. She went into the corner next to the doors and turned around.

"Come on, Kathy. Let's go to your room."

"The chickens," she said.

"In a couple days, Kathy, you will see your chickens. But you have to stay here until then. Just a couple more days, Kathy. Okay."

"Kay," she said.

We walked back to her room. She went over to the window and looked at a picture that was taped to it. It was a picture of our chickens. I brought it in because she was always talking about the chickens. It was Amber's idea to tape the picture to the window, because Kathy would frequently look out the window, searching for chickens.

"One, two, three, four, five..." she said, as she looked at the picture.

I opened the envelope, took out the letter, and read it:

Dear Mr. Stone,

Your wife, Kathleen Stone, is scheduled to be discharged on Friday, June 12, 2015. A post-discharge care meeting is scheduled for Wednesday, June 10, 2015, at 10:30 AM. As her primary caregiver, your attendance is required.

Thank you,

Jeff Miller, Head Nurse

On the way out, I stopped to talk to Amber, who was behind the counter at the nurses station.

"Who is Jeff Miller?" I asked. "Is he that big bearded guy that I see around here once in awhile?"

"That's him," she said.

"Is he the head nurse?"

She thought about it. "Supposedly. But some of us don't think so. Why?"

"He's the one that issued the subpoena."

"I was only kidding about that."

"No you weren't," I said. I punched in the code on the key pad, and left.

· · · · ·

I arrived for the meeting at 10:22 AM. I parked the PT Cruiser in the front parking lot and walked into the Jefferson Wing lobby.

"Excuse me, I'm here for Kathleen Stone's post-discharge care meeting," I said to Lori, the receptionist.

"The meeting will be in the conference room. Do you know where that is?"

"No."

She got up from her desk and came out to the main part of the lobby. "Go straight down this hall. Do you know where the main dining room is?"

"Yes."

"So," she said. "Go straight down this hallway. Down there—where the main activity room is—at that intersection, turn right. On the right, then, that's the main dining room—you know where that is, right? Well across from that, that's the conference room."

"The conference room is across from the main dining room," I said.

"Yes," she said.

"Thank you."

I walked down the hall and turned right. There was an open door across from the main dining room. I went into that room.

The conference room at Liberty Nursing Center was a large room with dark paneled walls. There was one picture window. Cabinets were around two sides of the room, and a large rectangular table—which was probably about twelve feet long—sat in the middle of the room. Chairs were set around the table on all sides.

I sat down in the chair at the end of the table that was closest to the door. There was one other person in the room—a woman. She was sitting at the other end of the table, in the first chair on the side which was to my right.

"Are you Mark Stone?" the woman asked me.

"Yes," I said.

"I should introduce myself," she said. "I'm Lisa Hartman. I'm with Ohio Hospice."

"I'm pleased to meet you," I said.

"I might as well get started," she said, as she got up from her chair. She came down to my end of the table and handed me a red folder. "This will explain our range of services."

"Thanks," I said, taking the folder. "I'll look it over." I set the folder on the table.

"Our name is 'hospice', but we also provide palliative care—and many other in-home nursing services. Here's my card."

I accepted the card from her and looked at it. "Okay," I said. Then I put the card in my shirt pocket.

"Call us if you'd like someone to come out and discuss our services with you, or if you have any questions whatsoever."

"I'll do that," I said.

"We accept most insurance plans, and, of course, we accept Medicare and Medicaid."

"That's good to know."

She went back to the other end of the table and sat down.

A couple minutes later, Jeff Miller walked in. He was followed by Polly, the social worker. He sat at the end of the table directly across from me. Polly sat across from Lisa.

Jeff leaned forward, resting his elbows on the table. "Why don't we start by introducing ourselves," he said.

Lisa went first. "I've already introduced myself to Mr. Stone, but I'm Lisa Hartman. I'm an RN with Ohio Hospice."

"I'm Polly Jenkins. I'm the social worker here at Liberty Nursing Center."

"And I'm Jeff Miller. I'm the head nurse here at Liberty Nursing Center."

The three of them were looking at me. "Oh," I said. "I'm Mark Stone."

"Mr. Stone," Jeff began, "I want you to know that here at Liberty Nursing Center, we truly care about our patients. We care about our patients even after they leave."

Polly nodded, but not with much enthusiasm.

Jeff was looking at me, so I said, "That's great."

"Kathleen is going to be discharged on Friday," he said.

"I already know that," I said.

"We have no medical reason to keep her past Friday."

"Right. I know that too."

"Pick up time is 11:00 AM. Now she has to be gone *before* 11:00 AM, or we will charge for an extra day at the private pay rate, which is currently three hundred and twenty dollars per day."

"It's three hundred and sixty-three dollars per day," Polly said. "It went up last month."

"Well, you don't have to worry about me being late. I will be here before 11:00 AM."

Jeff folded his arms over his chest and leaned back in his chair. "What we want to know, Mr. Stone, is what are your plans for Kathleen's care after she is discharged?"

I looked at him. "What do you mean?"

"I don't think that's a hard question," he said. "Or it shouldn't be."

"Well, I plan to take her home. Is that what you want to know?"

"Mr. Stone, I know you work, and I know you visit your wife every day. That's a good thing. But I'm told that sometimes you come in as late as nine o'clock at night."

"Once I came in at nine o'clock," I said. "Usually I come in at four or five."

"Do you plan to continue working?"

"Probably not as much," I said.

"Probably not as much? Mr. Stone, Kathleen needs twenty-four hour a day care. Someone has to be with her at all times."

"I agree," Polly said.

"At all times? I'm not so sure about that," I said.

"Well I *am* sure about that, Mr. Stone," Jeff said. "And I'll be honest: I'm very concerned about this discharge. I *will* be alerting Adult Protective Services and have them monitor the situation at your home—just to make sure that Kathleen is getting the care that she needs."

"Thanks for the heads up," I said, getting up from the table.

I was angry when I left the meeting, and, as I walked toward the lobby, leaving the building was the only thing on my mind. But then I remembered that I had not seen Kathy yet. So, instead of going through the lobby, I turned right and went down the hall that leads to Kennedy Hall.

I pushed the red button and went in. Amber was at the nursing station. I think she noticed that I was upset.

"Did you enjoy your meeting with Jeff?" she asked.

"That guy is an asshole," I said.

She started laughing. "I'd better not say anything," she said, and then she laughed some more.

· · · · ·

The next day—Thursday, June 11, 2015—was the last day that I installed carpet. Actually, it was the last day that I installed flooring of any kind.

We had an easy job. It was a pad replacement job in a basement that had flooded in late April. The customer called me right after the flood. I told him to take up the old, soaking wet pad, and throw it away. Then, when his carpet completely dries out, he should call me back.

He called me back in the first week of June, and I sold him some new pad.

Our job now was to clean up the floor underneath the existing carpet, install new padding; and, after that, to stretch the carpet back into place.

It was a nice day. The sky was clear. The air was comfortable— probably about seventy degrees, and dry. On days like this one, I liked to do as much work outside as I could.

I was cutting pad in the driveway. I needed three twenty-five foot runs.

Phillip came outside. He put a cigarette in his mouth and lit it. He inhaled deeply, and then blew out a cloud of smoke. "So you're really calling it quits, huh?"

"Yeah," I said. "I've been thinking about it awhile, and now just seems like a good time."

"It's a good time because that asshole male nurse is siccing Adult Protective Services on you."

"No," I said. "Well, that is something to keep in mind. But, no, that's not the whole ball of wax."

Phillip took a drag off his cigarette. "Why can't people mind their own business?" he said. "My next door neighbors are just like that asshole nurse. They're always calling Child Protective Services on the people across the street—and they don't know shit about what's going on over there. They just like fucking with other people. That's all it is."

"Yeah," I said.

"Does he blame you for the cut on Kathy's foot getting infected?"

"Probably," I said.

"Now that's a bunch of shit," he said. "Especially coming from the head nurse of a nursing home. You know, people get bedsores so bad in those places that they die. That happens all the time. And they never think they did anything wrong."

"Yeah, I know," I said.

"You know, if that asshole had run his mouth at me like he did at you, I probably would have kicked his ass."

I laughed, and said, "He's a pretty big guy."

"Well maybe I would've got my ass kicked, then," he said, laughing.

"No, Phillip," I said, "I think you could take him. I was just telling you why I didn't kick his ass."

Phillip laughed. He flicked the glowing end of his cigarette off with his finger, tapped the butt on the palm of his hand, and then put it in his pocket. "I'd better go help Zac move furniture," he said. He walked into the garage, and then down to the basement.

I cut my third run of pad and rolled it up. I carried the three runs of pad, one by one, down to the basement. I set them in a pile near the room where they go. Then I measured the next room—seventeen feet. I went back outside to cut two seventeen foot runs.

We finished the job a few minutes after two o'clock, and we were all—the three of us—walking back and forth between the basement and our vans, packing up pad scrapes and our tools.

When we were all packed up, I walked over to Zac. "Zac," I said, pulling out my wallet. "Here's a hundred dollars for your work today." I handed him a hundred dollar bill. "And, because we'll probably never work together again, here." I handed him another hundred dollar bill. "I've enjoyed working with you."

"Thanks, Mark," Zac said. He folded the bills and put them in his pocket. "I've enjoyed working with you. I'd give you a hundred dollars too, but I don't have it on me right now."

We both laughed.

"Phillip," I said.

"Yeah?"

I pulled two hundred dollar bills out of my wallet and handed them to him. "This is your share of the pot," I said.

"Thanks," he said.

"One more thing," I said, walking over to my van. I opened the side door and picked up my crab jack. "I want to give you this."

"You mean to borrow," he said, taking the tool.

"No. To keep."

"Are you sure about that, Mark? I mean, what are you going to do if you decide to do another carpet job some day?"

"If I ever need a crab jack again, I'll go to Southland and I'll buy a new one."

Phillip nodded. "Yeah, I suppose you could do that."

"Look," I said. "Anyone who calls me to do a carpet job, I'm going to give them your number. If it's a tile or a laminate job, then I'm giving them Ray's number. But I'm steering all of the carpet work your way. So I want to make sure you have all the tools you need."

"Well," he said, raising the crab jack to shoulder level, "you know I'll put it to good use."

"I know you will," I said.

. . . . .

On Friday morning, June 12, I woke up and got out of bed a few minutes after seven o'clock. I had set the alarm on the clock on top of my dresser for 8:00 AM—just in case I needed it. I didn't. I shut off the alarm and went out to the kitchen.

I pushed the power switch on the coffee maker. Then I got a Beggin' Strip from the bag on the refrigerator. I threw the Beggin' Strip out the front door. Rupert dashed out after it.

The coffee maker finished filling the coffee pot. I poured a cup of coffee and sat down at the kitchen table.

It was a sunny day. Kathy would not be home until much later in the morning—probably between eleven o'clock and noon. As I sipped my coffee, I debated whether to let the chickens out now—which, I'm sure, was what they wanted me to do—or to wait until I brought Kathy home, so Kathy and I could do that together—that was what I wanted to do because it seemed much easier.

In the end, the chickens won the argument.

I let the chickens out, collected the eggs, and brought them back to the house. I set the egg basket, which was full of dirty eggs, on the counter next to the sink. I figured I'd wash them later.

I went to our bedroom closet and pulled out Kathy's favorite suitcase. It hadn't been used in years, and it was very dusty. So I set it on the kitchen table and wiped it down with a wet towel.

Then I opened the suitcase. There were still some clothes in it from the last time she used it. I put those in her dresser drawer.

It was a few minutes after nine o'clock when I went out the back door with the suitcase. I got into the PT Cruiser, started it up, and drove to Liberty Nursing Center.

I went into Kennedy Hall. Amber was behind the counter at the nursing station.

"You're here early," she said.

"I know," I said. "I made it a point to be."

"Well Kathy's not up yet."

"That's all right."

I carried the empty suitcase around the corner, down the hall, and into Kathy's room.

"Kathy," I said softly.

She opened her eyes, sighed, and then closed them.

I put the suitcase on a chair and opened it up.

I stood next to the bed and looked at her. "You're going home today," I said.

She opened her eyes. "What?"

"Do you want to get going? Do you want to go home?"

"Get going?"

"Yes. Get going. Get going home. You're going home today."

She smiled, so I think she understood what I said.

I walked over to the closet. *What should Kathy wear today?* I glanced at Kathy. She didn't have any preferences—none that she could express, anyway. The decision was mine.

I took a pair of green pants off a hanger. Because she always wears green pants. Then I found her John Deere top. I took that off its hanger, because I liked the way she looked wearing her John Deere top.

I set the green pants and the John Deere top on the foot of her bed. Then I took all the other clothes off hangers and put them in the suitcase.

"Are you going to get up?"

She didn't answer.

I opened up the top drawer on the dresser. I gathered up all her

socks and sports bras and put them in the suitcase. There was a stack
of diapers in the drawer too. I didn't want to pack those, because
they belonged to Liberty Nursing Center, not us.

Amber came into the room. She got close to Kathy's face, and
said, "Rise and shine, Kathy. Time to get up."

Kathy got out of bed and looked at Amber.

"You need to go to the bathroom," Amber said.

"Do you have to tell her to go to the bathroom?" I asked.

"Don't you do that at home?"

"No," I said. "She knows when she needs to use the bathroom."

"Things might be different now," Amber said.

"She's only been away from home for five weeks."

"True—five weeks is not a long time. But Kathy has dementia,"
Amber said. "And, she had a bad infection. That's all better now. But
with dementia patients, their dementia gets worse when anything
else goes wrong with them—a cold, the flu, an infection—anything.
And those things might get better. But the dementia never does. I
know. I've been working with dementia patients for a long time."

"How old are you?" I asked.

"I'm thirty-two, smarty pants."

"You haven't even been alive for a long time."

Amber laughed. "I knew you were going to say that."

Amber picked up the green pants off Kathy's bed. She walked
over to the dresser and took a diaper out of the open drawer. "The
rest of these can go home with her," she said.

"I didn't buy those."

Amber looked at me. "Kathy's insurance company bought them,
believe me."

"Alright, I'll take them," I said. "Maybe I'll need them." I went
over to the drawer and got the stack of diapers. I broke them up into
three piles and put them in the suitcase.

I waited while Kathy and Amber were in the bathroom.

Amber pushed the door open a few inches. "Could you hand me
a pair of socks? And her shoes please?"

"Sure." I picked up a pair of socks out of the suitcase, and then I
began looking around for her shoes.

"Her shoes are in the bottom drawer of the dresser."

I got the shoes, and then I opened the bathroom door. I handed the shoes and the socks to Amber.

"Thank you," she said.

I watched as Amber disposed of Kathy's used diaper. Then she put the fresh one on her, along with her pants, socks and shoes—all while Kathy sat on the toilet.

When they came out of the bathroom, Amber pulled Kathy's nightgown off her over the top of her head. She picked the John Deere top up from the bed. "Is this what you want her to wear?"

"Yeah."

Amber put the top over Kathy's head.

"Isn't she able to dress herself anymore?" I asked.

Amber thought about the question. "I honestly don't know. We've been dressing her. Maybe we should have encouraged her to dress herself? She is here for rehab, after all."

"That's what I'll probably do."

"Encourage her?" Amber said. She helped Kathy get her arms through the arms of the John Deere top. Then she straightened it out.

"Yes. That, and she'll probably wear more button shirts. She has a bunch of those at home."

"Doesn't Kathy look nice today, Mark?"

"Uh-huh."

"I'm going to brush her hair." Amber went into the bathroom and opened the medicine cabinet.

All of a sudden, Kathy seemed very interested in what she was hearing—which was a cart rolling in the hallway. The cart rolled past the open doorway. It was a yellow cleaning cart, being pushed by a cleaning person. When Kathy saw the cleaning person, she walked out of the room to follow her.

Amber came out of the bathroom holding a hair brush. "Where did she go?"

I laughed. "A cleaning cart went by, and she took off after it."

"Oh," Amber said. "She left to see her friend."

"Should I go get her?"

"No. She's fine. You can finish packing her stuff. Just bring her up to the nurses station before you leave. I'll brush her hair up there. Also, I have some papers for you to sign."

"Alright," I said.

Amber left the room. I finished packing Kathy's things. Then I looked through all the drawers on the dresser, and I checked the medicine cabinet. The last thing I needed to pack was the picture of our chickens, which was taped to the window. I ripped it trying to peel it off. So I threw it away.

I picked up the suitcase and left the room.

Kathy was three doors down. She was standing outside a room, looking in. I walked up and stood next to her. Her friend, the cleaning person, was pushing the cleaning cart out of the room.

"Hi Kathy," she said, as she pushed the cleaning cart out into the hallway. She looked at me. "My name's Debra," she said.

"My name's Mark Stone. I'm Kathy's husband."

"I know," she said. She reached into her pocket and pulled out a Halloween sized Three Musketeer candy bar.

Kathy chuckled when she saw the candy bar. She reached for it, and Debra let her take it out of her hand.

"I give her candy," Debra said.

"That's okay," I said. I looked at Kathy. "Come on, Kathy."

Kathy followed me down to the nurses station. When we got there, she handed me her candy bar wrapper.

"Thank you," I said.

"What is she eating?" Amber asked.

"Debra gave her a candy bar."

"Oh. Of course." She opened the half door. "Kathy, come in here and sit down. I'm going to brush your hair."

Kathy went into the nurses station.

"Sit down, Kathy," Amber said, pointing to a chair.

"Sit down?" Kathy asked.

"Sit down."

Kathy sat down in the chair, and Amber began brushing her hair. "Mark, I put the papers you need to sign on the counter. There should be three of them."

"I see them," I said. I threw the candy bar wrapper at a trash can behind the counter and missed. "I missed your trash can."

"Don't worry about it," Amber said, brushing Kathy's hair.

I signed the top two papers. I looked over the third one and didn't see any place to sign it. "Where do I sign this one?" I asked, holding up the paper.

"Let me see that," Amber said. She stopped brushing Kathy's hair and came up to the counter.

Kathy got up from the chair.

"Hm. Well I'll be darn," Amber said, looking over the paper.

Kathy walked behind me.

"I could have sworn you had to sign that one, but I guess you don't."

Kathy opened one of the double doors and the alarm went off—beep, beep, beep, beep, beep.

"Kathy, come back here," Amber said. She came out of the nurses station and hurried out the double doors after Kathy.

When she came back with Kathy—probably less than a minute later—she punched the code into the key pad to shut the alarm off.

"Isn't it funny," Kathy said.

I laughed. "It is funny."

Amber started laughing. "Yeah, I guess it is," she said.

I picked up the suitcase and looked at Kathy. "Well, we're going," I said.

"We're going," Kathy said.

Amber pushed in the code on the keypad, again, and opened the door. "Now you may go," she said to Kathy.

We walked out to the PT Cruiser and drove home.

chapter 22

"So, Mark, how is retirement treating you?"

"Mom, this isn't exactly a dream retirement, you know. "I'm not golfing, or fishing, or traveling around the country in an RV. I'm sitting around the house taking care of Kathy. And that's my job—every single day."

"Yes, Mark, but Kathy absolutely adores you. That must be worth something."

"She adores me? What makes you say that?"

"Oh, Mark, I can tell by the way she looks at you."

It occurred to me that my mother's memories of Kathy were old memories. She hadn't seen Kathy in over two years—not since April, 2013. That's when Kathy and I went up to Sylvania to help move her into an apartment in the Mayberry Village Retirement Community. And the time before that was probably Christmas, 2011.

"Mom, I know Kathy loves me; and I love her too. It's just that we can't go anywhere anymore. Kathy has a lot of anxiety in unfamiliar surroundings, and her instinct is to just get the hell out of there—wherever it is. She's fine here at home. And she's okay in the stores that we go to. But that's it."

"I wish you could come up and visit with your family, Mark. I miss you. We all miss you."

"Mom, I can't take Kathy away from home for a whole day like that. She'd go nuts."

"And that's a crying shame, Mark. You spend your whole life looking for a loving relationship, you finally find it, and now this happens."

I heard a knocking on the back door. "Mom, I have to get going. Someone's at the back door."

"Okay, Mark. Take good care of Kathy. But take care of yourself, too."

"I will, Mom. Love ya."

"I love you too Mark. Bye."

"Bye Mom."

I tapped the hang up icon on my cell phone and put the phone in my shirt pocket.

I heard the knocking again.

I walked out to the kitchen. "Just a minute," I said, looking out at the woman through the back door window.

I got a Beggin' Strip from the bag on top of the refrigerator and went to the front door. I opened the door and threw the Beggin' Strip out to the front yard. Rupert dashed out after it, and I closed the door.

I went to the back door and opened it.

"Good morning," the woman said.

"Good morning."

"My name's Mary Cox. I'm with Adult Protective Services." She handed me a card.

I looked at the card. "Adult Protective Services. Hmm," I said.

"Does Kathleen Stone live in this home?"

"She does," I said. "But she's sleeping right now. I'll have her call you when she gets up." I started to close the door.

The social worker held out her hand to stop the door from closing. "Someone has expressed concern that Kathleen may be in danger here."

"Really? Now who expressed that concern?" I asked.

"I'm not at liberty to say," she said. "May I come in?"

"Be my guest," I said, stepping aside to let her in.

"Big kitchen," she said, walking through the kitchen. She frowned when she looked around the living room. "You have a lot of things in here," she said.

"We're hoarders," I said.

"Well, you do have a pathway to get to the door in case of fire. So I guess it's all right."

The social worker turned her head to look down the hallway. I looked too. Kathy was standing in the bedroom doorway, her eyes half opened.

"You must be Kathleen," the social worker said.

Kathy didn't respond verbally, of course. She just opened her eyes and looked at the woman suspiciously.

"Kathy, do you have to use the bathroom?" I asked.

"Yeah," she said.

Kathy walked into the bathroom.

I went to the kitchen to get a plastic bag, and then I went into our bedroom to get a clean pair of pants, Kathy's tennis shoes, a pair of socks, and a fresh Depend. I took the stuff into the bathroom and closed the door.

Kathy was sitting on the toilet, peeing.

"Are you finished?"

"Yeah."

I handed her a small wad of toilet paper.

Then I got down on the floor. I pulled off her pants and used Depend, putting the used Depend in a plastic bag and tying it. Then I put her feet through the leg holes of the fresh Depend. I slid those up her ankles a little bit, and took the dirty socks off her feet. I put clean socks on her, and then the clean pants, leaving them around her ankles. Then I put on her shoes.

"Stand up, Kathy."

Kathy stood, and I pulled up her Depend and her pants.

I washed my hands. Kathy opened the door and walked out of the bathroom.

When I came out of the bathroom, Kathy and the social worker were standing in the hallway looking at each other.

"My name is Mary," the social worker said, speaking very slowly. "I came her to see if you need anything." The social worker looked at me. "I look them in the eye and speak to them like their small children. It usually works."

"Oh, it's working! I can tell."

She looked back into Kathy's eyes. "Your wife has pretty eyes," she said.

"I've always thought so."

"Do you need anything, Kathleen?" The social worker stared into Kathy's eyes, waiting for a response. Finally she looked away. "I don't think she like me," she said.

"Can we have supper?" Kathy asked.

"Does she think it's suppertime?"

"No," I said to the social worker.

I went into the kitchen and poured some Honey Nut Cheerios into a bowl. I put the bowl on the table. Kathy sat down in her chair. Then I poured some milk on the cereal and handed Kathy a spoon. She began eating her breakfast.

The social worker looked around the kitchen for awhile, and then she wandered into the living room.

I followed her into the living room.

"You have a lot of cob webs," she said.

"I was just about to dust when you came to the door," I said.

She walked into the bathroom.

"I'm planning to clean the bathroom this afternoon," I said. I walked over to the bathroom doorway.

When she looked down into the toilet bowl her facial expression turned into a scowl. Then she looked over the bathtub. She picked up a bar of soap off a ledge on the shower wall. "This soap looks pretty dry," she said.

I couldn't think of anything to say about that. So I said, "Thank you."

She came out of the bathroom, peeked into our bedroom, and then she went back into the kitchen. She turned the cold water on and let the water run into the sink for a few seconds. Then she turned off the cold water and turned on the hot water.

"Why are you doing that?"

"Just making sure you have hot and cold running water," she said. "You'd be surprised."

I shook my head. *This is ridiculous.*

The social worker held her hand under the stream of water. When she was satisfied that the water was getting warmer, she turned off the faucet.

Kathy looked up at me. "Are the chickens out?"

"No. They're still in," I said.

Kathy got up from the table. She walked over to the back door and looked out the back door window. Her eyes moved back and forth, scanning the chicken yard.

"They're still in," I said again. "No one let them out."

"No one let them out," Kathy said quietly, to herself. Then she picked up the green gallon jug, and she took it over to the sink and began filling it with water.

"Is that for the chickens?" the social worker asked.

"Yes," I said.

(About a year earlier, Kathy had stopped adding the powdered stuff to the chicken's water. I noticed that she had quit adding the stuff, but I never asked her about it. Instead, I checked the shells on the eggs. The powdered stuff—whatever it was—was suppose to make the shells on the chickens' eggs harder. The shells didn't seem to be getting any softer. So I didn't worry about the powdered stuff not being in their water.)

When the jug was full, Kathy turned off the water and screwed the cap back on the top of the jug. Then she carried the jug to the back door.

I walked up to her, and she handed me an egg basket, which had been sitting on a table next to the door. "I think you take this," she said.

Kathy opened the back door and I gently pushed it shut.

"Kathy, we can't let the chickens out right now," I said. "We have a guest."

"Guessed?"

"Yes, a guest."

"What's 'guessed'?" She seemed confused.

"Someone's here." I pointed to the social worker. "Her."

Kathy looked at the social worker. "That one?"

"Yes. That one. We can let the chickens out after that one leaves."

Still looking at the social worker, Kathy said, "I think that one can leave."

The social worker looked at me. "Is she asking me to leave?"

I laughed. "I believe she is."

"Well I'm almost done here," she said. "I just have a couple questions."

"Alright, ask," I said.

"Do you have a job, Mr. Stone?"

"No."

She seemed surprised. "You don't have a job."

"That's correct: I don't have a job."

"I was lead to believe that you do have a job."

"Who lead you to believe that?"

"I'm not at liberty to divulge that information, Mr. Stone."

"Okay," I said. "This person who told you that I had a job—this person has the right to remain anonymous. Is that what you're saying?"

"I don't want to argue with you, Mr. Stone. It's our policy."

"If I were accused of a crime, I'd have the right to face my accuser, wouldn't I?"

"No one's accusing you of a crime, Mr. Stone. I have just one more question."

"Alright," I said, calming down.

"Do you ever leave Kathleen home alone?"

"No. If I go somewhere, she goes with me."

"That's all I wanted to know. Thank you, Mr. Stone."

"Your welcome," I said, opening the door.

Kathy walked out the door.

"It was nice meeting you, Mrs. Stone," the social worker said as Kathy was climbing down the steps of our deck.

After the social worker got out of the house, I stepped out and closed the back door. I looked over to the garage. Kathy was waiting for me at the garage entry door—even though that door was unlocked.

I walked across the yard and opened the door on the garage. Kathy and I entered the garage. Then I opened the door to the chicken house. We entered the chicken house.

The chickens were all on the floor. Kathy set their water jug down and opened their door to let them out. I set the egg basket on a bail of straw and picked up their water bowl.

When I took the water bowl outside to the spigot, I noticed that the county car was still on our property. As I rinsed out the water bowl, I strained to look into the car's windows. The social worker appeared to be writing something—probably a report, I thought.

I took the clean water bowl back into the chicken house and set it on the floor. Kathy filled it with water. Then she filled up their food bowl while I collected the eggs.

It was a good day for eggs. I collected ten: two green ones, two white ones, and six brown ones.

As we walked back to the house, I glanced over at the county car. The social worker waved at me. I didn't wave back. *Why is she still here?* I wondered.

We climbed the deck steps and went into the house.

"Can I play the music?" Kathy asked.

"Yeah."

Kathy set the jug down on the floor and went into the living room. She turned on her boom box.

I carried the eggs over to the kitchen sink. I filled one half of the sink with lukewarm water. One by one, I dropped the eggs into the water.

I washed, rinsed, and dried the first three eggs and placed them in a cardboard egg carton. Then, out of curiosity, I walked over to the back door and looked out the window.

The social worker was still there.

Now, I wasn't worried about what she was putting in her report. What's the worst thing she could say? That we both needed showers? That we were slobs? What bothered me was that someone—the social worker—was sitting in a county car, on my property, doing paperwork. It just didn't seem right. The police never do that. Cops drive to parking lots to sit and fill out forms and write reports.

I went back to the sink. I washed three more eggs, and then I went back to the window in the back door.

She was still there.

I decided to go out and have a word with the social worker.

I approached the car, not sure what I was going to say. I tapped on the driver's side window.

The social worker rolled the window down. The car was idling and the air conditioner was on. Cool air rushed out the open window. "Yes," she said.

"Do you want me to call you a tow truck or something?" I asked.

"Oh, I'm sorry," she said. "I'll leave if I'm bothering you. It's just so peaceful out here."

"Thanks," I said. "Kathy would appreciate it."

She drove to the end of the driveway. I waited until she pulled out on the road before I climbed our deck steps.

chapter 23

One of the things I noticed, after I brought Kathy home from Liberty Nursing Center, was that she was now in the habit of napping during the day. Almost every day, after we let the chickens out, she would come back to the house, play music on her boom box for a few minutes, and then go back to bed and sleep until two or three in the afternoon.

She might have been taking long naps back in the days when I was leaving her home alone all day and going to work. I wouldn't know.

Another habit that I noticed after I brought her home was that she would get up in the middle of the night and play music on her boom box. I know this never happened when I was working, but after I retired, it happened three or four times a week.

And she never asked my permission to play music—like she would do during the day. Although, to be fair, that was probably my fault.

On many occasions, I noticed her standing next to the bed on my side in the middle of the night. She'd stand there for awhile, looking at me, while I pretended to be asleep; and then she'd go out to the living room and play music on her boom box.

I could never sleep with all that noise in the next room—even when I'd get up and shut the bedroom door. So the next morning, I'd be tired, and the idea of taking a nap appealed to me too.

The trouble was: I wasn't used to sleeping in the middle of the day.

What I discovered—and I'm not recommending this. But I discovered that a few beers for breakfast made it very easy to fall asleep during the day. I should also mention that this beer-for-breakfast method to promote napping was most effective when beer was the only thing that I had for breakfast. If, for example, I ate sausage and eggs after I got up, and then drank beer on top of that, it would take seven or eight beers to make me sleepy enough to take a nap. On the other hand, on mornings when beer was the only thing that I consumed, then four or five beers would do the trick.

Needless to say, in the early days of my retirement, my beer consumption was on the rise. '

* * * * *

Around late February, or early March, 2016, I began having stomach problems. Now, for as long as I can remember, I have, occasionally, had heartburn or indigestion. And I'd take Tums for that. But these stomach problems were different than that.

For one thing, I couldn't hold down solid foods. Every time I'd eat something—like chili, or scrambled eggs, or a roast beef sandwich—I'd become nauseous, and I'd have to walk over to a trash can. I'd begin retching, and eventually I'd vomit.

I did hold down beer better than solid foods. But even beer I couldn't hold down completely. If, for example, I drank three beers, that would soon be followed by pain in my stomach, and then the retching and the vomiting. The volume of the vomit, however, would only be equal to one beer or less. (I know this because I began keeping a large bowl near me when I drank beer.) So I was still able to get some nutrients into my system—from the beer that didn't come up. But I don't believe that was enough, because I was beginning to feel lightheaded.

I tried eating different foods to see if there was something that I could hold down. Soups didn't work. Mashed potatoes didn't work. Even beef jerky with beer didn't work.

So, as a last resort, I decided to go to Urgent Care.

* * * * *

Kathy and I walked into the small Urgent Care building in Xenia. I walked up to the reception window.

"May I help you, sir?" the nurse, who was sitting at a desk close to the window, asked.

"I've been having stomach problems," I said.

"What kind of stomach problems?" she asked.

"I think I have a bleeding ulcer."

"I'll tell the doctor," she said. "You can have a seat in the waiting room."

I looked at Kathy. "Kathy, let's sit down."

"Kay," she said.

We sat down in the waiting room, which was empty except for the two of us. Kathy was surprisingly calm. That might have been because she knew that we were there for me, and not for her.

Anyway, we weren't there very long. After about a minute, the nurse came out to the waiting room and told me: "So, I talked to the doctor, and he said that we have no way of diagnosing a bleeding ulcer here. He recommends that you go to an ER."

"Go to an ER," I sighed. "Oh boy."

"If you have a regular doctor, you can go to him."

"I don't," I said. I stood up. "Come on, Kathy." I looked at the nurse. "Thanks anyway."

"Sorry," she said.

Kathy and I walked out of the building. We got into the PT Cruiser. But before I put the key in the ignition, I took a few moments to think about where I wanted to go.

I didn't want to go to the ER—if I could possibly avoid it. We were still paying bills from Kathy's trip to the ER, and that was almost a year ago. We couldn't afford another trip to the ER. On the other hand, the problems that I was having with my stomach might be serious. I hadn't been able to hold down solid foods for almost two months. I was lightheaded. I'd been noticing that I was getting weaker. So something had to be done.

I retched, and spit several time in a cup that I had been keeping in the PT Cruiser for that purpose. Then I started the car and drove to Drake Memorial Hospital. We parked near the Emergency Room entrance.

We went into the emergency room and walked up to a large desk where a nurse was sitting.

"Can I help you?" the nurse asked.

"I hope so," I said. "I've been having some serious problems with my stomach for the last couple of months. I think I have a bleeding ulcer."

"What is your name?"

"Mark Stone."

"Do you have health insurance?"

I handed her my insurance card, which was already in my hand.

She handed me a clipboard full of forms. "Please have a seat and fill these out, Mr. Stone."

"Okay." I looked at the clipboard, and then at Kathy. "Come on, Kathy. Let's sit down."

"Sit down?"

"Yeah," I said. "Let's sit down."

I walked over to an empty row of chairs in the waiting room. Kathy followed me. I sat down. She just stood there.

"Kathy, please sit down."

"Sit down?"

"Yes."

"Kay," she said, and then she sat down next to me.

As I filled out the paperwork, I glanced at Kathy now and then. She looked tired.

I finished the paperwork and took the clipboard back up to the nurse.

"You can have this back," the nurse said, handing me my insurance card.

"Thanks," I said. I put the card in my wallet.

When I came back, Kathy was lying down on the row of chairs. Her eyes were closed. Her feet were in the seat where I had been sitting, so I sat down in the next seat.

I realized that Kathy was missing her nap, and there was no way to predict when we'd be taken back to an exam room. So I let her sleep.

A few minutes later, a nurse walked up. "Please follow me, Mr. Stone," she said.

"Come on, Kathy," I said. "Wake up."

Kathy opened her eyes.

I stood up. "Kathy, we're going."

"We're going." She seemed pleased.

"Yes," I said.

The nurse waited for Kathy to get up, and then she led us out of the waiting room through some double doors, and down a hall to the rows of exam rooms. She opened the sliding glass door on the first exam room on the left.

"Right in here, folks," she said.

We went into the room.

"Please sit down. The doctor will see you as soon as he can," the nurse said. Then she shut the door.

I sat down.

Kathy remained standing. She looked around the exam room nervously. This wasn't the same exam room that we were in eleven months earlier, but the rooms were very similar.

"Kathy," I said, after a couple minutes, thinking that I smelled urine.

"What?"

"Do you have to use the bathroom?"

"Can I use the bathroom?"

"Yes," I said.

I opened the sliding glass door and looked out. A nurse was coming up the hall towards us.

"Excuse me," I said. "My wife has to use the bathroom."

The nurse stopped and pointed. "There's a bathroom right over there."

"I know where the bathroom is," I said. "But she uses Depend undergarments, and—"

"We have those," the nurse said. "What size does she wear?" She looked over my shoulder at Kathy, who was standing behind me. "About a medium?"

"Yeah," I said.

"I'll get her a pair. Just wait right here."

The nurse walked away. She came back a couple minutes later holding a Depend undergarment in her hand. "Does your wife need help in the bathroom?" she asked.

"Yes."

"I'll take her to the bathroom, then. You'd better wait here for the doctor."

"Okay," I said, and I moved aside to let Kathy out of the exam room.

Kathy stood frozen. She looked at me, then at the nurse, then at me, then at the nurse.

The nurse approached Kathy. She held out her hand, but stopped short of touching her. "I'll take you to the bathroom, ma'am."

Kathy looked at the nurse's hand. "I don't want that," she said.

The nurse pulled her hand back.

"Do you have to use the bathroom, Kathy?" I asked.

"Can I use the bathroom?"

"Yes. But the nurse will have to take you. I have to stay here and wait for the doctor."

The nurse held out her hand again.

"I don't want that," Kathy said.

"Why don't you walk her to the bathroom, and I'll help her when she's there," the nurse suggested.

"That will work," I said.

The nurse walked out of the exam room.

I looked at Kathy. "Come on, Kathy. Let's go to the bathroom."

"Go to the bathroom?"

"Yes," I said.

"Kay."

I walked with Kathy down the hall to the bathroom. The nurse was waiting next to the bathroom door.

I opened the door. Kathy and I went into the bathroom. I opened the lid on the toilet. "Go to the bathroom, Kathy," I said.

Kathy pulled down her pants and sat on the toilet.

I stepped outside the bathroom. "She definitely needs a fresh Depend," I told the nurse. "Hers is wet."

The nurse smiled. "I'll take care of it."

I went back to the exam room.

When I got there, all of a sudden, my stomach was having a fit. So I walked over to the sink in the back of the room. I retched and spat several times. My stomach was completely empty. So, fortunately, I didn't vomit.

When I was done, I ran some water in the sink. Then I sat down and focused my mind on keeping my stomach calm.

The nurse brought Kathy back. She sat down next to me.

After a little while, Kathy asked, "Can I have supper?"

"Pretty soon," I said. "As soon as we're done here."

"We're done here," she said.

At that moment a doctor entered the room. He was looking down at his clipboard.

I recognized the doctor immediately. It was the same doctor who looked at Kathy when the ambulance brought her in with a foot infection. He was the brilliant doctor who suggested that Kathy's dementia began with "a blow to the head", and he ordered a CT scan (which I refused to pay for) to prove it.

I was not happy to see Dr. Mason.

Dr. Mason looked up from his clipboard. If he recognized me, he didn't show it. "So, your stomach's been bothering you?" he said.

I nodded. "I believe I have a bleeding ulcer."

"Do you have nausea?"

"All the time," I said.

"Do you drink alcohol?"

"I drink beer."

"Do you drink beer every day?"

"Yeah."

"How much?"

"Usually a six pack—sometimes more," I said.

Dr. Mason nodded and wrote something on his clipboard. Then he left the room.

A few minutes later, a young man came in and drew a blood sample from my arm.

About ten minutes after that, two nurses—one who looked like she was about our age and the other about three decades younger—rolled a gurney into the room.

The older nurse handed me a hospital gown. "Dr. Mason wants you to get a CT scan on your abdomen. You'll have to take your shirt off and wear this," she said.

I began unbuttoning my shirt. "Can I leave my pants on?"

"As far as I know you can," she said.

I took off my shirt and put on the hospital gown. "Someone's going to have to stay with Kathy," I said.

"I'm going to do that," the younger nurse said. She was the nurse that had helped Kathy in the bathroom.

"Now get on the gurney," the older nurse said.

"Can't I walk to wherever we're going?" I asked.

"No. That's not allowed."

I climbed up on the gurney. "Do I have to lie down?"

"Yes."

I lay down on the gurney, and the nurse pushed me out of the room. We went down the hall and around a corner. Then we went down another hall and around another corner. We stopped in front of a set of double doors. Above the doors, in large black letters, it said RADIOLOGY.

The nurse pushed a button on the wall and the doors opened.

We entered Radiology.

She pushed me past the nurses station up to another set of double doors. Once we entered that room, she left.

Then a blond woman in dark blue scrubs walked up to the side of the gurney. "I need you to pull your pants down to your knees," she said.

"What?"

She laughed. "For the abdomen CT scan, you can leave your pants on, but you have to pull them down to your knees."

"Oh," I said.

"You sound disappointed."

I chuckled as I pulled down my pants.

"Now I need you to drink this." She smiled as she handed me a glass of thick, light blue liquid. "You're going to love it."

I drank half the glass, took a breath, and then finished the other half. I handed the empty glass back to the woman—or technician—and then I lay back down on the gurney.

Almost immediately, an alarming warmth spread from my stomach up my throat and down to my testicles. "What the hell!" I said.

The technician laughed. "Men tell me that it gives them 'hot balls'," she said.

"Ah…Yeah," I said. "That it does."

She pushed me into the next room and then into the giant white tube. Then she left the room.

I heard a buzzing sound when the machine was scanning. When the buzzing stopped, the machine was finished.

The technician came in and pulled me out of the tube. I pulled up my pants, and then she pushed me into the next room where the nurse who had brought me down there was waiting. The nurse took over and pushed me back to the exam room.

I climbed off the gurney.

The young nurse who had stayed to watch Kathy was standing there holding an IV pole. "You need to get up on the exam table," she said. "Dr. Mason ordered an IV drip for you."

"Can't I sit down next to my wife?" I asked.

The young nurse looked at the older one.

"It's all right with me," the older nurse said.

"Can I put my shirt back on?"

I didn't wait for an answer. I pulled off the hospital gown, laid it on the exam table, and picked up my shirt. I put on my shirt and sat down next to Kathy.

"I need your arm," the young nurse said.

I finished buttoning my shirt. "Sure," I said. I pulled up my sleeve and held out my arm.

She put a tourniquet around my upper arm. Then she tapped a vein with her finger. The needle, I noticed, was shaking when she jabbed it into my arm.

She taped the needle to hold it in place and smiled. "I'm getting pretty good," she said. "I got that on my first try."

"What's in the bag?" I asked, looking at the plastic bag full of clear liquid hanging from the IV pole.

"Saline solution," she said. "Basically, it's just salt water."

"Am I going to get that whole bag?"

"Yep."

"How long is that going to take?"

"About an hour."

"Great."

The two nurses left the exam room.

Kathy looked at the bag of saline solution, and then at the plastic tube going into my arm. Then she looked at my face and began to laugh. "Isn't it funny?" she said.

"Yeah, it's funny," I said.

A couple minutes later Dr. Mason walked into the exam room. "I have some good news and some bad news," he said.

"Okay," I said.

"The good news is that you don't have a bleeding ulcer."

"Are you sure about that?" I asked.

From the look that Dr. Mason gave me I could tell that he recognized me.

"And the bad news is," he continued, "that you have a spot on your liver."

"A spot on my liver?"

"Yes, a spot on your liver."

"What do you think it is?"

"We don't know."

"Cancer?"

"It could be cancer," he said. "Or it could be the beginning of cirrhosis."

"Cirrhosis of the liver?"

"Like I said, we don't know. But you should definitely have it checked out."

Dr. Mason left the exam room.

The older nurse came in a few minutes later. "You're going to be discharged as soon as the IV is finished," she said. Then she left the room.

So Kathy and I waited. I frequently looked up at the bag of IV fluid. Every time I did, Kathy would look up at the bag to see what I was looking at. The bag was getting skinnier and skinnier.

Finally the bag was empty and the alarm began beeping.

The older nurse came back into the room and pulled the needle out of my arm. She put a bandaid over the needle hole. "Stay here a minute," she said. "I'll get your discharge papers."

She walked quickly out of the room and returned, a moment

later, with a red folder and a clipboard.

She handed me the red folder, which was labeled *Drake Memorial Hospital.* Then she handed me a small piece of paper.

I looked at the paper. It was a written prescription

"Dr. Mason prescribed two medications for your stomach," she said. "With the carafate you take one before each meal and one at bedtime. With the Prilosec, you'll take one each morning."

I nodded and said, "Okay." I folded the prescription and put it in my shirt pocket.

She handed me the clipboard. "I need you to sign at the X."

I located the X at the bottom of the page, signed my name, and handed the clipboard back to her.

"You're free to go," she said.

Kathy and I walked out to the PT Cruiser. When we got into the car, I opened the red folder. I was curious: Dr. Mason said that I did not have a bleeding ulcer. So what, then, did he think was wrong with my stomach? I found my answer on the first page in the folder: "Diagnoses: Alcoholic Gastritis".

I shook my head. *He just had to use the A word.*

"Can I have supper?" Kathy asked.

I tossed the folder in the back seat. "Yeah," I said. I started the PT Cruiser. "Let's go home."

chapter 24

I took the Prilosec every morning when I woke up. On the bottle of carrafate, it said that I was suppose to take one before each meal and one at bedtime. But since I didn't eat meals, I took one in the morning with the Prilosec; another I took after we fed the chickens; I took a third one at six or seven in the evening (usually); and the last one of the day I took at bedtime.

I was hoping that the medication would make me feel better, but it didn't seem to be helping. I was still nauseous. I still couldn't hold down solid food. And I still vomited frequently.

In the middle of April, 2016, after being on the stomach medication for about three weeks, something else began to occur: For some unknown reason, I began to fall down a lot. And when I'd fall, I couldn't get back on my feet without a large object to grab onto to pull myself up. When I'd fall in our yard—which was where at least ninety percent of my falls occurred—my go-to object was the PT Cruiser. I'd crawl from wherever I fell in the yard to the nearest door handle on the car. I never hurt myself falling in the yard, although I did break quite a few eggs.

Once I fell in the Walmart parking lot. That was my most embarrassing fall. I had put our cart in the cart corral, and was walking back to the PT Cruiser, and then I went down.

I was in the middle of a car lane. A car had to stop. People were all around me.

I tried to get up without a large object, but my right leg wouldn't cooperate. So I crawled over to the nearest large object—a silver SUV. I grabbed the bumper with my right hand and pulled myself up a little bit. Then I grabbed the rear window wiper with my left hand

and pulled myself all the way up.

I stood there, for a couple seconds, looking at the SUV. My pants were ripped at the knee and my right knee was bleeding.

The SUV beeped and its lights flashed. Then a young woman pushed a cart full of groceries up to the rear bumper.

"I don't think I damaged your wiper," I said.

She checked it. "It's fine," she said. "Are you okay?"

"Yeah. I'm fine," I said. Then I limped over to the PT Cruiser.

On the way home I stopped at a CVS pharmacy and bought my first cane. It was a quad cane, which meant that it had four tips. It could stand up on its own, and it worked fine in the house, or on a level surface. But it was difficult to use in our yard, because there weren't very many spots where all four tips would hit the ground at once.

• • • • • •

It took me awhile to figure out what was causing me to fall down so much. At first, I thought it was a balance issue. I was lightheaded. So that must be it, I thought. But even when I walked very slowly and carefully, I'd still trip over nothing. So, while my balance might not be the greatest, it seemed to me that something else must be going on as well.

And there was something else going on. I discovered what it was, accidentally, one morning when Kathy and I were driving to the store. We were coming to a four way stop, I lifted my right foot off the gas petal. I intended for my right foot to press down on the brake petal, but I couldn't lift my foot high enough. After wasting two or three seconds, I finally grabbed ahold of my pants at the knee, lifted my lower right leg up, and dropped my right foot on the brake petal.

A car on the cross road of the intersection had begun rolling forward. He stopped suddenly when he heard my tires screeching, leaving his car in the middle of the intersection.

The nose of his car was directly in front of me. I wasn't going to be able to stop in time. So I pulled my right foot off the brake petal and swerved the PT Cruiser to the right. I managed to get around him.

When I was on the on the other side of the intersection, I heard his horn blast. I looked in the rear view mirror. His hand, which was clenched in a fist except for one finger, was outside his window, raised as high over the roof of his car as he could possibly get it.

We were coming up to another stop sign. I didn't want to rely on my right foot. So I decided that I'd use my left foot on the brake petal. I took my right foot off the gas petal, and then I pressed on the brake petal with my left foot. This worked fine. I stopped the PT Cruiser in the exact spot where I wanted to stop it.

When we took off I didn't do so well. I pressed on the gas petal a little bit too soon, so when I let my left foot off the brake petal, I squealed the tires. Oh well, I thought. Braking with the left foot was simple enough, but it was still something that I'd have to get used to.

I used my left foot to brake on the rest of the way to the store. We picked up a case of Budweiser and three Hershey candy bars, and then I used my left foot to brake all the way home.

When we got home, I went into the living room and sat down in a chair. I took my shoes and socks off. Then I put both feet on the floor, side by side.

I looked at both feet. Nothing appeared to be amiss with the right foot. It looked exactly like the left foot—except one was a right foot and the other was a left foot. Then I tried to move each foot individually. When I wanted the front part of the left foot to rise up, it rose up. When I wanted the front part of the right foot to rise up, it would stay flat on the floor. When I wanted the toes on my left foot to curl upwards, they'd curl upwards. When I wanted the toes on my right foot to curl upwards, they wouldn't move.

So now I knew why I was falling down so much: my right foot was dead, and I was tripping over it. Why was my right foot dead? That I didn't know. The right foot looked fine. So I didn't think the problem was in my foot. And I didn't think the problem was in my brain either. I thought, most likely, somewhere between my brain and my right foot there was a loose wire, so to speak.

Even so, just knowing that my right foot wasn't functioning allowed me to drastically reduce my number of falls. Because now, whenever I was walking, I was thinking about my right foot. And with every step I took with my right foot, I picked that foot up extra high. I did this because the front of my right foot dipped when

I lifted it off the ground. I was, of course, aware that when I was walking in front of other people (not Kathy), that my unusual walk appeared rather silly. But I thought that was much better than falling down in front of them.

· · · · · ·

One Sunday night, after Kathy had gone to bed, I sat in the computer room drinking beer and contemplating my condition. I could not ignore the fact that I was in poor health and I was getting worse. That morning, it took every ounce of energy I had to feed the chickens with Kathy. And so, later in the morning, when we went to the store to get a case of beer and a half gallon of milk, I decided to drive all the way to Xenia so we could go through a drive-thru. I felt too weak to walk around in a store. And then, at dusk, when it was time to shut the chicken's door for them, I didn't feel that I could make that long walk to the garage. So I stood on the deck while Kathy did it.

It didn't take a rocket scientist to know where all this was going to end, I thought. I was going to die. And probably pretty soon.

I finished my beer, grabbed ahold of my quad cane, and lifted myself out of my chair. Then I slowly made my way to the bedroom.

I turned on the light and looked at Kathy. Her eyes were closed and she was breathing softly. She looked peaceful. I turned off the light and lay down on the bed next to her.

Before I went to sleep, I thought about death. Being dead, it seemed to me, wouldn't be so bad. I wouldn't have nausea constantly. I wouldn't be tired and dizzy all the time. I wouldn't have a foot that doesn't work. I was probably going to die soon, I thought. And then I drifted off to sleep.

I was dimly aware, a couple hours later, that Kathy was standing next to the bed on my side. Then she left. A minute later music was coming from the living room. Kathy was playing The Gall Stones:

Babies are dyin' and mamas are cryin'
And my brain is fryin'
Yeah, my brain is fryin'
So please leave your message
After the bleep

I didn't get up to shut the bedroom door. I didn't have the energy.

The next thing I was aware of was the morning sun peaking through the curtains. I rolled over and sniffed Kathy. She didn't smell like urine. That was a good thing.

I grabbed ahold of my quad cane, which was standing next to the bed waiting for me, got my feet on the floor, and pulled myself up to a sitting position. I felt even weaker than I had on the day before.

Using a handle on a dresser drawer, which I could easily reach, and my cane, I pulled myself up to a standing position. I took two steps toward the door, and then I went down.

After I got on my feet again. I put the cane in my left hand, and I leaned against the closet doors with my right hand. I made it out of the bedroom.

Out in the hall, I moved very slowly, my right hand on the wall, my left hand on my cane. I made it out to the chair in the living room, which is always my first stop. I sat down in the chair and put on my shoes.

Rupert strolled over to the front door wagging his tail. He barked at the door. He wanted out.

I got out of the chair and stood, hunched over, looking at the front door, my left hand on my cane, the right on the arm of the chair where I had been sitting. The front door looked like it was a long ways away—even though it was only about ten or twelve feet from where I stood. I plotted my course. A couple steps to my left there was a wall which I could move along to get to the front door. I put the cane in my right hand, took the two steps, and got my left hand on the wall. I slowly made my way to the front door.

I unlocked the door and opened it. Rupert dashed out.

I closed the door and turned around. I was so dizzy, all of a sudden, that I just fell forward. My forearm caught the corner of the coffee table on the way down and I was bleeding.

I crawled out of the living room and into the kitchen, sliding my cane along with me, and leaving drops of blood on the laminate floor every three or four feet. I pulled myself up in front of the kitchen sink, and I turned on the cold water. Then I held the purple wound on my forearm under the stream.

I'm probably going to die today, I thought.

When I turned off the cold water, I happened to notice a cordless drill with no battery. It was back in the corner at the far end of the counter. I had bought that for Kathy back in the early part of 2014.

Kathy had wanted to buy a gun. And I kept asking her: "Why do you need a gun, Kathy? Why do you need a gun?" Her answer was always: "Hawks."

Now, we had had a couple hawk attacks on our chickens. One was back in 2010 (we lost a rooster), and another in 2012 (we lost a hen). But we hadn't had any attacks since then. So I didn't believe her answer.

One day, we were driving up to Xenia. We needed some Layer Crumbles. And Kathy brought up the subject again. "We need to get gun," she said.

"Kathy, why do you need a gun?" I asked.

"Hawks," she said.

"Kathy, the chickens haven't been attacked by a hawk in over two years. And I don't think you'd ever shoot a hawk anyway. So why do you need a gun?"

She was silent.

"Why do you need a gun, Kathy?"

Finally she told me: "You said, you're going when you're eight. If you don't go, I won't go. But if you go, I *have* to go."

"Okay," I said, nodding.

Kathy's intellect, by early 2014, had deteriorated significantly. But even so, in those months, she would, on occasion, surprise me with the soundness of her reasoning. This was one of those occasions.

Kathy was referring to a conversation that I had had with my mom on my cell phone. During that call, Kathy had stood next to me and listened, with interest, to my side of the conversation.

The conversation was about my dad. My mom had called me to tell me that my dad's doctor had found something that he believed was melanoma on my dad's ear. So the doctor wanted to cut off a little bit of the ear. But my dad didn't want the doctor cutting off any of his ear. My dad said—I was told—that since he was in his mid-eighties, and Stone men die in their eighties, he wasn't going to worry about the melanoma.

My mom wanted me to call my dad and talk him into letting the doctor cut off some of his ear. But I didn't know, if I were to make a call like that, what I could say to my dad to persuade him to let the doctor cut off a piece of his ear. "Mom," I said, "Stone men do die in their eighties. I expect to die in my eighties too."

Kathy heard me say that I was going to die. If I died, she felt, then she'd have to die too. So she wanted to prepare.

"We need to get gun," Kathy repeated.

"Okay, let's go buy a gun," I said.

I drove into Xenia, turned right on Main Street, and parked the PT Cruiser in front of a pawn shop.

We went into the pawn shop. I wasn't sure what we were going to do in there. But I was sure that we weren't going to buy a gun.

So we walked around in the pawn shop. We walked by the glass case in the front of the shop. The glass case displayed a few pistols, among other things. On top of the glass case, there was a cordless drill with no battery and no bit.

Kathy picked up the cordless drill and looked it over. "This thing is what we need," she said.

"Let me see it," I said. She handed me the cordless drill. I looked at the price tag. It was five dollars.

"Excuse me," I said to the clerk.

He walked over to us.

I held up the cordless drill. "I'd like to buy this."

"It doesn't come with a battery or a charger," he said.

"That's fine." I handed him the cordless drill.

He looked at the price tag. Then he looked up at me. "Five dollars," he said.

I pulled a five dollar bill out of my wallet and handed it to him.

He handed me the cordless drill. "It's all yours," he said.

"Thanks," I said.

When we got home that day, I put the cordless drill back in the corner on the kitchen counter. And there it sat, over two years later, with the price tag still on it.

I tore off a paper towel from the roll on the counter. I folded it in half, and then I folded it in half again. I pressed the folded up paper towel against the bleeding wound on my forearm.

I slid a couple feet along the counter and unplugged my cell phone from its charger. I put the cell phone in my shirt pocket. Then I reached for the kitchen table with my right hand and placed that hand on top of the table. I shifted my weight to my right side, pulled out a chair with my left hand, and then I plopped down in the chair.

I'd better go to the hospital, I thought.

I pulled my cell phone out of my pocket, tapped the button to light up the screen, swiped my finger across the screen to unlock it, tapped the green phone icon, and then I tapped in 9-1-1.

"9-1-1. What is your emergency?"

"Um. I'm very dizzy. And I can't walk. I think I need to go to the hospital."

"What is your address?"

I told her our address.

"What is your name, sir?"

"Mark Stone."

"I'll send the paramedics out right away, Mr. Stone."

"Thank you," I said.

I looked at the back door. It was unlocked. I had forgotten to lock the door before I went to bed. I'd better not make a habit of that, I thought.

"Can I have supper?" I turned my head. Kathy was standing in the archway between the kitchen and the living room..

I leaned over toward the cabinets and pulled open a drawer. "Why don't you eat a Hershey?" I suggested.

"Eat Hershey?"

"Yeah," I said. "They're in this drawer."

"What's drawer?" she asked.

I felt around the drawer until I could get my fingers into the package of Hershey chocolate bars. I pulled one out, unwrapped it, and handed it to Kathy. "Eat this."

She began eating the chocolate bar.

Then I heard the high pitch wail of a siren. The sound grew louder and louder, and then the pitch of the sound dropped. A second later the sound ceased.

I heard the paramedics talking as they climbed the steps of our deck. Then there were three taps on the back door.

"Come in," I said in a loud voice.

The three paramedics came into the kitchen. They were the same guys who had taken Kathy to the hospital almost a year before.

"Sorry to bother you," I said to the older paramedic. "But I didn't know what else to do. I'm dizzy, and weak. I can't really walk—or drive. So…"

"That's why we're here," the older paramedic said. "Can you walk at all?"

"Well, I got here, from the bedroom. But I fell down a couple times."

He looked at Kathy and smiled. "Ma'am, you seem to be doing much better than the last time I saw you."

Kathy looked at him and took a bite from her Hershey bar.

The older paramedic turned to me. "What about her?" he asked.

"She'll have to go with me," I told him.

"Do you want us to bring in the gurney?" one of the younger paramedics asked the older paramedic.

The older paramedic looked at me. "Do you think you can walk out to our truck?"

"Yeah." I put one hand on the table, grabbed my cane with the other hand, and stood up. I felt very wobbly. "I might need a little help, though," I said.

The older paramedic nodded. "Okay, we'll give it a try." He looked at one of the young paramedics. "Chip, you make sure she makes it out to the truck," he said. Then he looked at the other young paramedic. "Billy, you're the door man."

Chip walked up to Kathy and held out his hand. "Ma'am, could you come with me please?"

Kathy finished eating her candy bar, and then she looked at me. "Can I have supper?"

"Let's just go out to the truck, okay Ma'am?" Chip said.

Kathy looked at Chip for a moment, and then she looked at me again. "Can I have supper?"

I had one hand on the wall, the other on my cane, and I was shuffling toward the back door, which Billy was holding open. "Kathy, we have to go to the grocery," I said.

Kathy walked around me and went out the back door.

"Ma'am! Ma'am!" Chip said as he chased after her.

I made it out to the deck. Billy and the older paramedic followed me out. I pulled my keys out of my pocket and locked the back door. Then I grabbed the door knob and tried to turn it. It wouldn't turn. Then I shook the door. It was definitely locked.

"Get on the other side of him," the older paramedic said to Billy.

I quickly put my keys in my pocket, and then the two paramedics each got ahold of one of my shoulders. They helped me walk across the deck and down the steps. We stopped at the bottom of the steps.

The older paramedic looked at the ambulance, and then at Billy. "Let's do this the easy way," he said. "Get the gurney."

Billy started walking toward the ambulance. "Give me a hand with the gurney," he said to Chip.

"Can't," Chip said. "I've got to watch her." He was standing about five feet away from Kathy. Kathy was standing next to the passenger door of the PT Cruiser.

"She's not going anywhere," I said in a loud voice.

I was leaning against the post at the bottom of the steps. "I don't want to forget my cane," I said.

"I'll get it for you," the older paramedic said. He climbed the steps, picked up the cane, which was standing next to the door, and then came back down the steps. "Those are some steep steps," he said, handing me the cane.

"I plan to fix 'em," I said. "Just haven't gotten around to it yet."

"I hear that," he said.

Billy and Chip rolled the gurney up to me. I climbed up on it, with a little help.

"I can't get your wife to go to our truck," Chip said.

"Roll me over to her," I said.

They rolled me over to the back side of the PT Cruiser. I sat up on the gurney. "Kathy, we're not going in the PT Cruiser," I said. "We're going in that." I pointed to the ambulance.

"Taking van," she said. And she walked over to the van, which was parked close to the garage. She stood next to the passenger door.

"Roll me over to her," I said. "I'll get her."

They rolled me over to her.

"Kathy," I said. "Come here."

She walked over to the gurney. "What?"

I took her hand. "Kathy, we're going somewhere."

"What?" she asked again. She seemed confused, but she allowed herself to be led as they pushed the gurney to the ambulance.

When the gurney was up against the back bumper, I let go of Kathy's hand.

Chip immediately grabbed Kathy's hand and said, "Ma'am, you'll have to come around this way."

He led Kathy around to the side of the ambulance.

Billy and the older paramedic collapsed the gurney and loaded it into the ambulance.

After Chip and Billy strapped the gurney to the floor, and buckled a couple straps across me, I looked over to my side. Kathy was sitting on a bench seat looking at me.

I thought I should say something like: "Everything will be all right." But I didn't say anything. I just looked at her.

"Are the chicken's out?" Kathy asked.

"Yes," I lied. "I let them out."

She leaned forward and looked out the back window of the ambulance, trying to see into the chicken yard.

The ambulance started moving.

"Turn your hand over," Chip said.

I turned my hand palm upward. "What are you going to do?"

"Just a quick blood test," he said. Then he pricked my finger.

A couple minutes later, he poked a white capped needle into my arm. He taped it in place. Then he plugged a tube into the white cap. The tube was connected to a bag of saline solution, which hung on the side of the ambulance.

After about five minutes, I said, "I'm starting to feel better." And I was. I didn't feel nearly as dizzy.

"The stuff works wonders," Chip said. "After a bag of this stuff,

I've seen people jump off the stretcher and just walk away."

I knew we were in Xenia when the ambulance stopped, idled, and then began moving again. We stopped a couple more times. We made a couple turns. Then the low rumble of the engine ceased, and I heard doors on the ambulance opening and closing.

The back doors of the ambulance opened, and I was unloaded.

Billy and the older paramedic pushed the gurney as they wheeled me into the ER. Chip carried the bag of saline solution, and my cane. Kathy followed along a couple steps behind the gurney.

They stopped at the ER desk for a moment, and then they pushed me through the double doors, and down a hall, to an exam room.

Chip hooked the bag of saline solution to an IV pole that was already in the room. Then the three paramedics lifted me off the gurney and laid me on the exam table.

As the paramedics were leaving, the older one waved and said, "Good luck."

I nodded.

I looked over at Kathy. She was standing in the middle of the room looking at me.

"Kathy, why don't you sit down? We're going to be here for awhile," I said.

She just stood there looking at me.

"Kathy, there's a chair behind you. Please sit down."

"Please sit down," she said. Then she walked out of the exam room.

A nurse brought her right back. "Ma'am, you have to stay in here with your husband," the nurse scolded. "Do you understand?"

"Kathy, please sit down," I said.

"Sit down?" she asked.

"Yes. In that chair." I pointed to a chair.

"Kay," Kathy said. And she sat down in the chair.

"Make sure she stays in here," the nurse said to me.

"I'll do my best."

The nurse closed the sliding glass door when she left.

Kathy seemed antsy. She'd look at me, then she'd look at the sliding glass door. Then she'd look at me, and then she'd look at the sliding glass door.

"Kathy, we have to stay in this room," I told her.

Kathy got up and opened the sliding glass door. She stepped out into the hall.

"Ma'am! Ma'am!" I heard the nurse shout, and then she was shoving Kathy back into the exam room.

Kathy immediately sat down.

The nurse looked at me, and then at Kathy. "This isn't going to work," she said. "I'm going to move you two."

The nurse left, and a short while later, two male aides came in pushing a gurney.

"Do you need help getting on the gurney?" one of the aides—the tall one—asked me.

"I don't think so," I said.

I started to scoot myself toward the gurney. Then one aide grabbed my back, the other grabbed my feet, and they slid me onto the gurney.

"Get the IV," the tall aide said to the other aide.

"And my cane," I said.

The aide picked up my cane, grabbed ahold of the IV pole, and then the two of them began pushing the gurney.

"Come on, Kathy," I said. "We're going."

"We're going!" Kathy said. She got right up.

When we were out in the hallway, I asked, "Where are you guys taking me?"

"To the special room," the tall aide said.

"It's for special people," the other aide said.

Then they both laughed.

They pushed the gurney behind the nurse's station. Then a nurse unlocked the door to a room, and they pushed me into that room.

Kathy wandered in as they were leaving.

"You two will be fine in here," the nurse said. She closed the door and locked it.

The room had one bed. And that was it. No other furnishings. The floor was white VCT, and the bare walls were painted light blue.

The room had two doors. Kathy checked them both and discovered that they were both locked.

Then she sat on the bed.

I lay flat on my back, looking at the ceiling. Not much to see up there either—except a shiny black dome mounted about a foot out from the corner. I wondered what it was.

I looked over at Kathy and noticed that her pants were wet. I felt bad that I didn't take her to the bathroom when she got up that morning.

"Sorry Kathy," I said.

"What?"

"Nothing."

A few minutes later a nurse came in.

"Um. I think my wife wet herself," I said.

"I'm here to check your pulse and blood pressure. But I'll send an aide in to help her," she said.

As she was wrapping the cuff around my arm to take my blood pressure, I asked her: "What is that thing up on the ceiling?"

"That's our camera," she said. "That's how we keep an eye on you."

"Oh. Is this the room where you keep the crazies?"

"This is the room where we put patients who are mentally ill or suffering from dementia." She looked at Kathy. "She's been in this room before. Haven't you?"

Kathy gave the nurse a dirty look.

The nurse chuckled. "Yep. She remembers."

A couple of minutes after the nurse left, an aide came into the room. "Does she want to use the bathroom?" the aide asked me.

"Yes," I said. Then I looked at Kathy. "Kathy, go with her and use the bathroom."

"Use the bathroom?"

"Yes. Go with her and use the bathroom."

Kathy left with the aide, and then a young man came into the room.

"I'm here to get a blood sample," he said. "Can you sit up please?"

"Sure," I said.

I struggled to sit up, and he finally grabbed ahold of my shirt and pulled me up into a sitting position.

He took the blood sample from the same arm that the IV needle was in, and then he left.

The aide brought Kathy back. I could tell from the yellow tape poking over the waist of her pants that she was wearing a hospital diaper. And she was wearing a different pair of pants. The pants that she had on were way too big for her.

Kathy lay down on the bed. She curled up and closed her eyes.

I watched Kathy, and was starting to get sleepy myself. Then a nurse opened the door. "Is she sleeping?" the nurse asked.

Kathy opened her eyes.

"No," I said.

"I brought her something to eat."

Kathy sat up on the bed and the nurse handed her a white cardboard box.

"This is our box lunch," the nurse said to me. "It's got a peanut butter and jelly sandwich, some chips, and a cookie."

Kathy opened the box and took out the cookie.

"We're going to admit you," the nurse said. "Because your blood test is showing severe hyponatremia."

"Hyponatremia?"

"That means that the sodium level in your blood is low," she said.

"Oh. That's bad, huh?"

"A person's sodium level should be 135. Yours is 117. That's dangerously low. So yes, that's bad."

I nodded.

"So what do you plan to do with your wife?"

"Umm," I said.

"Do you have any children?"

"Yeah, we both have children," I said. "My daughter has her hands full already with two toddlers."

"And your wife is not her mother," the nurse said.

"Right," I said. "And her kids both live on the east coast."

"Is there someone else you could call?"

I shook my head. "I can't think of anyone."

"Well I'll send the social worker in to talk to you. Maybe she can help you come up with something."

A few minutes later the door opened and a woman I recognized walked into the room. "My name's Sandy Hawkins," she said. "I'm the social worker here at the hospital."

"We've met before," I said. "I'm Mark Stone."

"Oh yes. We have met before, haven't we? Under slightly different circumstances."

"Under drastically different circumstances," I said.

"I can understand why you'd say that, Mr. Stone. So—" She looked around the room. "I'm going to need a chair." She left the room, and a moment later, came back in scooting a chair. She scooted the chair to a corner and sat down. She set her tote bag down on the floor and pulled out a clipboard. Then she said, "The first thing I need from you, Mr. Stone, is information about the assets that you and your wife own."

"Why do you need information about our assets?"

"To see if your wife is eligible for Medicaid."

"She's not."

"You know that?"

"Yes. I know that," I said. "She has a 401k with over a hundred thousand dollars in it. And I have a little bit of money in the bank. So we're not eligible for Medicaid."

"Mr. Stone, if you don't have anybody to take care of your wife, she will have to be placed in a nursing home."

"I realize that," I said.

"And her insurance won't pay for the nursing home because it's not her that's sick."

"I understand that too," I said. "But if she is going to be placed, I wanted to see if you could place her at Liberty Nursing Center. You've placed her there before."

"I remember that," Sandy said. "Her name it Kathy, isn't it?"

"Yes," I said. "They know her there. So—this is not a good situation—but I think that would be the best thing for her."

Sandy stood up. "I'll see what I can do, Mr. Stone," she said. "I can't guarantee anything. But I'll call Liberty and talk to them first."

"I'd appreciate that," I said.

Sandy left the room and returned about a half hour later.

"Liberty Nursing Center is going to take Kathy," she said. "I talked to Lavern, and she said that the only reason she's willing to do this is that she knows you and she knows Kathy." She handed me a clipboard. "She faxed this over. You need to sign it."

I looked at the paper on the clipboard. "What is it?"

"It's a promise that you'll pay them," she said. "Normally they want two months paid in advance before they admit someone. But, since you're in the hospital, you can't go to the bank right now."

"Okay. So how much money are we talking about?" I scanned down the paper to a figure: "Nineteen thousand, nine hundred and eighty-three dollars." I looked up at Sandy. "That's a lot of money."

She nodded. "It is."

"Well, I guess I don't have much of a choice, do I?"

"No," she said.

I signed the paper and handed the clipboard back to Sandy. "Okay. That's going to empty all of our bank accounts," I said.

"Thank you," Sandy said, and then she left.

A nurse came into the room. "Mr. Stone, we're going to leave you in here with your wife until the transport service picks her up. And then you'll be moved up to the third floor."

"Whatever," I said with a sigh.

She closed the door and locked it.

A couple hours later, a nurse and a man in a blue uniform came in through the door in the back of the room. Another man in a blue uniform came in behind them. He was pushing a gurney.

"They're here for your wife," the nurse said to me.

Kathy was sitting in the chair.

One of the men approached Kathy slowly, like he was trying to trap a raccoon. "Kathy," he said. Then he looked at me. "Is that her name?"

"Yes," I said.

"Kathy, my name is Rodney. This other fella here is John," he said, pointing to the other man in a blue uniform. "We're here to take you to a nice place. Would you like that?"

Kathy looked at Rodney.

The other man, John, walked around to her other side. Kathy's eyes went back and forth between John and me.

"Do you want to go to a nice place?" Rodney asked her.

Kathy pointed at me. "I go with her," she said.

"Kathy, I have to go somewhere," I said. "I'll see you soon."

Rodney and John, at the same time, grabbed Kathy's forearms. They lifted her from the chair.

"I don't like that," Kathy said, struggling to get away.

"They said she might give us some trouble," Rodney said to me.

"I don't like that," Kathy said, as they moved her toward the gurney.

She looked over at me as they were strapping her down on the gurney. "I don't like that," she said.

They wheeled Kathy out of the room on the gurney, leaving the door on the back wall open.

A few minutes later, two nurses came into the room. They pushed the gurney that I was on through the open door on the back wall.

chapter 25

By the time I got settled into my room on the third floor of Drake Memorial Hospital, it was suppertime. And, oddly enough, I was hungry.

A nurse came into the room. She handed me a menu, which was for Tuesday. "This is tomorrow's menu," she said.

I glanced at the menu. "Is there any way I can get something to eat today?"

"They'll bring you something," she said. "I'm not sure what." She sat down in the chair next to the bed. "I'm told that you have pets in your home. Is that right?"

"Yeah. We have a dog and two cats. And we also have chickens."

"How do you plan to take care of those animals when you're in the hospital?"

"I've been thinking about that," I said. "I guess I'm going to call my daughter. She can feed the cats and check on things every couple of days. But I don't want to ask her to take care of the chickens. That's an every day and every night thing. That would be too much to ask. And I don't want her feeding our dog—not with her kids around. He might bite somebody."

"My dad works for animal control," the nurse said. "I'll have him come in and talk to you tomorrow morning. Do your animals have enough food for today?"

"Our dog's got a shed that he can go into, and that's got food and water in it. And the cats live outside. So if we don't feed 'em, they find food elsewhere. The chickens—I don't know. We didn't feed them this morning."

"Chickens can go a day without food," she said.

"They probably can," I said. "And if they get hungry, they can dig through the straw in the chicken house and find a little something to eat."

"Okay then," she said. "I'll have my dad talk to you in the morning." She got up from the chair, adjusted the bag of IV solution on the IV pole, and then left the room.

About an hour later, a hospital worker brought me in a tray of food. She put the tray on the overbed table and then pushed the table in front of me.

I picked up Tuesday's menu off the night stand. "Do you want this?" I asked. "I've circled my choices for tomorrow."

"I can take it for you," she said.

I handed her the menu and she left the room.

My first meal—in a very long time—was Salisbury steak, mashed potatoes, green beans, peaches, a roll and milk. I began eating.

A television sat on top of a dresser directly across the room from me. I decided to turn it on. I glanced around the room. I didn't see the remote. I opened the drawer on the night stand. It wasn't in there either.

I finished the food on the tray, and, surprisingly, I didn't feel at all nauseous.

When the hospital worker came in to pick up the tray, I asked her: "Does it cost extra in this hospital to watch TV?"

"No," she said.

"Then do you know where the remote is?"

"It should be on the night stand, right next to you," she said.

"It's not," I said.

"Maybe it's in the top drawer of the nightstand."

"No. I checked there too. It's not there."

"Then I don't know where it is," she said. She carried the food tray out of the room, and then she came back. "Maybe it's in a dresser drawer," she suggested. She opened the top drawer of the dresser. "Here it is."

She handed me the remote. I thanked her, and she left the room.

I turned the television on and surfed through the channels. For whatever reason, on the hospital's cable—at least on the TV in my room—there were only five channels. Three of the channels I wasn't familiar with. The other two were CNN and MSNBC.

I watched MSNBC, and sometimes CNN, until dark. Then I turned the television off and went to sleep.

· · · · ·

In the morning, before breakfast, the nurse came to the door of my room. "My dad is here to see you," she said.

A man about my age stepped out from behind her. He was wearing a gray uniform. He walked over to me. "Jerry Olson," he said, extending his hand.

"Mark Stone," I said. I shook his hand.

He sat down in the chair next to the bed. "I'll get right down to business, Mark," he said. "Barb tells me that you have some animals on your property that need to be rescued."

"Yeah. We have chickens. And a dog—something will have to be done with him."

"How many chickens?"

"Thirteen—twelve hens and a rooster."

"I have a friend who will take the chickens," Jerry said. "Now the dog, he's going to be taken by animal control—unless you know someone who will take him."

"I don't," I said. "Unfortunately, he doesn't take kindly to strangers."

Jerry nodded. "What kind of dog is he?"

"He's a Jack Russell."

"Well, we'll pick him up. But if he's not a friendly dog, I can't make any guarantees about what's going to happen to him."

"I understand that," I said. "I guess his future is up to him."

"That's the way to look at it," Jerry said. "Barb said that you had some cats."

"Yeah. But the cats will be fine. They live outside. And I'm going to have my daughter stop by every couple days to feed 'em."

"Okay, I won't worry about the cats then," he said. "Ah. I'm not going to charge you for the chickens—my friend's going to take them. So that's free. But I'm going to have to charge you a hundred and ten dollars to deal with the dog."

"Sure," I said. "I got that much cash in my wallet. But…My wallet's with my stuff, and I don't know where my stuff is."

Jerry got up and walked over to the door. "Barb, could you come in her please," he said in a loud voice.

The nurse came in. "What's wrong?"

"Do you know where his stuff is?" Jerry asked.

"That's all you wanted?"

"Yeah," Jerry said.

She opened the bottom drawer of the dresser and took out a large clear plastic bag. "Here ya go," she said, handing me the bag.

The bag contained my shoes and socks, the shirt, and the pair of pants that I was wearing when I was brought in on the day before. I took my cell phone out of my shirt pocket, and I took my wallet out of my pants pocket.

I pulled a hundred dollar bill and a ten out of my wallet and handed the money to Jerry.

"Thanks," he said. He folded the bills and put them in his pocket. "Now am I going to need a key?"

"You shouldn't," I said. "The dog's out in the front yard, so you don't need a key to get to him. Now, you will have to go into the garage to get into the chicken house. But the garage is unlocked—or it should be. If you can't get into the garage, you can still get the chickens. Just go around to the back of the chicken house and open their door for them. They'll all come out."

"What did you say the dog's name was?"

"Rupert."

"Okay, Mark, I hope you're back on your feet real soon."

"Are you going to take care of all this today?" I asked.

"This morning," he said. "Right now, in fact."

"Okay, thanks. I appreciate what's you're doing," I said.

Jerry nodded and left.

I picked up my cell phone, which was next to me on the bed. I tapped the phone icon, went to my list of contacts, and then tapped my daughters picture.

"Hi Dad, what's up?"

"Hi Virginia," I said. "Umm. I need you to do me a favor."

"Sure. What do you need me to do, Dad?"

"I need you to—today or tomorrow—come by my house and feed the cats."

"Why? Aren't you and Kathy there?"

"No, we aren't," I said. "I'm in the hospital, Virginia."

"What happened? Did you have an accident?"

"No, Virginia, I didn't have an accident," I said. "I just…I guess I just got sick."

"You're sick?"

"Yeah—well not sick sick. They admitted me for severe hyponatremia."

"I know what that is," Virginia said. "Are you going to be okay?"

"I think so."

"So where's Kathy?"

"In a nursing home."

Virginia was silent for a moment. Then she said, "I knew that would happen."

"I did too," I said. "I knew it would happen eventually. And, I guess, 'eventually' arrived."

"What hospital are you in?"

"Drake Memorial. I'm in room 326."

"Oh."

"So when do you think you can come up and feed the cats?"

"We'll do it this afternoon—right after lunch," she said.

"Okay. Do you still have a key to my house?"

"Yes. I think I still have it. If I can't find it I can get your key. We'll be coming up to the hospital too."

"Alright. But if you can find the key, stop by the house first. Because I need you to pick up my cell phone charger. It's in the kitchen, on the counter."

"In the kitchen, on the counter—okay," she said.

"And Virginia, the cats have food and water bowls on the deck and in the garage."

"I already knew that."

"And one more thing, Virginia: don't tell anybody that I'm in the hospital."

"Why not?"

"I just don't want anybody to know."

"Okay Dad. I'll see ya this afternoon. Love ya."

"Love ya too, Virginia."

They brought in breakfast, which was eggs, toast and jelly, grits, coffee and orange juice. I ate everything. Then I pushed the overbed table, and the food tray, to the side of the bed. I turned on the television. CNN came on.

A doctor walked into the room so I turned off the television.

"Good morning," the doctor said. "My name is Dr. Jarvis I'm a hospitalist here at the hospital."

"A hospitalist? What kind of doctor is that? Is that just a doctor who works at a hospital?"

"Basically, yes," Dr. Jarvis said. "If I practiced outside of a hospital, my specialty would be internal medicine."

"Whatever the hell that is," I said.

Dr. Jarvis chuckled, and then asked, "So how are you doing this morning?"

"Well, my stomach is feeling better than it has in quite awhile. And I can eat. That's a good thing," I said. "But I'm extremely weak. Especially in my legs. I don't have the strength to stand up. And I don't understand why all of a sudden I should be this weak."

"We think you might have had a stroke," Dr. Jarvis said.

"A stroke?"

"Yes. We think. We don't know. I've ordered an MRI."

"An MRI," I said.

"We want to have a look at your brain," he said.

"When's that going to happen?" I asked.

"This morning," he said.

A few minutes after Dr. Jarvis left, Barb (the nurse) came in. She took the IV needle out of my arm, helped me into a wheelchair, and pushed me out of the room. Then she pushed me down the hall to an elevator. We went down to the first floor.

When Barb pushed me out of the elevator, I knew where I was. I was in Radiology.

．　．　．　．　．　．

"Now there's a small window above where your head's going to be, and we have a mirror above the window that let's you look outside. That should help you feel less enclosed," the technician said.

"Let's do it," I said.

I was slid head first into the giant white tube.

And then I was looking at a tree. It was a young tree with healthy gray bark. It had nice, vital looking, green leaves. The tree was surrounded by grass. The grass hadn't been mowed recently. It wasn't too long, though. It was shaggy, with a dandelion here and there.

Then the noise started. It sounded like a train going by. A very long train—the sound went on and on. The train was endless. The sound got louder and louder.

Not one bird has flown past that tree!

The sound changed. It began to sound like an old land line phone. Except, whereas the ring of an old land line phone pulsed, this ring was continuous. It went on and on and on. If it were an old land line phone it would break. But it wasn't an old land line phone. It was an MRI machine. So it just kept going and going and going.

Not a bird n the sky! No squirrels near the tree! Why?

The sound changed back to the train sound. Only now, the train went faster and faster—until I thought it couldn't possibly go any faster. Then it went faster than that.

Not even a dog walks past that tree! What the hell's wrong with that tree?

"Fifteen more minutes," a voice from the outside said.

The sound inside the MRI machine changed two or three more times. It seemed to me that it had been at least fifteen minutes. I was beginning to think that they had forgotten about me. Then I heard from the outside voice again:

"Ten more minutes."

When they finally pulled me out of the machine, I wondered how anyone could expect Kathy—or any person with a cognitive impairment—to lie still during an ordeal like that.

The technician smiled. "Did you have a good time in there?"

"It was an interesting experience," I said.

·　·　·　·　·　·

When I got back to my room the lunch tray was setting on the over-bed table. Barb helped me get back into bed, and then she pushed the lunch tray in front of me.

For Lunch I had a hamburger on a bun with lettuce, tomato and onion, baked french fries, apple sauce and milk. It wasn't too bad—except the hamburger was very dry.

As I ate, I picked up my cell phone and looked at the screen. I had a missed call. It was from Virginia.

I called her.

"Hi Dad."

"Hi Virginia. I missed your call. What's up?"

"We just left your house. We're almost in Xenia."

"I thought you weren't coming up till this afternoon?"

"We left early. The kids wanted to see you."

"Oh, okay." I smiled. That made me feel good. "Was Rupert there when you were at the house?"

"No."

"Were the chickens there?"

"Yeah. The chickens were running around in their yard. Three guys were chasing them around and catching them with nets."

"Did they say what they were going to do with the chickens?"

"I talked to the older guy. He owes a farmer's market, and he said he already had sixty hens. But he needs more eggs. So that's why he wants the hens."

"What about the rooster?"

"I asked him about that. He said it all depends on how well he gets along with his rooster."

"Oh. Well, he's a friendly rooster," I said. "I hope he can make friends with another rooster."

"I hope so too, Dad," Virginia said.

"Yeah. Did you feed the cats?"

"Yes. And I put an extra bowl of food for them in the garage."

"Good," I said.

"And I got your cell phone charger. Dad, we're in Xenia now."

"Okay. I'll let you drive. I'll see you in a few minutes."

"See ya, Dad. Love ya."

"Love ya too, Virginia."

I had just finished eating when Virginia and her two kids, Aiden and Sarah, came into the room.

My daughter's youngest, Sarah, started to climb up on the bed. "Gampa!" she said.

"Sarah wants to give you a hug," Virginia said.

I pushed the overbed table aside and hugged my granddaughter.

"Do you want me to do something with this?" Virginia asked, as she pulled the overbed table away from bed.

"Just push it in the hall," I said.

Virginia pushed the table with the food tray out into the hall. When she came back into the room, Aiden was rocking the IV pole.

"Aiden!" Virginia scolded. "Stop that!"

"I was just looking at it," Aiden whined.

I chuckled.

"So why do they think you have hyponatremia?" Virginia asked.

I shrugged. "They think I might have had a stroke."

"A stroke? You mean like a 'silent stroke'. Is that what they think?"

"I don't know what they think, Virginia," I said. "But they did an MRI on my brain this morning."

"I'll bet that was fun."

"Oh, it was a blast," I said.

Virginia and the kids stayed and chatted with me for a few more minutes. Then the kids started to complain about being hungry. So they left.

I turned on the television.

· · · · ·

In the morning, after breakfast, on the third day that I was in the hospital, a different doctor came into my room.

"Good morning," the doctor said. "My name is Dr. Kruger."

"Are you a hospitalist?" I asked.

"No. I'm a cardiologist." He put the stethoscope in his ears. "I'm going to take a listen to your heart."

As he listened through the stethoscope, I asked, "Do you think there's something wrong with my heart?"

"Hmm," he said. He moved the chest piece of the stethoscope. "Hmm."

He stood up and took the stethoscope out of his ears. "You've had a heart failure," he said.

"What do you mean? Do you mean I had a heart attack?"

The doctor nodded. "Maybe. Maybe you had a heart attack."

"Wouldn't I know it if I had a heart attack?"

"Not necessarily," he said. "I'm going to have them give you a stress test for your heart. Only it won't be the normal stress test with physical exercise. Because you're too weak for physical exercise. This test—which is the same test—uses drugs to simulate the physical exercise."

"That sounds interesting," I said. "When are they going to do that?"

"Today. Maybe tomorrow," he said.

"Well that gives me something to look forward to, doesn't it?"

Dr. Kruger smiled. "Have a good day," he said. Then he left the room.

．　．　．　．　．

The room that Barb took me to to get the stress test looked like an ordinary exam room. A nurse stood next to a rolling table which had an EKG machine on it. And, for some reason, a doctor sat on a chair in the corner with his arms crossed across his chest.

Barb and the other nurse helped me get out of the wheelchair and up on the exam table.

When I was on my back, the nurse untied my hospital gown and put electrodes all over my chest.

"Now I'm going to give you a shot," the nurse said.

"Okay," I said. I turned over my arm and she gave me a shot.

After a few seconds, I felt nauseous. The nausea kept getting worse. And then the room began to spin. I thought I was going to vomit.

The nurse wrapped a blood pressure cuff around my arm and took my blood pressure. When she was taking the cuff off, she said, "I'll give you a couple of minute to recover and then I'm going to give you another shot."

I nodded.

She gave me the second shot.

The room suddenly felt very hot. It felt like I was being cooked in an oven.

The nurse, again, wrapped the blood pressure cuff around my arm. She took my blood pressure, and then she took the cuff off. "I'll give you a couple of minutes to recover," she said. "And then I'm going to give you another shot."

I looked over at the doctor. He was sitting in the chair, quietly, watching. "Is he here just in case you kill me?" I asked, jokingly.

The doctor smiled.

"No," the nurse said. "A doctor just has to be present when we do this test."

"Oh. Is this the first time you've done this?"

"No," she said, sounding offended. "This is not my first time."

"How many more shots am I going to get?"

"Two," she said.

The last two shots weren't nearly as bad as the first two. But they were still unpleasant.

When it was over, and Barb brought me back to my room and helped me get into bed, I fell asleep immediately. That test wore me out.

· · · · ·

On my forth, fifth, and sixth day in the hospital, they did tests on me every morning. On the morning of the forth day, they did a CT scan on my spine. The next morning, they x-rayed my lungs; and on the morning after that they did an MRI on my right knee.

In the afternoons, on those days, a physical therapist came in with a walker, and we'd go for a walk. I, of course, would use the walker, which had wheels on the front legs and split tennis balls on the rear legs so it would slide on a tile floor. The physical therapist would stand behind me, always wrapping a strap around my mid-section so she could grab me if I stumbled—and that happened a few times. We'd walk to the doorway, and then she'd tell me which way to go. We either went to the right and down the hall and back, or we'd go to the left and down the hall and back.

In the evening of my sixth day in the hospital, the night nurse came in and took the IV needle out of my arm. "You're done with the IV," she said.

"For good?"

"For good," she said. "You're going to be discharged."

"Oh. No one told me that. When's that suppose to happen?"

"Tomorrow."

"But I can barely walk—even with a walker."

"The doctors are recommending rehab."

"Really. Well I wish they would have discussed that with me because I do have a preference in rehab facilities. Liberty Nursing Center is my first choice because that's where my wife is."

"I'll make a note of that, Mr. Stone."

"Please do. I'd kind of like to see how my wife is doing. I haven't seen her for a week."

"I believe that doctors are aware of that, Mr. Stone. But I will leave them a note."

"Thanks," I said.

· · · · ·

The next morning, when Barb brought me my medications, I asked her about it: "Am I suppose to be discharged today?"

"That's what I hear," she said.

I put a pill in my mouth and then took a sip of water. "I'm suppose to go to a rehab facility," I said. "Do you know if they're sending me to Liberty Nursing Center?"

"Yes, you will be going to Liberty."

"Well that's good news." I took a couple more pills. "Do you know when?"

"That I don't know," she said. "I'll try to find out for you."

I took the last three pills and finished the cup of water. "Thanks," I said, handing her the plastic cup. "I'd appreciate that."

A few minutes later, an aide carried in my breakfast tray. He set it on the overbed table, and then pushed the table in front of me. "Enjoy," he said.

"I'm sure I will," I said, as he was walking out of the room.

I took the cover off the plate. The food looked good—scrambled eggs, hash browns, and ham. Although the ham looked pretty dry.

I turned on the television to keep me company while I ate.

I was still eating when Dr. Kruger came in. He stood at the foot of the bed.

I picked up the remote for the television and pushed the mute button. "Do you want to listen to my heart?" I asked.

"I don't want to disturb your meal," he said.

"No, no. I'm finished," I said. I took one last bite of scrambled egg and pushed the overbed table out of the way.

As the doctor listened to my heart, I asked, "Does my heart sound okay?"

He took the stethoscope out of his ears and picked up my wrist. "It's good," he said. "It sounds good."

He was counting my heartbeats so I didn't bother him. When he was done, I said: "So what's the verdict, Dr. Kruger. Did I, or did I not have a heart attack?"

"Maybe you had a heart attack," he said. "But I don't think so."

"Did something go wrong with my heart?"

"You had a heart failure."

"Okay. Well," I said, "I hope my heart succeeds."

"I hope so too," the doctor said.

"For a little while, anyway," I added.

"For a long time," he said. "If you take care of your heart it should succeed for a long time."

I nodded. "So am I good to go?"

"You're good to go," he said.

I didn't think he'd know, but I thought I'd ask anyway: "Do you know when they're going to move me to Liberty Nursing Center?"

"They should be here within the hour," Dr. Kruger said.

Then he left the room.

I got the plastic bag out of the top drawer of the nightstand and I was ready to go. All my stuff was in the plastic bag—except my cane, which was standing next to the bed, and my cell phone, which was in my hand.

I kept track of the time. Dr. Kruger left the room at 9:27 AM. The two guys from transport service—the same two who had picked up Kathy—arrived at 10:20 AM.

"Now its my turn," I said, as Rodney and John pushed the gurney into the room.

Rodney nodded. "Yep," he said. "I sure you don't mind saying good bye to this place."

"No. I don't," I said.

chapter 26

On the ride over to Liberty Nursing Center, I entertained myself by looking out the rear windows of the transport truck and trying to figure out where we were. I know where Drake Memorial Hospital is; and I know where Liberty Nursing Center is; and I know what roads I would take if I were to drive from one of those places to the other. We didn't go that way.

We seemed to be on Main Street. When I saw the Tractor Supply on the right side of the road (my right), I realized that we were coming into Beavercreek. Then we were moving in a big circle, which meant that we were getting on I-675. We stayed on I-675 awhile. When we got off, we drove through a residential area that I didn't recognize.

Then we arrived at Liberty Nursing Center.

We went in through the Jefferson Wing entrance. They pushed me through the lobby and stopped the gurney at a nurses station.

"We've got Mark Stone," Rodney told the nurse behind the counter. "Where do you want us to take him?"

"He's not going to Jefferson. I know that," she said. "Let me find out for you." She walked out of the nurses station, into the lobby, and then out of my view.

When she came back, she said, "He goes to Reagan."

"That's what I figured," Rodney said.

They pushed me up to another nurses station at the other end of the building.

"This is Mark Stone. I think he's yours," Rodney told the nurse.

"He goes in room 716," the nurse said. "Let me make sure it's ready."

The nurse walked quickly down the hall. The transport guys pushed the gurney behind her.

She stopped in front of room 716. "Just wait here," she told Rodney. Then she went into the room.

After a couple minutes, she came back out to the hall. "It's ready," she said. "You can bring him in."

As they pushed me into the room, I noticed that the covers on the bed were neatly folded back.

John put the plastic bag with my stuff on top of the night stand. He stood my cane next to the bed. Then he and Rodney picked me up from the gurney and put me on the bed.

After the transport guys left, the nurse picked up my cane.

"That's my cane," I said.

"You don't need a cane right now," she said.

"Maybe I don't. But that's still my cane."

"Mr. Stone, we don't want you trying to walk until you've seen the physical therapist," she said.

"Alright, when will I see the physical therapist?"

"You'll have to talk to the doctor about that."

"When will I see the doctor?"

"I don't know," she said.

She picked up a cord which was attached to the sheet on the right side of the bed. The cord had a red button on the end of it. "Do you see this?" she asked.

"Yes."

"This is the call button. Press it once if you need anything." She set the call button on the side of the bed next to me.

"What happens if I push it two or three times?"

"You only need to press it once."

"Okay," I said.

Then she walked out of the room with my cane.

The door to my room was left open. So, as I lay in bed, I watched people go by. Most of the people who worked there walked by the doorway quickly. The residents and the patients moved much slower. Most of them were very old—the residents, anyway—and most of them were in wheelchairs. One woman, who was probably in her forties, rolled by, wheeling her wheelchair, with both arms and both legs in bandages. I thought that she must be recovering from burns.

The food cart stopped outside the door, and an aide brought me a lunch tray. She put the tray on an overbed table and rolled the table in front of me.

"What would you like to drink, sir?" she asked.

"Do you have coffee?"

"Yes," she said.

She brought me a cup of coffee and set it on the tray.

I looked down at the food. The sandwich looked like tuna fish, but the bread was soaking wet. The coleslaw didn't look good either. It was shredded too fine. In fact, none of the food looked—or tasted—very good. But I was hungry, so I ate.

While I was eating, Lavern came in the room. "Are you enjoying your lunch?"

"Um. No," I said.

"Sometimes lunch is not very good here," she said. "Dinner should be better."

"Listen," I said. "About the money that I owe you guys. Now, I don't know how long I'm going to be in here, but I've talked to my daughter, and—"

Lavern raised her left hand. "Look, I didn't come in here to talk about money," she said. "When you get out, give us a check at your convenience. I'm not worried about it."

"Okay," I said.

She handed me some papers on a clipboard. "These are your admission forms. Fill them out some time today."

I nodded and took the clipboard. "How's Kathy doing?" I asked.

"She seems to be adjusting," Lavern said.

"Has she been trying to escape?"

"Sometimes she does. We tell her that Mark wants her to wait for him right here. That seems to calm her down."

"You see. That's what I thought. She's waiting for me," I said. "Now I noticed that most people around here have wheelchairs."

"Most of the residents have their own wheelchair," she said.

"Does Liberty Nursing Center have any wheelchairs?"

"We have a few."

"Well, how do get one? I'd like to go see Kathy. And I don't walk very well. And they took my cane away."

"You'll have to ask the doctor about that," Lavern said.

"Okay. I'll do that. But where is the doctor?"

"Dr. Whitman is not in the building right at this moment," Lavern said. "But he will be here."

"When?"

"Later on this afternoon. Maybe this evening."

"When the doctor gets here, tell him to come and see me right away."

Lavern smiled. "I'll tell Dr. Whitman that you want to see him, Mark."

"I'd appreciate that," I said.

"So how are *you* doing, Mark?" she asked.

"I'm here, aren't I?"

"You'll get better," she said, and then she left the room.

．．．．．

I was no longer expecting to see the doctor that day when, at nine o'clock in the evening, the nurse and a middle aged man with glasses walked into my room.

"This is Dr. Whitman," the nurse said.

"I'm glad you could make it," I said. "I didn't think you were going to show up today."

"An emergency came up this morning with one of my patients and I've been running behind all day," he said.

"Of course," I said. "You're a doctor. Things like that happen. I didn't mean to be rude."

"No offense taken," he said.

The nurse left the room.

Dr. Whitman stood at the foot of the bed reading a piece of paper which, I guess, was information about my medical condition.

"Are you experiencing lightheadedness?" he finally asked.

"No."

"Any nausea or diarrhea?"

"No."

"Headaches?"

"No," I said. "My main problem is weakness. Especially in my legs. I'm too weak to walk."

"I see," he said.

"I need a wheelchair—so I can get around," I said.

"Um-hum," he said.

"They told me I had to talk to you about getting a wheelchair."

"I don't have a problem with you getting a wheelchair," he said. "I don't assign the wheelchairs around here. They're not my wheelchairs. But I can tell the nurse that I don't have a problem with you getting one. That's all I can do."

"I'd appreciate that," I said. "Thanks."

"Your welcome," he said, and then he left the room.

. . . . .

The next morning, right after breakfast, a young man pushed a wheelchair into the room. "I'm Vernon," he said. "I'm your physical therapist."

"I'm Mark Stone," I said. I pointed to the wheelchair. "Is that for me?"

"You can borrow it," he said.

"Well, yeah. That's what I meant."

Vernon pushed the wheelchair next to the bed. I put my right hand on one of the push handles and slowly began to crawl out of bed.

"Do you need help?" he asked.

"No. I can do it," I said. I got my feet in position in front of the wheelchair and sat down.

When I was sitting in the wheelchair, I looked to my left side and then I looked to my right side. There was a lot of extra room in that wheelchair.

"This wheelchair was made for a bigger person," Vernon said. "But its all we have available right now."

"It will do," I said. I put my hands on the tires and pushed, moving myself forward.

"To propel yourself, put your hands on the outer rims," Vernon said. "That way you don't get your hands dirty."

"Oh." I put my hands on the outer rims of the wheels and wheeled myself to the doorway. "Like this?"

"For right now keep your hands in," Vernon said. And he took control of the wheelchair.

I lifted my hands off the rims. "What are you doing?"

"I'm taking you to the physical therapy room."

"Why?"

"For your initial evaluation."

"Do we have to do that right now?"

"Why? Do you have a date?"

"Yes," I said.

"Well we have to do it right now," he said. "It won't take very long."

He pushed me down the hall toward the nurses station. We turned right at the nurses station and went down another hall. That hall had a couple bends in it. Then we arrived at the physical therapy room, which was on the right.

The physical therapy room looked like an ordinary exercise room—except there was no weight bench. It had a treadmill, a stair climbing machine, and a stationary bicycle. There were also a few things in there that you wouldn't expect to find in an ordinary exercise room: such as the wooden bridge with a handrail on each side; or the two step up, two step down platform.

Vernon left me near the doorway for a minute. I sat in the wheelchair and watched another physical therapist as she tried to get an old woman to toss a beach ball. The old woman was getting frustrated because she couldn't muster up enough arm movement to toss the ball more than a foot or two beyond her knees.

Vernon came back with a clipboard. He pushed me over to a row of chairs. Then he came around the wheelchair to face me. He pointed to the side of the wheelchair. "Do you see that red lever?"

I put my hand on the red lever. "Yeah," I said.

"That's the brake. The brake should always be on when you get into or out of the wheelchair."

"Okay. It's like a parking brake."

"Right," he said. "Now put the brake on."

I put the brake on.

"Now, I want you to get up out of the wheelchair and sit down in a chair. Do you think you can do that?"

"Yeah. I can do that," I said.

I put my hands on the armrests of the wheelchair and stood up. Then I reached out and grabbed the armrest of a chair. I slowly shuffled around backwards. I grabbed the other armrest of the chair when it was behind me, and then I sat down.

"I noticed that you're dragging your right foot," Vernon said.

"That foot's been giving me a lot of trouble," I said.

Vernon set his clipboard on a chair, and then he got down on the floor and pulled off my socks. "Tap your left foot," he said.

I began tapping the floor with my left foot.

"That's enough. Now tap with your right foot."

We both stared at the right foot.

"Nothing?" Vernon said.

"No. Nothing. That foot doesn't move. It's dead."

Vernon stood up. "Before we declare it dead, I want to try something." He walked over to a closet, opened the door, and picked something up off the floor.

He came back with a black case. He set the case on the floor, opened it, and took out some kind of electronic device. The device looked something like a voltmeter, only it was bigger, and had more dials and buttons than a typical voltmeter.

"What's that?"

"It's an EMG machine," he said. "I'm going to test the conductivity of your peroneal nerve."

I nodded.

He plugged the machine into an electrical outlet on the floor. Then he taped two electrodes to the side of my right ankle. "You might feel something here," he said. He pressed a red button. "Did you feel that?"

"No."

He adjusted a dial, and then pushed the red button again.

I felt a tingle in my ankle and my right foot jumped up.

"That's a good sign," Vernon said. "A very good sign."

"Why? You can do the same thing to a dead frog, can't ya?"

Vernon put his hand on his chin as he thought about my question. Then he took his hand off his chin and raised his index finger. "Yes!" he exclaimed. "But only if being dead is the only thing wrong with the frog."

I chuckled. "Now I'm going to have to think about that one."

Vernon put the EMG machine back in the closet. He picked up a walker from a stack of walkers in the corner. He brought it over, opened it up, and stood it in front of me.

"Have you ever used one of these before?"

"Yeah. I used one at the hospital."

"Great. I'm going to have you do a little walking, and then we're done for the day." He walked over to a table, picked up a strap, and came back. "Do you need help standing."

"No. I can stand up," I said. I used the armrests on the chair to push myself up to a standing position, and then I grabbed ahold of the walker and stepped into it. I looked down at the legs of the walker. "The one I used at the hospital had wheels in the front."

"We have those here," Vernon said. "But I always start people out with the walkers that don't have wheels." He put the strap around my mid-section. "Okay. Move the walker forward four or five inches, and then step into it."

I hopped the walker forward, and then I stepped into it.

"Take another step."

I did it again.

"Good. Take another step."

I hopped the walker forward about a foot.

"Not that far!" Vernon said. "Take baby steps first. Keep that in mind."

I pulled the walker back a few inches and stepped in it.

"That's it," he said.

I walked across the room in the walker, and then Vernon said: "Stop right there."

I stopped and waited.

Vernon took the strap off my mid-section, and then he got the wheelchair and rolled it into position behind me.

"Okay, you can sit down," he said.

I sat down in the wheelchair and grabbed ahold of the otter rims of the wheels. I tried to move the chair, but it wouldn't budge.

"The brakes are on," Vernon said.

"Oh." I pulled the brake levers up on both wheels, and then I turned the wheelchair to point it toward the door.

"Just wait," Vernon said.

"I thought we were done for the day."

Vernon put the strap and the walker away, and then he came back to the wheelchair and started pushing. "We are, but I have to push you back to your room," he said. "That's my job."

"Alright then," I said. I held my arms in and he pushed me back to the room.

"Do you want me to help you get back into bed?" he asked.

"No. I'm good."

"Then I'll see ya tomorrow. Same time. Same place."

"Okay," I said.

I waited a couple minutes after Vernon left before I rolled the wheelchair out to the hall. I glanced over at the nurses station, which was to my left. I didn't see anyone. So I turned the wheelchair right, and, using the otter rims of the wheels, I began to roll.

I knew how to get to the dementia unit from where I was: I had to go all the way down to the end of the hall that I was on, turn left, and then take that hall all the way to the other side of the building. I had been this way before—when Kathy was in rehab, and I was walking.

Fifty feet down the first hall, I was thinking about how much quicker and less strenuous walking was compared to using a manually propelled wheelchair. By the time I was down to the end of that hall, my arms were completely wore out.

So I rested for a couple of minutes.

When I got going down the next hall, I used a technique that I had observed other people in the building using. Instead of pushing on the wheels to move the wheelchair, I used the handrail on the wall to pull myself along. This method was much easier on the arm muscles. Although, it couldn't be used in doorways. And I don't think some of the residents I passed along the way liked me being so close to their rooms.

The double doors leading to the dementia unit were at the end of the hall. Before those doors, on the right, there was a nurses station with a nurse sitting behind the counter.

I rolled up to the double doors, and then I reached up to press the red button.

"Sir!" The nurse came out of the nurses station. "Sir, you're not allowed to go in there."

"I want to see my wife," I said.

She walked up to me. "What's your wife's name?"

"Kathleen Stone."

"And who are you?"

"Mark Stone."

She looked me over, sizing me up. "Okay. I know who you're talking about. I guess I'll let you in." She pressed the red button and held the door open for me.

I rolled into the dementia unit.

Amber was at the other end of the hall. She noticed me rolling toward her, and she waited. When I was close, she said, "Well look what the cat dragged in!"

"It's nice to see you too, Amber," I said.

"You know I was only kidding, right?"

"Yes," I said.

"Are you here to see Kathy? Well, duh! Of course you are. She's in the activity room. Follow me."

I followed Amber into the activity room.

"Kathy, you have a visitor," Amber said.

When Kathy saw me, her mouth dropped open. She set her cup of hot chocolate on the table. A smile slowly came to her face. Then she began to laugh.

"You're over there," she said, laughing. She got up from the table and came over to me. "Isn't it funny? You're over there." She grabbed my hand and tried to pull me out of the wheelchair.

Amber grabbed ahold of Kathy's arm. "Kathy, let go of him." She gently tugged Kathy's arm away.

Kathy let go of my hand. "You're over there," she said.

"Yes," I said, chuckling. "I'm over here."

"Isn't it funny," she said, still laughing. "You're over there."

I began laughing. "Yes, it's funny, Kathy," I said. "I'm over here."

epilogue

I was a rehab patient at Liberty Nursing Center for three weeks. When I was discharged, I was still very weak, but I could walk with a walker and a drop foot brace on my right foot.

My right foot was still completely dead, and I wanted to bring it back—if that was possible. So I went to see Dr. Smith about it. She referred me to a podiatrist because my problem was with a foot. The podiatrist did an expensive test to confirm what was already known—that I had neuropathy Then, because he concluded that the source of the problem with my foot was not in the foot itself—which I already knew—he referred me to another doctor. It turned out, that doctor's specialty was pain management. When I told the pain doctor that my foot didn't hurt, he couldn't figure out why I was referred to him. So he referred me to a neurosurgeon. The neurosurgeon, likewise, didn't understand why I was referred to him. He told me that an orthopaedic surgeon might be able to help me. But he wasn't sure. He said I'd have to ask an orthopaedist about that.

While I was talking to the neurosurgeon, I happened to be sitting with my right leg crossed over my left leg.

"How often do you sit like that?" the neurosurgeon asked.

"Like what?"

"With your legs crossed like that."

"I don't know," I said, and then I thought about it for a moment. "I guess it's a habit of mine."

"Well don't do it anymore."

I put my right foot on the floor. "Do you think that has something to do with my right foot being dead?"

"Stranger things have happened," he said.

The neurosurgeon was the last doctor I went to see about my right foot. But I did take his advise about not sitting with one leg crossed over the other.

It took me awhile to regain my ability to walk without any mobility aids. I walked with a walker, and I wore a drop foot brace on my right foot, for a couple weeks after I was discharged. Then I bought a single point cane. I practiced with it around the house, and, after about a week, I ditched the walker and walked everywhere with the cane. Of course, I still wore the drop foot brace. But then, six or seven months after my discharge, feeling and movement began to return to my right foot. So I ditched the drop foot brace. I was still weak in the knees, though, so I continued to walk with the cane.

It was close to a year after being discharged from Liberty Nursing Center that I was able to walk, at all times, without a cane and without a drop foot brace.

I have wondered about the role the neurosurgeon's advice—that I not sit with one leg crossed over the other—played in the recovery of feeling and movement in my right foot. I suspect that it played a role, but I don't know for sure. Because sitting with two feet on the floor is only one of the things that I did differently. I also began taking vitamins. I also ate meals—two, sometimes three meals a day. I also limited my alcohol consumption to no more that two beers a day—taken at bedtime.

The bottom line is: I got healthier, and so did my right foot.

* * * * *

Unfortunately, Kathy's prognosis is not so rosy. Her disease continued to progress. A year after my discharge from Liberty Nursing Center, she was almost completely mute. Occasionally—but very rarely—she would utter a word.

The last word that I heard her say was on December 26, 2017—the day after Christmas.

The day before I had gone to a Christmas party at my brother's house in Sylvania, Ohio. Sylvania is a couple hundred miles north of where I live, so I left early in the morning and didn't get home until late at night. I didn't have a chance to visit Kathy that day.

The next day I went to see Kathy in the morning. I picked her up in the dementia unit, and I took her out and we wandered around in the building.

We walked into the main activity room, which is across from the physical therapy room, and we sat down. There was no one else in the room. Bonanza was playing on the television.

I hadn't heard Kathy speak for a couple months, and I didn't expect her to answer. But I asked anyway: "Did you miss me yesterday, Kathy?"

She didn't look at me. She continued to look straight ahead—not at the television, but at nothing. Then she opened her mouth. She closed it. A couple seconds later, she opened her mouth again. She closed it. Then she said, "Yeah."

She made her point: My visits are very important to her. So December 26, 2017 was the last time I went a whole day without visiting my wife.

about the author

M. G. Webb has been a home builder; he's owned a flooring business. He worked for the federal government for ten years-which is as long as he could stand it. Currently he is semi-retired and works as a substitute teacher. This is his first novel.

M. G. Webb and his wife Kathy, visiting his mother in August, 2008, on their way to a concert in Toledo.

www.ingramcontent.com/pod-product-compliance
Lightning Source LLC
Chambersburg PA
CBHW020542020726
47494CB00006B/1872